PETER'S

BURN

PETER'S BURN

K.C McCraw

ARPress
45 Dan Road Suite 5
Canton MA 02021
Hotline: 1(888) 821-0229
Fax: 1(508) 545-7580

Ordering Information:

Quantity sales. Special discounts are available on quantity purchases by corporations, associations, and others. For details, contact the publisher at the address above.

Printed in the United States of America.

ISBN-13:   Softcover   979-8-89330-278-3
              eBook   979-8-89330-277-6
Library of Congress Control Number: 2024901501

TABLE OF CONTENTS

PROLOGUE

The 747 Jumbo Jet had not begun its descent when the stewardess was already advising the passengers to fasten their seat belts. Baltimore- Washington Airport was but moments away. At once, seats were adjusted forward, literature laid aside, and the vibrant jitters of novice airline patrons became a noisy overtone. In the last row of the first-class cabin, a man sat with his wife, who'd been frowning since she'd heard the announcement by the stewardess. The flight had been uneventful. If anything, only minor air turbulence was encountered, but it had left the woman terrified. This was to be her first and last flight. Air travel was not for her, she confessed to herself. The next trip to the States would require a stateroom on a luxury liner or else her husband shouldn't expect her company. He could do what he wanted; her mind was made up!

The stewardess worked her way down the aisle, inspecting each passenger to see if all of the seat belts were secured. Casting a reassuring smile at the man and his anxious wife, she then gave her best perfunctory smile to the gentleman in the aisle next to where they were seated. The man sat alone, dressed to the hilt in a three piece suit, with a starchy white shirt and large flashy cufflinks that could do little else than date his outdated taste. He didn't acknowledge the stewardess. His mind was focused elsewhere. Nothing less than a crash landing might phase this man. He was older than most of the passengers. The stewardess guessed about sixty, but beyond that she hadn't the faintest idea. The "NO SMOKING" signal was on, and she resented his arrogance, when he removed a pipe from a breast pocket and began packing its bowl with tobacco. She said nothing. She knew she'd be in the forward compartment by the time he lit up. This man, she sensed, had not and would not be denied. Her shift was about over. In ten minutes, she'd be saying goodbye to all of the passengers, including the Grand Duke, as she had secretly named him. Then she would go to her apartment, clean up, and do the town. A confrontation with the old jerk had the potential of ruining her enthusiasm. She wasn't about to bother with him.

Upon landing, the stewardess wavered her game plan by staying in and watching sit-coms until past eleven. By then, her ambition to seize the town had died, but not the same for the Grand Duke. He went out. Taking a cab from the airport, he paid a handsome fare to Baltimore. From there, he rode a bus to a nearby city. To him the name of the town was Nowhere and the people who lived there were Nobodies. He was the Grand Duke. Unlike the citizens of Nowhere, he'd made his mark in life. Nowhere would be nothing more than a minor scratch. The Grand Duke would spend some time in Nowhere, brush up on his international skills, and migrate to better territory. Belfast had been nice. Jerusalem was even better. More than anything though, unscathed regions were what he desired. The stewardess, indeed, had him pegged. The Grand Duke was definitely one to light things up!

This story is a work of fiction. It is a product of the writer's imagination. Any similarities between the characters and other people who may exist now or ever is purely coincidental. Some facts have been used to enhance the story, but they are supported by historical documentation or else they should be considered as false. The names of some famous people and celebrities have been used but only in a fictitious manner unless supported by established facts or documentation. The names of all locations have been used in a fictitious way. Any similarities between places of business, meaning names or otherwise, is strictly coincidental. To the author's knowledge, they don't exist. In no way do philosophies, such as those having to do with criminal reform, reflect upon the author's own ideas or convictions. In no way are the author's biases, personal feelings, or past experiences part of this work.

CHAPTER 1

Vernon walked toward the highway slowly without gazing back. His strides were even and relaxed. He hardly bothered to turn as the door slammed shut from behind himself. From inside, Emmitt's eyes pierced through a set of flimsy blinds and watched. It was beginning to show signs of rain. Except for the fluttering gulls which circled about, the sky was gray and drab. As he dangled his empty coffee cup from his index finger, Emmitt assumed that Vernon would be fine. He thought of how the walk would be good for Vernon. It could be therapeutic. Emmitt was only half awake as he strolled into the bathroom and covered his face with shaving cream. The razor was somewhat dull but, because he had held it beneath the stream of hot water for so long, it felt good against his face. He began to move his hand in short, quick strokes which were hastened by the chimes from the clock in the den. Once again, they had pronounced him too late to open the doors at the bank.

Emmitt Braedeikk was the branch manager of the largest and most busy bank in his hometown of Malfaxe, a city where he had lived and never strayed far from since his days as an infantryman in Lyndon Johnson's nineteen sixties army. Occasionally, he would drive to nearby cities to transact business, but Emmitt was basically a creature of habit. His span of travel seldom encouraged a night in a strange bed. Emmitt's idea of a change meant a new computer or an updated cellular telephone

1

instead of a one year old model. He was, in many ways, typical of many others who might be hard-working, sincere, and gentlemanly. Emmitt was a bore. He knew it himself, and he also suspected that others were quite aware of the fact. Not that it really made very much difference to him. He could live with it easily enough. Although severe changes were not to his liking, there were times when he would have enjoyed a different image. Once he had considered longer hair. Later he dismissed the idea. It had been too drastic for openers. His hair was rather fine anyway , so he submitted to the wearing of a very thin mustache instead. It was dark brown and no more than a quarter of an inch wide. It crowned his upper lip superbly. Emmitt's mustache was more unique than most. One evening at a distant salon, he had paid a hairdresser two hundred and seventy-five dollars for it. Naturally, he had chosen to be discrete about its originality, so he had waited until after his vacation to wear it. The banker had never before felt so virile. Everybody praised it, and nobody dared hint that it might be unreal. Emmitt, himself, would often stand in front of his full-length mirror and look upon it in awe. He cherished the way that it confirmed his masculinity.

Emmitt seldom missed Sunday morning church services, although Vernon had caused him to miss two consecutive sermons in April. The banker had been up all night on each occasion waiting for Vernon's return. Of course, there were never any questions from Emmitt, nor answers from Vernon, about the details. Emmitt wasn't altogether naive about male drives. It was only when Vernon had flaunted his ugly animal instincts that Emmitt became angry. Two months before he had caught Vernon doing it right in back of the kitchen. It had been very late that night, but the moonlight had peeked into the patio and revealed the vulgar gyrations of Vernon's vivacious body in motion. Emmitt had merely gone back to bed jealous and shaken. He refused to worry over unchangeable events. He wondered, however, if Vernon should see a different shrink. It seemed the prudent thing to do. The idea nagged him, because Emmitt didn't need another mouth to feed and that was always a possibility. As he was dwelling on the matter, he directed his conservatively dressed body toward his parked sedan. In six more nights to come, he would ponder on how Vernon would likely screw up another Sunday morning. Today was Monday, and Emmitt was committed to five more solid days of work at the bank.

Emmitt walked forward in his driveway to his car. He then extended his hand and removed a note from the windshield. As he read from it, disappointment shadowed his face. His cleaning lady had quit. He looked away from the note. His eyes veered toward the thin crack which severed the gray cement sidewalk. From behind his gold framed glasses, his eyes squinted. The wrinkles which layered a high forehead appeared deeper. His cheeks seemed drawn and his lips remained tightly together. He folded the note neatly and pushed it into his shirt pocket; then he started the car and pulled it onto the asphalt road.

If he made the speed limit, the drive into town usually took the banker only ten minutes. Today, he drove slower. His pattern of life was about to be changed and now he had the burden of making adjustments. He was in deep concentration, as he unknowingly and by way of a semi trans divorced himself from the other traffic. He didn't see the green cedars which barricaded the small farms from the highway. Nor did he notice the edge of the river, which had consumed his one-time favorite fishing pier. Now it was only a broken down relic in the black mud. He heard no sounds of discontent from the hungry cattle grazing in the open fields along the highway. The mist, which kissed so very lightly the surface of his engine's hood, went undetected. His first solid thought was that of opening the bank's front door.

As he stepped through the vestibule, he lifted his head and looked toward the tellers. The girls had all taken their stations more than an hour ago. John Kirby, the assistant manager, was at his desk talking to a man and woman. The man was husky in build with very strong features. But it was the woman who had caught Emmitt's attention. She was no more than twenty-two. Her hair was dark brown and hung straight, trimming her narrow shoulders. Her face was browned by the sun and her eyes dipping into her high cheekbones seemed to slant off at severe angles. As she sat erect with her legs crossed, she appeared content to let the man do the talking. When Emmitt went by, she looked up and smiled. Her teeth were unusually straight. When Emmitt nodded his head, he wondered if they were real. He walked on by until his thoughts were interrupted by a regular customer.

"Hello, Mr. Braedeikk," the customer spoke.

"Good morning, Mr. Kelly," he returned, while still moving on.

When he reached his office door, a voice called out in a low monotone, "Hello, Emmitt." The banker gave a faint hello without looking over. It was Margaret Simpson, who had called him by his first name. He resented every syllable of the way she spoke to him. John Kirby was to be transferred within the month and Margaret was to take his place as assistant manager. Margaret's record at the bank had been splendid. Her energy was without end, but her personality was somewhat aggressive. To Emmitt, she was little more than a vulture hovering over a piece of dying meat. She was offensive, he thought, as he passed through the door to his private office. He then very gracefully lowered his one hundred forty-pound body into a revolving chair.

"Mr. Braedeikk."

Emmitt looked up to see Kirby's head emerge from behind the door.

"Yes, John?"

The young man approached the manager's desk. He handed his boss a loan application which he had carefully avoided wrinkling. Emmitt's eyes scanned the paper as a wry look invaded his face. His left hand moved up to touch his jaw. He started moving his head back and forth in a horizontal direction.

"No, I can't approve this loan, John," he said.

"That's what I thought you'd say, Mr. Braedeikk."

"So then, John," Emmitt grumbled, "Why in the hell did you bother me with it? Sometimes I can appreciate caution, but this is insanity and you know it. Why is it that I always have to be the hardcore bad buy?" His voice became even more condescending. "Look," he said. "These people want seventeen thousand dollars for a used automobile. They don't even have a token down-payment. You saw this, John. Their combined income is only thirty thousand, seven hundred dollars per year. And look here," he blasted, "They have no previous credit listed either. If I gave out many loans like this, do you know where I'd be? I'd be out on Hamilton Avenue next week waving my skivvies to all the people driving by. And they would all probably have brand new automobiles, too! Now is that where you'd like to be? How bout it John?"

Kirby looked away as Emmitt handed him back the loan application. "No, sir," he said. "I guess not."

"Good," Emmitt said, "now go out there and tell those people you're sorry, but you can't extend our services as things stand." Kirby turned and started to walk away as Emmitt called him back. "John," he said.

"Yes," Kirby answered as he stood sideways to Emmitt, almost looking back over his own shoulder.

Emmitt's voice became mellow. "I know you hate to refuse those people, but if you're going to stay in banking, you'll have to get used to it. We have a lot of other people counting on us to protect the investment they've made here. Money's too tight. Besides that, you don't think those people sitting in your office actually expected a loan from us, do you? Not likely. They only came in here to find out if you had your brains jammed in reverse. Now go out there and handle them."

"All right," Kirby answered, as he turned and walked out into the bank's front office. He was feeling much like a kid who had been forced by his father into locking horns with the neighborhood bully.

Emmitt then looked down at the stack of papers on his desk. It was messy. Spontaneously, he thought about his home without the cleaning lady. He wondered if his brother's filthy habits could have been responsible for her leaving. He began to stack his papers neatly as the phone rang.

"Hello, Emmitt Braedeikk speaking." He listened tentatively for only a few seconds before he spoke. "No, I don't think so. I already give to various charities." Emmitt then offered a warm goodbye and put the land phone back onto the receiver. He stood up and went to the door which separated his office from the rest of the bank. He noticed how professional the tellers looked and how adeptly they helped the customers.

Kirby was inviting a disheveled man into his office. The man was quite old and poorly dressed. Emmitt imagined that this man also wanted to buy a car, probably a limousine, and then his eyes suddenly shifted to Roxanne's legs. They were thin but shapely and carried her goddess like figure with the grace of a fashion model. Her nylons had been cursed by an ugly run though. Emmitt traced it up as far as the edge of her knee length dress before looking away. George, one of the armed delivery guards was smoking again. Emmitt approached him.

"Are you comfortable, George?" He asked.

"Yes, sir," the guard answered, as he attempted to go about the business of securing the previous weeks monetary transactions.

"Can I get you an ashtray or anything?" Emmitt asked.

"No thanks," the guard said. He looked straight ahead, as he lifted his foot and blunted out the cigar on the heel of his shoe.

"Good, don't forget what you're supposed to be doing."

Emmitt turned and walked back into his office in time to hear the telephone ringing. He reached for it, squeezing it tightly. "What is Vernon stealing today?" He wondered.

"Hello, Emmitt Braedeikk speaking." He paused. "Yes, of course, we do. Can you come over to the bank later this afternoon?" He inquired, scribbling a notation on the bottom corner of a pad. "Excellent," he said. "I'm going to arrange an appointment for you with our assistant manager. Is two o'clock all right?"

Again, the banker was silent and, as he looked around the office, he exhaled deeply before he spoke. "To tell you the truth, I have an appointment this afternoon. But if there's any problem, I'll personally review your application myself."

There was another hesitation, then Emmitt continued. "Then the man you want to see is a Mr. Kirby, that's John Kirby. I'm sure he'll be able to help you. Now is there anything else I should know before I tell him to expect you?" Emmitt was quiet. "Okay, thank you very much for calling," he said, as he put the phone down. Sitting motionless, he gazed at the phone briefly. Emmitt wondered why it had been Vernon and not himself who had been spared from life's so numerous and trivial burdens. Vernon was such a free spirit, taking from life only what he wanted, and disregarding the stupid hassles. Emmitt suddenly leaned forward and grabbed a magazine. It had been concealed between a financial report and a large folder. The cover of the magazine had an illustration of a huge bear towering over a man with a rifle. It had been one of Emmitt's favorite issues. He loved stories concerning man against the wild. They excited him to no end. He opened the magazine and began to read as the phone disturbed him once more.

"Hello," he said, "Emmitt Braedeikk speaking."

The voice on the other end of the line jabbed at his nerves instantly.

"Are you the owner of a brown and white mongrel with a distorted ear?" A woman asked.

"Maybe," Emmitt said, with only a faint hint of denial.

"Good, Mr. Braedeikk, this is Miss Cole from the city pound. I believe that we have your dog down here, if you care to pick him up."

"What's he doing down there?" The banker was puzzled.

"He was found this morning in a shopping center."

"A shopping center?" Emmitt repeated. "What business do you people have snatching up my dog from a shopping center?"

"Well, apparently he spends a lot of time down there, especially in the drugstore. The management has put him out several times. But this morning, he knocked over some bottles. That's why we have him. We'd like you to come down here for him some time this week." She paused and then spoke again. "Now when you do, come to building 2A. There's going to be a seventy dollar per day boarding fee, and we close the doors at six-thirty every night."

"Are you finished?"

"Not quite," she said, "at the end of the week, we turn the gas on."

Emmitt slammed the phone down. "Miserable dog," he said, letting his anger flare. He sat silently for only an instant, as he stared at his office door. His hand was vigorously rubbing the contour of his chin before it hit the button on the intercom. "Kirby," he said, "send Margaret in here."

Within the time it had taken him to breathe deeply twice, she was in his office and Emmitt turned his entire chair somewhat to greet her.

"Margaret," he said. "I'd like you to take a cab over to the city pound and bail my dog out."

"Why me?" Margaret objected, truly annoyed.

"Margaret, please, you'd be doing me a great favor. I have an appointment this afternoon."

Margaret tilted her head slightly and folded her arms as she scrutinized the situation. "If you mean the one with the minister of your church, John said to tell you that he called, and it's off. He wants to know if he can catch you on the road again.

"Absolutely," Emmitt said, "but I still want my dog retrieved."

"Sometimes those people make mistakes. How can I be sure I have the right dog?" Margaret continued to fret.

Emmitt swung his revolving chair around to his desk again. He held on to his magazine and began thumbing through the pages, not even bothering to glance up as he spoke. "Just ask for Vernon," he ordered.

CHAPTER 2

It was only the 29th of April. The warming temperatures had been breached by rain, and a mild breeze glided over town carrying with it all of the promise of a beautiful spring to come. Emmitt closed his office door and locked it. He darted briskly to the end of the teller's counter and stepped around to the other side. Everything seemed in order, so he terminated a complete circle by walking back to his office door. There he picked up his attaché case, which was sitting on the floor and carried it to the bank's front door. Peter Ghudd, the bank's cleanup man, had just wrung out a mop that he had been using to clean the floor. He was pouring the remaining soapy water into a drainage sink as Emmitt called out. "Let's go, Peter. It can wait until tomorrow. I have to scramble."

The old man appeared from inside of a utility closet and waved his hand slowly to show acknowledgment. Then he went over to Emmitt and began to wipe his damp fingers across a piece of shredded rag. "OK," he said, as he reached for a thin jacket that was hanging loosely across a metal coat rack. "I hate to complain," he said, "but do you suppose the women could keep things a little neater in there?" He looked accusingly toward the ladies' restroom.

"Peter," Emmitt argued, "whatever they're doing to mess that place up is the reason why you have a job. I don't need them wasting any more time in the ladies' room than necessary, even if it is to tidy up. In short, that's why I pay you."

Peter turned his back on Emmitt and went over to the large front window. Emmitt watched as the old man drew the curtain, a ritual that he had witnessed every night for almost two years. Peter hobbled with a slight limp, but up until now, Emmitt had never questioned why, not even in his own mind. Now he was wondering if the janitor hadn't suffered from a birth defect. He began to feel sorry for Peter and felt badly about the way he had talked to him. Emmitt set the alarm system, and the two men went out onto the concrete steps.

It was still raining and, had it not been for the overhanging canopy, the two of them would have been drenched instantly. Peter stepped aside, allowing Emmitt to turn and lock the door. Emmitt's hands were fidgety. He wiggled first the door and then the key trying to synchronize them together. Peter stood there contemplating how Emmitt ever made it out of his own house in the mornings without help. To Peter, Emmitt was a combined piece of intellect and clumsiness. Peter began to guess to himself that it might be a slightly common condition in the world of white collar intellects.

Emmitt finally turned to face the older man who was standing under heavy raindrops from the downpour. The canopy had been ripped above Peter's head and the water was saturating Peter's hair. Emmitt clasped his hand around the older man's upper arm and gently moved him from under the leak.

"I didn't mean to get curt with you a minute ago, Peter," Emmitt apologized.

"That's all right," Peter returned. "I shouldn't have bothered ya."

"No, you're right, and I intend to speak to the women the first chance I get. You deserve more consideration. You know, Peter, you've been with us for a couple of years now, and I've never had any problem with the way you take care of things around here."

Emmitt tried to sound noble, but what he said was very true. Peter always showed up for work on time and his jobs were completed with the utmost of pride. That was Peter's calling card. He cleaned the lavatories, polished the floors, and kept the windows shiny all the time.

These were just a few of the countless duties he performed in addition to the many other things he did. Peter would have worked forty hours a week, but the bank's policy only allowed for a part time custodian. As far as help went though, most of the women in the bank considered him invaluable, especially because of their little smoking nooks which they tried keeping rather secret from the boss. So if their private spots ever needed attention, or as little as a dirty crevice had to be wiped, it was he who raced to the scene to jubilantly finger the job. "Anyway, Peter," Emmitt concluded, "I'd be the first one to miss you if you ever left us. I'll see you tomorrow."

"Tomorrow," Peter took his hand and smoothed it across his gray matted hair. By now, it was water-soaked and was hanging wildly over his ears. He turned and walked away, disappearing into the oncoming darkness. A darkness that he felt more than he saw.

It was almost six o'clock when the banker checked his watch. He had just fastened his seat belt and started the car. The rain was coming down harder now, and Emmitt's shoes had become waterlogged while crossing the parking lot. Had he been on time for work, he could have parked closer to the bank. Emmitt had no regrets. He had needed the extra hour's sleep. Besides, it had always provided him with a sense of aristocracy to come strolling into the bank late. His morning had been perfect, he thought, as he slid his shoes off and placed them carefully to the side. His socks were drenched and felt, to the banker, as they had been pasted to his feet. He removed them slowly and laid them neatly over his shoes. He, then, put the car into gear and drove onto the main drag of the town in his bare feet.

As Emmitt wheeled through the heart of Malfaxe, his eyes began to scan the buildings. Except for a steady and constant deterioration, they never seemed to change very much. Many of them had been built from brick and were very old. Over the years, their original reddish color had faded to a dingy brown. They were rapidly becoming shrines to a forgotten past. As he condemned them to himself as being eyesores Emmitt lit up a cigarette. He made a right hand turn by the YMCA building and a sharp left turn by an Army surplus store. The traffic had been detoured because of road construction. There was always road construction in Malfaxe. Emmitt couldn't understand why. The roads never got smoother or larger. They were just always torn up. He stopped at a traffic light and prepared to turn left. Another car had stopped right next to his own. He casually looked over, trying to pretend aloofness. Four teenagers were passing a cigarette around. When the remaining stub had finally returned to the driver, he blunted it out. It reminded Emmitt of the military. He suddenly remembered how many times he had relished a good-tasting cigarette. He began to feel lucky that he could afford a pack of his own. It never occurred to him what they were smoking, at least not until the light changed to green, and Emmitt had made the turn. He was back into the mainstream of traffic once again.

The banker hated his drives across town. What he disliked even more was the reason for his evening journeys. If Peter had only known who Emmitt was catering to. The thought kept reverberating in his mind until he finally admitted an outward feeling of shame to himself. He wanted to end the relationship that had always kept him in such emotional turmoil. It wasn't possible. Sure there were arguments, but nothing too serious. Once Emmitt had even dared to raise a fist, but that was as far as any disagreement had ever gone. He wanted to fool himself without much success by believing it was usually just the lack of mutual understanding that had strained his amiability so. A year earlier, he had considered calling the entire arrangement off at a financial loss. He had dwelled on the idea somewhat, and finally decided not to. To him, at the present, a bad relationship was cheaper, and maybe even better than none at all. He kept driving and as he neared his destination, he continued to evaluate his ever changing feelings.

The road was better now. It had changed into a highway. He was driving more comfortably. He passed a high school and then a gas station. It occurred to him that his own gas tank was getting empty. He decided to have it filled near his usual point of rendezvous, which was right across the corner from his pick up place. He turned and pulled into a filling station displaying a large sign that advertised plus gas at a reasonable price. It was one of the few remaining stations with an attendant who pumped. As Emmitt lowered the window with his hand, he turned the ignition off with the other.

"What'll you have, Mister?" A gruff man asked.

"Fill it up with plus."

It was then that he saw them. A man and woman were relaxing across the street. They were on one of the many park benches which decorated the perimeter of a nursing home. The woman had never looked better to Emmitt. She had long blonde hair which cascaded halfway down her back. She was beautiful. It was obvious to Emmitt that her tag-along friend had dubious aspirations. It was written all over his conniving face. Emmitt was full of resentment. He wished they would stop talking and notice that he was waiting. The man was such a slob, Emmitt thought to himself. The woman began to move her legs sideways, and gracefully leaned back against the bench. She propped her forehead in her hand, twisting to engage the man's face. Her profile revealed a few freckles against her fair complexion. She had a sharp nose. It was nice, and Emmitt even thought it to be charming. He couldn't see the color of her eyes, but he'd known from first glance that they were blue. She balanced her free hand over the curved handle of an umbrella. Her extremities were delicate, and Emmitt focused his own eyes on her sandaled feet. The rain had stopped, but the ground was still wet. Emmitt hoped that the girl wouldn't get her feet wet. Suddenly, they turned and acknowledged his presence. The banker began to feel disgusted, as the man walked over and got into Emmitt's car.

CHAPTER 3

Stepping from inside of the bank and looking briefly about the streets, Emmitt wanted to be outside. He walked over to the vender where he usually bought his morning paper. It was empty. Normally, he could have counted on having the news anytime before nine o'clock. It was almost nine-thirty. He looked down Hamilton Avenue until he could see no farther. There wasn't any sign of the delivery truck. He turned and walked directly to the bank. His skin had become sticky in just a few seconds. Air conditioning was priceless, he thought as he pushed open the bank's front door.

A sudden, "hello", startled him. Emmitt turned to see a round faced Blackman offering his hand.

"Oh, hello, Reverend," he said, reciprocating with his own. "What evil deed brings you out on such a hot day?"

"I want to talk to you about the church, Mr. Braedeikk." the man said with a friendly grin.

As he withdrew his arm, the Reverend Jameses looked very much at ease. He stood somewhat crooked, projecting an air of relaxed composure. He smiled, which was usually the case, and Emmitt could never understand why. The preacher's wife had died only four months earlier, as a result of a stroke. Along with numerous medical expenses, the minister had been left with the burden of a young college age daughter.

"Good, I've been trying to reach you all week, too. I was wondering if we could arrange a meeting sometime?"

"What about right now? I've got time, if you do."

"It's not quite that simple," Emmitt said. "There are other people involved."

"What other people do you mean? You're still giving my congregation until the first of the year to catch up on the mortgage payments, aren't you?"

"I was," Emmitt said, as he looked toward the street. "But I went out on a limb for you, Reverend. One of the vice presidents didn't appreciate me giving you that additional time."

"And," the upset preacher paused. "Exactly what are you telling me?"

"I guess what I'm saying is this. If the mortgage payments aren't caught up with by the end of the month, the bank will be prone to foreclosure."

There was an awkward lapse in dialogue before Emmitt began to speak again. His voice became soft and, as he attempted to excuse his embarrassment, his eyes strayed from the minister's distraught face.

"Look," he said, "I'm not insensitive about this issue. If my bank had that piece of real estate tomorrow, I don't know who'd want it. Anyway, it makes me feel uncomfortable to have to repossess a church property."

"Maybe you won't have to," the black man appeared upbeat.

"What do you mean? If you have any cards to play, tell me. You know a lot of investors are running from real estate around here. It's too far underwater. It's not worth the aggravation, Reverend. Why don't you rent a hall or a vacant movie theater for your services?"

"We still have a few weeks."

"That's right," Emmitt said, removing a handkerchief from his shirt pocket. He wiped his brow with it before tucking it away again. "Don't hold me to this Reverend, but I'll call my boss. Maybe I can get him to hold off on foreclosure proceedings until mid-September."

"Do you think it would do any good for me to give him a call?"

"No," Emmitt returned emphatically, "I wouldn't advise it. He's unpredictable. If he got the impression that we were ganging up on him, he might react adversely."

"I'll let you see to it then. Only I'd appreciate it if you'd call me at my home, and let me know what he said."

"I'll call you as soon as we talk." Emmitt was glad to oblige, as he extended his hand a final time.

The two men parted, and Emmitt continued his retreat into the bank. It felt good, he thought, to be out of the heat. He walked over to the large front window and peered out. The black man had just crossed the street and jumped into the back of his pickup truck. He was moving garden tools around. It wasn't until the minister caught the banker watching him maneuver the equipment that Emmitt stepped away from the window.

Emmitt approached Kirby at his desk. "John," he said, "get this mister Beck on the phone. He's the district representative for Icon Oil." Emmitt reached over Kirby's desk and grabbed a small piece of paper. He jotted down a name and phone number and handed it to John. "When you get him on the line, I'll take the call in my office." Emmitt left immediately and went back to his own desk. He was there for only a minute when his phone signaled his incoming connection.

"Hello," Emmitt Braedeikk speaking."

"This is Richard Beck," said a voice on the other end of the line.

"Mr. Beck, I think I've got some good news for you. How would you like that large lot that we were discussing last week? You know, the one I said would be a marvelous spot for your new convenience store, and gas station."

"Certainly I'd like to see it. If it's suitable, maybe we can talk about it. Is it zoned for commercial use?"

"No, not yet, but that won't be a problem. You've got my word."

"Where is it, Braedeikk? I'll cruise by and check it out tomorrow, before I report in downtown."

"You'll be temped," Emmitt said, "just go down Hamilton Avenue until you get to a restaurant called Weaver's. Make a left at the light and go one block down to North Avenue. There's a porn shop next door. You can't miss the lot. It has a church building on it."

CHAPTER 4

It was easy coasting down the long narrow stretch of highway, although Emmitt believed the air in his tires was a bit low. The evening had just begun, but he felt as though it should have ended hours earlier. He was perspiring heavily. This time, his entire body seemed to be melting right out from underneath of himself. He was at the end of a short downward ramp. He would have to pedal his bicycle harder now to reach the top of the oncoming hill. Emmitt drew in one more very deep breath. The mild evening air felt unusually good as it began to fill his nostrils and replenish his lungs. His legs began to pump faster, and his body took on a vertical posture. Delicate hands squeezed at the handle grips fiercely; and he leaned forward, trying to drive the gentle breeze into his body. His sweatshirt stuck to his skin, so he wiggled his shoulders, hoping to free them from the clinging cotton. When he turned his head only somewhat backward, his hood slid down and fell over his neck. There was no traffic in sight, prompting him to cross over to the other side of the street with hardly any effort. His second wind had arrived, and he was ready to challenge the pain of the next two miles.

Dusk was only an hour away, and Emmitt anticipated a coolness that would escort him home, as it had the night before. June had been hot, but July would be agonizing, he decided, as he approached another turn and cornered it slowly. A loose Doberman nipped once at his heels, but Emmitt picked up the pace and left the half-hearted dog far behind. He crossed over a cement bridge and drifted down another hill. Sitting erect, he felt good at last. The wind assaulted his face, making it vibrant and flushed. As he reached the next intersection, the light turned green. Emmitt exploded with a sudden burst of energy and hurried through it. At first, he ignored the other rider who was following him. Only the road mattered, and Emmitt watched it peel beneath his front tire even faster now. Soon the two men were riding abreast. Emmitt propelled ahead once more, but the other biker was relentless. They were side by side. As he attempted a new charge, the banker felt his legs begin to weaken. It was no use. The pain was overwhelming. He dropped back and allowed the other man to capture the lead.

The two men rode another mile on paved road before Emmitt, following the other biker's lead who turned onto a dirt route. It was barely a path, and Emmitt had never come this way before. The bumps in the ground were becoming a hazard, but he didn't complain. The changing landscape was refreshing, especially the open fields of towering green corn erupting with golden tassels. The path was also trimmed with tiger lilies. They were orange and dangled on the end of long narrow stems. The banker had never liked flowers, but these were different. They resembled small flames dancing happily in the fleeting breeze. A crow flew overhead and then perched on a nearby fence. It remained still and its black outline looked one dimensional against a fading horizon. Emmitt and his companion turned left at a fork in the trail. It was a downhill ride from there and another rest for Emmitt. He sat up straight and tried not to think about the return trip up. When they reached the bottom of the hill, the trail ended. The two men got off of their bikes and sat down in a small clearing.

"You know, Bert," Emmitt said, after drawing in a long, labored breath, "I think if that dog had gotten me back there, it might have been more merciful."

"I know. I'm hurting, too," the other man answered.

"What do you know about hurting? You've only come half the distance that I have, and that dog is always chasing me. Everyday he gets just a little bit closer to my ankles. One day, he's going to yank me off my bike like raw horse meat."

"Why don't you raise some hell with the owners?"

"I don't know who they are. Even if I did, people don't care Bert, not here."

"You're forgetting it's not the sane town I grew up in either Emmitt."

"It's more than the town, Bert, and you of all people should realize what I'm trying to say."

"I do." Bert stepped over to a large oak tree and leaned against it. They were near Clear Bottom Lake, which had been named many years earlier even before Malfaxe had been nothing more than a one street cow path.

Now that very name was a sheer mockery to the lake's true condition. The water was always brown and murky, but it had nothing to do with industrial pollution, as one might guess. The lake had suffered more from some of the few small surrounding farms than anything else. Every time it rained, the runoff would take with it the soft dirt and fresh fertilizer, dumping them right into what had once been perfectly clean water. Before the farms, there had been timber, which had protected the water from natural pollutants. Now only a few remaining areas were wooded. Emmitt joined Bert near one such stand of trees. Bert stroked the fingers of his left hand through his curly blonde hair. With one upward notion, he lifted the hood of his windbreaker over his head.

"Emmitt," he asked, "are you interested in Malfaxe or is it just a place where you happened to of had the misfortune of being born?" He continued, never waiting for an answer. "It wasn't just by chance that I brought you down this way."

"Just exactly why are we here?" Emmitt gasped.

Bert extended his index finger and pointed out toward the large body of dirty, choppy waves that had been kicked up by the increasing wind. "Emmitt, what do you see out there?"

The banker was puzzled. Other than a junkyard that flawed the open view, there was nothing unusual for him to comment about. Emmitt gazed at the distant shoreline. Then he looked over to Bert for a clue. It was futile. Bert's face was blank. His eyes were fixed, and his lips were sealed. Bert stayed quiet, as if he were in a trance. "I'm not sure I know what you're talking about, Bert. I can see clouds and birds. There's a boat to the left of that sandy reef. There's a lot of water out there, Bert, a heck of a lot of water."

"What's there?" His friend prompted. He pointed to a distant side that emptied into a narrow pond. "Beyond the water," he encouraged.

"A lagoon?" Emmitt responded, as though he were questioning his own answer.

"Yes, and do you know what else I see?"

Emmitt looked once more. He was becoming annoyed with Bert, but they had been friends for many years. Actually, Bert was the only friend that he had ever had. He wanted to please him, so he decided to play the game through. There was nothing more than what appeared to be a half of a mile of wasted quagmire. The reeds sticking out of the water were tall and very dense. There were cattails, too. The banker noticed how they resembled large brown cigars. When he was a kid, he had tried smoking one, but it hadn't worked out. It was fuzzy and tasted ronk. He had gotten the idea from his brother, who, himself, had smoked one. Just another Norman prank, he was telling himself, as Bert brought him back to the present.

"Well?"

"Oh, yes," Emmitt said, really wanting to gratify Bert's patience. "What's that? It's a duck blind, isn't it?"

"The new city prison! That's what I see over there, Emmitt."

Emmitt's eyes squinted at the duck blind. It was standing on four pilings, which had been driven beneath the water and into the lake's firm bottom. The sides and top were made from dead reeds and were attached in undetermined directions. There was a slight opening through which Emmitt could barely make out a decaying floor. On one side hung a piece of decrepit boat canvas. It appeared to be concealing an aperture. The entire structure was the crudest piece of handiwork that Emmitt had ever surveyed. He'd been considering an addition to his house and amused himself with the unlikely prospect of acquiring the same builder.

"Bert," he said, not once looking away from the duck blind, "You've got a really wild imagination. Are we going to keep all of the convicts there or just the really hard cases?"

"We're going to need a new penitentiary," Bert proclaimed, "And I think right there is where it should be." He waved his hand, gesturing toward the rolling hills of pasture and cultivated soil that lay just above the reach of the swamp. "The only trouble is that nobody wants it built in their district. We have two congressmen in this city right now who are barely speaking because of the issue. Did you know that Hays isn't going to run for mayor this year? He's done. That last heart attack almost put him under, and the next one probably will. Urban renewal, along with the new prison site, was going to be part of his campaign. Can you imagine who would oppose anybody for wanting to move the city prison to a remote spot like over there? Get the convicts out of town , that was going to be his next victory slogan. What candidate in their right mind would oppose the logic? Nobody, Emmitt. It can only leave anybody else sucking up to the idea, wishing they had thought of it first."

"I see what you mean."

"Not yet, you don't, but you will. The lower corner of that farm out there cuts straight across the city line. If that facility is going to be built right, it's going to take all of that city side property, every inch, plus more. Otherwise, it can't be done. Now we both know very well who owns that ground, so it's nothing more than getting our influential ducks lined up at this point. Believe me, the man who first introduces the issue of an alternative prison site in that very spot is going to be a shoo-in. My people are prepared to back that candidate to almost any extreme."

Emmitt reached down and began jerking up his loose sweat pants. They had slid from his narrow waist considerably, and were drooping from his hips almost down to his buttocks. He looked at Bert inquisitively, trying to think of the next appropriate thing to say. Finally, he spoke. "Tell me, who is it that you're going to promote this time?" He asked.

"Come on, Emmitt," Bert said, as he watched the boggled little man cover his backside. "Don't be so modest."

CHAPTER 5

"**O**uch!" Dammit, Norman, you just made me cut myself!"

"Sorry."

"Why is it that every time I'm in here shaving, you have to come around and crowd me? Can't you at least wait 'til I'm finished before you start?"

"I'm in a pretty big hurry," the other man replied.

Emmitt looked over at his younger brother, who outweighed him by an honest sixty pounds. He thought about just telling him that it was all right, that he would vacate the bathroom himself, if Norman would only stand back and give him two more minutes. Not this time, though. The blood on the side of his face would take at least twenty minutes to coagulate. He felt like smearing the red all over Norman's new shirt, but he knew better. The younger brother might get physical with him, as he had so many times before. It had been a rough way to grow up, having a younger sibling who could actually make you leery of his presence. Norman was stockily built, and had it not been for his protruding waist and nineteen fifties pompadour haircut, Emmitt would have envied him.

When they were kids, Norman controlled everything, even the other neighborhood boys. They never respected Emmitt, and Norman didn't ask them to. In fact, it was quite the contrary. Sometimes they would all sneak over to a local quarry and engage in skinny dipping with some of the more free-spirited girls. Everyone, that is, except Emmitt. Norman would have the other guys tie his older brother to a tree somewhere out of sight. Then he would threaten to beat him up if Emmitt said anything to their parents about what had happened. Emmitt never told. It would have meant another sibling thrashing, and he knew it.

Even their clothes, which they shared, were passed from Norman to Emmitt. Yes, because he was always at least two inches taller and so much more robust than his older brother, Norman got the new clothes first. Norman didn't wear hand-me-downs. Emmitt wore hand-me-ups.

"Are you in a hurry because you have to meet that woman again today?" Emmitt asked.

"Yes."

"She didn't look like your type to me."

"I know."

"Well, why bother with her then, Norman?"

"Well, Emmitt, I wouldn't, but she helps to take my mind off of my problems."

"You don't have any problems, Norman."

"I know."

It was another conversation speeding to a finish, but Emmitt was used to it. It was always fun trying to out wrestle Norman verbally. He thought he was so smart. Norman had barely gotten out of high school. In fact, he couldn't hold a job for any more than six months at a time. Heavy construction was his occupation when he did work, but building had been slow lately. Norman mostly loafed these days, and in his own words, he was draining the system for everything that he could. Sometimes he would moonlight down at O'Shea's Tavern. This was mostly on Friday and Saturday nights, whenever a pick-up band would get together and play to a full house. Norman loved playing, and he was good. Actually, he was very good. The uncanny truth of the matter was that he had never had one music lesson in his entire life. He loved drums, but he could play strings, too. Horns were his favorite, though. All he had to do was choose one and start playing. It made no difference what kind of instrument it was. Trumpet, clarinet, or saxophone, the music would flow like beer from Charlie O'Shea's taps. Sometimes, Charlie would stay open until dawn, simply because the crowed wouldn't go home. The band would get better all the time, and if there was anything that Norman liked, it was holding center stage. He was an exhibitionist. He absolutely thrived off of the attention. That was exactly what Emmitt was thinking when he began to jockey for position.

"Norman," Emmitt said, as he continued to run the razor up the lower side of his throat.

"Yeah?"

"You know, Norman, that woman you're seeing really is very pretty."

"I know.

"Are you interested in her, or is she just another bang in your demolition derby?"

"I don't know."

"By the way, why don't you shave before you put your shirt on, instead of afterwards?"

"Normally I do, Emmitt. To tell you the truth, I wasn't going to shave at all, then I changed my mind when I saw you doing it."

How smart, Emmitt thought. He couldn't stand the idea of me having the bathroom all to myself this morning. Emmitt felt the anger building from within. "I have to tell you one thing, though," he went on with a small note of sincerity. "I really like that shirt you're wearing."

"Really?"

"Yes."

"What color would you say that is anyway, beige?"

"I guess."

"Well you know, Norman, that fabric is kind of unusual, too. Is it silk or what?"

"I don't know."

Emmitt produced a sly look, as he moved in for the kill. "I do like it, though."

"Honest?"

"Yes, really," Emmitt made light, snickering to himself. "My old girlfriend had a pair of useless panties made out of the same kind of material."

Norman stepped back momentarily. He allowed his hand, which held the razor, to drop to his side. He stared at Emmitt for a moment and then went back to his shaving. "I know!" He informed his older brother.

Emmitt had nothing else to say. He wiped the excess shaving cream from around his ears and flung the damp towel onto the sink. He hated being bullied by an uneducated tyrant, but being outwitted was inexcusable. No matter how Emmitt tried to handle his brother, Norman usually came out on top. Emmitt felt like filleting Norman's tongue and feeding it to the dog, but Vernon would never touch such a sordid thing. He dismissed the ugly notion for the absurdity that it was and made his way down the hall to his own bedroom.

His room was small, however, it was a large house, and the largest bedroom had been occupied by his parents. They had both been dead for years, and their will had been somewhat conditional. It had stipulated that both sons could live in the house until one or the other wanted to sell it. At that point in time, the house would have to be sold, and the proceeds divided between the brothers. Neither of the two cared to budge. Out of a mutual respect for their parents, their bedroom had simply been closed up and left the way it had always been while they were living. Naturally, Norman had kept the next largest room, leaving Emmitt with the small one. It was ten by twelve feet long. Had Emmitt been sixteen it wouldn't have seemed cramped at all, but he was almost sixty-four, and the décor was much younger than the banker's years. As he slammed the door, a baseball glove slipped from a carelessly driven nail. A chest stood directly across from the door, and on it were two plastic airplane replicas. Both were World War Two vintage. Emmitt had glued them together when he was nine years old. At the adjacent wall was his dresser. It had a mirror over it, and from where Emmitt stood, he could barely see his fragile image. Down below were rock samples that he had never bothered to build a case for. He wished that he had felt more comfortable working with his hands. Those specimens belonged under glass, he told himself. Besides, they were scratching the finish on the dresser from constantly being moved. If he were lucky enough to get a new cleaning lady, he hoped that she would be more careful. Between the dresser and the chest was Emmitt's bed. It was small, but he still had enough room between the headboard and lower end to accommodate himself.

The walls were painted blue, two of which had pictures of baseball players hanging on them. The wall opposite the door was different, though. This wall held the banker's prize possession. It was a huge color poster of "the King." He loved the way Elvis dressed in those really neat outfits with the high collars and unique capes. Years before, Emmitt had gone to a banker's convention, just outside of Baltimore. Elvis was doing a concert there. The banker never had any idea of getting a ticket, but one did become available due to a long chain of events. Emmitt paid four times the original ticket price and considered himself fortunate. He could have sold that ticket himself at a profit, but this was one time that money didn't count. The entire show had been nothing less than spectacular, and when Elvis had ended it by singing "I Can't Help Falling In Love With You" there was complete silence. You could have driven an eighteen-wheeler right through the middle of that audience and nobody would have moved. Elvis really was "the King", Emmitt told himself, as he began to pull his tee shirt over his own frail chest.

Seeing his window was left open, Emmitt was quick to slide it down and secure the latch. He gazed out of the window and formed a mental picture of the addition that he was going to have built onto the back of the house. It would be fantastic, and the only access to it would be through his own bedroom. That meant that Norman couldn't get there unless, of course, he were invited. The back bedroom wall was going to be knocked out and the entire space would be extended eastward into the backyard. That way, he reminded himself, the sun would come up right over his deck every morning. The deck wasn't there yet either, but it would be. It would be built right onto the back of his enlarged bedroom. The thought of it all delighted Emmitt to no end, because the back yard began to slope rapidly where the deck would begin. There would be no stairway from the ground for his brother to climb and likely harass him.

Emmitt was going to buy an outdoor dinette with some padded chairs, too. He would probably sit up there until the early hours of the morning just playing his radio and drinking whiskey sours, especially on weekends. He imagined himself leaning over the railing and waving to his neighbors across the way. Maybe some of them would join him. He would greet them at the front door and escort them, hopefully right past Norman, to his palatial and private perch. It was going to be wonderful. All he needed now was the right builder, one who would give him everything he bargained for, and maybe more. Fortunately, and for some unusually strange reason, that's exactly who he got.

CHAPTER 6

The service was about over, and Reverend Jameses was looking out toward his congregation, as the choir sang the last stanza of 'Peace, Like A River'. A closed hymnal had just fallen from a small girl's hand, making a loud bang echoing simultaneously with the final chorus of the song. Then it was quiet. The preacher gave an "amen" as he shifted a solemn glare at some of the empty pews. There would be more of them. Jobs were going south and a lot of the people with them. The cycle was shifting. Sixty years ago, people of all colors and ethnic kinships had migrated to the northeastern part of the country to find work. Huge factories had sprawled everywhere. Airplanes were mass produced and cars rolled off of assembly lines, like soldiers marching in close quarter cadence. The impact of the automobile age seemed as though it would last forever, but it didn't. There were still jobs to be had building cars, only fewer, and with the foreign competition, it would never be the same as before. It was difficult to compete, especially with the Chinese. The automobile industry and its spin offs, along with other businesses, were bidding for a solid position in a global setting. Often this meant heading for the Sun Belt, where taxes might be lower and labor cheaper. The reverend wondered if men might not be driven by a way of life that had introduced the beginning of the twentieth century. A time when union muscle challenged company empires. To

Lester Jameses, it had been an even match until big business decided to pull out the brass knuckles and send much needed jobs elsewhere.

The minister watched a small girl, as she folded a Sunday morning bulletin into a corrugated fan and waved it repeatedly under her chin. It reminded him that he had ordered the electric blowers turned off in order to minimize the utility expenses. The area had short summers anyway, he thought to himself, as he casually unsnapped the middle button of his sports jacket. He stood up and signaled for his congregation to do the same. Then he bowed his head and folded his hands together, hesitating only momentarily before he began to pray.

Reverend Jameses asked for forgiveness for his sins and begged for inner fortitude. He gave thanks for blessings. Then he begged that the sick be healed. If they weren't to be healed, he asked that their pain to be short. He prayed for the poor man, who had no worldly riches, and the rich man, who might not understand what real wealth was. He asked for help in solving the financial problems of his church. Then he closed his request by calling for a revival from within the hearts of his parishioners. When the congregation opened their eyes, the minister told them to remain standing for the next song. It was faster. The organist began to play, and the gospel music echoed off of every tiny corner of the sanctuary. It was so loud that it could be heard on the surrounding streets. The preacher noticed an emotional uplift beginning to appear. Some of the people were moving their legs to the time of the music. Others moved only their shoulders and arms. Some, however, were swaying while keeping their feet firmly on the floor. He heard an "amen" from a man in the second row. One woman raised her arms and shook her hands, allowing her fingers to vibrate upward. As the hymn ended, the clergyman looked back down to his congregation and motioned for them to take their seats. He was happier now. He knew they too were upbeat.

"We're going home shortly," he said, "but before we do, I want to do a little talking about money. Yes, I know that you're all getting tired of hearing about money. Well, I'm tired of naggin' about it. It's buggin me just the same as you."

He raised his voice, and the congregation got very quiet. They realized what was about to come next. They knew his words could pour out like hot molten lava. If they thought it was warm now, there was more heat on the way. It had happened before, so many times before. They watched as he paced sideways and slightly behind the lectern to the left, then back to the right. At first, he let his hand rest on his hip loosely. Then he reached up and clenched the back of his neck. His face looked perplexed. It was only an act though. He was preparing to turn on them, as they feared he would.

"I had a premonition the other day," he said. "Yes, that's right. I had a premonition." He closed his eyes tightly, as though he was straining for the memory. "It was peculiar. I'll tell you why it was peculiar if you want to know."

"Why, preacher?" He heard a voice call out from the fourth row, echoed by another closer to the front.

"Tell us," someone else called.

"All right, all right, I'll tell you," he answered, as if he had been coerced into disclosing a well-kept secret. "In this vision, I saw a large wheel. Yes, this wheel came soaring down from who-knows-where right in front of me. Now, friends, I'm not talking about a flying saucer. I'm not referring to one of Ezekiel's wheels, either. You know, the ones that were controlled by the bronze creatures with the faces and wings and straight legs. You remember, of course, you do. Those creatures had fire blazing out of them, and everywhere they went the wheels followed. My wheel was nothing like that. In fact, you've never seen a wheel such as this. This wheel stood on its end. At first, it was turning so fast that I couldn't tell how it was put together. Then it slowed down and, finally, it just stopped. Well, when this wheel came to a halt, I saw that it did, in fact, have lots and lots of spokes. Every spoke on that wheel was just like those on all other wheels. This was important; because, as you know, if one spoke becomes weak or broken, the entire wheel loses its integrity. Sometimes, it comes completely apart. I have to say, though, that this wheel was strong. Did I tell you that the spokes all had names? One spoke was love. Another was compassion. I saw understanding, brotherhood, forgiveness, selflessness, fidelity, and many more. There was a hub. Every wheel has a hub. Am I right?"

"Right, preacher," someone volunteered.

The black man stepped toward the congregation, who by now had completely forgotten about the temperature and waited intensely to hear the end of his story. He held his hands up, trying to form a large circle. At best, he formed two arches, because his fingers and thumbs never met to close the gap. "This wheel not only had a big hub," he said, with a lot of emphasis on the 'big'. It had a big hole in the center! I walked over and stuck my head through this thing. It was high off the ground. I didn't even have to bend down. I just kind of raised my chin a little and I was looking in." He began rubbing his eyes slowly. "Do you know what I saw?" He asked.

"An axle?" A small boy proclaimed from the first row.

"No, Jimmy," the Reverend Jameses answered, as he buffed a handkerchief across his wet, brown cheeks, "I saw a church. I won't bore you with the decor. I only want to tell you about the people who were in there. You see, there were no empty seats. I saw people who had high cheek bones and slanted eyes. There were light-skinned people there, too, with blond hair and fair skin. The red man was, also, represented. Oh yeah, I saw people with dark brown skin, pearly white teeth, and heavy lips. Now, who do you suppose they could have been? The minister chuckled. "I, also, had the feeling that I was the only one who paid attention to the fact that these people looked different from one another. They didn't see it. They didn't know it!" He raised his voice. "They didn't care! They were a family in God! They were very special people! Now I want you to know that I tried to get into that church. I pulled myself up and squeezed real hard against the sides of that hole, trying to push myself in. At last, I realized, it was impossible. I just didn't fit. That's right! I couldn't make myself go in. My head made it, but my shoulders were really tight against the hub. By the time I got my fat waist to the same spot, I found that it was useless!" There was a slight laughter from the membership. "I didn't tell you that there was another reason why it was impossible for me to get into that church. The truth is, and I should have known it from the beginning, that it was not my kind of church. It's difficult for you to believe, I know. You see, that parish and the people in it were just as beautiful as they could be. Remember the spokes on that wheel? That's what held those people and that church together. All of those spokes were there holding tight and keeping things intact. They didn't need me. My job is here!" The minister yelled out. "Here, where some of our spokes are gone and the rim dangles loosely around the edge of things! Here, where the people, who make up the hub of this church, are crying out for the support that they can't do without! Here, where every time I gaze among my loved ones and see empty seats, I'm reminded of Luke, Chapter Fifteen. You remember that parable. Christ told the story of the woman who had ten silver coins and lost one of them. She swept her house and went to a great deal of trouble to find that coin, didn't she? When she found that coin, what did she do?" The preacher's voice trailed off so that it was barely audible. "She rejoiced!" His words now became mingled with temperance. When I can fill this building up with, not just the beautiful people, but also the drug addicts, the prostitutes, the wife beaters, the crooks, and the ones who you might consider to be lost souls, then and only then will I rejoice. Our wheel has a hub. What we need to do is secure our spokes to an outside rim, no matter how bad its condition might be. If we can do that, if we can straighten that rim out, then our wheel, this church, may continue to roll along with adequate support.

There was an inflated silence as the reverend picked up an empty offering plate and flashed its brass interior at the group. "I told you that I was going to talk about money today, but Luke, Chapter Fifteen, was not exactly what I meant." So now, it was coming. They thought that the worst was over, but actually it had only begun. He was going to press for larger contributions. Just as a master chef mixes all of the exotic spices and vegetables to make the perfect dish that only he can prepare, the preacher had blended imagination with words to cook up his own recipe. Along with that, he was about to turn up the heat, and for the congregation there was no way out of the kitchen.

"I guess you could think about the situation we have here for a little while longer and hope the man sitting next to you makes a real big donation this week. That way, maybe next Sunday, it won't get so uncomfortable in here for you. I'm not talking about the weather either, friends," he said, as he stared around solemnly. "I'll tell you what," he continued, "why don't we say a little prayer, and just ask that there won't be foreclosure proceedings? Sounds good, right?" They were on the defensive, and the preacher's face was marked with undiluted disenchantment. "Wrong!" He threw back. "That's not the way it's done. I've often been asked, 'Who is God? Preacher, does God look like us? Could God be a space alien? Does God have a light color, or is he dark, like us? Is God real, preacher, or are you just putting us on for the money?' People, you can believe two things. Beyond any question of a doubt, God is real!" He hollered. "And I am obviously not standing up here in these nineteen seventies' worn out suit every Sunday morning because I like the pay! 'What pay?' You ask. Good question, folks. I haven't drawn a paycheck in months. As a matter of fact, it's costing me part of my personal income to keep this church from going under."

Nobody in the congregation moved. From where the minister stood, a twitch couldn't be seen or a clearing of the throat heard. To him, they almost looked plastic, as they sat quiet and motionless. They were afraid of him. They were afraid of his insight. He knew each one of them. He knew their capabilities, but more than that, he had been studying their souls for years.

"Now, I want each and everyone of you to think about how you're going to help us keep our church," he resumed. "I'm going to be dropping around to see some of you through the week. Eventually, I will contact all of you. I want to know what you plan to contribute. As for myself, I'm working two part time jobs. My daughter is working to help out, also." He removed his glasses and leaned over the lectern, as though he were going to pull a large fish into a boat from the open sea. "Now, if my family can do it, so can yours!" He said, with the force of a crashing wave. "Now, it would probably be appropriate to mention at this time, that our choir is now under contract to sing on Sunday mornings. You won't be hearing them here in church for a while. But they can be heard singing hymns over the radio between nine and ten o'clock. They're going to be with 'Reverend Mickey's Gospel Hour'. Tune them in before you come over here. I might, also, mention that we're considering a small church fair in September. Any ideas that you might have on the subject will be welcome. Just get in touch with either myself or Brother Turner.

The minister put his glasses back on and gestured for the congregation to stand. "Now before we close our services," he said, "I'd like us to sing hymn number two hundred and forty-six, 'Help Us To Help Each Other, Lord'. Yes, nice and loud!" He urged. The many faces began to melt from their frozen calm. The singing was more subdued than it was before. He looked around to the choir and then over to the organist. Marian looked so angelic, he thought. She played so professionally, her delicate, light fingers gliding from one key to the other. In the past, she had always pleased him so, but lately, he had noticed a change. Rapidly leaving her was that halo of innocence that had always shadowed her every move. She was beginning to wear more makeup and jewelry these days. Her language had slipped a few times, and her hair was about as groomed as some of the loose company that she was keeping. He wondered about the change in this girl. She had always been so faithful and willing to serve. He hoped that part of her wouldn't change. She looked up and noticed him watching her. He raised his hymn book closer to his face, as if to hide his thoughts. It was making him feel good to sing out loud.

The final prayer was said, and the congregation was dismissed soon afterward. Reverend Jameses stood by the door to shake hands and wish everyone a good day. He smiled and said many things in jest now. His presence became one of tranquility, and his words were soothing. Marian was almost the last person to pass by him. He grabbed her hand firmly with both of his. "You played well today, Marian," he said.

"Thank you, Daddy," she replied.

CHAPTER 7

The party at one seventy-nine Oakwood Court was gaining momentum, as the evening retreated into midnight and then threatened the slumber of an awaiting dawn. Even Norman had hung around for the affair, not to mention the strong liquor and single women that were surely to be available. It was Emmitt's night. He was entering the primaries. Malfaxe needed a new Mayor, and Emmitt wanted a stab at the job. He knew the position was demanding, but there would certainly be rewards. If he were able to get the city council on his side, his power within the town would be awesome. Bert had promised him that. The primary election was only his first hurdle. From there, it would be just a matter of time. Emmitt was charging into the political arena, just as a drunken sailor enters a house of ill repute. He was promising to satisfy everybody. All he wanted in return was to show how really big and wonderful he could be. It was getting late and Emmitt was primed, ready for action. He was starting to worry however that the inquisitive press might not be there in time to aid in his exposure.

At first, there had been a lot of calls. People he hadn't heard from for months, even years, were now promising their support. Emmitt had been on the phone for what seemed to be hours. He had sat in the stairway talking vivaciously and loved every detail of every conversation. He felt positively magnetic, and never before had he felt so accepted.

The guests were still arriving, only in closer intervals, and often by the carload. The noise was getting louder, and Emmitt questioned just how much more the neighbors would tolerate. There was music, too, thanks to Norman. His brother had brought the band over to help push the campaign into high gear. "Why not," Emmitt surmised. Everything was free. It would be another good time at his, Emmitt's, expense. That was Norman's style.

At 3:15 A.M., two patrol cars cruised down Oakwood Court and stopped across from Emmitt's house. A young looking policeman got out of one of the cars and began to approach the band, which was being lead by none other than Norman who didn't see, or hear the police arrive. Nobody in the band was sober, and the music was no longer in tune. Had it not been so loud, it might have been amusing, but the serious officer heard nothing funny.

"Who's in charge here?" He began.

Bert stepped forward. It may have been Emmitt's party, but Bert had all of the expertise in damage control. Everyone present was aware of that; everyone, except for Norman. Norman who was sloppy drunk moved right up to the annoyed policeman with the grace of a baby elephant that might be fending off a serious stupor. From all indications it had the signs of an awkward confrontation. The officer, with his jaw firmly set, appeared undaunted.

"If this is your party, mister, you're going to have to tell your guest that it's time to be quiet or go home."

"Listen, kid, "Norman lashed out, "nobody is going anywhere, except for you!"

Three more policemen got out of the cars and began walking up to where Norman and the policeman were digging in their heels.

"Does that mean you refuse to cooperate?"

"It means that I don't like sissies, who dress up like honest cops and try to interfere with adult fun!" Norman blurted out.

Bert stepped over by Norman. "Why don't you get in touch with Captain Burnz and tell him you're trying to shut down Bert Dixtzon's party?" He suggested. He's an understanding man."

"I'm sorry," the policeman said, "I'm afraid it really doesn't make any difference. I hear that sort of thing from a lot of unhappy blow hards. The truth of the matter is that most of them have about as much pull as this man's zipper." He looked at Norman accusingly.

Norman peered across at a young woman, who was standing right in back of the officer. She was wearing a low-cut blouse and an extremely tight skirt. Norman had planned on making a pass at her all night but had never really gotten around to it. "Don't ever knock my zipper, pal. It's under a lot of strain right now, and it's doing one hell of a good job," he griped.

The officer reached for Norman. "I believe I've heard enough."

"Get your lousy hands off of me," Norman snarled, as he gave the policeman one hard shove backwards into a white post that ascended under the front porch. The officer went off balance and slid from his feet, landing directly in a rosebush that clawed at his flesh viciously. He worked his way loose from the thorns immediately but his uniform was punched full of ragged holes, and his hands were spotted with blood. He angrily bounced back at Norman and grabbed him from around the center, using both arms. Another policeman took hold of Norman's neck and another his right leg. The fourth officer cuffed Norman's left hand and then his right behind his back. Emmitt and everyone else had watched helplessly, as what was to be a beautiful evening was now being destroyed by a contest of muscle and cheap shots. As he looked out into the many bewildered faces, Emmitt was relieved. The press still wasn't there, and for the present time he was glad not to be the center of attention. There were no cameras, only faces and bodies. Unfortunately, Norman was once again making a scene. Emmitt knew he would eventually have to bear the blunt of things. He wanted to dig a large hole and crawl into it, but he knew that, as far as escaping Norman was concerned, no hole could ever be deep enough.

Everyone seemed paralyzed. Norman was being dragged toward the patrol car and, except for the toes of his shoes rubbing against the sidewalk, it was totally quiet. Just as the group towed Norman to the end of the walkway, two more patrol cars arrived.

"Wait a minute!" Norman bellowed. "Stand me up! Stand me up!" He slurred. It was a command, and for some unknown reason, as if a drill sergeant had delivered the order, the officers responded. Norman was on his feet. He turned toward the onlookers and began to gaze at all of the shocked faces, only stopping to meet Emmitt's bashful eyes. The stare continued for no more than a few seconds, but to Emmitt, it seemed like three lifetimes. It was as though time had cast them all in stone. Emmitt would have breathed easier even if that had been the case, for he knew that Norman wasn't finished yet. Everyone waited for Norman. He looked Emmitt over with nothing less than raw detestation. "And you call yourself a brother!" He scorned. Emmitt's eyes dropped to his own not so sturdy feet. He felt more shame and humiliation from those six words than he had ever thought possible. Norman was placed in the back of a police car and driven to the end of Oakwood Court. The patrol cars came back down, and, as they passed by on their way out, Norman turned his face in the opposite direction. He was, no doubt, sulking. Emmitt, for a flash of a second, wanted to pick up a brick that was next to his foot and give it one long heave right through the window and into Norman's fat head. Instead, he submitted to a guilt trip. He knew what Norman had meant with his degrading comment, and maybe Norman had been right. Emmitt had neither raised a hand or cracked a lip to help his own brother. If he would have intervened, the entire situation might have been avoided.

"The party is going to continue," Bert announced as he gestured for everyone to head back to the portable, outside bar. Within minutes, it was as though nothing bad had ever happened. Bert made a phone call downtown, and the rest of the policemen left. Emmitt was nauseous. He went to the backyard and grabbed a lawn chair. He positioned it behind the trunk of a huge elm tree and sat quietly. It was just like when they were kids, he thought. Once again, Norman had him behind a tree. Nobody seemed to notice him there. He was glad. The moon and stars faded into the morning sky and eventually everybody was gone, except for Peter. Emmitt had hired him to stay around and keep things in order.

Peter was pushing trash into a can with his foot, when Emmitt began to notice that Peter was still there. The old man almost stumbled, as he removed his foot from the container. Emmitt watched as he twisted and hopped to keep from falling. Peter was wearing a dress shirt. Not a very good one, at least Emmitt acknowledged Peter was trying to make a good appearance though. Peter's pants were too loose, and his shoes were vintage loafers. Emmitt wondered how a man could get to be Peter's age with so little to show for himself.

Emmitt approached the old man slowly. He could tell that Peter was embarrassed by his own clumsiness, and Emmitt didn't want to add to his humiliation by running to his rescue. Peter was standing at ease now, so Emmitt gave him a light pat across the back.

"Good job, Peter," he encouraged.

"Thanks."

It was Emmitt who was truly thankful and noticed a sense of responsibility in Peter that he had often admired before. Peter had been there all night. While the others were enjoying themselves to no end, the old guy had never stopped working. Peter had carried drinks, served food, kept the yard clean, and, now, he was getting rid of the trash.

"Let me help you move those cans, Peter."

"I'll manage."

"Not without me, you won't; they're heavy."

"If you insist," Peter said.

"I insist."

The two men carried the cans out to the road for the garbage truck. Then, together, they moved six more bags of waste. When they finished, Emmitt sat on top of a can and looked at Peter. He could see that Peter was tired, but Peter would never admit to that, anymore than he would to a variety of other things. Being old was one of those things. Being lonesome was another. Emmitt suspected that he was anyway. He saw how Peter's eyes always lit up whenever one of the women in the bank called his name, even if it was to do a smutty job. Beyond that, Peter was an enigma. Emmitt, nor anyone else, seemed to know or care to know much about Peter Ghudde. He was reliable, anxious to help, and, for the most part, taken for granted.

"Peter, I have one more favor to ask of you," Emmitt said.

"You got it," Peter answered.

"I have to go down to the jail and get my brother out."

"Maybe you should leave him there a little bit longer."

"I can't do that. If I don't get him out soon, I'm afraid your idea will become very appealing to me, and it wouldn't fair well with the papers if they found out about it."

"I hear ya?"

"He's my brother, Peter!" Emmitt felt compelled to explain.

"He's your brother." Peter patronized Emmitt. "What can I do for you?"

Now it was Peter, who was making the observation. He noticed a reluctance in Emmitt's voice. He believed it to be fear, although Emmitt had tried to disguise his preceding comment as anger.

"How about if I finish up here, and then I can drive downtown to pick him up," Peter offered. "You give me the bail money, I'll have him home in an hour."

"No," Emmitt didn't hesitate, "he's my headache. Besides, you already have one rotten job right here, remember? Please do me one last favor before you leave. Vernon's food is in a can on top of the kitchen cabinet, the one by the sink. Would you feed him and then lock the house up on your way out?"

"Sure will," Peter replied.

Except for the other cars on the road, the ride home from the city's overnight holding facility was qiiet. Neither Emmitt or Norman said anything to one another. The atmosphere was typical for the pair. It was no longer awkward for Emmitt or fun for Norman. It was simply habit.

"Don't get out." Emmitt said, as he parked the car in front of the house. "I have to talk to you about something pretty important to me."

"Go on."

"It's the job I'm running for, and you know it."

"So what does that have to do with me?"

"Until last night, nothing," Emmitt clarified.

"Are you gonna keep me sitting here forever?"

"Norman, I want to be the mayor very badly. You shouldn't have to make me say it for you, either. I'm perfect for the position. I can do a lot of good for this dreadful city, that is, if I ever take office. You realize that, too."

"Do I Emmitt?"

"Yes, you do. Aren't you tired of seeing how corrupt things are run? Nothing ever changes in this town. It's been the same old people playing the same old politics, and giving the same old promises for years. Now, I have a chance to get in there and really change things. I can honestly say that all I want is to accomplish a worthwhile job."

"I'm impressed."

"Do you know who was at the party last night?"

"I can't imagine."

"Mike Howartd, he's retired now, but he's politically involved, maybe even important."

"Not to me."

"Norman, it was his cousin you took to the high school prom."

"I remember. We were stoned bad. We were young."

"She could've died. She came close. I think that car accident you had did kill the old man. He thought the family was about to loose everything he'd worked so hard for! You take a huge toll on people Norman. Doesn't it ever weigh on your conscience?"

"Sometimes."

"Norman, I want you to move out for a while. Disassociate yourself from me."

"No."

"As the city's top executive, I'll be able to make certain appointments, Norman. You like construction work. I can probably get you a building inspector's job. I know we've never seen things in the same light. but I need you to walk a mile in my shoes, Norman, just this once. I think then you'll see why I'm always so sore."

Norman looked over at his brother. As far as he was concerned, Emmitt was still the skinny little nerd that he'd always been. Sure, he drove an expensive car and dressed fashionably. He also had a good job. Other than that, he saw little to respect. No matter how nicely Emmitt could fiddle, Norman was still calling the tune.

"You should wear your hair more like me, Emmitt. It would make you look taller."

"How about it, Norman?"

"Did you mean what you said about the job?"

"One hundred percent."

"Look, hoss, we'll do it your way for now, but you're going to miss me!" Norman was pleased to threaten.

CHAPTER 8

Emmitt checked his watch. He still had thirty minutes before his date was expected to show. She had asked over the phone to meet him in front of the motel office. He would then check in and get the key to a room, a room that he imagined to be just as drab and musty as any he had ever been in. It was raining fast, heavy drops, making it difficult for him to see any further than the end of his car. At last someone turned on a neon sign in front of the office. The word "VACANCIES" stood out in huge pink letters and the parking lot became illuminated with a pastel glare that reflected in the wet asphalt. Emmitt pulled his hat down lower on his forehead.

There was gin in the glove compartment. He removed it and held the pint bottle with moist fingers. The cap on the bottle was tight, so he knocked it against the dash to make it come loose. He poured a couple of ounces into a small paper cup. It was good, so Emmitt poured himself some more. He then returned the gin to its original hiding place.

Actually, Emmitt had misled his date about the arrangements. He wouldn't be waiting near the office. He had decided earlier to check into the room at midday. That way, he might only appear to be a worn traveler looking for a needed rest. Besides that, he could get into the room at his convenience, watch from behind the shades, and commit himself only if he liked the woman's looks. Clever idea, he thought to himself as he got out of the car and headed for the room. Even if the woman didn't show, he pondered a good night's sleep. Nobody knew where he would be. There would be no knocks at the front door or late night phone calls to disturb him. The only thing that bothered him vaguely was his dog. He wondered if Vernon would be all right at the house by himself.

He walked from the car and went straight to the lodging. As he opened the door, he was suddenly aware of an odor. It was like being in a crowded elevator on a hot day; the kind of day when everyone's sweat permeates the air. It was difficult not to admit disappointment to himself, but he did. Instead of the usual hundred dollar a night room at a highly competitive motel, he had settled for much less. He consoled himself that only a spendthrift would have done otherwise.

Emmitt removed his raincoat, trying not to let the water dampen his new suit. He laid the coat across a vinyl chair. The chair's rusty metal legs were situated so the chair would conceal a torn portion in the worn carpeting. A small desk with a table lamp was pushed against a mildew stained wall. He quickly walked over to the lamp and turned it on. Curiosity made him open every desk drawer and examine them to see if anything were inside. Each drawer was empty. If nothing else, he had wished to find a free magazine. He looked over to the front window and saw that the shades were not completely shut. Feeling conspicuous, he wondered why he had not taken the precaution to close them upon entering. Immediately, he yanked the frayed cord. His privacy was now secured, but he still felt anxious. Almost five minutes had passed since he had entered the room. He was allowing his eyes to scan the lodging.

The room had green plasterboard walls which were buckling in places, especially at the baseboard. The baseboard itself did not meet the floor evenly, and Emmitt watched as a cockroach ran underneath one of the openings. There was a bathroom to the right side of the bed. The banker wondered if the unseen was as equally depressing. He walked over and pushed the door open only far enough that his head might enter. At first glance, Emmitt saw that it was a sanctuary of filth, and neglect even beyond his initial expectations. After watching two more roaches run out of the grimy sink and retreat into the protection of a dirty bathtub, Emmitt closed the door tightly.

He went to the bed and began to check its condition. It looked barely six feet long and not half as wide. At the upper end of the bed was a headboard that allowed a pillow to nestle against it. The pillow was covered with a ruffled white cotton case. It was refreshing to see. Two blankets had been neatly placed over a clean white sheet. Emmitt pondered that they wouldn't be needed. He pushed against the mattress, first with his fingertips and then with the flat of his palms. It was pliable and not suitable for a back to lie on. He wasn't concerned, for he knew that it wasn't his back that would endure the discomfort. After turning and sitting on the bed, he bounced slightly and listened for the sound of telltale springs. He noted that they all squeaked, but at least in unison.

It was almost eight o'clock by the time Emmitt finished looking the premises over. Once he was convinced it was suitable, he reached into his dress pants pocket and removed a worn, but thick, billfold with numerous credit cards. Twenty and fifty dollar bills overlapped one another, and Emmitt watched carefully as his thumb hurdled the top edges for an accurate count. All together, he was carrying seven hundred and sixty dollars. He knew it was dangerous carrying that kind of money on himself, but like the gin, the money also made him feel strong. Alcohol and money were two of his favorite companions. They could both offer immunity from the dismal burdens of everyday life. He took out two fifties, folded them neatly, and slid them into his vest pocket. It was a lot of money for one night's entertainment. He felt guilty, but soon gave in to simple justification. He told himself that this sort of thing was nothing more than an essential male drive. It was necessary, because he had been under unfair pressure lately. Being the manager of a bank was not easy. Running for political office was even tougher. He envied the way so many of the big boys in Washington handled themselves with such little concern for the feasible consequences.

It was eight fifteen. The woman was nowhere in sight. Emmitt could tell because he had moved closer to the window. He stood there motionless, watching discreetly from behind the blinds. He toyed with the idea of her being only a few blocks away.

Another vehicle pulled into the parking lot, and the banker watched curiously as a couple got out of a sports car. As they hurried for another room across from Emmitt's, they were laughing and talking feverishly. Emmitt looked back down at his watch, tracking the second hand. It rotated into another minute, he was beginning to feel forgotten.

While he watched, one thought soon led to another. It really had been a very tiring week, and he sometimes felt like just giving up. A traffic citation on Monday morning had gotten him off to a bad start. It was his third in a year. Now his insurance rates were sure to increase. It would have taken something very good to cancel out his sour mood. Instead, the very next day, he was given instructions from the main office to promote Margaret Simpson to assistant manager. That was when he had decided to take Wednesday off. If Margaret wanted the job so badly, she could have it all to herself, he told himself, at least for her first day. When Emmitt had called all of the tellers into his office and made the announcement. She had pretended to be astonished. She was quite an actress. To him, only a smug little snip like herself could have pulled it off so well.

Wednesday morning, however, did bring some lighter news. The press had chosen Emmitt as the most promising candidate for Mayor. His background in money matters and his citizenship were considered to be of the highest level. It was, also, noted that Emmitt was a Vietnam veteran, who had received a Purple Heart. Yes, it was true! The incident never left his memory. He was the fourth man in a detachment of approximately ninety. Each man was anticipating his own death, when the first man in the company stepped on a land mine and was blown apart. Emmitt had been hit by both shrapnel and flying anatomy. He shivered at the recollection.

When Emmitt began to notice the room again, he was no longer excited about the evening. The ugly scenery was staring him in the face from every angle. It hardly seemed the place for a person such as himself. What had started off as something to give himself pleasure was now pecking away at his nerves. His skin was itching, and his increasing feelings of guilt were becoming more acute by the second. It didn't seem fair to him that he should be suffering like this. Why did he have to worry so much anyway? Didn't other prominent members of society do this also? Of course, they did. Politicians, entertainers, even clergymen were caught indulging in this sort of behavior. But that was exactly the point! He didn't want to be caught. Life, he thought, was filled with dilemmas. On one hand, he yearned for power, influence, and a position that would gain him respect. Upper social mobility was what he craved. On the other hand, he harbored a contempt that urged him to disregard society and all of its silly morals, not to mention the stupid code of ethics that men were tied to. He yearned to turn his blindside to the refined world while he romanced, no marveled, his partner into a state of pure, carnal ecstasy. He needed the release. He needed to become altogether physical, like an animal of the worst, sensual kind. He wanted to be like Vernon, unrestrained, if only for one night.

Emmitt heard footsteps on the pavement and took a deep breath when they stopped. Had the woman known where he was? The sound of another door opening and then slamming shut elated him. He changed his mind. Emmitt wanted out. Telling himself that his constituents had a right to expect better, he made a dash for the door. He wasn't going to let them down. He hesitated only long enough to grab his coat before rushing out of the room.

The front seat of the car had never felt better to Emmitt. He pushed himself back into the smooth contour of the black upholstery, trying very hard not to crease his still dry suit. When he turned the ignition on, the wipers immediately began to clear the drops of diminishing rain that were tapping on his windshield. He moved his car to the far corner of the parking lot, where he might not be noticed. He waited five more minutes to see if his date would ever turn up. He drank another shot of gin and waited some more. Still there was no sign of her. Still he waited. Emmitt knew that he could not leave until he had seen who his fear was warning him, so earnestly, to avoid. All of a sudden, she appeared. He wondered how he had missed her arrival. It must have been when he was putting his paper cup into a small brown plastic bag that he kept under the seat. She was standing right in front of the office. Yes, he remembered, he had deliberately not given her the room number in advance! Her hair was short and tapered neatly at her ears. Long earrings decorated the sides of her cheeks. Her facial features were petite, but accentuated by a fancy choker that trimmed her neck. Her dress was cut low, and Emmitt watched, like a night owl casting its gaze toward an unsuspecting prey. She stepped somewhat out of the light. It was then that Emmitt saw what he really appreciated. There was an air of confidence in her movements. He liked her long legs. They were so delicate, feminine, and inviting. She was fine featured with narrow shoulders, and her skin was mildly tan.

It wasn't until tonight that he was sure that she was black. Not that it made any difference to him. He thought that maybe she was. She wouldn't have been his first. It wasn't until she turned her head sideways to look down to the other end of the parking lot that it struck him. He knew this girl! He had seen her in town quite often. She worked part time at an all-night diner. Once or twice, she came into the bank with the owner to drop off cash receipts. Norman knew her, too! Emmitt recalled that a gang of motorcyclists had stopped by the house about three months earlier. They parked in front of his place and had never gotten off of their bikes. Norman had gone out to the road to meet them. At the time Norman hadn't seen fit to tell Emmitt why they had come by, but this girl was with them. She stood out then, just as she did now. Emmitt was sure that she had come from a fine home. He didn't understand why Marian Jameses was doing this!

CHAPTER 9

"I don't like this place, Bert. It's unnerving."

"If it's any comfort to you, Emmitt. I don't either. We're going to have to do this sooner or later, we're running out of time. Let's get it over with."

It was one thirty in the morning. The pair had checked into the central security headquarters with the same enthusiasm as two frightened worms about to dive into a tank full of hungry piranha. It was close quarters, and friends were rare. The only thing that separated some of the worst degradation of human life from the rest of Malfaxe was the city's penitentiary. Most inmates were not worthy of any more than local notoriety though. Some were mere thieves, thugs, or even armed robbers. Not that those offenses were to be taken lightly. However, in comparison to other convicts, the former were no more than the average, run of the mill jailbirds. It was men like Harvey Dempps or Sam Rhiggs, who stood head and chest above the others in a long line of some of the city's toughest criminals.

Harvey had been in prison for over eighteen years. Oddly enough, when he was a kid, he had wanted to become a doctor. After graduating from college magna cum laude, he had applied for acceptance at a medical school, only to be turned down. Convinced that he was rejected because of reasons other than academic, he went on a rampage. He had kidnapped several of the medical school's senior students, three to be exact, and killed them one by one. Afterwards, he dissected their bodies and left the dismembered portions scattered over different parts of the campuses tiny, secluded streets. Victim number three was Harvey's favorite. This one probably had the highest IQ and the most promise of any of the others. It was Henery Van Slectcher the third. Harvey was in the process of leaving Henery's eyeballs on the windowsill directly outside of the dean's office when the police had grabbed him. The encounter, however, was not the result of good police work. Harvey, or "the road kill clipper", as the police had code-named him, normally left a trail a mile wide and twice as long. In truth, Harvey never cared if he were caught or not. If he couldn't be a doctor, he confessed, maybe a prison butcher would be possible. To gratify his passion, he asked for and was granted a job in the prison's kitchen, where he was put in charge of slicing all the meat. The accommodating and understandably appalled officials hoped never to see or hear from him again.

Sam Rhiggs had a different lust. At the age of thirteen, Sam was sent to reform school for purse snatching. At fifteen, he went back for more of the same, plus breaking and entering. At nineteen, he went to prison for armed robbery. By the time Sam got out, he was twenty-six and totally ruthless. Following his release, he laid low for a total of four months before realizing that all of his best talents were resting idle. Not the lazy type, Sam decided to earn some money by robbing a bank. Just for practice, he walked into a savings and loan one Friday evening. Before he left, the manager, four employees, and two customers were dead. One of the customers, a young woman, who was recently divorced, was trying to borrow enough money to buy a refrigerator. Her six-year-old son was with her. Sam killed him last.

Status at Sutler Penitentiary like other prisons was often acquired by one's purpose for being there. The only trouble was that the prisoners, who occupied the slots right beneath inmates like Harvey and Sam, were growing in double digit numbers by the week. It was a scary problem.

"Couldn't we view slides?" Emmitt went on, as the pair attached themselves to a guard named Larry. He would be their escort into and out of all the cell bays.

"It wouldn't be like being here, Emmitt. You need to gain a feeling for the place. Let it seep into your fiber a little. You'll get used to it. Besides, everybody's sleeping."

The three men walked to another security area, where a huge black guard in a drab blue uniform greeted them politely from behind a desk. He was scanning the closed circuit television with careful application when they arrived. This man had nothing to worry about under the worst of circumstances, Emmitt thought to himself, noting the guard's size. When he stood up to shake hands, Emmitt was almost compelled to compare the guard to a huge balloon at a New York holiday celebration.

"You'll be clear to go in there in a moment," he told them. "I have to see your identifications before I open up." The pair of you have been authorized to stay until dawn. Tread lightly. "He cautioned after he checked their credentials.

Once the big guard checked Bert and Emmitt's prison passes against their driver's licenses. He, then, removed a key from his desk drawer and stepped over to the heavy iron gate that separated his security station from cell bay one. He tried to open it as quietly as possible, but to no avail. It made a screeching noise that spurred Emmitt's panic. The last thing that Emmitt wanted now was undue attention, especially from the convicts. Larry went into the cell block first, with Bert close by. Emmitt lingered in their trail.

Bert encouraged him in a whisper. "It's not that bad."

An inmate, who was sleeping in the shadows, rolled over on his side before letting out a long, and loud snore. It spooked Emmitt; and Bert, himself, began walking more carefully.

"How many men would you say are confined on this floor?" Bert whispered.

"I can tell you exactly," Larry obliged. "We have seventy-two cells, and each cell has a man in it."

"Then," Bert concluded, "if we have six floors and each floor has seventy-two inmates, that means we house, let's see, four hundred and forty. No, that would be about four hundred thirty-two inmates.

"Your math is fine," Larry wanted to be polite, "but these prisoners are the lucky ones. They've been given individual cells for special reasons, processing, protection, transferring, etc."

A laugh was heard from halfway up the cell block. As the noise jabbed at his insides, Emmitt's body got stiff. "Some of these bums, we don't know what to do with them," the guard admitted. "Eventually they'll all be moved to the elevated confines where quarters are tighter. New comers will take their places here."

"So every prisoner doesn't have his own cell?" Bert queried.

"I'd say that's an understatement. The truth of the matter is that most of the cells have at least three men in them. Some have as many as five and six."

"How big is each cell?" Emmitt asked.

"About nine feet by twelve feet."

"Don't they fight?" Bert wanted to know.

"Like Frazier and Ali," the guard joked.

"Let's quicken the pace," Bert insisted. "I'd like to be out of here before sunrise."

The three men took the elevator up to the fourth floor, skipping the second and third. "I had a reason for bringing you up to this particular bay. I wanted you to see something," the guard bragged. They checked in, just as they had on the first floor. "This used to be our death row, years back." They went into where the cells looked no different than the ones on the previous level, except for being further apart with a noticeable gap in between. Several men were in each of those cells also.

"I didn't know this place had a death row," Emmitt admitted.

"Years ago, it did. Some executions were carried out here. I'm referring to the Thirties and Forties," Larry explained. That was until the death penalty was abolished. The state penitentiary at Linsburg was doing our heavy work."

"Why, I mean why, would they do executions here, in a city prison?" Emmitt asked.

"Because," Bert took over, "up until nineteen forty-three, Emmitt, this was the state prison. It just reached a point where they needed a bigger facility. Sutler Penitentiary could no longer accommodate the number of criminals they were receiving."

"That's true," Larry reinforced. "Only now, the big house can't handle them either. That's why we're so packed here. We have inmates that should've been shipped straight to Linsburg after their conviction. There just isn't enough room anymore." He toned down, as though not to offend a sharp ear.

Emmitt looked down at the cement floor. Even in the dark, he could see that it had been painted gray many times over. The walls were gray, too.

Only the bars were black. It was depressing. He thought that if he had to remain five more minutes in this prison, he would be forced to vomit.

"Is that all you wanted us to see?" Bert finally asked.

"No, step over here," Larry gestured. He walked over to a double steel door that wasn't locked and nudged it open. Then he led them into a room blackened with the pitch of night. Using the tiniest amount of red ceiling light from cell block four, he was able to locate and flip on the electric switch. Larry closed the door, but the new light was hardly a blessing, for with it came the reality of every perverse idea Emmitt may have entertained about capital punishment. He was standing no further than six short feet away from a gallows. It was higher than he would have ever imagined. He was dumbstruck by its size. Larry approached it without the slightest bit of hesitation and gently kicked one of the four main supports that elevated the platform. "Old reliable," he said. "It made a lot of long men out of wrong men. They used to call it the Sandman. I like the yank o plank, myself."

Bert circled around it in a counter clockwise direction. He was evaluating every bolt, nut, and screw for its purpose. When he got to the steps that led to the top, he began to climb them. As his friend moved upward, Emmitt counted the steps to himself. The last step was the thirteenth. Definitely an unlucky number, Emmitt acknowledged to himself. He wondered why Bert felt the desire to go up there. Bert stood at the top and looked down. He was being careful not to get near the center, where the floor was separated by a gap in the boards. He looked over the front side cautiously and then to the front wall. Like all three other walls, the front wall was nothing but unpainted cinder blocks. A picture of Christ was the only exception. It was the crucifixion, and it hung directly across from where the condemned man would draw his final breath. Larry saw Bert staring at the picture and explained that it must have been placed there to give the dying person some last minute solace. Feeling no need for the guard to elaborate on the obvious, Bert had already concluded the same.

Emmitt's had focused in on the picture, also. He finally looked back at the gallows. These two things were the only marks of mankind in a room that was taller than it was long or wide. One offered nothingness; the other eternal life. The interim, Emmitt derived was reincarnation. He was plugging in on the idea of purgatory when the trap door banged open and startled both himself and Bert.

Larry was standing by the trap door lever with a smirk on his face. "After all these years it still works like a charm," he said with deep satisfaction. "I kind of relish the feel of this thing. Maybe, if times were different, I'd ask for the job."

Bert skirted around the sides of the platform and started back down the steps. Emmitt saw he was irked. Larry, who was fidgeting with the lever, remained composed. At first, Emmitt had been indifferent to Larry, but Larry was beginning to seem obnoxious. Emmitt didn't see why they had to be brought into this particular room anyway. To him, it was impressive, only in the wrong way. He wanted out, and he never wanted to see a gallows or anything like it again.

"Let's go, Bert. I want to see some happier workmanship," he urged.

"How 'bout it?" Bert asked the guard.

"No problem, the machine shop's awaitin."

"All right, let's see it," Emmitt said.

The machine shop was off to itself, in the far extremity of the prison. Bert didn't appreciate the extra effort required to walk the entire distance, however. Emmitt was curious enough to insist. Once again, Larry hit the lights, and when he did, Emmitt was confused. He had never seen such an assortment of tools and machinery. At the risk of sounding ignorant, he began to pry Larry for information.

"What's this do?"

"It's a milling machine. You can cut all kinds of configurations on that machine. Some of the men in here are actually pretty good with this equipment." Larry picked up an object that was sitting in a vise and handed it to Emmitt. It was a steel plate about one inch thick and five inches square. Cut into the plate were multitudes of holes and slots. It was explicit craftsmanship to Emmitt. He held onto it, trying to imagine how something like this was formed. Some of the holes were elongated at angles. Some were counter bored. There were threaded holes for bolts to screw into. There was, also, a square cavity in the plate with steps cut into the sides. To Emmitt's untrained eye, it appeared to be a masterpiece. He couldn't imagine how someone could conquer these skills, but still not be able to cope with society. His thought was amplified when Larry pointed out an intricate gear that someone had machined.

"We should all be so gifted," Bert said impatiently. "Show us where the license plates are made."

"They're not made here," Larry answered.

"Oh, really?" Bert said.

"They bang those out at the state pen."

"Bert asked, "what's turned out here?"

"Very little, it's all specialty type work. There's no mass production. We don't have the room."

Bert attempted to tread on more solid ground. "So, then, you're talking about community jobs that just serve to keep this facility operational, maybe?"

"Basically, that's right. We have an electrical shop and a carpentry shop on the north end. The laundry is down below. You want to go down?"

"What about recreation?" Emmitt asked.

"We have some exercise equipment and a lounge. Outside, in the yard, there's a couple of basketball nets."

"They moved on through the prison and by the time Bert looked at his watch it was already 3:00 a.m. For the most part, the tour was over. Neither Emmitt or Bert were used to keeping the graveyard hours. They chose to call it a night after seeing the auditorium and a few other points of interest. Bert asked why there was no security station or steel doors present there. Larry explained that it was seldom that the auditorium was ever used. He mentioned that whenever it was occupied by inmates, guards were posted like coyotes over lame deer. Any attempt to break free would be futile if not a death wish. Emmitt wouldn't argue the matter, knowing full well that whatever he had to say would likely fall on deaf ears.

When Bert and Emmitt returned to the main security station, it was past 3:20 in the morning. Both men were tired. Emmitt didn't anticipate getting out of bed any time before 2:00 p.m. that afternoon, maybe later. The tour was over. He was glad. He was intimidated by Sutler. Sure all of the inmates were locked behind sturdy bars, but a killer in a cell was still a killer, and Emmitt kept in mind that Sutler had its share of them. When they reached the security office, Emmitt almost kept walking. Had it not been for the guard calling out to him for his pass and signature, he would have trotted straight out into the prison yard by himself leaving Bert behind in the office.

Bert asked for his camera back. It had been taken away from him by central security. They had informed him then that it was against prison policy. He acknowledged to himself that it wasn't a very good idea and had given it up without an argument. All that was left to do was to leave. He and Emmitt went into the prison yard freely and without the protection of a guard. Bert had wanted it that way. Normally, a walk like that would have been impossible, but most people were never allowed to inspect Sutler. Emmitt himself was always aware of Bert's yank. Wherever Bert tugged, something was sure to bend. Tonight, it was some of the prison rules.

They were standing by the building that housed hundreds of the city's worst criminals. It could have been any one of many buildings that Emmitt usually passed on his way to work during the week. The only apparent difference was the bars over the windows. Even that was not totally unique. Some of the other buildings in town had bars, too.

Emmitt surmised that one day most buildings, even homes, would be fortified with them. It was then that Bert drew Emmitt's interest to the ivy growing up the side of the crusty brick walls. Emmitt responded with, "I wonder why they planted that?"

"They don't plant ivy, Emmitt. It just grows, kind of like spontaneous generation. The next thing you know, it's all over the place."

As far as Emmitt ever knew, there was no such thing as spontaneous generation. Everything had a beginning, no matter how small or how large it might be. Nothing just appeared on the face of the earth, or anywhere else, without some reason for it being there. Like the ivy, everything needed a host or something supportive to cling to. In his own case, Emmitt thought it might be his work. On second guess, it had to be Bert. For the first time since he had known him, he began thinking of Bert Dixtzon as his wall, a wall that he could sink his roots into and climb with to unlimited destinations.

"Look over on that side." Bert gestured with a straight arm toward another part of the prison.

"The stuff is three quarters of the way up on that wall. If it weren't for the bars, this place might pass for a college dormitory."

"If it weren't for the bars," Emmitt responded, "it probably would be a college dormitory. That's part of the curriculum, isn't it?"

"I guess, but not all prisoners get that, Emmitt, and besides, it takes a lot of work to get a degree, no matter where it comes from. You know that yourself." Bert reminded his friend.

"True."

"Emmitt, the problem here is not the bars or the lack of them. It's not the programs, either. This prison is just too old and too small to be housing the number of inmates that it has. It's right here in the middle of town; and believe me when I tell you, that nobody, but nobody, wants it here anymore!" Bert was being emphatic. "You want a campaign issue, Emmitt? There it stands. It's a monument to every pussyfooting executive who's ever served this city. It loses an average of one prisoner every two years!" Emmitt looked surprised. "That's right!" Bert continued. "Nobody knows because the press never finds out about it. I know, Emmitt, because they want me to know."

"Who's they?"

"They, Emmitt, are the people who invest in this town. The pace setters who dictate everything outside of the weather. The people who buy and sell other people anytime they darn well please, the powerbrokers. Emmitt, they want this property, and they're going to have it."

"What for?"

"A high-rise office complex. What you see here will be leveled. Visualize it. Nine levels of state of the art architecture taking the place of this monstrosity."

"What's the source of financing?"

"That's no problem. The only two things needed are another prison location and an executive with the grit in his guts to say "let's do it!"

Emmitt's eyes surveyed the six-level structure that jutted out of the earth's skin like a cancerous sore. No matter how you tried to look at it, common sense dictated the truth. The city prison was the epitome of decadence. Malfaxe could do better for its citizens. Nobody deserved to have dangerous criminals harbored in their own back yards This had been the case for years. Emmitt was astonished that complaints had never been registered before concerning this unthinkable, precarious situation. Possibly there had been.

During the primaries, Emmitt had brought up the prison, along with other problems, he felt were pressing. Tax cuts and more traffic lights were two of them. Bert was right, though. Sutler Penitentiary was not just a windmill for some Don Quixote type politician to tilt his lance at. The prison needed to be replaced, but it would probably become a messy endeavor before it was over. Emmitt, also, realized that he needed Bert to guide him into the battle. Otherwise, if not handled strategically, the prison issue was apt to kill him politically.

"Let's do it then, Bert, but first, I have to get myself elected!"

"No, first I have to go home and get myself some rest, Emmitt."

"Why the sudden hurry?"

"Tomorrow's Sunday, or have you forgotten? I have a sermon to prepare."

CHAPTER 10

"I go by Koepy."

"That's an unusual name," Emmitt remarked, as he held the man's business card between his index finger and thumb. He tilted it slightly, as if trying to capture just the right amount of sunlight to get the full effect of the written words. "So you're in home improvement," he continued. "How'd you know I was looking for someone?"

"Could be this is my lucky day," the man said. "I began scouting this neighborhood out on Friday. What're you interested in having done?"

"Could be that depends. What kind of work do you do?"

"Like the card says, home improvement."

"Yes, I know what the card says!" Emmitt snapped. It was 11:15 AM on Saturday, and he was still worn out from the night before. The prison tour was not necessary, he had told himself, as he tried to focus his sleepy eyes on the man in front of him. "You'll have to bear along with me for a few minutes, while I try to wake up. I wasn't expecting the doorbell to ring this morning." He was beginning to calm.

"I'm sorry I woke you," Koepy apologized.

"I wasn't meant to sleep in anyway. What I want to know is what's your specialty? Do you prefer certain types of jobs, or do you work in a wide range?"

"I do it all."

"One of those guys, huh?"

"What I do best is cabinetmaking and carpentry. I'm versatile though. If you want block work or electrical hook-ups, I can do those, too. I, also, do roofing."

Koepy removed his wallet from the back pocket of his clean white overalls. As he began sorting through his cards, Emmitt observed how young he looked. He was tall and wiry, probably six feet three at least. He had a full head of hair. It was light brown and untrimmed. It hung over his ears, making his gaunt face appear somewhat broader than it actually was. He had a mustache, too, a real mustache. This kid couldn't have been more than twenty-seven, Emmitt reasoned. He also thought that Koepy was kind of bold, believing that he could pass himself off as a jack of so many trades, simply because he possessed an overwhelming abundance of male hormones.

"Here," he produced another card and handed it to Emmitt. It was an electrician's certification.

"Okay," Emmitt's own doubts began to come back to mock him. "I guess you are an electrician. That's your right name then, Stanley Scott Koppenhous?"

"Koepy. It's just Koepy."

"Fine by me. I'm curious," Emmitt said, "How long have you been doing this type of work?"

"Since I was fourteen."

"Come on now!"

"My father was a carpenter. I apprenticed for him. When I got old enough, I went on my own."

"Was your father an electrician, also?"

"He didn't have to be. Framework was easier to come by then."

"Maybe so, but I'm sure any good carpenter could find his share of jobs today without all of this other stuff you say you can do."

"Wintertime can be a corker."

Emmitt looked straight into Koepy's eyes. They were such a pale blue that any less hue would have made them colorless. He considered breaking off the conversation, then thought twice about it. There was a sincerity there that challenged his distrust, "Do you have any references?"

"I have a list of names and phone numbers of people I've worked for."

Koepy walked back to his truck and returned with a printout of his recent clientele. It was computerized and showed the type of work he'd performed at each different location. "You can check these people out if you like," he offered.

"I appreciated the option, I probably will," Emmitt returned. "As long as you're here, I'd like a rough quote." Emmitt started walking around the side of the house with the younger man in pursuit.

"It's either an addition or a porch," Koepy said.

"How'd you know?"

"Anytime somebody leads me to their backyard, it's either one or the other."

"In this case, it's both."

"You'll make me a busy man," Koepy beamed.

"You haven't been given the job yet," Emmitt retorted. "Here's what I want," Emmitt said, when they reached the rear of the house. "That up there is my bedroom. I want that brought out this way to about where I'm standing." Emmitt extended both arms from each side as far as he could to make himself clear. "Once that's done, I want a deck attached. A big deck about eight by twelve feet. My bedroom is twelve feet long, so that's how long I want the deck to be."

"What do you want the deck made from?" Koepy asked.

"Something hard that makes a nice appearance. I was thinking about redwood."

"Redwood looks fine, but it's not one of your harder woods. It's a conifer. Conifers are the softwood trees."

"What are the hardwoods?"

"Gum, maple, birch, oak to mention a few, but they're for furniture, not jobs like this. If you don't mind spending the money, redwood is still a good choice. It's weak though in comparison to some timber."

"Why use it?"

"I was going to say that it's very resistant to insects and diseases. It even holds up against decay. The other choice is pressure treated pine. That wouldn't be nearly as expensive, and, practically speaking for you, it might be the best wood to use."

"All right," Emmitt said, "let's talk pine for the deck. Give me an estimate on the extension to the house, plus the deck."

Koepy pulled a steel tape off of his belt and laid it across the ground from the edge of the house to where Emmitt was standing. "You're talking approximately eighty-four square feet being added to that back room and then the deck. By the way, where do you want the steps?"

"What steps?"

"The ones to the deck."

"I don't want any steps going up there."

"You don't?"

"No, I don't."

"Are you sure?"

"I'm sure."

"It isn't going to cost very much more."

"It's not the money!"

"Oh."

"The problem is," Emmitt complained, "there are chice people I won't have up there."

"Neighbor problems?"

"I wish it were."

"I'm good with burglar alarms, if you want to have one installed."

"No, in this instance, it's my own brother. He lives here with me. He did, anyway. He's gone for now, but probably not for any real length of time. So the last thing that I want is for him to be up there bothering me. That place is to be my sanctuary."

"Is he that bad?" Koepy asked.

"He's a bona fide jerk." Emmitt put his hand to his forehead, as someone who were in deep thought might do. "You're an electrician," he said.

"Suppose we did put steps going up, with a railing of course. Do you suppose we could have a gate with an electrical stinger attached?"

"That could be dangerous."

"I don't wanna lay him out. I only want to jolt him. You know, keep him at bay."

"I think you're right," Koepy agreed. "Let's just forget the steps for the time being. How does twenty-one five sound?"

"I'll have to let you know." Emmitt sulked.

"Is it that bad between the two of you?"

"I'm going to check on you," Emmitt said, ignoring the question. "I also want to get some other estimates. Maybe we'll do business in the future."

Koepy smiled. He reached out with his hand to Emmitt, who took hold of it lightly with his own and shook it. Emmitt was still contemplating the electrified gate. "Listen," Koepy said. "No matter who does this job, make sure it's built to last." He then walked to his truck, got in, and very slowly drove away.

Emmitt was confused. If the man wanted work, then why didn't he go next door or stop anywhere else on the street, he asked himself. Was he a con-man besides everything else that he claimed to be? Did he hear that Emmitt was an easy mark? No, not likely. Everybody knew that Emmitt could squeeze the green right out of a dollar bill. There was something about this guy that was puzzling, but Emmitt couldn't understand what. He was friendly enough, but that wasn't it. His price didn't seem overly attractive, but it was enticing. Emmitt would have to check that out and make some comparisons. Perhaps it was nothing more than his good looks and apparent honesty that lured Emmitt, but still, Emmitt was reluctant to hire the young guy. Sure, he acted like somebody who had it all together. He didn't though, and Emmitt had known from the very first instant he laid eyes on Koepy that the guy was somehow troubled. Why else would he have such terrible gashes across his wrist and both arms?

CHAPTER 11

If ever anybody could cram five decades of life into nineteen years, it was Marian Jameses. Being the daughter of one of the town's most influential, but poor, black ministers was demanding. On Sundays, she played the church organ, taught Sunday school, and gave people who needed rides a lift to and from church. That was never any problem for Marian. In reality, she, more or less, liked it. The mingling could be fun. It was the rest of the week, however, that was starting to drag her down. She always considered working Mondays through Saturdays at the diner and truck stop a downright drag. Her hours were from 1:00 p.m. until 9:00 in the evening; and if the relief shift didn't show, sometimes she stayed later. When it did, she was free in the sense that more lucrative work might be accomplished. Marian enjoyed being a prostitute. It wasn't only because of the money. It was the excitement. The mental rush was what she really craved the most.

In more ways than not, she was a righteous girl. Marian visited the sick, consoled the grieving, and gave as much money to the church offering as she could spare. It was tough, because college credits were expensive, and she was working towards an associate's degree that might not ever materialize. All of that, and there were still chores to be done around her father's sixty acre run down farm. It was draining to the point where it sometimes crushed her spirit. That's how she was feeling as Emmitt drove up in front of her father's house and got out of his recently waxed and polished car.

"Is the Reverend around?"

Marian stopped loading bushel baskets of corn onto the bed of her father's pickup barely long enough to acknowledge Emmitt's presence.

"He's inside the house," she said, letting out a long breath. She then lifted up a final basket and gave it one labored jostle onto the back of the vehicle.

"I'll get him for you," she offered.

"Thanks, aren't you his daughter?"

"Seven days a week, fifty-two weeks a year, but today, I'm doubling as his field hand."

"I guess you have to make hay while the sun shines," Emmitt tried to excuse her circumstances.

"In case you didn't notice, that was corn I was wrestling with."

Emmitt walked over to the truck and looked briefly at all of the tiny green ears that were pushed tightly into the baskets. They were parched on the outer edges. He slid his thumb under the leaves of an ear, causing some of the sparse yellow kernels to show. "I guess you're right. It's corn," he said jokingly.

"Very funny! It's been a dry summer. We're trying to salvage some of this corn before it all dries up. And if you're a fertilizer salesman, we've got plenty of bull manure."

"No," Emmitt admitted, "I'm the manager of the bank your father does business with."

"Offhand then, I wish you were selling manure."

"I'm not that bad, personally!"

"I know a lot of people who might disagree," Marian argued.

"Like who?"

"Like people who go to my father's church, but it really doesn't matter, does it?"

"But it does matter. In fact, that's what I came out here to see your father about. I'm doing my best to see that the church doesn't go under."

"It won't. You may take the property, but my father's church is more than simply a hunk of cement and building material."

"Easy now," the minister said, as he let the screen door close shut from behind himself. It was attached to a spring that pulled it inward with a frightful bang. Emmitt almost cringed at the interruption. The minister was trying to straighten the suspenders to his faded bib overalls, as he approached the pair. "I hope you have some good news for me," he said.

"So do I," Emmitt answered. "Can we talk?"

"You mean alone?"

"Not necessarily."

That's fine," Marian said, "I have things to do inside, unless you'd rather gab in there."

"No, right here's good, and you are, too." Emmitt tried to sound convincing.

"I'll get you something to drink," Marian disappeared into the house. When she returned, Emmitt was jotting numbers down in a small paper tablet. He looked engrossed. Her father appeared fully absorbed in the figures.

"I hope you like iced tea," she asked, not at all caring whether Emmitt did or not.

"I love it," Emmitt said. "Did you add much sugar?"

"No, I try to keep it as bitter as possible."

"Just the way I like it," Emmitt returned with little element of sincerity in his voice. "I'll bet you make good pastries too."

While her father and Emmitt continued to talk, Marian went into the house and turned the radio on. At eleven a.m., she came back out to remind the Reverend that if the corn was to be sold at the produce stand, it must be there by twelve. Her father didn't look so happy, and she wondered what the banker was trying to pass off as good news.

She had thought that Emmitt was a shylock as soon as she laid eyes on him. Supposedly, he was not ready to collect his pound of flesh yet. So why had he come? It was hot, and she watched as her father, flanked by Emmitt, walked over to the truck. Both men wore very serious expressions. They had been talking for a long time, and the sun had turned Emmitt's skin to a soft pink. Marian wondered, if put to the test, how he would hold up to a real job. As far as she was concerned, her father was the only man of the two. She called him once again and pressured him to hurry along.

"Alright, alright, I'm going!" He waved his large calloused hand to her, as if he wanted her to be quiet. She remained firm though and watched him eventually get into his truck. She told herself that dealing with him was not the sort of thing a daughter should have to do. Sometimes he wasn't just slow, but downright obstinate to the core.

A moment later, he was gone. Marian and Emmitt looked on, as the truck disappeared down the winding dirt road and beyond the high stalks of corn that were rapidly turning brown.

"We need adequate rain soon," Emmitt said, "it looks like everything is going to dry up otherwise, not just the corn."

"You're the one who said you have to make hay while the sun shines,"

Marian retorted. She wanted to seem sarcastic, but she sounded more indifferent than anything.

"Well, I guess I'm not much of a farmer," Emmitt admitted. "Besides, corn's healthier."

"So what are you then," Marian asked, "a banker or a politician?"

"Today, I'm a little of both. How did you know, anyway?"

"You mean about you're running for office?"

"Yes."

"My father told me. I read the papers once in a while, too."

Emmitt's eyes wandered to the house. It was very old and needed outside repairs from the roof on down. Some of the shingles on the side of the house were cracked. The screen door was torn, and the windows were in dire need of repair. As his eyes dropped, he noticed the cellar blocks were without mortar in some areas. He tried to feel sorry for the Jameses. It wasn't in him, although today he was glad that he didn't have to pass a loan appraisal on their home.

"Is that your motorcycle?" He asked, sizing up the bike leaning against the side of the house. It didn't appear to be in the best of shape, and even Emmitt could see that it was flirting with obsolescence.

"What did you say to my father?" Marian asked, without answering the question.

"I said that I would allow him more time on the mortgage payments."

"Why?"

"Why not?"

"I have a feeling this town better keep an eye on you." Marian brought her hands up to rest on her waist. Even though she didn't trust Emmitt, she chose not to press the issue. If Emmitt was allowing the church more time, that was all that counted for the present. She would get the details from her father when he got home. For a few seconds, neither Emmitt or Marian spoke. From a distant room in the house, Emmitt could vaguely hear a radio. He didn't like the music. It was about as agreeable to his ears as the iced tea was to his taste buds, and by now he wanted to tell her so!

"I'd better be leaving," Emmitt said. "Thanks for the tea."

"How was it?"

"It killed my thirst," he said, walking over to his car. He got in and started the motor.

Marian took two steps from where her, and Emmitt had been talking. She then turned halfway. "Yes," she said.

"Yes, what?"

"Yes, that's my motorcycle."

The banker raised his head and met the girl's eyes. They were large and penetrating. He, himself, felt transparent and wanted to throw up a shield. Marian then turned again, and walked towards the barn. Her waist was so trim that her fleshy buttocks seemed almost out of proportion. Emmitt watched closely. When she reached the entrance to the barn, he called out to her. "Marian!"

"What?" Was all she answered.

"You'll have to give me a ride sometime!"

CHAPTER 12

Hypothetically, it's possible to reason that cities like individuals have their own defining characteristics, or even unique personalities. Some are colossal and slow-moving. They can also have a violent reputation. Sometimes a city may try desperately to hold on to a past rather than move into the future where its identity could be lost or its capacity strained. Others appear sleepy or even tired during the day, but awaken at dusk. They are the towns that garb themselves in the pleasures of the night and wear a crown of a million neon signs. They sometimes either attract the adventurous or repel the prudent.

Strangely enough, there are urban areas that are conceived, developed, and mature just as a person does, and then, for some unknown reason, refuse a futuristic destiny. A city like this can rest in the slumber of an unchallenged time and eventually decay under the weight of its own apathy. Malfaxe was one such place. Nobody knew or actually cared where or when Malfaxe began. Most people may have assumed that it started as the result of post Civil War migration of Southerners to the north. Perhaps it was a rare combination of poor farmers and plantation aristocracy who together lost almost everything they had in the South that first settled in the area. There were strong indications to promote this line of thought. Several large mansions of historically southern architecture stood at various locations on the outskirts of the city's limits. They were sparsely located, and all but hidden by a conglomeration of small factories, shabby houses, and narrow cobble stone streets. This was not the heart of Malfaxe, though. These hereditary traits were only the first clues of a giant about to be born.

An aerial photograph would show geometric figures, mostly squares and rectangles, of different sizes. They were formed by the roads, highways, and main arteries that crossed through town from opposite directions. A closer view would reveal building complexes. Some of these might have smoke stacks, many of which were idle. This was primarily because of the environmental movement of the nineteen-seventies. A few of the older manufacturing facilities had simply been abandoned when the companies were relocated for more favorable, and friendly business sites. A drive through town would have turned up three hospitals, two comparatively small and one large. Parks being abundant, on Sunday's families could be seen playing ball, riding bikes, or just meandering over the grassy slopes in casual bliss. Some of the recreational areas had softball fields and tennis courts. There is, also, a minor league baseball stadium of respectable size. In 1945, the municipal planners allocated property for a golf course. It covered a huge plot of ground at the northwest boundary near a cloverleaf exit. Everyone was invited to play there, although the fees were considered to be unusually high.

Ninety percent of the school buildings were old, and several stories high. Their entrances were marked in cement for either boys or girls. Nobody had paid attention to that, at least not for the last half of the twentieth century and along with the beginning of the twenty-first.

If one were to look carefully, Sutler Prison could be seen. Its several stories of reddish-brown brick is in no contrast to the rest of the view. Nevertheless, closer inspection would show a twenty-foot wall girdling a cement apron. Barbed wire was coiled over the top of the wall. Its keenly honed sharp teeth ready to grab and rip into the flesh of anyone desperate enough to test its bite. Two guard towers extend several yards above the wire. They are in all four corners of the prison yard. The watch always consists of young men who have superb eyesight and cast a steady glare downward into the confines. As a rule, they're conscientious and committed to their jobs, knowing full well the responsibility that rests with themselves, but not today. Today is different. A parade will be passing nearby soon. The guards have put their caution on furlough and tend to watch on only two outer sides of the wall. Like children, they've anticipated the colorful decorations and bright, shiny instruments. They've waited patiently, and after a while, the first marchers could be heard about to arrive.

A tired giant was beginning to stir. The previous winter had been terrible. The snow was deep. The ice treacherous. It lasted through April. Suddenly, it was hot, very hot, and it seemed to be without end, although summer was winding down now. A slight hint of autumn was present in the air and the labor day parade would arouse the cumbersome sleeper if only for a few short hours. Then, after the festivities were over, the weary, and unconcerned giant would be allowed to slip quietly back into its peaceful rest again.

Malfaxe was awakened, and now its heart seemed to be beating to the sound of the oncoming drums. They were getting louder. The trumpets, clarinets, and trombones were blending in. Then the tuba sounded off, resembling the warning blast from a distant out of port freighter. It was in a rising ocean of music, demanding to be recognized. The bands were spread out. After the first one appeared on Central Avenue, another band could be heard making its approach. In between came the floats covered with artificial flowers and carrying pretty girls who were dressed in long gowns. Their gloves were all the way up to their elbows, leaving little else but their upper arms and cute faces to be bathed in the warming sun. They would pass three roads over from the prison and continue five blocks down to 63rd Street to where the parade was to officially begin.

Clowns narrowed the gaps between the floats. The auguste clowns were outnumbered. They had unhappy faces, unlike the clowns who pulled their foolish or carefree pranks. Those clowns were the merry jokers, who threw candy to the children or tossed water balloons randomly into the crowds. White makeup covered their faces and on the top of the white, the blues, yellows, and pastel greens accentuated their cheerful moods. Like the auguste clowns, the hobos were few and far between. They moved slowly with tearful eyes and large red noses.

Their clothes were tattered and their minds seemed absent from what was happening around them.

By mid morning, the parade was in full swing. The American Legion led the way for part of a National Guard unit that was driving jeeps and dropping harmless fireworks in its wake. They were loud however, and startled some of the people, causing them to back up and move further away from the curbs. Then more bands and marchers appeared, not to mention, beautiful majorettes, who were throwing batons in the air and catching them with ease. Their uniforms were short, the tops fitting close to their chest, and decorated with brass buttons. Just in front of a motorcade were three such girls and their hats were sprouting rainbow tinted plumes that curved upwards and tall.

Gordon Hays sat on the back of a convertible facing the front of the car, with his feet in the rear seat. He had been the mayor for eight years. For Gordon, it was time to step down. His health had failed rapidly, and it was believed by everyone close to him that another term in office would be fatal. Mrs. Hays sat near him, as they both smiled and waved. They seemed jovial, and at ease. Behind the Hays' car was a float with a big man dressed up like Uncle Sam. He was sitting in a rocking chair marked "Free Ride." A weary looking midget stood behind him, moving Uncle Sam's chair backward and forward. The midget had taxpayer stamped on the back of his shirt. Occasionally, Uncle Sam would turn and grin at the little guy, who would make ugly facial expressions in return.

Soon afterward, came another convertible with Art Towson. Art was a black man, who, also, wanted to run the city. He was well thought of and moved cleverly in prominent organizations. His wife sat close, too. They presented the image of the perfect couple. Art was always so well-dressed. He was wearing a light blue summer suit along with aviator gold-framed glasses. He was a handsome man, and his wife, Schelly, obviously adored him.

More floats came by and, eventually, the Boy Scouts followed. A Democratic congressman, Bill "The People's Will" Kelly, walked down the street, shaking hands feverishly. He was like a fast-moving pinball, bouncing from one person to another. His seat was up for grabs. It was anybody's guess what the election's outcome would be.

Soon it was mid-morning. The vendors were vividly pushing their souvenirs, pretzels, and soft drinks; while children munched and drank all that their parents were willing to buy.

Emmitt's slow-traveling convertible ushered in a gradual increase in the temperature, as it turned onto 63rd Street. He, also, sat above the rear seat. Emmitt didn't have a woman with him. Instead, Vernon sat at his side. As the crowd watched, it would have been difficult not to notice the big ears and droopy eyes, which were highlighted by a dumbfounded gaze. Vernon, too, appeared much the same. Emmitt was out of his element. He was trying hard to look suave, however, his hand movements and happy facial expression seemed forced. Had it not been for his sweat, he could have passed for a big wind up toy. All in all, it was a sad thing to watch. At one point, the dog attempted to raise his leg. Emmitt had to slap it down. He vowed to himself never again put Vernon on public display.

Two more aspiring congressmen passed by, James Hill and John King. In between, came three engines from the volunteer fire department and several Girl Scout groups. City policemen on horseback were riding close behind them donning their dark blue suits and pure white helmets. They carried themselves majestically.

Eventually, the sound from the bands began to die. People were going home. It was time to leave the giant undisturbed. He would sleep deeply tonight, and tomorrow, he'd likely dwell in a state of serenity.

Hardly anybody saw the old man at the end of the procession. Whoever did see him may have laughed or simply pointed out how ridiculous he was. Like the tee-shirt that hung loosely from his shoulders, his face was aged and wrinkled. His pants were vintage 1960's and rather snug. A rectangular cardboard sign hung over his neck. It covered the better part of his torso. Had only he come along earlier, there may have been hundreds of spectators, instead of a mere few. They may have only smirked at him, or disregarded him completely. Fortunately, there were only a dozen or so left to assume that this man actually was serious about becoming the mayor. That's what his sign had said. His name was printed in big capital letters, and was underlined with different shades of crayon. "FOR MAYOR" was quite large also, and placed down toward the bottom of the sign. He could have been mistaken for a final act. Maybe a maverick clown, trying to get one last laugh. There was a lot to suggest that he was. His presence mimicked that of a mentally disturbed person. Two inches of socks were showing under his high water pants, and his tennis shoes were much too large for his feet. His hair was badly mussed from the sun's heat and his scalp's perspiration. Because of all of that, nobody seemed to take into account that his face was like weather beaten rawhide. His eyes were fixed too. They constantly peered straight ahead, never yielding to distraction. They were filled with a cargo of sheer determination for everyone to see. Perhaps someone did. Maybe not, but this guy was for real alright. Everything considered though, Peter Ghudd had never looked so bad.

CHAPTER 13

"All stand!" Norman heard the officer at the front of the courtroom order. "The Eleventh District Criminal Court of Malfaxe is now in session. The honorable Joshua Harris is presiding. You may be seated."

The day of reckoning had arrived. After weeks of brief stays in squalid rooms, borrowing money from friends, and attempting to keep a meek profile, Norman was now going to trial. Time had slipped by fast since the night of the party, and with a little luck plus a stiff fine, Norman's future would be brighter. He'd go back home. That is if Emmitt refused to cooperate. Norman slouched sideways on the long wooden bench and anticipated Emmitt's reaction. He could hardly wait to tell his older brother what he wanted in return for his own absence. It was going to be fun, especially since Emmitt was not in the bargaining position. Not so deep inside, Norman was becoming ecstatic.

As Norman gazed about the courtroom he was bored. It was nothing new. He had seen it all before. There was a window right next to him. It was big enough to be two doors wide. When he was a kid, he had once watched an old western on television with a similar layout. An innocent cowboy was being unjustly tried and managed to escape through a window much like this one. It had been sensational for a five year old boy to watch a man leap through shattering glass, fall two stories, and complete his getaway on a swift running horse. Norman grinned at the idea. He then trained his attention on the judge, who was to the front and center.

Judge Harris had been a stevedore on the Baltimore docks when he was in his twenties. He had no doubt seen his share of skirmishes in his life time. A gash on his throat and one ear that resembled a smashed tomato lent credence to his nasty temperament. With the exception that a female defendant always did better than a man, he was formidable and unpredictable. On one side of the judge was the American flag, to the other, with its black and gold displayed in a tasteful contrast, was the state's banner. The room was well lit, and Norman allowed his eyes to drift from one person to the other in search of a familiar face. There was none to be found. It wasn't like the old days. That was a time when Norman could run across a buddy or two and make bets as to who might get off with the lighter sentence. The old friends had certainly dwindled since then. Ironically, Norman chose to view himself as a survivor.

The first hearing dealt with a domestic fight between a husband and wife. The man had learned that his wife was cheating on him. He had lost his self-control and savagely attacked her. She was a mess. Her scars were still evident, and her nose had been fractured in two places. Norman listened half-heartedly, while the woman testified about the hardships and cruelties that she had suffered at the hands of her brutal husband. According to her, she had been driven into infidelity and felt no shame.

When the man gave his version of what had happened, Norman thought about how it all reminded him of a bad soap opera. He wanted to turn them off. He remembered the time that his own nose had been hurt badly. It had happened one Monday night three years earlier inside of a local tavern. A heated altercation between two other men evolved into a fist fight. Norman was trying to leave when he was hit squarely on the beak by a wild overhand right. He was sent to the floor immediately and sprawled there, pretending to be unconscious until the ruckus was over. His nose had never really looked the same since then, and the pain had been excruciating. Norman was extremely glad it was the woman's nose that had been slugged this time instead of his own.

Two more offenses went before the bench, and Norman started wondering about Emmitt's delay. His brother had promised to be there, and now he was already forty minutes late. Another case was called, and Emmitt finally entered the courtroom, taking a seat behind Norman. The judge had been peering over the top of his bifocals at a squeamish young man, who had been picked up for nonsupport. The magistrate looked stern, as he cast a mean glare toward the defendant, who was quite subdued. The expression on Judge Harris's face told it all quite clearly. He had already placed two husbands on probation, and his patience was wearing thin. It was later in the day. It was also becoming obvious by now that the judge was fed up with the rift raft traffic that was pouring through his court room. He was appearing angrier by the minute. Along with nursing a bad headache he was rapidly developing the disposition of a prospective road kill caught in middle of a busy intersection as he began to hate anything that moved. Emmitt watched the judge's eyebrow arch into a vortex, as he yelled, "What?" to a diminutive, yet shrinking defendant who remained withering beneath the bench.

"Where've you been?" Norman confronted Emmitt.

"I couldn't get here any sooner. We're having an audit next week, Norman. There are a lot of things to get in order. Where's your lawyer anyway?"

"That's not important. Did you bring some cash, like I asked you to?"

"If you don't have an attorney, what's the money for?"

"I don't need a lawyer. I need a doctor. I've got a virus."

"You're not in a very good position with or without an attorney Norman, but right now, having one seems to be your best bet for staying out of jail."

"Don't worry about the lawyer, just hand me a few bucks."

"How much?" Emmitt asked, reaching into his back trouser pocket.

"Twenty-nine hundred dollars."

Emmitt froze. "What?" He said, searching for a hint of falsehood in Norman's voice.

"Twenty-nine hundred dollars."

"How about three thousand, Norman? I think I have some extra left over from the last audit."

"I thought you might," Norman sneered.

"You own a late model Corvette," Emmitt heard the judge addressing the man again. It was his first conscious reminder of where he was since Norman had made his demand. "I'm sure that you could be more frugal than that," the magistrate scolded.

"Norman, I really think you could be more frugal than that," Emmitt finally mumbled. in a pathetic little voice.

"No, I can't, Emmitt. I've been scrounging like a field mouse for weeks. Now either you give me the help I need, or else I'm moving back home."

"I'll have to make a withdrawal. Give me a day or two."

"I ought to lock you up," the judge said loudly. Everyone, including Norman, looked straight ahead.

Emmitt leaned forward and spoke softly. "I think he's hot. You'd better be careful up there," he coached.

"Charlie says," Norman looked around taking heed to make sure that nobody was sitting close enough to hear. "All I have to do is plead guilty."

"Guilty? Are you nuts?"

"That's right. It's all taken care of."

"Sell your car, mister!" The judge said, making sure that everyone there could hear him. "Because the next time I see you in here, you're leaving in metal braces."

"Norman, if this man finds you guilty, you're not going to need twenty-nine hundred dollars."

"Three thousand."

"Whatever."

"Besides, I'm pleading guilty, Emmitt. I have to. You don't think he's going to let me stand up there and make a monkey out of the cop, do you? That's not the way the system works."

"The State versus Norman Braedeikk," the bailiff announced.

"There's nothing for me to be concerned about. Charlie knows a lot of people downtown," Norman said, without hearing his name called. "You just have the money ready by the day after tomorrow. I'll drop by the house and pick it up."

"Norman Braedeikk, please stand and approach the bench." The bailiff was louder.

"I still don't see why you need quite that much money, Norman. It could be dangerous having that much cash around. Why don't you let me give it to you in small installments?"

"That's exactly what you're doing, Emmitt, giving it to me in small installments. The first installment is in two days, three thousand dollars. If you're late, there's a ten percent penalty."

Emmitt went pale. "I can't afford this!"

"You can always repossess me."

The bailiff cleared his throat and yelled Norman's name for the third and final time. At first, it seemed to linger in the air like a terrible odor waiting to dissipate and eventually be forgotten. A prolonged stillness occurred, and the courtroom was soon overtaken with a sense of judicial mysticism, while every mind became alert, trying to capture the intensity of the moment. Then, and to everyone's surprise, came an answer. It was as sudden and precise as any military officer could have delivered. Emmitt was moved. General George Armstrong Custer himself may too have done as well after straddling amount for hundreds of miles with a blistered and sore butt, however this was Norman's scene. He, also, had a sore derriere, and he rubbed it exuberantly, as he stood to make his presence known for all to see. "Yooooh!" he articulated, hobbling toward the front of the courtroom.

The police officer took his place, flanked by the prosecutor, who began charging Norman with numerous counts of disturbing the peace, drunkenness, and assault on an officer. Emmitt began watching his brother in dismay, wondering how Norman would once more try to maneuver his way through the legal system.

"You're entitled to a defense, Mr. Braedeikk," the judge said. "Is this something you are choosing to abdicate?"

"What do you mean, Your Honor?"

"Do you want to give up your right to an attorney?"

"I believe so."

"Why would you do that, Mr. Braedeikk?" The judge warned, as he tapped several of his fingers in a gesture of irritation.

"I'm guilty, Your Honor."

"Mr. Braedeikk, were you listening to the charges against you? I'm wanting to admire your honesty, in the face of some very serious offenses."

"Thank you, Your Honor."

"So you are telling me that after being cited for disturbing the peace, you willfully and without provocation assaulted a police officer. Being drunk you also resisted arrest. Is this what you wish to be held accountable for?"

"I didn't intend to get out of control, Your Honor."

"I'm certainly glad to hear that," the judge said mockingly. "Policemen can sometimes be bothersome, that goes without saying. I suppose I can understand the awkward position you may have been caught in, being drunk, and full of folly. Do you know, Mr. Braedeikk, that I've served on the bench now for almost seven years? I have to say that you are one of the most audacious people I've ever had the privilege of meeting. I believe you're a very impervious fellow. In fact, I've never before encountered this kind of crudeness. Not from anyone! You beat up a police officer and then you think that you can come into my courtroom, plead guilty, and just prance right on out again."

Norman lowered his head and finally spoke, aligning his answer with a carefully measured portion of humility. "I'm homeless." He lifted his head sheepishly, wanting to catch a glimmer of sympathy from the judge's face. There was not the slightest sign. He wished now that he had hired a lawyer like Emmitt had suggested. Somebody who could have spoken eloquently. Norman looked back at Emmitt, who seemed to be calculating the situation, like a spectator watching a fire dance, and anticipating when the performer would get burned. He hated Emmitt for it, but the show would have to continue anyway. He only hoped that it wouldn't get too entertaining.

"Six months, Mr. Braedeikk. That's what I'm sentencing you to. Six months in the city prison. Now you have a place to stay."

"Your Honor, I'm a sick man!"

"I think everybody in this room today would agree to that, Mr. Braedeikk."

"How about three months?"

"How about getting him out of here?" The judge ordered the two court officers, who were standing close by. In only a few seconds, Norman had disappeared, leaving behind a quiet and stunned room full of people. Emmitt sat motionless. He told himself that his problems with Norman were temporarily over with. He trusted that the newspapers wouldn't find out about any of this. For the first time since deciding to run for office, he felt relieved. It was almost like having a railroad spike pulled from his side. It was years since he had felt so good, and he wanted to scream with joy. Instead, he reached backward one more time and pushed his wallet deep into his rear pants pocket. Then he left.

CHAPTER 14

Tell me, how's the market for premature corn these days?" Emmitt asked, as he followed Marian through the interior of her father's house.

"I wouldn't know," Marian answered. "We're specializing in hybrid cantaloupe this month." She said it softly, looking down at her father, who had fallen fast asleep on a makeshift hammock. She was about to awaken him when Emmitt stopped her.

"Don't. I'll comeback another time."

"It's all right," Marian assured him. "He'll have to get up soon anyway. He has to visit someone before dark settles in."

"We'll give him a few more minutes," Emmitt suggested. "You can show me the cantaloupes. I'd like to see how they grow if you don't mind."

Marian didn't hesitate. She turned and walked to where they had passed through, stopping only once to pick up a catalog that was lying on the floor.

"He sleeps more and more all the time," she confided gently tossing the book onto the sofa. "I think he's depressed."

"He's taken a lot on himself, "Emmitt replied., still following her close by.

The two of them stepped outside. It was almost dusk, and the air was humid and sticky. Emmitt removed his jacket and let it rest over his left arm, they walked past the barn and towards the fields.

"Where are we going?"

"You said that you wanted to see my cantaloupes."

"I was only kidding," Emmitt laughed. "I just wanted you to leave your father alone for a while."

"Now what do we do?"

"Since we've gotten this far, let's go on with it. I could use the exercise."

They went further, until they came to a hill with a small shed on it. A fence made of meshed wire surrounded the dilapidated structure. Emmitt knelt down and picked up a small stone. He bounced it off the side of the wall closest to him, causing a noise much louder than the one he had anticipated. With an explosion of high-pitched squawking, chickens by the dozens began scurrying wildly. Most of them retreated into the pen, feathers fluttering and flying in various directions.

"Wow! They get pretty carried away!" Emmitt said, trying to put more distance between himself and the coop. He made a faster stride and continued following Marian who had gotten ahead of him by now. She was on the crest of a ridge. Below was a field of thick green runners intertwined and crisscrossing. They dwindled apart about a hundred feet from a small shallow stream. Until then, it was all but impossible to tell where one plant ended and the other one began. In between the heavy foliage, Emmitt could see the tops of thousands of the brown, oblong fruits, eclipsing themselves within their caressing leaves. Emmitt was amazed. "You have a fortune in melons! Who planted them all?"

"My father and I."

"Are they difficult to grow?"

"This summer, I'd say they're easier than corn. You don't know a lot about agriculture, do you?"

"My knowledge of farming doesn't go beyond the two plants I have in my back yard."

"What kind are they?"

"Big Girls."

"You mean Big Boys," Marian corrected him.

"Big Boys, Little Girls, what's the difference? They're all tomatoes."

"You mean Early Girls."

"You're not very enchanted with me, are you?" Emmitt said, throwing his coat over his right shoulder as he looked off into another direction completely opposite from where they'd come.

"I don't like your type," Marian confirmed.

"And what type am I?"

"Prim, proper," she stalled before she finished, "shifty."

"You don't even know me. How can you be so judge mental?"

"Why are you out here right now? I'll tell you why. It's because you're trying to size up what you can hustle away from my father."

"Oh, I guess I came up here with you in order to start with the cantaloupes, didn't I?"

"You want the short story version?"

"Tell me."

"You want part of his farm."

"No, I don't." He reconsidered, "I do, but it's not for me. Didn't he tell you?"

Marian's sarcasm overflowed. That opulent manor we left a few minutes ago and this prime fertile property you're standing on are the last remnants saved from a ton of hard work, both black and white."

"I'm aware of the history here." Emmitt submitted, "Your father will keep his major part of the land, plus quite a sum of money for his trouble. He'll keep his church too, if we can pull this deal off. Look Marian, Malfaxe needs an alternative prison site. Your father can use the finances. It's nothing more than a couple of gears meshing with one another to move things along."

"And what do you need, nothing, I suppose?"

"Marian, I need a platform."

"A gimmick."

'No, a platform. A genuine promise that I can deliver on. You know Marian, if your father's willing to part with just a small portion of his farm, he'll be paid handsomely. I realize it's not an easy thing for him to do, or even think about, but it is an answer to a large chunk of his money problems."

"Where's the money coming from?"

"The city will apply for a federal grant."

"I see, you're going to use government money to buy my father's land, so that you can get elected. You really are a politician, aren't you?"

"Marian, it's a solution."

"You're playing two ends towards the middle."

"You're not being fair," Emmitt sighed. "Besides that, everything I'm telling you is an oversimplification. I'd like you to keep this to yourself."

"Why?"

"Because it's important to me that I reveal it at the proper time."

"You make me furious."

"I've tried to be straight with you."

For a moment, it was quiet. Emmitt removed a pair of glasses from his shirt pocket and put them on, letting his eyes scan the fields. He looked much like a general trying to develop a battle plan over questionable terrain. The farm was vast, he thought to himself. He tried to see the lake, but it was useless. Hills and thick timber met the horizon, blocking off the rest of the farmland that lay beyond.

"Marian, the section of land by the lake," he asked, "has it been cultivated, or is it coarse and rocky?"

Marian turned and began to answer. At first she couldn't make the words come out. When they did, she surprised even herself. "Wait here," she said. She turned and went back down the way they had come. Emmitt's eyes traced her until she disappeared into the barn. Soon, the rumble of an engine preceded Marian's return, as she sped through the double doorway on a motorcycle and headed up the dirt path straight toward him. When she reached the place where Emmitt was standing, a dusty haze had already enveloped them.

"Get on," she said, twitching her head to indicate the rear of the bike.

"I don't believe I can. I've never done anything like this before."

"Just sit on the back and hang on," Marian told him. "I'll do the rest."

Emmitt was barely seated when Marian released the clutch and began moving over the rough terrain at a vicious speed. It was difficult for Emmitt to stay on, especially after they made it to the narrow stretch of woods that divided the farm into two different tracts of land. Marian stopped for nothing, not even Emmitt's pleas to pull over so that he might get a better grip on the seat. It was open throttle for Marian, and no looking back for Emmitt. Every bump seemed more challenging than the last, causing the two of them to strive diligently to keep the cycle in an upright position. When they came out on the other side, they hit a slope. Marian stuck to a path that eventually ran smooth. Soon it led them through a patch of parched corn that spanned for acres and died noticeably by the edge of the lake. Marian stopped and allowed Emmitt to dismount first. She then pushed the bike under a big sycamore tree that clawed the half barren sod with it's immense roots. Never before had Emmitt been so jarred. He began walking in circles aimlessly, until Marian at last spoke.

"Are you injured?" She asked in an unconcerned tone of voice.

"Next time, let's walk!" Emmitt complained while trying to regain his composure.

"It's a long way."

"How far would you say it is from that stretch of wooded area to here?" Emmitt pointed in the direction of the lake hidden by the heavy timber.

Marian shrugged her shoulders.

"Just give me a decent guess. How many acres across?"

"Nine, maybe ten," Marian surmised.

"We probably wouldn't need any more than fifteen."

"For what?"

"The entire prison complex."

"You'll be lucky to get half that much."

"Why are you fighting this?"

"My family has had this land for decades. It was given to my great grandfather by the widow of a tobacco millionaire."

"Sounds much too altruistic."

"Maybe, but my family's had it ever since. I don't like the thought of having a prison this close, either."

"I understand, emphatically "

"You, also, know that I'm going to try and talk my father out of selling any of the farm, don't you?"

"Yes, but you should try to remember that the idea does have merit. Besides, we don't even know if it's possible until the testing has been made. This whole conversation might be useless."

Marian appeared to be taken off balance. "Because?"

"Things have to be done. In a few weeks, you'll likely be seeing a lot of activity around here. This place could be crawling with people."

"What kind of people?"

"Civil engineers, probably hydrologists, too. Marian, I have no idea of what the outcome of all this is going to be. Nobody has a crystal ball. Let me ask you a question though, if you don't mind."

"Ask it," Marian was indifferent.

"I don't know exactly what your financial status is, but is it possible that you could use a change of work that's not so demanding?"

Marian ran her fingers across her face to remove some of the dust, as she allowed her eyes to survey the farmland that had eaten up so much of her time and youth. "Do I look like a girl who needs more work? She asked. "I guess you mean a position at the bank?"

"No," Emmitt said. "Actually, what I need is a new cleaning lady for the time being."

The walk back to his car wasn't quite as bad as Emmitt had figured it would be. The mosquitoes weren't biting like they had been on previous nights, and the moonlight, which was guiding Emmitt's return trip to the farmhouse driveway, covered the dirt path with a milky glaze. Marian's departure had been so abrupt that she hadn't given him an answer, not verbally that is. Obviously, she was angry, maybe even hurt. Emmitt wanted her to think his offer over and reconsider. He needed her on his side, otherwise the relocation of the prison was doomed. As far as he knew, there was no option other than her father's farm. Emmitt decided that he would give her a day or two to calm down before he called to explain himself. In the meantime, he needed to consider another problem. Peter Ghudd, the political meddler, was still working at the bank.

CHAPTER 15

Peter sat across from Emmitt with his hands folded. He'd been focusing on a dirty streak that marred the glossy linoleum floor. Peter had barely begun his chores that Tuesday, when Emmitt had called him into his office and asked him to take a seat. It was Tuesday morning, and Monday evening had done little to brighten his spirits. Hand billing was draining. He'd walked until he could walk no longer, giving out printed sheets of paper with his name on them. They were nothing extravagant. All they said was "'Peter Ghudd for Malfaxe Mayor, Vote Independent." After the fatigue had set in, he'd found a busy corner to stand on and handed his papers to anyone that would accept them. A few people had read them. Others wadded them up and cast them aside, like mere trash. It was especially displeasing if they'd ignored him entirely, or worse, pushed his handouts away. It had happened a lot. Monday night had been a real downer, and Peter was in no mood for meaningless conversation.

"Peter," Emmitt began, "I want to take a moment to update your personnel record, if it's suitable. Some fast answers will do it."

"Shoot."

"Okay, is your present address still 1119 Langford Avenue, or have you moved?" Emmitt asked. He was sizing up the old man from across his large mahogany desk.

"Still the same."

"Any medical problems we should know about?"

"Nope."

"And last of all, Peter, you've never listed any next of kin. Isn't there somebody, anybody, we can reach in the event that a situation could require it?"

"Not without a séance," Peter informed him. "All done?"

"Just about. Your middle initial, what's that stand for?"

"I'm sorry you asked," Peter seemed on the brink of being fussy.

"It's only for my personal knowledge," Emmitt appeased him. "You don't have to tell me unless you want to."

"It doesn't matter," Peter complied. "Try Barnabus."

"Okay to me," Emmitt said, "I only thought it might be helpful."

"Is that all?" Peter asked, raising out of his chair.

"Please don't go, Pete." Emmitt gestured for the janitor to sit back down.

"We need to talk for a few minutes."

"What about?"

"About you, about me, this job we're both going after. I didn't know that you had political aspirations," Emmitt said, trying not to sound overly interested. "Why didn't you say something about it?"

"I wasn't sure myself. I guess this has put you in kind of an awkward position."

"Not at all. It'll be fun. I believe what bothers me, as much as anything, is that I know more about Art Towson than I can ever hope to learn about you.

And it's you that I see almost every day. All I know about you is that you're seventy-one years old, hard-working, and you live in a city apartment.

"Then, what do you know about Art Towson?"

"If I tell you, Pete, we'll both know, won't we?" Emmitt tried to tease.

"Maybe so, but then we could chip away at him from both sides." Peter grinned.

"I think I'd better beware of you."

"I'm hardly worthy of that, Mr. Braedeikk."

"Emmitt, as long as the girls don't hear you, and lets keep it clean." Emmitt made himself stay jovial. "I have a lot of respect for you. When this thing is over with, I'd like us to remain friends."

"Clean is my specialty. That's one thing you can depend on," Peter said, as he lifted himself from the chair and simultaneously dumped Emmitt's filthy ashtray into a wastebasket next to the desk. "I like you, too, Emmitt. Maybe we ought to sign a truce."

"As long as you're not after my money, I'll take your word for the truce, otherwise I'd require a signature." Emmitt said, pretending to go back to his paperwork.

Peter didn't leave the office immediately. Instead, he walked over to a window next to Emmitt's desk and slowly ran two of his fingers across the vertical blinds. After inspecting the office thoroughly, he left without another word. Emmitt's eyes, along with his suspicions, followed the janitor through the doorway. Why would he, of all people, run for an official position, Emmitt asked himself. The thought gained momentum in his mind. He felt transfixed by the very idea of it, and wondered how could he possibly run a serious campaign against somebody of Peter's stature. It was out of the question. The man was little more than a tramp, and if he weren't careful, Emmitt's anxiety could easily turn to contempt. Peter was right about one thing. It was awkward for Emmitt, since the two of them worked at the bank. A strategy would have to be developed against the old man, or old fool, as Emmitt found himself thinking.

'Braedeikk Unveils Plan to Move City Prison'

In a bold and surprising announcement on Wednesday evening, Emmitt Braedeikk, Vice President of Coronet Alpine National

Bank, disclosed a plan to move the Malfaxe City Prison to the extreme outskirts of the city limits. Braedeikk, who is running for the office of Mayor, says the prison should have never been constructed at its present location, and he feels the move is long overdue. Mr. Braedeikk, who also claims he has the inside track on the executive position, is personally supervising the investigation to conclude whether the penitentiary can be relocated to a portion of a farm owned by the Reverend Lester Jameses.

"Etcetera, etcetera, etcetera," Bert said, after reading only part of the article that had been published in Thursday's paper. "I'll tell you something, Emmitt. It makes excellent print. Now all we have to do is follow-up. Keep baiting the nastiest hook."

They were in Bert's study. "That's not easy," Emmitt remarked, "since I don't know what's happening until you tell me."

"You will," Bert answered, as he cast the newspaper aside, "but for the next week, try to keep a low profile. We don't want any reporters bugging you."

"It's getting tough, Bert. That interview you just read took place in the bank's parking lot. I was heading out for a diner."

"Nobody ever said it was going to be easy, Emmitt."

"I'm running short of things to say, and you know how reporters are. You can never jabber enough to make them happy."

"Just make sure you choose your words carefully. More than one campaign has been destroyed by a slip of an unrestrained tongue."

"What can you tell me about Art Towson, Bert?"

"He's bright, attractive, and, as you must be learning for yourself by now, well-liked."

"I know all those things. I need to know his habits."

"You mean weaknesses."

"I'll settle for those."

"Personally Emmitt, I don't know of any. Politically he lives in the left hemisphere, but that's well known." Bert grabbed the remote to the television set. His wife had left it on. He hit the mute button. Prior to the commercial, the sound had been barely audible. He laid back into his recliner and looked at Emmitt, as though Emmitt were a bomb that had to be defused. He was showing signs of unwarranted distress. "If I were to tell you that Art Towson brushed his teeth with scouring powder or ran around nude, chasing young girls through the park with his jumbo joystick. Would you believe it?"

"Get serious, Bert."

"Of course, you wouldn't believe it, but you might find the story somewhat amusing. Now if we watered that story down to where it was believable."

"What if we could somehow link him to porno."

"You didn't let me finish," Bert said. "Look, Emmitt, running for any office can be dirty sport."

"So?"

"So nobody walks away from politics smelling like a bed of roses. The best thing that everybody can do is stick to the issues, and let it go at that. Art Towson is a good and decent man. I merely want you to develop some tough skin. You'll need it. I think some of the problems with your brother has put you on edge. Forget it, Emmitt!"

"I'm sorry, Bert. I should've never recommended the idea."

"Never mind. You Can't know. If we do have to get down into the trenches with Art, we'll keep that one handy," Bert laughed. "By the way. Is Norman adjusting to prison life? Have you seen him?"

"No," Emmitt answered. "I don't have the vaguest desire for another visit to the prison. I wanted the time I went with you to be my last."

"I understand," Bert consoled him. "Has he called you?"

"No." Emmitt made his way to the door, and then turned abruptly to face Bert once again. "Oh, Bert, there is one other thing. This business with Peter Ghudd, we haven't seen fit to talk about him to the smallest extent."

"Exactly what kind of a fellow is he Emmitt?"

"Energetic, crude, blunt to the point of being brash. He's puzzling because he's extremely private. He's very difficult to get next to."

Emmitt's anguish was apparent. Bert could visually tell by the squinty eyes and blush that invaded the end of Emmitt's nose. It was rare that it happened, although whenever it did, Bert always knew how to handle his words. "Look, if you want my advice, here it is. Treat this Mr. Ghudd with the same respect you give anyone else and avoid problems. You may have to stroke him a little. Don't snub him, Emmitt, and definitely don't make up stories about him," Bert went on to say. "You'll only hurt yourself, if you do."

You know me better than that. On top of my private reservations I don't believe he's into porno anyway. I'm a trifle concerned though that his involvement will make the election seem stupid."

"Emmitt," Bert said, "he won't last! I've seen this sort of thing happen before. At one time or another, everybody has thought about entering politics. He's a part-time cleaner, and right now, he's probably bored to death with his life. He'll amuse himself with the notion for a couple of weeks and then move on to something new, probably some kind of charity work. Most of the time, it's that way with these old chiefs. Ignore him, and he'll take his war dance somewhere else."

When they departed Emmitt had hardly been convinced that Peter was experimenting with political life on a whim. He and Bert promised to keep one another informed more often. They agreed to meet again in a few days. Marian, also, was weighing on his mind. Emmitt thought about how they had parted and felt guilty about it. He wanted to call her to let her know that he couldn't give her a teller's job in the bank at this time basically because there were no openings. He, also, wasn't proud of the way he had expressed himself and was craving the opportunity for redemption. Even if Marian was against his tactics, she had been honest about it. However, the new prison sight was becoming a "must have" and needed a push. Combined with all of the other mounting turmoil, Bert had given him a separate piece of information that was stabbing away at his peace of mind. Possibly it shouldn't have. It did, though. He never liked violence. Killers worried him, child killers, in particular. To Emmitt's way of thinking, a person who could kill children was the absolute pits. Malfaxe really did need another prison, so that scum like Sam Rhiggs could never escape again, as he had the day before.

CHAPTER 16

"Keep the noise down will ya, Koepy? I'm on the phone!" Emmitt hollered out from his bedroom window. "Take a break. You deserve it!" Instantly it got quiet, and Emmitt was able to hear himself speaking again. Koepy had turned the power saw off. After three hours of steady hammering, sawing, and climbing up and down his extended two-story ladder, Koepy had at last, with Emmitt's encouragement, become more tolerable.

Emmitt's ears were better now and his nerves less frayed. If he were able to turn the carpenter back on as easily, the job would be completed in no time at all, he thought, three or four quick weeks at the most. Instantly, Emmitt admitted to himself the idea wasn't exactly fair. Koepy was a fine worker. Even if he was a slow starter, he abundantly compensated for that fact alone. For the last five mornings, he had arrived promptly at 7:00 am and toiled into the evening hours, taking only two snack breaks in between. Emmitt knew this because his next door neighbor had told him so. Jay Bileyd may have been a busybody, as far as Emmitt could tell, but people like Jay had their purpose. So Koepy showed up at the same time every morning and sometimes spent as much as forty minutes to an hour hauling tools around to the back of the house. Then he would lay everything across a flattened canvas tarpaulin as neatly as he could before commencing to stare at the second floor of the house, as though it were some magnificent mountain that he desperately needed to climb. Emmitt had seen him doing this just two days earlier. He was leaving for the bank when he checked on the progress being made, and there was the carpenter, hands hanging idle, gazing toward the roof. It had occurred to Emmitt that Koepy was in deep thought, so he didn't interrupt him. The man's eyes were so fixed above that Emmitt, as much as he wanted to, couldn't bring himself to interrupt Koepy. What he saw up there was beyond Emmitt's recognition. Since Koepy wasn't being paid by the hour, Emmitt chose not to let it bother him. That was Thursday. Saturday had come like there was not even a hint of Friday, and now Marian was trying to get off the phone with Emmitt.

"I told you that you don't have to apologize. It's my fault. I wasn't very polite," Marian tried for a third time.

"But it wasn't your fault, Marian. Personally, I'd love to have you working in the bank, but there aren't any openings."

"As it stands, I'm already trying to wear too many hats. I'm sure you understand where my priorities happen to lie."

"I do. Believe me, I do. If you'll bear along with me, I know that I can make it worth your while. Marian, I'm not going to mince words. My original proposition" Emmitt had used a word he was sorry for, but went on with it, "stands." If you can find the time, I'd like you to help me out at my place. I promise you that the first opening at the bank is yours."

"How do you know I'm qualified?"

"You're a high school graduate, right?" Before she could answer, Emmitt continued. "You can be trained."

"Let's do this," Marian returned. "If I can help you at your house, I'm beholding. I don't want to work at your bank though. It's not me."

Now it was Emmitt who was offended. He wasn't in the habit of extending job opportunities to people he knew so little about. Because of his peculiarities, sometimes he would take weeks to fill a job slot, leaving the other employees to work more than their regular hours. As he continued to appease Marian, he was asking himself who this young twerp thought she was.

"Marian," he said, "don't give me your final answer as to the bank until you've reconsidered. We'll be searching for steady help soon enough, Your names at the top of the list."

"What's your address?" She asked.

"One seventy-nine Oakwood Court. Coming from your place, stay on the highway heading south for approximately six miles. Turn right at exit twenty-eight. Go three blocks down, until you come to a stop light and make another right, and you're there."

"That's easy."

"Finally, she's on board." Emmitt was able to convince himself. "Can I assume you'll try and make it?"

"I'll see. It strikes me as a compassionate endeavor." She laughed at Emmitt's pleading.

"Marian, please don't disappoint me."

"I'll do my best not to," she said, bolstering Emmitt's hopes before hanging up the phone. While talking to Marian he had made his way to the kitchen. Emmitt grabbed two cups, one for himself and another for Koepy. He then filled the two cups almost to the brim with freshly brewed coffee. "Koepy," he called through a partially opened window. "Want Your share of this morning's brew? I made extra."

"Black and piping hot?"

"Yeah," Emmitt returned, "I hear it puts lightning in your rod this time of day, if you drink a sufficient amount. Don't start anything you can't finish in thirty seconds.

"In that case the rafters can wait." Koepy had briefly ended the sentence when Emmitt came strolling around the side of the house with the two steaming drinks in his hands.

"How's it coming?"

"You're the boss. What do you think?"

"To tell you the truth, Koepy, fall is almost here. I'd like to have this job finished. You're not exactly taking off like a racehorse."

"I don't know much about horses, except they've got hearty appetites."

"Koepy, I'm amazed! You mean I've found something you're not up on?"

"But look how long it's taken you, I've been working for you for six whole days, You've taken close to a week finding out I hav'ta be watered."

"Maybe your next break should be from a feed bag," Emmitt joked. He hadn't kidded around like this with anybody in years, and it occurred to him that it was refreshing.

"The oats won't be necessary," Koepy objected with a wide smile. "The coffee will do quite fine."

"It is rather good," Emmitt seemed proud in saying. "There's more inside go help yourself. I'll be in and out most of the day." Emmitt aimed his attention back to the house, and the addition that was to be. "Koepy, seriously, when do you think it's going to be finished?"

"We're almost through August," Koepy pondered out loud. "I'd have to say it'll be getting done sometime in October."

"Early or late?"

"Mid."

"Why so long?" Emmitt inquired.

"High quality" Koepy pointed out. "Every nail that I drive and every board that I cut has my signature on it. Believe me, you'll be more than satisfied.

"We can skip the monograms. I just want it to start taking shape. Up until yesterday, I didn't see anything other than this concrete base." Emmitt eyed the three-sided foundation that extended from his house and stopped about two feet away from where he and the carpenter were standing.

"Is the footer far down?"

"Forty inches."

"Pretty deep isn't it?"

"The county code calls for three feet putting it slightly below the frost line."

"So why go four inches below that?"

"I believe in a strong foundation. Otherwise, how much integrity can you expect the rest of the room to have in the distant future?"

"But Koepy," Emmitt was condescending, "why should it matter? I'm not prone to give a hoot in another hundred years."

"True," Koepy agreed.

"I don't need that kind of moral insurance," Emmitt responded. "Doesn't that enter into your code of ethics?"

"Yes, but I do, and I have a feeling that's the reason why you hired me."

Koepy pleasantly returned. "You have to realize that my work's meant to endure systematic deterioration, abuse too."

"Oh, I get it," Emmitt decided to be sarcastic. "You mean like the smart little pig?"

"Yep. That pig lived past a bad confrontation," Koepy answered.

"Maybe," Emmitt was lost for more words. Certainly, the analogy about the pig was uncalled for, but the way Koepy had chosen to respond was needling him. Emmitt didn't like it one little iota. It would have to wait, because of the odd rebuttal, he chose not to show any more interest in what his hired help had to say. Originally, he had wanted to be congenial. However, he felt as though Koepy had taken control of the conversation and left him with nothing additional he could converse over. What bothered him more was the fact that realistically, Koepy was right on target. It was true that Emmitt had hired the man because he believed him to be a perfectionist. Why then make an issue of the time involved. The price wasn't going to escalate. Thus far, this zealous work hand talked a good job. If he was a third as good as his confidence dictated that he was, Emmitt was sure that he would get his money's worth. He just wasn't prepared for what was in store, not to mention the rest of the chaos that was about to take place.

CHAPTER 17

Frank Cobb was scribbling notes at a rapid fire pace. The newscaster, with one sudden notion, swung open the door to the van and leaped to the sidewalk. From there, it was three long, quick strides to the bank's entrance and one fast turn on an antique brass doorknob that delivered him through the doorway and into the main lobby where Emmit and a technician were waiting. The interview wasn't Emmitt's idea, and he was doing his best to appear unshaken.

Bert had called him without adequate notice, telling Emmitt that a news team was on its way and to stay put. "Don't forget to smile a lot." Bert had reminded him. "You need to look your best." It was a reasonable request, but Emmitt was panicstricken.

"Calm down, Mr. Braedeikk," Frank said. "This whole thing won't take over ten minutes, and that includes the time it takes for me to pack things and clear out."

"Is this live?" Emmitt asked.

"No, we wouldn't do that to you without a warning," Frank assured him.

"Do I look all right?"

"Great!"

"What kind of questions are you going to ask me?"

"Nothing that you can't answer. Just general stuff, your age, what kind of home life you have. Do you believe that you can change City Hall? We just want the public to be familiar with our next Mayor."

Emmitt eased up. "You're jumping the gate a little, aren't you?"

"You're hot in the polls."

"So was Dewey," Emmitt commented, searching for a touch of humility.

"Here we go," Frank said, prepping Emmitt for the interview.

"This is Frank Cobb. I'm here at the Coronet Alpine National Bank, located at the corner of Hamilton Avenue and Spring Street. Emmitt Braedeikk is standing right here. He manages this bank, and, as most of you already know, Mr. Braedeikk is running for mayor. Right now, what I'd like to do is bring the camera a little closer, so that everybody can get a good look at the man whom, some people believe, to be the number one candidate."

The camera went on Emmitt. In order to capture both Frank and Emmitt, it then receded. Emmitt was caught fixing his tie.

"Mister Braedeikk, approximately two months ago you started campaigning for the job of running this city. Would you tell us why?"

"Well, Fred."

"Frank."

"How about if we both be frank?" Emmitt tried to land on his feet after making the grand blunder. "There's plenty of work to be done here. Frank, how many potholes did you drive over on the way here? You don't know, because after the first two dozen, you probably stopped counting them. The city streets are in the worst condition I've seen them in years. While we still have a city to live in, we've absolutely got to shift some of our money that we're spending on useless endeavors and put it back into urban renewal. Now, potholes are a trivial example, Frank, compared to many other discrepancies. I want to tell you something. This city needs more than a facial. Cities all over the country are digging into their resources, and doing what has to be done to divest themselves of decadence and slums. If this city is to survive, Frank, we have to do likewise."

"Where would you start?" Frank asked. "That is assuming that you were elected."

"What's the first thing most people do in their own home, Frank, whenever they remodel? I'll tell you. They discard the junk and begin again. That'll be our challenge."

"Meaning?"

"Meaning slum housing, dilapidated buildings, and vacant factory sites must be rehabilitated or torn down. We'll level what we can."

"And next?"

"We start rebuilding."

"Who would be in charge of this magnanimous undertaking?"

"The city council, along with the mayor."

"We're talking millions and millions of dollars here. Who is going to pay the bill for all of this?"

"Frank, federal dollars will foot the bill for at least two thirds of the money required."

"It's that easy?" Frank Cobb was astonished.

"No, it's not." Emmitt added. "Our particular plan will have to be blessed by the U.S. Department of Housing and Urban Development."

Although Frank Cobb had mislead Emmitt as to the nature of the interview, it seemed as though it was advancing quite well. It was beginning to appear as though Emmitt was somewhat knowledgeable and wasn't merely hiding behind a fake smoke screen.

"If we're going to tear down the city's slum areas and build new housing projects, where are the displaced people going to live?" Frank was interested, but also appeared confused.

"Frank, that will have to be worked out in the master plan. I don't have all of the answers now," Emmitt admitted, just then a mop sloshed by and grazed his heels. The man taping the interview turned the camera off and laid it on a cart beside some of the extra lighting fixtures.

"Maybe we should have roped this area off," he huffed, giving the janitor a hateful glance.

"Don't worry about it," Frank said. "I want to pick up on the prison issue. Let's roll."

"Let's call it a day," Emmitt protested. "We'll cover that one another time."

"I'll take that one," Peter said, as he leaned his mop handle into a corner.

"Why'd we want to ask you anything, pop?" The agitated technician asked.

"I'm a candidate myself, sonny!" Peter proudly proclaimed, as he reached inside of the utility closet and pulled a toilet plunger out for everyone to unwillingly view the filthy rubber bulb on the business end of a stick.

"I'll bet you're pledging waste removal," the technician ridiculed.

"Leave him alone," Frank ordered. "Mister Braedeikk, we had some important questions for you concerning the new prison. What if we touch on that, and then we'll close on something soft, like your family life?"

"He doesn't have any family life." Peter interjected.

"Neither do you!" Emmitt retaliated, before he could catch himself. The last thing that he wanted to do was attach importance to any of Peter's words. "Actually, what I mean is that we're both bachelors."

Frank looked over at the old man who was still glued to the handle of the rubber plunger. Both his hair and fingernails were badly in need of trimming. He had no intention of giving the custodian an interview, but he didn't like the way Smitty, the technician, had treated him either. His own father, years before, raised five children on not much more than a pauper's income. He, too, had been a cleaner for a small company that had long since gone out of business. It was an honorable living. Just as Peter was wearing his shirttail on the outside of this trousers and a beret turned a little to the side of his face and down some, his own father had dressed in much the same fashion. Those years had been marked by financial hardships. The climax occurring when they had lost their small two-bedroom bungalow. The bank, which held the deed to their home, was forced into foreclosure. The family was evicted, and, because there was no one place where they could all live, they had to be split apart and stay with different relatives. Those were trying times. Eventually, the family had been reunited, although the circumstances weren't much better than before. By that time, Frank was the main wage earner in the household. His father's health was not only shot, but his pride was ravaged. Frank's father finally succumbed to alcohol. After years of hard work to get an education and make something of himself, Frank managed to come out on top. He was right where he wanted to be in life. Engrossed in broadcasting, and journalism had paved the way.

"What about a picture of the two of you shaking hands?" Frank asked, wanting to pacify Peter. "It'll be in tomorrow's papers."

"Sure, why not?" Peter said, dragging his plunger over to Emmitt. This was not what Emmitt wanted. He saw it as crude and demeaning. It was embarrassing. Now he, Emmitt Braedeikk, bank manager and probably the leading candidate, would have to be identified with Peter Ghudd, the downtrodden big mouth.

"I don't think so," Emmitt declined. "I take a lousy picture."

"Don't worry about it," Peter insisted, "I'm not photogenic either!" Shouldering his plunger, he stepped beside Emmitt and stuck his hand out to meet Emmitt's. Emmitt knew that he would have to distance himself from Peter, however now was not the time. As their hands met, he seethed. The flash went off, and Emmitt turned to find refuge in his office.

"The next time you guys come, we'll talk about the new prison," he promised.

"Sounds all right to me," Peter said. "Maybe we can talk about eminent domain while we're at it."

Emmitt stopped cold. "Eminent what?" He asked.

"Eminent domain," Peter reiterated.

"Yes, I heard you. What about it?"

"If elected, are you going to exercise it?" Peter asked.

"There's not going to be any need for eminent domain," Emmitt said.

"What are you talking about, Peter?"

"According to the appears," Peter answered, "the property that you want to use for the new penitentiary is part of the Jameses farm. I drove down there just two days ago and talked to the owner. He's a preacher, so I figured he was telling me the truth. He said he hadn't made up his mind as to whether or not he's selling off any of his land."

Emmitt's pulse soared. Peter had put him in a position of either lying or appearing as though he didn't know what the facts were. There was no doubt about it, he had to be as evasive as possible.

"There isn't anything on paper now," he admitted. "We're in the fundamental stages. The first thing we have to do is verify the viability of the property in question. Once that's accomplished, I, or whoever is mayor at that time, can pursue whatever course of action that they deem appropriate. I know the Reverend quite well," Emmitt almost blustered. "I believe he'll do what is genuinely best for the city." Smitty was operating the camera again, while Emmitt stared directly into it.

"So you're saying, as far as the new prison site is concerned, you don't anticipate any problems?" Frank asked.

"That's right, Frank. I've been nothing less than encouraged by Reverend Jameses, and I'm very excited about the concept of moving the prison to the outskirts of the city."

Peter moved closer to Emmitt. He was still holding onto the toilet plunger, as he made a bid for the camera. Smitty almost shut it off again, but Frank elbowed him. "You know," Peter said, "even if the minister does agree to sell the property, we still need to have a public hearing before the city can purchase it. It seems like a lot of hassle for a bunch of cons."

"Peter, you know very well it's not for the convicts! They're breaking loose!" Emmitt returned, with frustration attacking his composure.

"Have you read the crime sheets lately? It's more like they're trying to squeeze themselves into prison instead of out!"

"Peter," Emmitt condescended, "I've been in the prison, and I can't imagine anybody consciously trying to get into that dive. Let's not be ridiculous, okay? I was never so happy to get out of a place in all my days."

Peter cast a suspicious glare at Emmitt and folded his arms. "I don't know how long it's been since you were in there, Emmitt, but maybe they have different ways of doing things since you left. Did you serve much time?"

"Honestly, Peter, you know what I meant when I said I was there! I toured the penitentiary! Let's get serious here."

"Precisely," Peter argued, "but nobody in public office wants to. Politicians have been squawking about anticrime issues for years. It gives them something to complain about. Nothing's gotten better. Is a different prison gonna help the situation?" Where would criminal attorneys be if we didn't have soaring crime?" Peter raised his plunger high for all to see. "It's a farce is all it is!" He slammed the plunger hard against a nearby teller's counter, making a hollow sound that snapped Emmitt's patience.

"That's it for today," Emmitt said. "Come back in a week gentlemen, and probe me. Peter, after you wipe that counter top off, see if you can get my office next.

"I'll do that," Peter promised.

Emmitt approached his office. Before he reached it Margaret Simpson intercepted him and handed him a brown folder containing several papers.

"This requires your written response before the week's up," she informed him.

Emmitt looked at the newsman, who was still speaking with Peter. They were getting awfully friendly, he thought. He couldn't understand the attraction. What could Peter possibly be saying that was worth listening to, he wondered. Not much it seemed, because everyone else was going about their business. Peter had his hat tilted to the back of his head. His glasses were perched precariously on the end of his bent and oversized nose. Emmitt wanted them to fall off and shatter into a hundred little particles. Without taking his eyes from the duo, he grabbed the folder from Margaret. Imitating a man of unquestionable authority, Peter was waving his plunger in different directions and talking feverishly to Frank. "Why don't you harass commissioner commode?" Emmitt gestured towards Peter with a disgusted scowl on his own reddened face. "He has all the answers."

The bank's manager mumbled something vulgar and incomprehensible before angrily storming away.

CHAPTER 18

From where she was standing, Marian didn't see very much. The room was dark. She could already smell the same rankness that filled many of the other dumpy joints she'd been in. As Marian pushed the door, it squeaked. Still, there was no sign of anyone. The idea of a struggle came to mind. A big, muscular arm reaching around from inside of the door would be all it would take to fling her to the floor and render her helpless. Too many times she had toyed with fate, always wondering if her life would come to an end in a bazaar act of lustful violence. At barely twenty years of age, Marian was seeing her life as an X-rated movie, but it failed to stop her. A role in a dirty, off-screen drama was still better than barely existing on her father's much-demanding, vegetable farm. If this was going to be the last act, she would play her part to the curtain. Marian's instincts were good though, and she felt ready to share herself one more time with whoever was paying. She sensed his presence. He was there, but not like a cat ready to spring, more like a scared rabbit who needed to be cuddled. She pushed the door open all the way and turned a small lamp on before closing the door behind herself.

Marian's vibes were reliable. Perhaps Emmitt wasn't a rabbit, but he was, also, a far cry from a tiger. She considered walking out, but hesitated.

"The voice on the phone was familiar. I had a weird feeling it was going to be you," she said.

"Are you disappointed?"

"What difference does it make?"

"None, I guess." Emmitt looked at his watch. "You're on time tonight."

"What do you mean, tonight?"

"Nothing," Emmitt said, deciding to skip it.

Marian switched the lamp off again and stood motionless in the dark for a few seconds. She then opened a small closet and removed her blouse. Emmitt watched as she slipped out of her shoes and approached Emmitt, who was still sitting in the corner of the room. He was on a hardback chair, wearing an expression of boyish discomfort. She went to him and began to unbutton her skirt. "Would you like to help?" She asked.

"Marian, I don't feel good about this," Emmitt said, getting up and moving closer to the door. "This is more awkward than I thought it would be."

Marian didn't appear surprised. She let her skirt slide to the floor and moved gracefully toward him. They didn't touch, but Emmitt could sense the warmth of her body. It was more than seductive. It was magnetizing. Emmitt was withering with each breath. It made him ashamed. She was one-third his years. "Doesn't it worry you that we know each other?" He said, trying to repel her allure. "This strikes me as kinky."

"Relax," she said, "I'm not going to tell anybody we spent the evening together if that's what you're afraid of."

"I can't afford the mess it would create."

"And that's why you wanted me, because I can't either," Marian assured him.

"No, you're wrong. I wanted you because you're very tempting. On the other hand I'd be a fraud if I told you I wasn't nervous."

"Oh, sneaking around here with me isn't being deceitful is it?" Marian took Emmitt's place in the chair and crossed her long slender legs. She then turned the radio on. It was under the lamp, right next to where she was sitting. "You don't mind, do you?"

"No," Emmitt said, "but at least play some good music."

"What's that…classical? I prefer stripteases."

"Fifties will do just fine."

"Just how old are you?" Marian asked from behind her mask of hard steel. She didn't change the station from where it was. Emmitt thought he recognized it as country. However, he wasn't sure, and he found it difficult to care as much as he had pretended.

"Marian, your father would be brokenhearted if he knew what you were doing."

"So who's going to tell…you?"

"You're missing the point," Emmitt retreated in the opposite direction.

"Doesn't it rankle you that what you're doing goes against everything he stands for?" He said, while unbuttoning his shirt. "It's sweaty in here. "I normally get my sermons on Sunday," Marian remarked, as she got up from the chair and went over to where the bed was.

"Am I boring you, Marian?"

"Quite the contrary." Marian let the fingertips of her right hand drift slowly down the inside of her bare thigh, prompting Emmitt to respond. He wouldn't, so she reached behind herself. With one snap, her brassiere dangled loosely, allowing Emmitt a better look. "You know, if I wanted to, I could hold you partly accountable for me being in this line of work," she said, as her breasts became fully uncovered. They were large, much bigger than Emmitt had originally believed. He felt a throbbing from below. He wanted Marian. She was the forbidden fruit, and tonight she was his for the taking. What she said bothered him, though, and he felt the anger growing from within his very guts and working its way up to his throat. He understood what she meant and felt compelled to call her on it. Otherwise, his desire would change to contempt, and he would have to leave what he was not about to forget. It would torment his memory for the rest of his life.

"I have nothing to do with you being in this line of work," he excused himself. "You do this because you want to."

"Oh, Yeah, well I've collected a lot of church donations right here in this very room."

Emmitt surveyed the room momentarily. It was a rat's nest, probably the worst that the poor side of town laid claim to. He felt guilty for his insensitivity about Marian and wanted deeply to make amends. Her life had obviously been tough, and Emmitt yearned to be the one to somehow help this girl. He could think of only one solution for the time being. Emmitt let his pants drop down past his knees and furrow hideously over his ankles. "Marian," he said, "I know things haven't been all that easy for you or your father. I'd really like to make a significant contribution to the church."

Marian reached down and felt the bulge through Emmitt's underpants. It was less than significant. If good things came in tiny packages, then Emmitt promised to be no less than terrific. She giggled out loud at the prospect. "Okay," she said, "you know what they say about every little bit helping. Suit yourself."

So Emmitt went all out to make a donation. The trouble was it amounted to little more than a drop in Marian's awaiting bucket.

CHAPTER 19

Bert was a master with words. He'd delegate his flock to the fiery pits of Hell, shower them with The Almighty's forgiveness, and within seconds deliver them to the Pearly Gates. He practiced a driving passion for oratory such as most people had seldom heard. It was no wonder he was the minister of the largest church in Malfaxe. On his worst day, Bert Dixtzon was nothing less than a sensational speaker.

Few people were as committed to their Sunday morning traditions as much as Emmitt. For twenty-seven years, he had been a deacon in the church. Along with that, he had headed the board of finance, and controlled the distribution of every dollar the church had taken in. Regulating money was his passion. That's actually what brought him out to church these days, it was the power of maintaining a familiar type of control. Emmitt had learned well from his father how to handle money. His father, too, had been a banker, but not a church addict. That was just another reason why Emmitt in the past had always accompanied his other to church on Sundays. It was a ritual in the Braedeikk household that lEmmitt had never shunned. It lasted for years, into his adulthood, and ended only after his mother had expired at the age of seventy-eight. He'd served his mother and the church diligently, even if he were agnostic. Today, church ended early, and Emmitt was glad. Burning the candle at both frazzled ends wasn't meant for him. Trying not to be conspicuous, he chased the sleep from his eyes with subtle buffs from a wadded tissue. He would be fourth from last in a long line, as he rose and began to make his way to the exit of the church. Bert was there with an outstretched hand to greet him. The service was over.

Not wanting to appear drowsy, Emmitt enthusiastically met Bert's inquisitive gaze. It had scarcely been four days since they'd last seen one another, but the two men shook hands like it had been half-a-century. There was much to be hashed over, obviously though, this specific forum was in no way isolated enough. When he parted from Bert he went to his car, stopping twice to exchange brief conversations. He was right in front of his car when he heard his name called. Emmitt was happy to see Bert trailing after him in apparent haste.

"Emmitt, I've been trying to get a hold of you. We've got to meet." Bert was tense. "What about tonight?" Bert inquired, expecting an affirmative.

"I can't Bert. Why not tomorrow afternoon at the bank?"

"I have to be somewhere across town. Look, Emmitt," Bert said, sounding more anxious. "We've got to talk." Bert was fidgety. Evidently, he had something important to discuss, and it forced Emmitt to submit to Bert's initial request.

"Bert, there's nothing I can't drop for you anytime."

"Do you have ten or fifteen minutes now?" Bert pressed. Emmitt propped his foot up on the bumper of his car and leaned down over his knee signaling Bert that he was available. "You've got my ear."

"How are things progressing with Lester Jameses?" The edge in Bert's voice was noticeably sharp.

"He's non-committal."

"I'm somewhat deflated, Emmitt. I saw the interview on the news. I've been trying to reach you since Friday."

Emmitt felt a sense of unworthiness. If Bert was willing to express disappointment in him, he worried just how inept he had come across to the masses who'd also seen him on television.

"We need his name on a contract." Bert whispered.

"Bert, he's already signed off to have the excavation work done. Believe me, I'm moving as quickly as I can with him. He's the obstinate type."

"Look, Emmitt, once you get him to promise to sell, we're past a giant hurdle. Otherwise, you're going to look like you started something you couldn't finish, then you might as well fold."

Bert was right, but Emmitt hated to hear the truth just the same. He would have to get out to the farm to see the Reverend Jameses soon. He couldn't help wondering how much more complicated his life was going to become. If it got any worse, the idea about folding may not seem so far-fetched even if Bert hadn't meant it to be.

"Bert," he said, "I guess I could've been more agressive with him. I apologize. I may have allowed too much water to flow under the bridge in the last few days."

"A lot more has gushed over, Emmitt!"

"Bert, I'll tell you something. I knew that man was trouble."

"So did we, Emmitt, but we never expected him to break loose, let alone kill somebody."

"Who are we talking about, Bert? Peter Ghudd isn't a killer."

"I don't mean Peter Ghudd. Who cares about Peter Ghudd? I'm talking about Sam Rhiggs!"

Emmitt was totally perplexed. He'd planned on feeling Bert out on some ideas of toning Peter down, but Bert's revelation had caught him by complete surprise. What if Sam Rhiggs had escaped from prison? The fact that he had killed someone was not to be taken lightly. However, why should Bert be so upset? It wasn't his problem.

"Emmitt," Bert complained, "you're going to have to start lighting a fire under out friend's hind end!"

"Bert, I don't know what I can do! He keeps hitting me with he needs more time to think it over. I'm afraid I'll scare him out of signing if I become too pushy."

"You know, Emmitt, I like Lester Jameses. Did I tell you we went to high school together years ago?"

"No, Bert, I'd a thought he was older."

"Afterwards we went through seminary together. We'd shared a wonderful friendship in our dawn. He's a fine person, Emmitt. He always was. He's got one problem though. With Lester every decision is monumental. Emmitt, if you give Lester an inch, he'll take three decades to get there. Now all we need, for the time being, is a contingency contract. Tell him it'll be risky trying to develop that property. Explain to him that we need a commitment from him in order for the testing to take place. Ah, Emmitt, why am I telling you this? You're smooth. You know what to say. I'll bet he even likes you by now!"

"I wouldn't rely on it."

"Why not?"

"He's polite with me, Bert. He isn't friendly."

"It doesn't matter. He needs the money and don't let him forget it. Bert's eyes narrowed, and his shock of curly blonde hair was beginning to droop down over his ears. He was a strong-featured man who, unless he smiled, could be mistaken for angry. Not many people of any sort went up against Bert Dixtzon. That was another reason why Emmitt cherished their friendship. He wanted to please Bert more than he wanted to please anybody. To Emmitt, if Bert seemed overpowering at times, it was because he had to be in order to accomplish whatever it was that he'd set out to do. Working to get the penitentiary out of the inner city was commendable on Bert's part, and Emmitt respected him for it. Bert's crusade was as noble as any Emmitt had ever witnessed. The people who had lived near the prison had been at the mercy of a perilous thread. For the ones who couldn't afford to move from the area, it was a life of constant fear. Emmitt imagined that they, too, were serving their own kind of sentence, one of anguish without the possibility of parole. Win or lose, Emmitt would help Bert by being his political tool, even though it was often gnawing at his own peace of mind.

"I will, Bert. I'll start blitzing him today," Emmitt said, fully aware that he was already tired from the burden of trying to manipulate his sparse personal time. He looked around, wanting to shake his worries off by losing himself in the scenery. People were still standing in small clusters talking to one another.

Emmitt struck on a face that didn't seem to fit with the regulars. In a split second he recognized one of the casual stragglers as Koepy, his builder.

"How long's he been coming here?" He asked Bert, gesturing with a twitch of his head toward Stanley Koppenhaus.

"Who? Do you mean Stanley there?"

"I call him Koepy. That's the fellow I hired to do some work at my place. He's adding on."

"I'd say," Bert hesitated, "I don't know, Emmitt. I guess he's been coming here for four or five weeks now. He's real interested. Says he'd like to teach Sunday school."

Bert and Emmitt watched together as the builder stood under a crimson red maple tree and mingled with some of the children. At first, there had been no more than two or three, however, the group was increasing. Emmitt saw twelve in all, eight boys and four girls.

"He's a charmer, isn't he, Emmitt?"

"I don't know, Bert. With kids, it doesn't always take that much."

"Emmitt, do you think that he's alright? I mean, you don't think he's a pervert or a head case of a sort, do you?"

"No, of course not. He's okay."

"He's not married."

"Well, neither am I."

"True, but you're not the one hanging around the kids." Bert answered, remembering that he might soon find himself in an embarrassing situation. He thought he had been kind to Stanley or Koepy, as Emmitt preferred to call him. He seemed likable. That's why Bert had taken him around that very morning to meet some of the church's finest. Although Koepy conveyed a peculiar demeanor at the time, Bert, just as Emmitt had, recognized a certain appeal to the stranger. It was difficult to describe. Everyone that Bert had introduced Koepy to insisted that the newcomer join the church. Koepy was not only young and attractive, he was anxious to join in. The church needed people like this. They were the seeds that would keep the church infinite. Now Bert was beginning to have second thoughts on this new person who had the children so whole heartedly captivated.

"I'll watch him anyway, Emmitt."

"It never hurts," Emmitt agreed. "What's he doing that for?"

Koepy bent down and reached inside of a small boy's jacket. As he did, Bert became frantic. He started to approach the group when the carpenter's hand reappeared. Somehow, he had managed to pull a soda out from underneath the boy's coat. Koepy popped the tab and gave the drink to a little girl. Then he stuck his hand back inside the boy's jacket once more and pulled out another drink. Before he was through, four drinks had mysteriously appeared. The children were most pleased, and at this point, considered the drinks quite special. They began passing them around until they had all enjoyed some of the beverage. After that, Koepy moved right along. He placed his hand next to a girl's ear and delighted her as he flashed a silver dollar from between his fingers.

"I think he's wasting his time in construction," Emmitt remarked in fun.

"I need a man like him at the bank."

Bert remained quiet. The chance of him being taken in by a second rate entertainer had put him in a touchy mood. Koepy may be alright, Bert reconciled to himself. There was no telling. It was going to take close observation to be positive. He was a puzzle, but Bert took pleasure in the fact that, in the end, the pieces would all come together. He began scanning to see how many others were taking an interest in the seemingly caring visitor.

Without saying a word, Koepy stretched his hands out from his sides as far as he could reach. They were empty. Suddenly he brought them together and cupped them into a ball. As he gently separated them, a sparrow appeared from between and began fluttering about the children who were, by then, altogether amazed. As the bird moved about, it chirped and flapped its wings as though it were about to take flight. Emmitt was transfixed. Not since he was a kid himself had he enjoyed such a display of magic. His mother had taken him to the circus once, and it, too, had a magician. Emmitt remembered him as being very good, but, like Koepy's group of onlookers, Emmitt was quite young himself. He thought again about how children were so easily impressed, although this time it was different. At the moment he didn't understand why. It just was. The bird had made its way to Koepy again and perched very comfortably on his left thumb. Then the carpenter rotated his hand. The sparrow at once nestled in Koepy's palm. Emmitt's sensitivity was spurred at what he saw next. Koepy walked over to a boy who was standing by himself. He had Down's Syndrome. The boy had been watching the magical display from the inside of a nearby gazebo. He had no idea that Koepy was aware of his presence. Emmitt could see the boy's face clearly. It seemed as though he wanted desperately to hide from the man who was approaching. Without speaking a word, the carpenter bent down and placed the bird in the boy's soft hands. The bird was content with where it was, prompting the boy to smooth its feathers affectionately. It remained there for the longest time leaving only to perch itself back onto Koepy's shoulder.

Afterwards, Koepy returned to the other children and gave them some small pieces of hard candy that he had removed from an inner compartment of his truck. Bert, Emmitt, and several of the parents continued scrutinizing Koepy's behavior. It was evident that Koepy certainly had a way with the children, but the fact remained, Bert had told himself, his motivations would have to be scrutinized. He was pondering the consequences when Emmitt spoke up.

"He's kind of good," Emmitt said.

Bert disagreed, reinforcing Emmitt's original response of it not taking much to charm kids. "He didn't do anything neither of us hasn't seen a dozen times before. Deceit's nothing we want to be teaching our children, Emmitt."

"Bert, you missed the trick," Emmitt protested without thinking twice.

"What?"

"I said you missed the trick."

"What trick? I saw the tricks, all of them."

"The one with the bird."

"I saw the trick with the bird," Bert insisted, as the two men caught a final glimpse of the builder before he got into his vehicle and waved goodbye to the children.

Emmitt turned to Bert. He was baffled by his friend's oversight. Normally, it was difficult to get anything past Bert. Bert's mental, along with his visual, perception fell within the extremely, acute range. This time he had been blind to something that had momentarily caught Emmitt's complete attention.

"Bert, did you ever try to teach a sparrow not to fly? That bird was outdoors and not once did it ever attempt to fly away."

"Emmitt, he probably clipped its wings."

"Not that one. That bird had its whole span. It fluttered right to Kopey when the lad released it. I kept waiting for it to go airborne. I'm sure it could have."

"It's not that important, Emmitt. Let's forget the sideshow and get down to business."

Emmitt felt foolish. Bert was right. They should have been discussing political savvy, not the finer points of illusion, although sometimes Emmitt stumbled over the difference. Deception didn't belong exclusively to magicians, he admitted to himself. Politicians, given the opportunity, were reputed to be equally talented.

"Get the signature, Emmitt. We need it." Bert wrapped a firm grip around Emmitt's upper arm and squeezed it hard. Emmitt understood that the gesture helped Bert to communicate. Whenever he embraced a fellow human being. It was Bert's way, and it was Bert's wish for Emmitt to know how much he was counting on him. Bert didn't take well to being disappointed, either. One way or another, Bert would get what he wanted. There were no exceptions. This week, it was a few acres, next week it might be the entire farm. At any rate, Emmitt would have to be well-received by Lester Jameses.

The drive to Reverend Jameses farm Sunday afternoon took Emmitt exactly twenty-five minutes. On the trip, he contemplated seeing Marian. He fantasized her in dungarees and carrying baskets of produce across her father's foul smelling earth. He assumed it was the fertilizer that made the air out there so unpleasant to breathe.

Emmitt, as Marian had previously corrected him, didn't know much about agriculture nor did he desire to. It was Marian, however, who did keep his interest. That in itself served to incite him even more into doing Bert's will. He kept telling himself that seeing Marian would make his day happier. The Idea of getting her alone came to mind. Then he dismissed it. He knew better than to try that right under her father's suspicious nose. There was too much at stake. Besides, she had an independent nature and would likely be difficult on her own turf.

In contrast, Marian was often accommodating. She turned Emmitt on as much as any woman he had ever been with. Not that there were that many, but Marian occupied the highest plateau in Emmitt's opinion. Emmitt concluded that it was her free spirit and knack for keeping him off balance that had him altogether infatuated. He liked it.

As Emmitt cornered the Jameses house, he caught the reverend checking the oil level in his pickup tuck. The heat was blistering, and Lester Jameses was wearing cutoff shorts that were tattered around the edges. A tee shirt hung loosely over his waist and perspiration was forming under the preacher's arms. A silly looking, wide, brimmed hat drooped down past Lester's eyebrows and shadowed his reciprocating glare towards Emmitt. He seemed out of place and quite different than before. When Emmitt greeted him, the minister gracefully pulled the oil stick through a wad of paper and rested it across the top of the truck's engine. It reminded Emmitt of a fencing master laying his weapon aside.

"How's the oil checking out?" Emmitt smiled.

"Not too good," Lester answered. "I'm one gusher shy of surviving."

"There's a way to remedy that," Emmitt said, making an effort to read the intent in Lester's expression. Lester's words were affable enough, however Emmitt didn't know how to continue on without being direct. "Mr. Jameses, this city needs your help. If you'll agree to sell us the land we need, you can build yourself three churches, if that's what you want."

"One will do me just fine," Lester said, taking his hat off and fanning himself with it. "Besides, it's already built."

"Built yes, paid for, no." Emmitt countered, attempting not to sound too harsh.

"Do I have a choice?" Lester asked. "I hear the city might try to take the land. You didn't say anything in regard to that."

"As far as I can tell, eminent domain is a remote ploy. Bad karma in my book. The city can afford to offer you a nice deal."

"I heard what that feller, Ghudd, said on the news." The minister replaced his hat. Then he pushed the oil stick into the truck's motor.

"Peter Ghudd has a wild imagination. He doesn't have the vaguest idea about what's happening.

"It doesn't make any difference," Lester said, casting his attention over his dwindling and parched fields.

Emmitt's insides were shaken. Everything he had just said in reference to imminent domain was true. As far as he was aware, the city had no plans of confiscating the minister's property to erect the prison. That was a short while ago. Now it appeared to be a whole new ballgame, at least to Lester, and Emmitt was winding into his next pitch when the reverend's words made him balk.

"I'll sell."

"Thank you," was all Emmitt could manage.

"Same price, though. I won't take anything less."

"I'll arrange for a contingency contract, Reverend. The people in city hall will be fair with you. They have generous feelings."

"That's comforting," Lester said, "because I just dumped a bunch of mine."

"I admire your courage." As soon as the sentence had left his mouth, Emmitt regretted his own truthfulness. It took plenty of guts to have a prison placed right at your home. It required an inner strength that Emmitt realized he knew little about. Hr felt weak in the other man's presence and wanted to avoid any more thought on the subject. "I'm glad you see it out way."

"Our way, your way, their way, I'm only doing what I have at do."

Emmitt raised his foot and scraped the sole of his shoe against the front tire of the pickup. Unlike the truck itself, the tires were in good condition. When it occurred to him that he may have been offending Lester, he withdrew his foot immediately. He ran his hand over the contour of the fender as if he were admiring the blue paint that had long since faded into a dismal gray.

"Reverend," he said, "the right thing doesn't always have to be the unselfish thing. How many miles do you have on this?"

"The odometer says ninety thousand. Double it, plus ten."

"Why don't you do this?" Emmitt prompted. "Come down to the bank this week and take out a loan for a new one?"

"Don't you think my credit is a little bit questionable?"

"Not anymore. Once the city buys your ground, you'll be doing fine. I'll co-sign for your loan myself."

"I'll think on it."

"I'll even drop the interest rate."

"I'll let you know." The minister wasn't overjoyed at the prospect of getting a new truck, and it showed. Once again, Emmitt had put himself in a bad light. It had been but a few weeks earlier that Lester Jameses was practically begging Emmitt for an extension of time for his church's mortgage payments to be met. Emmitt had come across as indifferent. Now that it appeared that Lester would soon acquire a sizable amount of money, Emmitt was wanting to help Lester buy a truck that Lester, himself, had no desire for. Emmitt was ashamed of himself for making the suggestion. He wished to part on a good note and could think of nothing other than Marian to talk about. He didn't bring her up right away. He got into his car first and sat behind the wheel. As his engine came to life, the radio blared in his ears, and he lowered the volume.

"By the way," he began, loud enough so that Lester could hear him over his car's idling, "how's your daughter doing?"

"Not bad," the minister said, "she's in the house snoozing. Has to go into work late tonight and stay until the morning."

Emmitt was saddened. For a brief period, Marian had given him a happiness that had been unrivaled. It was ill founded, and Emmitt accepted that for what it was. He had no misconceptions about being handsome, but Marian, in her kindness, had persuaded him that he was somehow deserving of her loyalty, even if it were to the smallest extent. It wasn't going to be easy for Emmitt to sleep tonight. He despised how much the nightshift meant to the difficult young girl that he was falling so hard for.

CHAPTER 20

The trailer park in Malfaxe County contained more than four hundred closely-situated mobile units. It was a low-income neighborhood, where essentials were the basic commodity. Telephone poles were scattered along the premises, integrated with a few randomly-lit street lamps. The faulty lamps were not a reflection of poor electrical maintenance, but rather a condition inflicted by rowdy teenagers, flaunting their marksmanship with air rifles. Whether the lamps were working or not was of little consequence. Tonight they had all been shut off. Traffic entering the park had been detoured by the police department. Local residents were detained from going into their homes by black and white units enforcing blockades.

It was 1:00 AM and dozens of policemen were feeling the effects of the overtime hours that were chiseling away at their endurance. That included ten men, who were part of a S.W.A.T. team. They were holding a position around one trailer. It was a silver eighty-four model with a maroon canopy decorating the front door. From within, a dim light was making itself known through a dingy curtain. The curtain sagged from a kitchen window. Nobody could be seen. That is until Sam Rhiggs moved slowly under the florescent bulb, and temporarily darkened the frosty glow with his menacing image.

"Do you think he'll bed down tonight?" A uniformed officer asked a plainclothesman. The two men were watching Rhiggs from another trailer window. For five hours, they had been occupying that trailer. It was one block down an adjacent street. A third policeman, Mike Barns, was keeping surveillance from a bedroom in the rear. He, too, was out of uniform. His white shirt was loose around the collar, and his tie dangled down the front of his chest in two separate columns. Mike's left hand was squeezing a walkie-talkie, causing it to become warm and slick from his moisture. The lieutenant's state of mind was tense. Four hours had passed since Mike had taken charge of the operation. After three weeks and two additional murders, Sam Rhiggs had been pinned, but it wasn't due to efficient police work. Luck was the key factor, just as it had been the first time they had caught Sam. That time, he was recognized while changing a flat tire. He'd enjoyed sending seven people to the undertaker on that day. The video in the savings and loan had recorded the event. Sam was blatant enough to pose for the camera.

Sam's escape from Sutler Penitentiary had been purely accidental. While a couple of low risk inmates were taking advantage of a rare opportunity, Sam happened by. He'd been pushing a cart of dirty clothes to the laundry. The three men had gotten into the refrigerated compartment of a half empty food delivery truck and stacked crates of milk and yogurt around themselves. Since there was no guard or driver in sight, the rest was easy. The convicts rode four miles before they opened the door of the truck and jumped free. The first two men went straight for a vacant building, where they were seen and picked up by the police without incident only a day latter. Sam did something different. He commandeered a car and vanished for twelve days. He came out of hiding once. It was for only twenty short minutes, but ample time for Sam to get what he so badly needed, cash. That's when he killed the two people in the all-night market. One person was a clerk, the other was there only to buy a cup of coffee when Sam had barged in. He robbed the cash register, shot both men through the back of the head with the clerk's own gun and then left with the customer's cup of coffee in his hand. It was evident that Sam was in a huge hurry that night because he hadn't taken the time to smile for the store security video. Since the murders, the police had been relentlessly stalking his faltering trail.

"Get Hicks on the phone," Mike Barnes ordered. Thirty seconds later, the uniformed cop handed a wireless phone to the detective.

"I want every road, every sidewalk, and every ant path covered" Mike Barnes blasted. "If this guy gets past you, you're going to be painting speed bumps 'til doomsday! Have I made myself abundantly clear?"

Mike put the phone down on the small bed that was next to him and continued staring up the street. It was pushing 2:00 AM, and Sam Rhiggs was still awake. The detective was irritable, not to mention anxious. Following an anonymous tip on where Sam was spending the night, Mike had been on the alert for eighteen hours straight. Apparently, Sam had been given a key to a friend's trailer and had planned on letting himself in. Unaware that his friend had relocated, Sam let himself in, as he had always done in the past. What Sam didn't expect to find was a new owner. She was a sixty-three year old woman living with her grandson. Sam was surprised, but by no means discouraged from staying the night. He tied the woman and boy to a chair. Then he made himself a nice meal from out of the pantry. While watching the evening news he topped it off with a snack of sardines. His plan was to get a decent night's sleep and then leave Malfaxe, never to return.

That one last resting spot was an oasis that Sam needed. With a different car and some pocket change, he figured on making it to the Bronx or possibly Boston for a short stay. Sam had remained in Malfaxe one night too many though, and his extra-sensory perception began to kick in, and tell him so.

Sam Rhiggs pulled the curtains apart cautiously. He scanned the streets, using all of the limits of his keen eyesight. A blanket of clouds mingled with the somber night. At other times, the night had been a welcome arrival for Sam. He used the dark effectively to travel about, sometimes changing cars or buying drugs. More often, he searched for a shop or store that promised to be an easy hit. Nothing was without risk though. Sam, as a present rule, preferred to stay off the streets.

When Sam hid out, he'd use his always sharp instincts and sinister, gray, skull matter to develop what he liked to refer to as his survival itinerary. He would rehearse them hundreds of times in his head, going over the smallest details until they were implanted firmly in his brain. That's what Sam was doing before he felt a presence. It had fallen on him and tingled his consciousness like ice water over his spine.

Occasionally, a stalked animal will reverse the order and circle behind the hunter, taking him off guard. Tigers are one such breed. Sam Rhiggs didn't have that kind of maneuvering room. Besides, the odds were hardly in his favor. Yet, to Mike Barnes' way of thinking, a savage animal, even if trapped, was still more than just a little dangerous. There was no doubt that Sam was a preying beast, and Mike worried about who's life would be ripped apart next.

"Calm down, Mike. He's not going anywhere," a younger plainclothesman said. He surveyed Mike's condition, as though he were in disbelief. The two men had been partners for eight years, and Phil wasn't used to seeing Mike so disturbed. Mike leered at the opposite end of the trailer. The uniformed cop had his back turned and was squatting. He was watching for Sam from a window in a small bathroom. His name was Joe Moreland. He was a sergeant, and Mike knew him well also. He was a good man, but what Mike had to say wasn't for Joe's knowledge. Mike gestured with a sly wink for Phil to slide the bedroom door shut.

"What's wrong, Mike?" Phil asked his senior partner, trying to keep the conversation low. "You were kind of mean with Hicks, weren't you?"

"It was just talk." Mike was barely audible, as he began checking through the window again.

"So what's the problem? We've done this same thing together dozens of times before. You've never been this jumpy, Mike."

"The problem is this, Phil. It's not Hicks' whose job is teetering on the line here. It's mine."

"Why's your job hanging on this jerk?" Phil was truly appalled and was finding it difficult to keep his voice down.

""I'm not sure. I just know the pressure is on to get him, no matter what it takes."

"You told me that before. That's why I've never complained about all the extra hours we're putting in. Mike, he's an escaped murderer.

This town's seen some pretty bad cases. What's so special about Sam Rhiggs?"

Mike rapped his knuckles on a folder. It was on a bed close to where he was standing. Some of the papers that had been in it were partially spilled toward the outside and overlapping one another, much like a hand of disfavored playing cards. Phil shrugged his wide shoulders. Sam Rhiggs' record, for the most part, was no great revelation to him. He'd read the entire document three times over.

"Mike, the man's got a very mean personality disturbance, and he won't hesitate to kill," Phil acknowledged. "If we have to fill him full of holes, he'll go horizontal like the others did."

Phil was contemplating Sam's demise, when Mike interrupted his mode of thought. "Phil, read the sentence that's been underlined twice in red ink!"

Phil began reading out loud. "It says classification of subject can primarily be categorized as antisocial, but frequently manifesting tendencies of residual deviancy." Phil didn't want a lesson in psychology, but it was certainly obvious the term 'residual deviancy' was a clue to Mike's behavior. "I guess I didn't do all of my homework, Mike. Why's this pestering you?"

"Phil, there's no accounting for what this Rhiggs might do. The doctors can't even hang a label on him. I've been asking questions," Mike said in a distraught voice. "I started at the prison. I've talked to guards and inmates both. I saw the prison psychologist, too. Rhiggs should have never been incarcerated at Sutler."

"All right, so what? Mike, it happens!"

"Sure, it happens…sometimes."

"It was poor judgment. We can't change that."

"No, but I'll tell you what I think."

"Go on," Phil said picking the folder up from the bed and neatly inserting the papers.

"There's been a big push to get rid of the city prison," Mike said in a forced whisper. "I think the two cons who got out with Rhiggs were meant to escape, but not Sam.

"Why?"

"Those other two guys were nothing but a couple of petty thieves. They would have been paroled soon. They made the front of the papers, Phil!"

"Along with Sam Rhiggs."

"That's right; but until he got loose, I think the whole mess was supposed to be nothing more than a planned threat to the public."

"So you think when Rhiggs got out, the wake-up call turned into a panic scream."

"Yeah, I do, and it's been pounding against my gourd ever since."

Mike dropped down to his knees and placed a pillow under his shins. He kept half of his face behind the window frame, while letting his right eye engage the small dwelling where Sam Rhiggs hid. Initially, Phil thought that Mike would be there too for a while. He wanted to tell Mike not to worry about Sam Rhiggs. Sam had no place to go. He couldn't possibly get free. Phil wasn't able to say the words. In circumstances like this, no one could guarantee the outcome. Phil had witnessed some bizarre incidents during his hitch on the force. Mike had been around longer. There was no excuse for Phil or Mike to lull under the shadow of a madman.

"Can you see anything that's going on?" Phil asked.

"Get me Hicks on the phone," Mike ordered. "Rhiggs knows we're out here!"

"You sure?"

"Yes, hurry, do it!"

Within half a minute, Mike was on the phone yelling into the mouthpiece. "Move everybody in close! Who's your best sharpshooter?"

"McCurry," Hicks answered, "but he's on vacation." Mike blew his cork. "Well then, he can't do us very much good if he's not here, can he?"

"I'll have Landuss get you on the radio."

Soon the radio in Phil's hand came to life. Jimmy Landuss spoke with a slow southern drawl that usually had a calming effect. This time, it was grating on Mike and the static was terrible. He wanted Jimmy to accelerate his dialogue. When Jimmy didn't, the detective fought the urge to become rabid. "Damn you Landuss!"

"Yes, lieutenant," he was relieved to hear, "this is Jimmy."

"Landuss, I hear you're an ace with the rifle."

"Much obliged, Lieutenant," Landuss said, emphasizing the three words, as if he were completely astonished by the compliment.

"Landuss, listen to me."

"I can't hear you too well, Lieutenant."

"Landuss, get the corn pones out of your ears! We don't have much time."

"The corn's what?" Landuss said, as the interference got worse.

"Landuss, if Sam Rhiggs gets any further than twenty feet from that trailer, I want you to put a bullet straight through his temple."

"Okay, Lieutenant. I guess I can do that. Can you tell me exactly where his dimple is located?"

"Temple, temple, temple!"

"Gotcha, temple."

"Put Hicks back on," Mike said, resisting the temptation to pull his own revolver out and turn it on himself. Landuss was beginning to frighten him almost as much as Rhiggs. There was no telling where Landuss might put a bullet or who would be unfortunate enough to get shot. Hicks didn't wait for Mike to ask him if the men were positioned. "This is Hicks. The rifle team will be set in two minutes. Landuss knows what to do."

"When that half wit comes out, I want plenty of light on him, and I don't mean Landuss either!"

"Lieutenant, we have a chopper ready. As soon as I notify the pilot, he'll be overhead within seconds. You'll have all the beam on Rhiggs that you need," Hicks promised.

"Good, be ready. I can't wait much longer. I can't wait for Rhiggs to kill whoever's in that trailer before we do something.

"Settle down, Mike," Phil said, trying to convey a not so phony self-assurance.

Mike shoved the two-way radio into Phil's hand. "The only way Sam Rhiggs is leaving here tonight is in irons or sporting a rubber bag!"

"I'm all for the bag," Phil said, "But I don't think it's coming to that."

"You read his history," Mike all but shouted. "The man refutes all analysis."

Mike began making his way toward the front end of the trailer. As he reached the door, he removed a thirty-eight caliber revolver from under his jacket. Aiming the gun down as he moved through the doorway, he let the cylinder swing out and appraised a full load of hollow nose bullets. He then slammed it shut.

"Stay behind me, Phil," he ordered, charging out to the steps.

Mike immediately went to the other side of the small dwelling and trotted briskly toward Sam's refuge. Using the other trailers as protection he was able to work his way around the vigil that he was certain Sam Rhiggs was maintaining. He was aware of the fact that neighbors living close by had been discreetly and orderly evacuated by the police. It had all been accomplished through phone calls. Mike's only concern now laid with the people that Sam had inside with himself. He harbored a sick feeling from down below, as he took cover behind a van parked directly across from Sam's shelter.

"Rhiggs!" He called out. "Sam Rhiggs, this is the Malfaxe Police Department! We want you to come out, Sam; with your hands empty and lifted over your head!"

"You won't have any trouble with me." Sam Rhiggs sounded more subdued than anything.

Phil had been right all along, Mike thought to himself. In another hour, the two of them would probably be drinking a hot cup of coffee and trading jokes, while they were waiting for the morning news to broadcast their arrest of the killer. Then Mike would go home and take his wife out to breakfast. Thereafter, he would sleep for the remainder of the day. For the first time in a long time, he was confident. Then Sam Rhiggs opened the trailer door and destroyed Mike's optimism. Sam was holding the sixteenyear- old boy from behind. He was gripping the boy's neck firmly with his left arm. The two of them descended the small set of block steps and Sam came boldly into the open. Sam held a gun in his right hand. Mike reasoned that it was a forty-five automatic. The muzzle was jammed into the boy's mouth.

Beads of sweat were forming on Mike's face, but the detective didn't feel them. Nor did Mike hear the helicopter whipping loudly in the sky directly about. Instantly, a large circular light appeared and everything within its border was illuminated. Mike approached the pair carefully, and it was his hands, and not Sam's, that were raised and empty. He'd laid his gun on the road. His legs trembled with weakness, and, for the first time in years, he wanted someone to tell him what to do. He had never had the support of so many lawmen in his entire career with the department. Thinking about it should have bolstered his strength. He wanted it to be that way, but it wouldn't happen. Regular patrolmen, sharpshooters, and plainclothesmen had all turned out to bring in one man. They had been dispatched in mass numbers, and now, with Sam Rhiggs in the spotlight, Mike saw exactly why.

Physically, Sam wasn't a big man. Being on the short side gave him the advantage of using his hostage as a forward shield. His response hardly seemed typical of a man with a one hundred sixty IQ, nor were his unprotected body zones causing him any agony besides. Sam was a pure, undiluted exhibitionist who thrived on attention. It bothered Mike that Sam displayed no apparent fear. There was no crackly voice or blinking eyes. Instead, he taunted the policeman by making light of his circumstances.

"I changed my mind. Go ahead, let your men unload! Junior's gonna need one helluva dentist though."

"No, Sam, that isn't what we want to do," Mike answered.

Sam pulled the kid closer to his own torso, yanking the boy's vertebrae into a painful arch. The convict was keeping a tight finger on the hair trigger of the gun. It's nickel-plating was polished, and it glistened like a brilliant crystal in the convict's hand. Mike stood motionless, not retreating or advancing, knowing any wrong move might cause Sam to react. The boy's legs appeared nimble, and his torn jeans were pulled upward over his ankles from Sam's wringing grip. His complexion had paled, and Mike hoped that the kid would pass out. That would take Sam off-guard, possibly setting him up for Landuss or any other sniper with quick instincts. It was merely wishful thinking, for Sam Rhiggs was calling all of the plays, and nobody there would dare bat an eye or skip a heartbeat unless Sam gave the nod first.

Sam began pushing his hostage toward his parked car, but Mike stepped in his way. Somewhere, between his common sense and his fear of inadequacy, the detective had come to terms with himself. He blocked Sam from going any further.

"Try me!" Sam snapped, shoving the pistol harder into the roof of the boy's mouth.

"You can't leave, Sam!"

"If I don't, mister, they'll be mopping Junior off the street!"

The chopper above had descended giving a steady beam of concentrated light. Mike looked around. He could see six other policemen. Every one of them had their guns trained on Sam. It was useless, he thought, to talk to Sam. About the only other alternative was to let Rhiggs get so far, and before he could make his way to his stolen car, the sharpshooter would bring him down. That, in itself, would be murder. Mike knew that the slightest flinch from Sam would likely jolt the gun's trigger, killing the boy.

The noise from the helicopter was thunderous. Mike's perception was becoming dull. He swiped the wetness off of his eyelids. Mike stepped closer to Sam. They were two feet apart when the two men locked stares.

Twice before, the veteran detective was in similar standoffs. They were nightmares, but this time was worse. Sam Rhiggs was not human, and sure death was right there in his stone cold, and glaring pupils.

"Sam," Mike began to plead, "unless you give me that gun, there's no way you can leave here alive. How about it, Sam? Let him loose! I'm begging you, Sam!"

"Mister, you bore me!" Sam ridiculed the cop.

"Sam," Mike was solemn, "give me the gun." He reached, his confidence nullified. Then he touched Sam's forearm lightly with his bare fingertips. They were trembling. "Come on, Sam. It's late. We should go."

"You've got that right!" It was the last thing the detective heard before the first shot. Blood splattered on Mike's face, causing his eyes to shut and his fist to curl tight. Before Mike could recover, the sound of another shot exploded in his ears. The second shot had come from a rifle, and Mike hardly had time to collect himself before Sam's body was swung into him by the impact of the projectile. For an instant, Mike felt as though he wasn't there. He had the sensation of watching from a distant perch. It was a place where nobody could see him. He could drift. He floated out over the highway to the new housing development that occupied the better side of the county. It was safe there. If he wanted to, he'd lay down on one of those thick, green lawns, then slumber in the cool blades of the moist grass. They'd smell so very sweet. When he awakened, he wouldn't be Mike Barns. He'd be somebody else, perhaps only a child playing, happy, solemn.

Suddenly, he was feverish. Two bodies lay at his feet in opposite directions. The boy was disfigured beyond recognition. His life was gushing onto the road so fast that some of it found Mike's shoes before he could step around it. Men are mortal. The reality of it never had affected Mike. He, too, had killed before. Police work could be filthy business. He believed that every new day in this world was a gratifying bonus for redemption. Mike had learned to live with that notion years earlier. There was nothing inside of him that helped this time. The boy was dead. Moments before, he was alive. He might have become a musician, or a doctor, or nothing more than a penniless vagrant, but he deserved an honest chance. Sam Rhiggs chose to destroy that chance. The almighty Sam, Mike boiled, deserved a fate worse than he could ever dream up.

An old woman came running from her trailer into the street. Mike knew it had to be the boy's grandmother. As she sobbed uncontrollably, a policeman grabbed her and dragged her from the body. Mike knelt down. A pointed rock was wedged under his knee so tightly that days later he would question where the bruise came from. He was numb with confusion.

Mike took his jacket off and laid it across the boy's corpse. He was overwhelmed with anger and grief. Nausea filled his stomach, and a pain grabbed at his larynx. He turned his eyes from the teenager. Two paramedics were on the scene. One of them had uncovered the boy. He quickly covered him again. Then he spun around to assist with Sam. Sam's wound was bleeding profusely. The bullet had ripped through his trapezius muscle and exited through his right chest. Nowhere near his temple, but what was left resembled a small crater. The first medic had given up on Sam. The other tried in vain for a pulse. Mike stood over the convict's body. The chopper still hovered low. It's gusty wind blowing their hair wildly. Mike was glad that Sam was dead. He was festering with hatred. He wanted to kick Sam's bones into splinters. He would have, too, if a paramedic hadn't stopped him.

"I've got a vital!" The attending medic cheered.

CHAPTER 21

Did you furnish the cleaning agents?" Emmitt questioned, as he escorted Marian through the downstairs. In a single day, his quarters had been transformed from an untidy and dusty blend of Mediterranean and contemporary furniture into a noticeably different state of existence. The smudgy armchairs, along with the stained door frames, were all polished and waxed. Marian shampooed the living room carpet also. When that was done, she tackled the walls. The windows were made squeaky clean, and the shades were unrolled completely, sponged off, and hung under curtains that had been left to bask in the sunny outdoors. The fragrance of potpourri spread through every room, sweetening the air like expensive perfume. Marian's touch was angelic. Emmitt was delighted. Rejoicing inwardly, he temporarily contained his gratitude. His shyness served well to aid his constraint. The last time they'd been together, their room was unlit. Emmitt's instincts urged him to flick the switch to cut the light. It was only six inches above his right elbow when they strolled through the archway separating the living room from the dining room. A second later, they were in the dining room, and Emmitt had abandoned his original impulse. "Marian, you're wonderful!" He praised, forgetting the light altogether.

Emmitt opened his mother's china cabinet to examine the unused dishes. Holding up a glossy plate for inspection, "How much do I owe you for this?" He asked.

"Figure on a couple hundred," Marian answered, patting the edge of Emmitt's suit collar, smoothing a partial crease.

"You're expensive." Emmitt clutched the china tighter, scrutinizing the Autumn Leaf pattern that his mother had thought so highly of.

"I'm not done working," Marian informed him, "that is unless you'd rather I leave." She rotated the dimmer knob to the crystal chandelier, causing Emmitt to tense as Marian crept closer. "Why don't you stop fondling the china?" She asked seductively.

Emmitt replaced the plate on the shelf as Marian glided her arm around his waist. He turned to meet her will. They kissed, and Emmitt become aroused as he embraced her. She was like an over ripened piece of fruit begging to be enjoyed to its fullest capacity of satisfaction.. He felt the soft rotunda of her buttocks moving her abdomen close against his groin. Emmitt had had Marian on four previous occasions, none of which excited him as this did. It had always been planned, almost routine, a mechanical reaction that had stopped as swiftly as it had begun. With a quick jerk, Marian undid the clasp on Emmitt's belt and began opening his pants. She kissed his neck slowly, working her searching hand into his shorts. "I'm fond of you," she said, embracing his manliness to the fullest extent.

"Is this included in the two hundred dollars?" Emmitt asked, wishing not to sound hesitant.

"I'm a good deal," Marian remarked, knowing full well he was in no position to allow the matter at hand to simply drop.

"Marian, I'm nuts about you! I mean it, but you've got to stop messing with my mind!"

"So that's where it's at, "Marian tightened her hold before they kissed once more. When they locked their mouths together, Emmitt sucked on the warm , sweet delight of her irresistible tongue. She stroked him repeatedly while their kiss became a molten bond. Marian broke the bond only to slip to her knees and bring Emmitt to his. There they remained but for seconds, melting themselves into the forthcoming ecstasy as Marian guided Emmitt on top of herself. He was feverish. He slid his hand under her skimpy dress, removing her erotic, scented undergarments. Marian gasped, as Emmitt plunged forward, rocking her tender body incessantly. She clawed at his ribs and clamped her lips onto his flesh, begging uncontrollably without using words for Emmitt's relentless passion not to end. They were different, and their affair had erupted as a journey of lust through a forest of obstacles. It was in the dawn of their love that they sealed their union with a groan of rapture tempting Emmitt to an awaiting threshold. One that he sensed was undeniably dangerous. "Marian, I need you to be mine," he murmured.

Marian held Emmitt protectively. He was weak, or tonight he appeared to be, and she was strong. Emmitt seemed starved for affection. Marian had dealt a lot with his type. What bothered her was his self-righteous attitude whenever he was in control. There were several occasions when she preferred to hate him. When Emmitt had come out to her father's farm and pressured her father into signing papers was one such time. He'd demonstrated a shrewd and aggressive side of himself that afternoon. To circumvent her suspicions would require a short memory, and an iron clad determination. As they lay on the dining room carpet, Marian inadvertently followed the pattern of Emmitt's ear with her freshly painted nail. She wasn't sure if Emmitt was as attracted to her as he pretended to be, or if he was cleverly maneuvering her into the enemy camp. For now, she'd remain guardedly loyal, but whatever the case, Marian was no fool. She'd have the truth one way or another.

Emmitt's breathing diminished. His body was in such a state of lax that Marian laid her head by Emmitt's face to detect his faint need for air. She listened patiently. It was barely audible. Soon she, herself, succumbed to the exhaustion of a hard day's work.

Sleep for Marian meant peace until the wee hours of dawn. When that came, she'd be gone, away from Emmitt, back to her father's farm. She'd be a caretaker for her father, his humble servant; the one person in the entire world he'd never stop counting on. Inwardly and shamefully during her awakened hours, Marian often daydreamed about a release from her father's dependence. She'd try to calculate his life span and estimate how much longer she'd have to trade her youth for the privilege of ridding herself of guilt for wanting to leave him. Sleep for Marian was precious. It rendered a nullification of her unfulfilled fantasies. They were desires that sent her conscience to the lowest gutters and then some. When she slept, she was unaware. It was the only relief she had. How could she have possibly known that right next to her, on the dining room rug, Emmitt was indulging in a historical event of great magnitude. It wasn't unusual for Emmitt to revisit the past. Important wars were no exception. Tonight, a battle was at stake. Not a meaningless battle, it was a battle of the utmost consequence. It was 499 BC. Greece was under siege, and it was Emmitt who'd bolster the decisive attack, putting himself in the middle of two of the greatest civilizations in the ancient world.

Darius, King of Persia, was invading Greece. He'd decided to do this because the Ionians had revolted against Persia, and the Greeks had aided them. The Greeks would be made to pay. A Persian army of twenty thousand soldiers was dispatched from ships at the Marathon plain, where a mere ten thousand Greeks were waging a front. Grossly outnumbered, the Greek general, Miltiades's army had clashed head on with the enemy. It might have been futile except for one little deviation of the episode. To Emmitt's amazement, he was there. He'd been waiting patiently to engage the Persians. They may have been invincible for any other respectable army, but Emmitt's proved to be a whole different story. Before he was done, the Persians would know what it meant to encounter the underbelly of war. Emmitt's intervention wasn't to be on foot, or even horseback. His army rode on the backs of hundreds and hundreds of rhinoceroses. They were his secret weapon, which he had hid to the rear of the Greek formation. At the sound of the trumpets, the Greeks opened their ranks. The land vibrated to the mountaintops with the roar of a terrifying thunder. It was frightening, no horrifying. Emmitt's troops tore into battle atop the ugliest beast ever created. They were huge and exceedingly rank, trampling onto the scene with their fierce tempers, bulging eyes, and overlapping skin that swords and spears had no chance of penetrating. These rhinoceroses were quite fast, and they rammed their massive horns forty miles per hour into the retreating Persians. It was the world's bloodiest blood bath ever, for Emmitt rendered no mercy.

Afterwards, Emmitt, himself, gallantly trotted on his personal rhino, Bubba Tuck, across the battlefield to honor the fallen Persian soldiers. He, the victorious general with the triple-decker, silver helmet, had spared Greece. The chronicles of the ages would have chapters in time marked by all types of men, unforgettable men. Hannibal, Alexander the Great, Richard the Lion-Hearted. Combined, they all deserved immense recognition. Emmitt occupied a class of his own though, for he'd be labeled by history as Emmitt the Imponderable Limit. He loved these dreams better than reality itself.

CHAPTER 22

When the door to Lefty's Rollicking Rudder Bar and Grill came ajar, the jingling of doorbells always brought joy to the owner. That meant he was one customer closer to paying off the mortgage on his seemingly ancient investment. Seventeen years and eight months earlier, he and his wife, Dotty had sold their dwelling and moved into a smaller one. They took the profits, along with the money they borrowed, and went into owning and operating a tavern. It wasn't ornate, nor did it have to be. The clientele were mainly blue collar workers who stopped by after work or dinner to relax in an atmosphere of shuffleboard, loud talk, and heavy smoke. Lefty tended bar while Dotty worked the grill, cooking every short order from polish sausages served on fresh rolls to fried oyster platters. To some of the regulars, Lefty's was a second, if not a primary home. It was a comfortable place to unwind and be one's self. Yet there were people who avoided Lefty's place because it often catered to a variety of rowdy personalities.

An obese man, Hugo Myers, sat at the front of the bar with a half-empty glass of draft beer clutched tightly in a callused hand. It was his fourth. Five were typically his limit. Hugo looked forward to downing the last beer and hauling his three hundred pound body two city blocks down the street to his efficiency. There he would spend the remainder of the evening searching through his recently acquired bags of coins. He was a collector. His collection was one of the finest. It was representative of several European countries, as well as America, and dated as far back as AD 300, when Constantine reigned as Emperor of Rome. Among many of his contemporaries, it was an accepted rule of thumb that if Hugo didn't possess a certain coin, getting it would be an extremely arduous task.

Bruce Ryan, a lanky automobile mechanic, occupied the stool next to Hugo. An unlikely pair they were. Conversation between the two men seldom transpired beyond Hugo's coins, or Bruce's women. The latter fancied himself as a magnificent lady's man. To Hugo, who was a content celibate, Bruce was as interesting as a dirty book would be in a cold shower.

It was always a relief for both men when Sammy McCoy left his shuffleboard game to take a spot beside the two of them. Sammy had adopted the men that he had nicknamed "Micro" and "Nitro." As he spieled off jokes and slapped their backs, few of Lefty's patrons were aware that the three were not life-long friends. If Hugo proved to be a difficult audience, it was never the case with Bruce, who was constantly overtaken by fits of laughter. It was true that Sammy's jokes weren't always that funny, but Bruce thought of Sammy as hideous looking, which added to his appeal as an aspiring comedian. It was an ordinary gathering for the three men, when the bells danced again, and Peter Ghudd darted in from apparently nowhere.

Peter handed each person a flyer as he continued toward distant tables that were sitting empty in an unlit corner. Weaving through the customers with his corduroy coat unbuttoned and his beret hat cocked sideways, he leered arrogantly. There seemed to be no regard for the old man with the bundle of papers under his arms. Most people moved out of his space, in order to avoid him. A stout woman did drop his circular to the floor, but that was hardly the reason for Peter's anger. He was on the brink of hating all mankind. Life on the campaign trail had never proven to be this challenging before, anywhere. He chose an isolated booth where he could sit alone and try to restore a puny grain of his severed pride.

"What'll you have, friend?" Lefty called over from behind the bar. He was working a soft towel on the top of the counter. Peter grimaced at his words. Quick service was not what he'd expected. Peter twisted himself in the direction of the bartender, who had what appeared to be a twenty-inch neck, and a hard set jaw. Lefty was working the towel vigorously. His sleeves were rolled up above his elbows, and the growth on his arms reminded the old man of coarse steel wool. If Lefty was all that concerned about what Peter was thirsty for, he didn't betray himself. He began moving the cloth in a tiny rotating fashion, as if something small under the rag were irritating him. Peter hesitated to answer. He was tired of ignorant people. If the bartender was serious about wanting to serve him, he had a strange manner of conveying it. Peter was determined to make Lefty ask again.

"What can I get you, Pal?" Lefty expelled with a cough.

"A draft," Peter answered bluntly.

"What kind?"

"Any kind, as long as it's tonight."

Lefty soon came over with a large glass of beer on a tray. With it was a bowl of unshelled peanuts and a short stack of napkins. "You can pay when you leave," he said. "The peanuts are free."

"Let me guess. The beer costs four dollars?" Peter replied, being lost in his annoyance.

"I read your flyer," Lefty retorted. "You can consider the peanuts an early bribe, big shot. You politicians like that stuff."

"I'll put this hole on my friendly list," Peter said from the side of his barely opened lips, "That is if this dive survives past midnight."

Lefty was gone in a flash. Peter saw him round the counter and grab his towel. He gave it two hard shakes, threw it aside, and approached the three men who were clustered at the bar. As Lefty was speaking, Sammy reached past Hugo's massive stomach and snatched hold of one of Peter's handouts. The men gazed at Peter, and he could feel their eyes picking him apart. To Peter, it was a wordless act of shameless ridicule. He took a sip of his beer. Pretending not to hear their laughter, he took another. He pondered leaving. If that's what they cared for, the jerks could have their fun. He drank more. It tasted better. Why leave, he asked himself. His vanity damaged at this point, there was little else to sacrifice. Peter guzzled the remainder of the brew, and, tilting the glass in the air, he signaled Lefty that he expected a refill.

Lefty was busy, and in no hurry to please the crude old man. The tavern was becoming filled up with noisy aggressive men, many of whom were young and boisterous. At one table, they began arm wrestling for ten dollar bills. Peter's tendons hurt each time he saw a hand leveled. He was warmed by the fact that thirty years earlier it would have been his arm making the money. He gathered strength by knowing that a portion of his spirit was still intact. It was only searching for a different kind of sport. It was soon to be satisfied. The three men were hawking in on him from the end of the bar. When Peter realized that the heavier man was delivering his drink, he toyed again with the impulse to leave. It had been only a brief second of slight procrastination that had cost him the opportunity.

"What are you running on?" Hugo asked, lowering the tray with four full glasses of beer onto Peter's table.

"Hand me one of those boosters there." Peter said, pointing to one of the beers.

Hugo positioned the tray to give Peter easy access. "That's not what I meant," he said. He lifted a drink for himself and sucked on the foamy head. Hugo repeated the question. "What are you going to do for this town?"

Peter greeted the assault on his intentions with indifference. "What can any one person do with a town this size?" He half heartedly remarked.

"Strike a sore nerve here and there. That's about it."

"He don't impress me as the ambitious type," Sammy criticized Peter. He and Bruce had strolled over by this time.

Peter trained his sights on Sammy, who appeared to be bathing in confidence. To the old man, it seemed a remarkable endeavor. Sammy's complexion was powder white. His profile was hollow, and his chin protruded out like a splatter guard on a urinal. He had a lean nose, angling to the side of his cheek, tempting Peter to push it into its rightful position, and somehow flush the entire atrocity away. "Mister," he said, with the sincerity of an alter boy, "if I had your face, I'd plumb it to the wall in the men's room, and let people dribble against it."

"You won't get any votes that way," Bruce jumped in.

Peter casually waved the comment off with a free hand before taking a healthy gulp of beer.

"You're a fool," Sammy rebounded. "You'd never amount to a wart on a witch's snout!"

"I'll drink to that," Peter toasted, "and as far as snouts are concerned, try restraining yours. Now, if you'll excuse me," Peter started to lift himself up, "I've had about as much as I can take for one day. You fellas are starting to bore me."

"We just got here," Hugo said.

"And I'm just leaving," Peter returned.

"I think if he's running on anything it's a lack of heart." Sammy replied.

"What you think doesn't impress me," Peter said, loud enough for everyone in the place to sense a scuffle in the making.

"Settle down." Lefty took control. He had been monitoring the men from two tables away. "I won't tolerate any fighting!" He focused an accusing pair of bifocals in Sammy's direction. "This is the last time I'm telling you!" He warned.

"This bozo thinks he's a politician," Sammy huffed.

"He is a politician!" Lefty threw in. "He's been here for just thirty minutes, and I've already bought him off with a dish of peanuts! I think that says a lot about his possibilities."

"I never touched your lousy peanuts!" Peter said, brushing shell particles from his nine-o-clock shadow.

"He's a bold-faced liar!" Bruce said, as he opened a peanut between his own thumb and index finger and tossed it into his cavity riddled mouth.

"Why mull on it then?" Lefty asked. "Why can't he be a politician?" The proprietor spoke in apparent jest, hoping to lighten the atmosphere. "He's already proven he's up to the job."

"Sounds reasonable," Hugo proclaimed, "and I'm buying!"

There were five more rounds served to the four men, who bickered nonstop. At ten o'clock, two men toting bowling equipment in dark blue duffel bags joined in. They were accompanied by a young lady. Another three rounds were marked on the tab, totaling eight all together. Peter paid for two. Lefty was pleased. Lately business was on the upswing. It didn't bother him who argued or what they disagreed over as long as it didn't get physical. Lefty was humored by Peter's looks anyway. They weren't proper for a man seeking public office. He went to the cash register, rung up the bill, and was closing the drawer as Peter passed him on his way out. "Good night," the owner said.

"Same to you!" Peter answered, letting a little belch swindle his patched up self-esteem.

"Peter," Lefty had caught Peter's attention just as the door was opening again and the overhead bell rang and faded into the jumble of the incoming street noise. Peter's acute stop took the burly bartender off guard. Lefty hadn't expected Peter to hear his name being mentioned. Lefty was simply thinking out loud, when he had said it. It was a habit of his. For the present, he would have to follow up, or feel foolish. "Peter," he said, "hurry back. You're one of us!"

"Get your tongues honed," Peter said. "We'll make a brawl of it next time."

Lefty wasn't sure if he detected arrogance in Peter's words or not. For him, it was difficult to tell. He hadn't laid eyes on Peter until three hours earlier. The man proved he was able to go toe to toe with the amateurs. Lefty assured himself that the pros could be a lot tougher. However, if there was one thing that was undeniable to the barkeeper, it was as clear as the crystal brandy snifter that nestled in his oversize palm. Lefty could tell right off. This Peter guy could be a real scrapper!

CHAPTER 23

"Grant me one wish, and I'd ask to be six feet tall, heavier too," Emmitt said, as he emerged from the shower flexing his scrawny biceps in the foggy bathroom mirror.

"I don't think it makes a lick of difference. It's more in the way a person carries himself."

"Is that so?" Emmitt asked. "How then, do I carry myself?"

"Why don't you carry yourself in here?" Marian coaxed from the adjoining bedroom. She was nursing a creamy thick pina colada that Emmitt had mixed earlier in his blender. They'd downed four each with dinner. Emmitt made them extremely well; and when Marian bragged on how delicious they were, Emmitt was delighted to make another batch.

"What's on TV?" He asked, as he ran a comb past his vanishing hairline.

"Nothing to be minding over. I'll turn the radio on. I just wanna relax."

"Marian, see if you can find a decent station."

"These drinks kind of creep up on my want for more.," Marian returned, ignoring the remark. "Where'd you ever learn to conjure such a tasty potion?"

"It's easy. Who can tell? The next time, we could be enjoying them in Hawaii. That's where we ought to think about."

"Oh sure, this is coming from the same guy who hasn't bothered to take me out to a restaurant. I'd settle for Little Italy."

"And you'll have Little Italy." Emmitt promised. "You'll have the whole town after I'm elected!"

"That ain't what I'm wantin', so don't be so free with something you don't own," Marian came back. She had accepted the fact that Emmitt was keeping her hidden from public scrutiny for his own ambitious reasons. Reasons that he was not prepared to deal with. For her to demand that he flaunt their relationship would serve no purpose. She held no desire to destroy his ego cruise either; but what hurt the most was that she was losing a bit of herself to him. A part that she never saw herself giving to anyone, least of all Emmitt Braedeikk. She didn't like to use the term 'love' for any man beyond her own father, and naturally that was different. Emmitt was hardly in the same league in any imaginable scenario. He was strictly hurray for himself. Letting him use her body didn't strike her as a dangerous game before. The game was advancing though, and Emmitt was invading her stronghold. In the past she'd created a fortress that forbade affection for men, especially picky little clients who complained about her music preference. "Is it me you're ashamed of, or is it the two of us together?" She simmered.

Emmitt sauntered into the bedroom and embraced her gently. "We have more at risk here than my election, Marian. I'm very proud of you, however, your father isn't exactly nuts about me. After I'm elected, he'll appreciate the trouble I'm going through in his behalf. Then we'll have our day in the radiant sun."

"Lame hogwash," she said. "What you're doing, you're doing for yourself."

"Marian," Emmitt consoled her, "what we can't lose sight of is the end result. Your father will keep the church and the better chunk of the farm. He'll be financially set. He's too old to be working as hard as he does, and you have no future in being an underpaid field hand."

"Farm work's not what's festering me!" Marian let her anger bubble over.

"Well, it does me," Emmitt objected. "You're everything I've always admired in a woman, and I don't plan on seeing you erode out there on that farm like just another clod of dirt!"

Emmitt had shrewdly turned the conversation in a direction more to his benefit. Glibness was his specialty, and the liquor wasn't slowing Emmitt's wit. He had the rhetoric of a refined diplomat. If he could be evasive on such a personal confrontation regarding his affection for her, Marian decided that Art Towson had better be on his toes.

"You're a fine talker," Marian said. "What about me being, you know, a little on the loose side."

"I'd worship you even if you weren't."

Again, he was being foxy to the hilt. Marian increased the volume on the radio. "We shouldn't be fussing," she retreated. "How's that?" She asked Emmitt, who was about to manifest the effects of seven pina coladas. He was unconsciously swaying with the beat of the sixties, seventies, and eighties. The disc jockey went into uninterrupted songs, and Emmitt became ecstatic when a recording of 'Suspicion' blared past his fading senses and pinged wildly at his new revival.

Nothing aroused Emmitt's mood quicker than a vivid song by Elvis. Drowning in his own carefree folly, Emmitt mussed his sparse hair and jumped on top of the bed. "Marian," he was keeping pace to the music, "I learned this one from the 'King". Emmitt twisted his body and kicked his bare feet madly into the air. He curled his upper lip and plunged into wild karate chops, none of which had the force to squash a rotten berry. He was, although, becoming more drunk as the music played on.

When the song ended, Emmitt remained on his imaginary stage thanking Marian and countless numbers of loyal fans, who were not present, but to his own mindset were most certainly and totally engrossed in his fantastic appearance. They were foggy, but Emmitt just knew they were there. It wouldn't be until the night was over that they would let him go, nor he them. Appropriately enough, the man who dared be king found himself singing the song Elvis so often closed with. For Emmitt, every word was true. He couldn't help falling in love with Marian. He was her hunk, and now he was in supreme harmony with the whole universe and then some.

"Shake on down from there, baby doll," Marian quieted him. "You're drunk!"

Emmitt thanked everybody for coming to see his show and mentioned how flattered he was to share their company. He descended stardom at Marian's request and settled his heels firmly on the brown sculptured carpet of the bedroom floor. Marian temporarily placed his robe over his back and steered him back onto the bed. Emmitt was exhausted and that was his last performance of the night. Soon afterward, he and Marian expired into a deep unconsciousness. It was asleep that carried Emmitt further into stardom. He was dazzling the Emmitt-starved hordes with all of his favorite hits. In his slumber, he sang in concerts. He wore fancy capes and captivated billions of fans, who hung on every note that flowed from his fifty-inch masculine torso. Emmitt was coming to them live from Madison Square Garden, when a scraping noise filtered through the acoustics and blurred his concert out.

Frantic and not fully awake, Emmitt missed Marian. She hadn't set the alarm and was able to leave without disturbing him. He pounced to his arthritis riddled feet. Dashing for the front door, the pain ached like broken glass jabbing through his fragile heels.

The disturbance was from Koepy who was removing long pieces of siding away from the rear of his truck and laying them on the front lawn. Emmitt returned to his bedroom and retrieved his wrinkled robe that Marian had tossed on his dresser the night before. Then he hurried back to meet Koepy, who was finishing the unloading.

"I can't have that stuff laying there," he griped.

"I'll stack it wherever you like," Koepy volunteered. "It'll be installed soon."

"What's soon?"

"Supper time fast enough?" Koepy asked, expecting an affirmative.

"Don't let me down," Emmitt continued to grouch. "I need to run a mover through this jungle. He went on, peering around at his shaggy, previously neglected yard.

The flag on the mailbox was dropped, drawing Emmitt's interest to what awaited inside. He ambled to the box. The box was fashioned like a barn and had an oversize post supporting it. The previous box was not so strong and had been screwed to a hollow pole. Reaching in for the mail, Emmitt appreciated the sturdiness of the existing upright. It was only a few nights earlier that he saw fit to test the original post by ramming into it with his car. He'd been under the influence, something that was becoming more frequent in his life.

"Ah ha!" Emmitt said, extracting a letter. It bore the return address of a collection agency on the upper corner of the envelope. "Norman's accumulating a nice ledger of unpaid bills. I hope they keep him where he is for another ten years, and these people can inflate the interest."

"Where is Norman?" Koepy asked.

"In jail," Emmitt answered, waving the letter in a happy fashion, and traipsing toward the house.

"Why's he there?" Koepy inquired, causing Emmitt to turn and confront him.

"He's ugly," Emmitt declared, "and he's a stupid person!"

"They don't lock people up for that."

"I don't know why God lets the ogre live!"

"That's heavy language."

"It's meant to be."

Koepy bent forward and plucked an oversized dandelion that was growing in a dug-out plot of shredded mulch. Earlier in the season, mums had been there. They were just starting to wilt in the cool autumn air. Koepy held the dandelion close to his face, admiring the golden flower that seemed to be bursting open like a puff of sunshine. "Genus Taraxacum," he specified.

"I know that," Emmitt said, not wanting to be informed. "I try to get rid of them."

"People can be as obnoxious as weeds, but even some weeds blossom."

"Koepy, Norman's had forty-some years to bloom. He's not a flower. He's a blooming idiot , a degenerate, and I don't relish the fact that he'll return one day more ravaging than a bad disease!" With that,

Emmitt marched into the house, leaving Koepy to his work. He slept the remainder of the morning and through the afternoon. When he awoke, it didn't strike him as being worth the effort to start the mower. He had to meet with Bert for a while. They needed to touch base and exchange information. Marian would be available later. The yard work could wait until spring.

"The caboose is what I wanted, Bert. This broken down coach isn't me." Emmitt preceded his friend hastily past the portal of the rusted railroad car and dutifully ushered him inside.

"It's hardly cramped, is it Emmitt?"

"The caboose was perfect. It had a small office I could have cluttered with no effort. I don't know what to do with myself here, Bert. It's too spacious!"

"No, Emmitt. The caboose doesn't project the forerunner image. This is fine," Bert said, taking in the drab décor of the ghostly relic. "These old coaches have a ton of charm. Has the press been here yet?"

"They weren't invited."

"Have your staff plaster this Wabash lizzy with posters of yourself. Drape them in rolls of crepe paper."

"I'll pay my tellers overtime."

"Whatever it takes. I'm sorry for not being on top of this, Emmitt. We'll do the exterior with banners."

"The press hype will have to be your department," Emmitt moaned.

"The P.R. will be great! Trains are the foundation of what this land stands for. They have a reason, a theme. Full steam ahead and no rambling back. That's what trains do, Emmitt! You'll have to campaign on that same type of philosophy.

"Why not airplanes?" Emmitt pretended to care.

"They're symbolic of progress all right," Bert conceded, "but they're high tech. These iron stallions grunted over the entire nation with their immense wheels and powerful engines. They delivered civilization. Isn't that your reason for running, Emmitt, to bring in progress?"

A turbo train stormed northbound, shaking the local terrain. Bert quieted, as the train's heavy vibrations gradually grew faint. His point had been verbalized, and now emphasized on cue by the earthquake rumble of the rushing commuter.

"I'll bet this coach carried seventy passengers a haul," Bert pointed out. He was strolling through the center aisle, taking note of the seats that were long since removed.

"Ninety," Emmitt corrected him.

"Ninety, Emmitt! It's no wonder the country was settled by the twentieth century. If this car were restored, it would be a museum piece."

"It's in dangerous condition," Emmitt said, not sharing Bert's enthusiasm.

"They told me the axle became overheated. The wheel's wobbly."

"Journal box, Emmitt. It wasn't lubricated enough. It used to be a common problem with rail cars."

"You don't say," Emmitt fought his boredom.

"These days, the axles have bearings." Bert repositioned a wicker chair backwards and straddled it up close to Emmitt. "What's eating you, Emmitt You're distant. Lost your flare for politics, maybe?"

Emmitt gave in to Bert's lead and flopped onto a heavily padded seat that was lodged comfortably near a dormant kerosene lamp. He lit a cigarette with his gold monogrammed lighter. It glowed in the eerie shadows of the advancing sunset, prompting Emmitt to rouse, get up again, and bring the lamp to life.

"Flare?" He reiterated, tucking his lighter snugly beneath the outer layer of his wool jacket and inside a tiny compartment. "Politics isn't what I ever aspired to be involved in," he muttered.

"Keep on. I'm listening."

"Bert, Art Towson's snatching the election right from under our noses. I don't stand even a peep's chance in a cock fight."

"That's ludicrous!" Bert lunged at a three-foot square map that was pinned to the coach wall by four tacks with oversize heads. "Art's stronghold is in the black and southwest regions of town, Emmitt. He'll walk off with sixty percent of those votes. We've discussed that. He's a flagrant libber," Bert said, as he frowned and pressed the flat of his hand stiffly over a blotted portion of the city.

Emmitt blew a stream of chalky whiteness. His mood wasn't improving.

"This, Emmitt, is no man's land," Bert insisted. He pointed to other various broad divisions on the map. "The polls here are flexible."

"It won't be a cake walk."

"No, more like a crap game. There's twice as many registered voters in our high rent districts than in the bulk of Malfaxe altogether."

"How's that work for me?"

"The business community's given you its blessings, Emmitt. You're their key player."

"Art's dealt me some serious blows, Bert. The worst was when he refused to squabble over the prison shifting."

"That can't be fixed. Your toughest hurdle lies in the debate. Art can be a real crocodile. He'll chew you to pieces if you don't get a grapple on him."

"He cheated me out of making Sutler a personal crusade, Bert."

"That he did. It was clever of him to side with you early on."

"Was he tipped off?"

"Maybe, but when it comes to scurrying the prison rats out of their nest, this town views you as its pied piper. Political life is quirky," Bert said, detecting a higher degree of dismay in Emmitt's attitude.

"How do the inmates regard the transfer?"

"Not too well, from what I know. But who cares, Emmitt? They won't be pulling the levers."

"Any clues as to why the discontent?"

"It's normal to resist change. Plus, the kingpins are fearing tighter security."

"Too bad!" Emmitt mocked.

Bert continued to assess Emmitt's lack of gusto. He was dejected, and it wasn't over the convicts. It wasn't over Art Towson, nor was it over his poor self-confidence as a prospective city official. Emmitt was wrestling with concerns to which he, Bert, was not privy. How deep beneath the surface of Emmitt's thin, tender skin they resided, Bert wasn't sure, but he began to lift the layers of that touchy skin one by one.

"Have you had contact at all with your brother?"

"Nope."

"Is it a woman, Emmitt?"

"Bert, I'm not with you."

"Friend, I'm reading the signs. You're impossible to reach unless I can catch you at the bank. I've been after you relentlessly for this hash session, and as inconvenient as it may be, we've got to keep in touch."

"I'm sorry, Bert."

"We could settle important issues, Emmitt, if you'd answer your phone at night."

"The media's ringing me at all hours, Bert. It bugs me!" Emmitt snuffed his cigarette out in an upright ashtray glass insert that was nestled in an ornate stand. "It's Peter Ghudd!" He blurted.

"Come again?"

"Bert, the media treats me as though I'm campaigning for president. And who am I running against but a derelict who's a couple of paychecks shy from residing in the nearest soup lines!"

"Emmitt, I'm flabbergasted," Bert said, savoring the revelation. "They're snickering at him."

"Who?"

"Everybody. I hear he's dressing the part though, and they say his combat boots are even equipped with wireless burglar alarms." Bert chuckled to himself.

"Not funny."

"Well anyway it's irrelevant. He's irrelevant!" Bert's patience began to unravel gracefully. "Emmitt, Peter Ghudd happens to be a fly in some gritty, political ointment, that's the extent of it."

"He has to be eliminated!"

"He'll buzz himself out, Emmitt. In the meantime, it would be wise to remember that you don't go after a fly with a ten pound oversize maul."

Bert found himself at a window. It was tainted and cloudy. A discarded soda bottle aged for decades would have been more transparent. He leaned toward the glass, as if to analyze the imperfections. "Emmitt, this Sam Rhiggs affair is becoming vile."

"You sound laden yourself."

"He's filing a fifty million dollar law suit for damages sustained in his capture."

"That's a perverted joke!"

"It is!"

"Who's he gunning for this time?"

"The city and Mike Barns, the arresting officer."

"He won't get a counterfeit nickel!"

"Emmitt, the nation's running wild with foolish litigation. I'm afraid we've carved out a judicial nightmare for ourselves. Nothing is sanctioned. No one has anything other than their own good character that can't be taken away. With a sharp attorney and a sympathetic jury, who knows?"

"Bert, it's harassment," Emmitt complained, as he fumbled with his keys and prepared to depart. "A man goes to prison for multiple homicide. He breaks free. The police box him in. He doesn't cooperate. Instead of returning to the clink, he blows some poor sixteen year old kid to who knows where, oblivion I guess ! What did he expect them to do, Bert? Let him tip his hat and skip along? Only here, Bert! Only here! Does common sense ever prevail?"

"That's the shame of it," Bert professed, still deeply lost in the obscurity of the fading glass.

CHAPTER 24

Her silver hair fringed her neck and flowed neatly over her hidden ears. It was still thick, after decades of diligent care and undiminished pampering. She trained it to sweep upward, but every so often it would get caught under the high collar of her coat. Unconsciously, she flipped it out and a wave bounced into sight. Years earlier, she had lost it, all of it. Her life also had hung by less than a strand of that hair then. She lived. It was a miracle. Now she held the hand of her youngest granddaughter tight within her own. They had taken the bus into Malfaxe. It was to be a shopping trip. The woman bought the girl new dresses, four to be exact. They ate sandwiches at a nostalgic, retail store lunch booth, and afterward browsed through the various departments that were advertising clothing sales. Every dollar would have to be spent wisely. It was her unspoken rule. As a general practice, they didn't risk a trip into town. Malfaxe was not a safe city. Violent crime was rampant.

Daylight savings time advanced what was yesterday's four o'clock into the hour of five and prompted the woman to leave a sales rack marked fifty percent reduced. The woman's feet were sore, and she'd have to persistently tug at her granddaughter if they were to catch the next bus. The girl poked along. She was intrigued by the store windows that were garnished with snazzy clothing woven into bright autumn plaids. They soon found themselves behind schedule. Their bus had already left them, and it would be pushing dark before the next one arrived. In her haste, the woman had turned her ankle. She sat down temporarily to check the condition of her swelling foot.

In the distance, she saw a burn barrel. Its glow made her notice the fresh vegetables piled in the outside bins of a Greek market. The orange haze, with its assurance of warmth, pried the woman up and drew her to its lure. They were sure to be safer there. Upon reaching the container, the elderly lady sat her bargains down and peeked over the rim of the barrel at the charred wood. It was beginning to resemble white powder. A man, probably an employee, brought a piece of a used crate to the barrel and dropped it in. He left, not waiting to see the box decompose in the flames. Soon the granddaughter huddled next to the woman. They remained together around the rising ardent of the mounting cinders.

When he first came into sight the name cards he was carrying were not visible. He was holding them tightly in his closed hand. He had appeared from nowhere. Dubious as to his character, the grandmother remained near the young girl. Her initial thoughts of investigating a short aisle near the barrel were now forgotten.

The man pulled a card from the stack and gave it to an expectant mother. Another one went to a taxi driver who was loading groceries into his trunk. His fare was a heavy man with a wooden cane, who was bundled prematurely in winter attire from head to toe. He took a card, also. When she saw Peter approaching, the woman flicked at the end of her hair. It was merely a nervous reaction to an unfamiliar person. He handed her the card and smiled politely.

"I'm Peter Ghudd," he said, in a comforting way. "I'm running for Mayor. I'm Independent, miss. Would you please vote for me in the November election?"

He patted the granddaughter's head, then remarked about the strong family resemblance. "Here's one for you, girlie," he added. "That's just in case they lower the voting age and don't let me in on it!"

Originally, the woman had suspected that Peter was a salesman or a business person out for a casual stroll. He was dressed in a gray pinstripe suit and a flashy tie that was wider than the style of the time. From what she was able to tell, most of the tie was pink. A multi-buttoned vest was preventing her from seeing the brown, toothy monkey that was swinging under the palm tree on the lower half of the tie. If Peter was lacking anything in dress, he compensated for it in affability. He revealed a soothing manner and subtle charm that put her at ease. She felt humiliated when the proprietor of the market came from inside and asked the old gentleman to leave the premises.

There was no trouble. Peter crossed the single lane street to where a marble statue of Lord Calvert towered above a knoll of untrimmed grass. It was bordered by a rusting fence of wrought iron. Peter took a place below the statue. To the woman, it was as if he were an actor waiting on a vacant stage for a scene that would never be played out. He was alone, but didn't seem to be affected by the inconvenience. It was short-lived. Some men approached him, possibly a dozen. When they surrounded him, the woman became alarmed. She'd scream for help if they tried to harm him. It wasn't to be. Peter opened the gate to the fence and ascended the two steps at the base of the statue. He was obviously in control.

He began talking to the men. His enthusiasm seemed to be gaining momentum. She strained to hear Peter. It was to no avail. A college girl lugging some books went over to the gathering, and the grandmother envied the girl's bravado. Meantime, her curiosity was pecking away at her will. Some men in worn dungarees and clunky shoes appeared. From beneath their hard hats, their attention remained beamed on the old man, who stood askew and rambled on tirelessly. It was fascinating to watch his body language, as Peter kept his audience spellbound with louder words that were still not audible to her distant ear.

Peter's message, whatever it was, never transpired beyond the knoll. Rumbling car engines clashed with the nearby pounding of a road repair crew's hydraulic hammer. It muffled Peter's words. The woman was tempted to cross the road, but she didn't. Her bus would be along soon. It was late as of two minutes ago. She couldn't afford to miss this bus, too. Her daughter and son-in-law would be ill at ease. They didn't encourage these city trips, and it would be difficult to explain missing more than one bus.

With no warning, a man crossed the street. Using his foot, he kicked the smoldering barrel, weaving it between the traffic and at the same time just daring some of the city drivers to hit him. He was able to position the container at Peter's flank. Peter's concentration was not diverted by the clanging metal or the hot sparks that rose into the sky like a million lightning bugs. His voice seemed to be rising with the flames. The air was becoming thick with a spreading heat. More people trickled into the gathering. A sinister expression accompanied Peter's words, and the woman held her granddaughter's hand tighter. As the bus arrived, the two of them eased up to the curb. Upon boarding the bus, the woman experienced a bit of relief. She was ready to go home. The bus made a groaning sound as it began to discharge exhaust and roll slowly forward. Taking a seat, the woman found herself contemplating Peter's style. It was similar to someone else's. Apparently, Peter was not the meek, laid back sort that she had first imagined, but, then again, what aspiring politician could afford to be, she reasoned?

There was no mistake about it. This Ghudd character was some sort of a catalyst. Reoccurring memories flooded her mind from when she was no older than her granddaughter. It was unavoidable. She wanted to hurl her ugly recollections aside. They were repulsive, and it wasn't healthy to dwell on old matters that couldn't be changed. Still, they poked at her constantly. She began to blame the mouthy stranger for making her trip turn sour. Somehow, part of his theme had filtered through the clamor of the busy streets and pierced her dullest nerves. It had left her cringing, even worse. Why, she commenced to torture herself, would this man encourage the extermination of anybody?

CHAPTER 25

Emmitt's head throbbed to the tune of Koepy's hammer, which was vigorously pounding nails into a freshly shingled roof. Emmitt was beat. He pulled himself sluggishly from beneath the cover of his warm flannel sheet and went to the bathroom. He took two aspirin and, cupping his hands, trapped several ounces of spigot water for a chaser. It was to be a vacation day. Some vacation! He utterly resented the itinerary Bert had dictated for him. After spending three hours in a mall introducing himself to strangers, he was to greet patrons at Roma's Outside Market. There, at precisely 2:30 PM, he'd be smiling into a news camera while munching on an oversized pretzel, how homey, he thought. Bert had instructed Emmitt to buy a few groceries following the shot. He was to maintain a frugal image. That meant the bulk of Emmitt's purchase was to be vegetables, a loaf of plain white bread, and a carton of grade A medium eggs. The press could be very scrutinizing.

Emmitt thumped to the outside wall of his bedroom and strained to raise the window. "Koepy," he fumed, "knock it off! D-Day wasn't that noisy!"

Koepy climbed off the roof, toting a twenty-six-ounce hammer and a cloth bag containing shingle nails. Emmitt's guilt began to soothe his anger. It was a rare occasion.

"Sorry I spoiled your fun, Koepy. It's a shame the ruckus is in violation of our public ordinance."

"In the future, I'll pound my hammer more discreetly," Koepy said.

"Me, too," Emmitt responded, trusting the neighbors hadn't seen Marian leaving shortly after 4:00 PM.

"I should've warned you," Koepy said. "I woke up in the middle of the night with the wind in my ears."

"What do you mean, Koepy? There's hardly a breeze."

"You must've slept through the gust. This roof wasn't secured. I never throw caution to the wind deliberately."

"Or shingles?"

"You got it. At least this part's done," Koepy said, with apparent pleasure. He holstered his hammer inside a leather tool belt, and let the bag of nails fall by his feet.

Emmitt trotted to the yard in his slippers. The dew on the grass was heavy, prompting him to step high. When he reached a thick cement pad, he stopped abruptly. "What's this?" He stammered.

"It's the foundation for the steps to your deck."

"I told you, Koepy. I made it perfectly clear there were to be no steps. I'm not paying for this block. Bust it up!"

"Let's compromise. Since I'm going to take a loss on the block, you'd be wise to reconsider the steps. It's a nice deal."

"Get rid of it, Koepy. Norman's stupid, nonetheless, he climbs steps as well as any other primate. If it weren't for him, I'd have that whole house to myself. I wouldn't be paying for a deck!"

With that, Emmitt proceeded to the kitchen where he was met by Vernon. He removed a pork chop from the refrigerator. "Speak to me, boy," he said, tempting the dog with a hunk of meat. "What's the matter, tough guy, cat steel your tongue?"

Emmitt stooped. He relinquished the entire pork chop to Vernon. The dog scampered under the kitchen table with the prize tightly between his teeth. The aroma of coffee was growing stronger, and Emmitt bounced up again to see a full pot of coffee steaming on the counter top. Marian had thought to set the timer for his favorite blend, French Roast. He was literally warmed by the gesture. She was a sweet and caring girl. She'd, also, programmed the radio to activate at 8:00 am sharp. The music was country, a breed Emmitt wasn't fond of. It wasn't that he hated it. He didn't connect with it, that's all. Marian was diversified. She'd randomly listen to classical and swear that it was plant-friendly. She often claimed that the potted cactus was doing better because of what she was letting it hear. Emmitt dismissed the theory as ridiculous. He was baffled, however, by the Wandering Jew. It had perked up considerably and soon it would have to be transplanted into a gallon crock. Emmitt attributed its recent surge to regular care, as he cut the power button on the radio.

The silence was brief. The telephone rang. Emmitt left it alone. He saw no reason to be bothered. It was too early for Bert, and Marian was busy. Her father had recruited her for the grand task of gathering pumpkins. There were mountains of them to be harvested...truckloads! Emmitt hadn't been aware of their presence in the fields when the corn was green and sprouting skyward. Their leafy vines coiled and twisted perfectly through the stretching stalks of silver queen, so as not to be detected. Now the fruit was ripe. Many of them were huge. They were golden-orange, like the October moon that was setting aglow the exhausted fields at sunset.

Customarily, the Jameses sold their produce to roadside stands and supermarkets. They'd reap a meek profit to pay the bills, then winter would harden the ground. Emmitt tried in vain to imagine that type of life. It had to be tough, digging your livelihood out of the dirt and bartering for it. He refused to blame Marian for selling herself. He told himself it wasn't her fault. Besides, she'd have no reason to revert to her previous wage earning practices. The two of them were an item, a secret item, yes. Still, no less an item. The last several weeks were heavenly. They were the best of his entire life. Marian was enjoying them, too. Emmitt could tell from the way she'd been pampering him.

To the rest of the city, he was a sturdy businessman, a pillar to be leaned on. His mission was to save Malfaxe from a state of decadence and fear. The women at the bank called him "Sir." His intellectual assets at times were overpowering. He knew his muscle was predominantly financial. His power base was position. Emmitt had jockeyed for power the major part of his life. He reveled in the sweetness of the respect it brought him. Emmitt insisted that prospective voters call him Emmitt." As for Marian, she was different. She'd nicknamed him "Night Crawler." He referred to her as his Bunny Fluff. Emmit grieved over her wandering nest though. A position with esteem was what Marian needed. Emmitt was set on helping her. If that wasn't sufficient, the money her father stood to gain from the land deal promised to be plenty.

Emmitt sipped at his coffee. A hair curled on the cup's brink. He plucked at the hair suspecting that it was a prelude of things to come. Before the election was over, he'd be lucky not to need a major transplant.

The race for mayor was winding into full throttle. Art Towson maintained strong support in the black community. He was well embraced by the city's moderates. It was destined to be an election with the potential for surprise. Emmitt's cry for urban renewal was synonymous with his name. The trouble was Art wasn't the type to allow Emmitt all the thunder. He advocated Emmitt's plans and presented a few of his own. One proposal was the construction of an inside civic coliseum where live entertainment and sports activities guaranteed to draw thousands of spectators. There was, nevertheless, one major dividing line separating Emmitt's and Art's campaigns. It was in relation to the prison. Art was a reformer. He believed in giving the inmates the opportunity to fulfill their potential by preparing themselves for meaningful work. Anything less, according to Art, meant the revolving door of justice was bound to spin drastically out of control. This required schooling, and additional space, not to mention the extra personal required to administer the training.

Emmitt opposed elaborate conditions for the sake of rehabilitation. He dismissed Art's plan as a costly endeavor that mocked the premise of criminal restitution. "Art Towson's Taj Mahal will drain money from critical city projects. My prison will be composed of essentials that inmates have a right to expect and nothing more." His comment was made at a press briefing attended by himself and Art one week earlier. The briefing was at the Jameses farm and intended to reveal the remoteness of the prison site. Something that Emmitt and Art were both in total agreement with.

Excavation was due to begin prior to the last days of October. Testing of the farm's subsurface was to be extensive. The results of the land analysis would then be disclosed to the responsible parties. Afterward, the farm would be surveyed and divided. Emmitt made all of those points very clear, trying to sound as if he were the one dictating the chain of occurrences that, in reality, were legal preliminaries that inflamed his patience. He'd worn gigantic rubber boots to the farm that day. They were Norman's, and four shoe sizes too large. Bert had encouraged him to get them "nice and grimy. Wallow in the mud, Emmitt," he'd told his friend. "The voters want a regular, down to earth man. Give them a good show!"

Unfortunately, Emmitt wasn't certain where his aspirations were leading him. He sought rank. He craved authority. The two would accompany his installment as City Executive. He'd be the boss then. When left alone, however, his mind drifted. Marian was what he longed for. Often he became despondent and lost himself in the petty thrills they discreetly shared. At night, they traveled the bar circuit and the dives, but never anywhere that might be well lit. To Emmitt, it was an adult game of 'hide and seek.' He loved the element of personal jeopardy. He'd win the game. He'd handle the election. No kiss and tell for Emmitt. That had always been part of his code of ethics. Now it was his golden rule. Unfortunately, the gold was becoming tarnished. He was aching to be with Marian when he was distracted again by the sound of Koepy's saw, whining a piece of six-by-eight in half. It was irking him, but the carpenter was a hard worker. He was doing what he'd been hired to do. Emmitt's headache was gone rather quickly, therefore, he could think of no reason to detain Koepy any longer.

A growling stomach soon informed the banker that the wolf was scratching at the door. Realizing he hadn't eaten, he twisted a banana from a bunch sprawled on the kitchen table. Emmitt devoured it without giving thought as to how tasty it was. His concerns soon went to Peter Ghudd.

Bert had recommended to Emmitt that he tolerate Peter. "It's the Christian way," he condescended. "There's no alternative. I'd say he's mimicking his idol…you. He's a child, Emmitt." In their previous gab session, he'd left Bert's comments about Peter unanswered. It was at a political fund rally. The two of them were feasting on hundred dollar plates that served two dollar portions of steak. The mention of Peter's name served only to sting Emmitt twice in a night. Peter was a derelict, as far as Emmitt could tell, nothing else. Emmitt did try though. With Bert's blessings, he had taken Peter to the Willy Comb Memorial Stadium to see the Malfaxe Comets play their season finale. It was late September, and the two men had skipped supper. Emmitt did the driving. They went straight from the bank to the ball field, where they ate hot dogs smothered in mustard and relish. The buns were steamy, just the way Peter liked them. Emmitt was grudgingly buying. Peter refused nothing. Before the gratuities ended, Peter had consumed five franks and seven beers. Emmitt, by then, was resenting Peter to no end.

Peter had brought a brown cloth bag with a drawstring. When Emmitt inquired as to what was in the bag, Peter first claimed that they were to be his private little jewels. Then he admitted to Emmitt that he had eleven baseballs stashed in the bag. He claimed they were "jewels, but jewels in the rough." "I'll get Manny Pedroiesk's signature on these for the rowdies on the street," Peter had bragged. "You watch, Manny'll be in the majors next season. It was an understatement. Manny was a left fielder with an exceedingly hot bat. Three teams were negotiating for his contract. The Nationals had the inside track. To Emmitt's way of thinking Manny would rather sacrifice a hit other than use up the time it would consume autographing eleven baseballs for a decrepit, pestering nag.

"What makes you think he'll bow to your wishes, Peter?" Emmitt had remarked rudely and not caring.

"He's a regular guy. I know 'em."

The two men had sat on the bleachers for three innings, Peter engrossed in Comet mania, while Emmitt secretly persecuted him for his illusions of grandeur. Emmitt pondered how neat it would be to brag about his Manny Pedroiesk baseball, especially once the star was in the majors. Manny possessed natural ability that Emmitt had never seen equaled on any minor league team. Emmitt knew he'd excel as a major leaguer, too. It irritated Emmitt that Peter might see fit to bother a celebrity of Manny's stature. Peter, he constantly told himself, was a psychotic dreamer.

When the top of the fourth inning arrived, Alex Sharkey, number twelve, led off with a line drive to the center field wall. It put him on second base. Manny Pedroiesk batted second. The game was tied one to one. A low curve made Manny swing and miss. A ball was called on the outside. Peter was on the edge of his seat forming words with his lips that Emmitt wasn't able to hear. Emmitt may have been a die hard Comet enthusiast, but he hoped they'd stink for this one game. He wanted Manny to stink even worse. Emmitt needed to see Peter's gleaming eyes sag in dismay. Emmitt gloated to himself, how it would take the overbearing intruder down a couple of pegs. The third pitch to Manny was thrown at sonic speed. Emmitt cringed when Manny's bat slammed into the white dot with a terrific bang. The crowd roared and a high fly went past the far right center field wall and into the seats. The leading run scored clearing the way for Manny to tag the bases and broaden the gap three to one. Manny sauntered down the third base line, then crossed home plate. He whirled around and waved his hat to the home crowd, who was still howling. A minute later, Manny was at the bleachers for autographs. He presented an easy manner, as he mingled with the patrons constantly flashing bright, chunky teeth that no doubt would be dazzling in a toothpaste commercial one day.

Feeling his own pride was at risk, Emmitt battled the impulse to request Manny's signature. In only a year, the player's name on a used napkin would be a great conversation piece. Emmitt restrained himself, as Peter went to the fence.

"What do ya have for me today, Pete?" Manny bubbled.

"More little gems for the gang," Peter returned. He was gripping the bag in front of his droopy waistline. "This'll do it for a while."

It had happened weeks ago. Emmitt remembered how he'd looked on in pain-coated envy, while the presumptuous agitator had held his bag out to the star. It became clear, however, and in no time at all, that when an audience was present, Manny's skills weren't purely athletic. He was a born entertainer, who'd found the feisty scoundrel's private little jewels easy to manipulate. He went right to the old man's sack and after close inspection fondled his jewels with careful attention. Then with no warning he began to juggle them furiously. The fans went wild, as screams of approval coaxed Manny into proving, without any doubt whatsoever, that he and the custodian were more than just a little familiar. Before the event was complete, Manny'd have to relinquish his valuable name, however on the best of terms. It was with eleven strokes aided by the lightning quick flicks of a limber wrist, which had given the old lump of skin the thrill he'd come for. Emmitt was livid. He'd wished it had been his balls, if he'd had any, and not his companions that Manny had signed. Something worse was needling Emmitt's peace of mind, though. It was a prolonged reminder that whether flaunting his precious jewels or not, the crude narcissus was nothing more than a dried up trace of humanity. Unfortunately, he was still remaining in there to have his share of the action.

CHAPTER 26

When a guard with a nasty scar across his cheek and flared nostrils escorted Norman to a renovated storage compartment, the door was closed, but unlocked. Norman knocked, then entered for his parole hearing. He left the guard casually leaning against an upright beam in the hall reading the sports section of the daily paper. The interview had been sprung on Norman. He'd served barely one quarter of the six month sentence the judge had invoked. This was his first day of eligibility, and the board was wasting no time. The administration had neglected to notify him of his release hearing. Consequently, instead of the preferred suit and tie, Norman appeared in his blue jeans and tattered prison shirt. Rather than a fancy handkerchief protruding over his left breast pocket, he'd displayed his black stenciled identification number. He was also told at lunch to wash and prepare to present his best attributes to the board. According to the guard who'd taken him there, the board was tough to sway and not to expect longer than a five-minute audience. Who could tell, if he went over well the odds for release at the next hearing might be increased drastically.

Norman wasn't impressed by any of the surroundings. He slouched in a metal folding chair waiting for the parole board to address him. The flavor of spearmint gum was vivid in the air from Norman's mouth which had been working four pieces at the same time. He chewed vivaciously, accessing the sparse surroundings. They were sparse except for a seaside mural depicting rocks, whitecaps, and a lonely lighthouse. They were all alike, he silently criticized. If he'd painted the stupid thing, he'd have brushed a whale under the dismal overcast sky, spouting a humongous geyser. Norman respected whales. They were able to exist off of their stored blubber for months in an atmosphere of blissful tranquility. Whales, Norman reasoned, were terrific athletes, too. He'd visited Sea World in '96 to watch them jump and dive. In due time, he wanted to return.

A woman in the center of two men began speaking. "We see you've been incarcerated for assaulting a policeman, Mr. Braedeikk."

"I was soused!"

"Do you grow ugly when you're drunk?"

"No uglier than yourself," Norman grinned, not planning on a lengthy interviev.

"I don't trade punches with cops."

"You'd a tricked me," Norman returned, with a bigger grin. He wanted to leave.

"We don't have time to squander, Mr. Braedeikk," Simms, one of the two gentlemen came to the woman's rescue. "Miss Collins isn't here to be subjected to your witless insults. We'd hoped to give you the opportunity to be released early from prison."

In adversity to good manners, Norman continued to chomp on his gum.

"Suit yourself?"

"Well, you can't leave this prison without our approval until your sentence is served, Mr. Braedeikk. Aren't you looking forward to a parole?" Simms peered at Norman over his reading glasses.

There was a pause. Norman's honesty was being summoned, and, at this point, he neglected to stun them. "Nah."

"You're working in the laundry. Is this correct?"

"Ten-hour days."

"Other activities include weightlifting, auto mechanics correspondence lessons, and prison wrestling?"

"They forgot glee club."

"Sarcasm isn't necessary. I'd say you're keeping a close schedule."

"It makes the days pass."

"Assuming that we were to give you a parole, what would you do?"

"I'm a musician."

"Yes, and I'm, an ex-public defender. You'd be banned from bars. There'd be no drinking. We all have to sacrifice, Mr. Braedeikk, in order to achieve steeper pinnacles. You'd need a daylight job."

"It wouldn't fit me."

"I'm a retired naval pilot," Collins jumped in. "I flew F114 jets in the Gulf."

"Wow!"

It was impossible to tell if Norman was still acting facetious when Torres, the second man on the board, decided it was his duty to intervene. "Mr. Braedeikk, I'm a doctor. I'm, also, the son of a migrant fruit picker. I learned English when I was eight years old. Kids used to steal my lunch money in school. They drafted me for Viet Nam as soon as I graduated from the twelfth grade. Afterward, I attended college on the GI Bill, where I was thrown into a hyena's cage during a malicious fraternity hazing. Mr. Braedeikk, I've been beaten up, shot at, and almost mauled to death by an enraged hyena. I've never stopped trying to make something of myself. Today, when I'm not reviewing inmates, I specialize in gynecology at the state woman's facility in Frederick."

"You're a female specialist, huh?"

"It's my profession, yes."

Norman seemed appalled as he rubbed his fat, stubby chin. "I gotta admit, Dock, you've probably been in some mighty tight not to mention unusual places. My niche is instruments, though. It'd take me forever to find a paying job I'd be as good at."

"We won't twist the rules," Torres rebuked Norman.

"I got a ton of laundry to wash. Am I dismissed?"

"With extreme pleasure," Collins almost cried out.

Contrary to their personal misgivings, the three people on the parole board had previously decided in favor of Norman's release. They disliked Norman immensely. He was brash, indifferent, and foxy; but the board's dilemma was deteriorating on a daily basis. The overcrowding at Sutler Penitentiary was grossly escalating. On the congeniality scale, Norman was easily a minus ten. It was a shame that Norman was one of the best of a bad bunch because Collins, in particular, would have liked to have buckled his bottom lip to his bulbous snout using a hard uppercut. The interview had been a desperate formality. Norman's days at Sutler were to be brief. His behavior may have been miles from commendable, only when it was compared to the core group in the penitentiary, Norman looked like a prince. There was one underlying comment written by the prison psychiatrist. It was italicized in Norman's records and was a strange statement in view of Norman's disgusting attitude. It was also very accurate. "Norman Braedeikk does not lie." It served as his trademark in life. Norman despised both liars and lies. The psychiatrist went on to say that being honest was Norman's defense against what he might sometimes consider cowardice. On various occasions, Norman was questioned in regard to unscrupulous acts culminating in a relinquishment of privileges for himself. Under those circumstances he always came cleaner than the spotless laundry he'd washed for the rest of the inmates. His admissions, whenever solicited by the prison administrators, came without hesitation. Norman, despite all of his faults, was a truthful human being. Such was not the case with Sam Rhiggs who at this very moment was being visited by his dapper attorney right down the hall.

"We have ten minutes."

"I'm flattered." Sam Rhiggs penciled a Mickey Mouse figure on the Formica tabletop. He wasn't distracted. "You should be applauding yourself, Sam. I collect two hundred dollars on hour from my reputable clients."

"My last job earned me twice as much, Counselor. Thirty seconds of my time reaps much better pay. Tax free, too!" Sam laughed, "You oughta see if you can finagle a reimbursement for that expensive education of yours."

The lean attorney in the tailored suit removed a note pad from his briefcase. He then slid the case under the corner of the sturdy three by six table occupying the center of the prisoner conference room. They were on the first floor in Sutler.

Henry Siber picked up the dialogue, situating his impeccably groomed self at the distant end of the table away from Sam. "You're the one who's in jail, Sam. Can we stop measuring one another, or is it going to be eight more minutes of tit for tat?"

"Who's measuring? Do ya see a ruler anywhere?"

"Sam, you're childish. You're trying to get the last stupid word in, and it's time consuming."

"Childish, huh? Childish? Forging ahead with rodent tenacity, Sam repeated the term totally enchanted with the possibility of a hidden meaning. "A jury'd swallow that whole with the proper trimmings, don't 'ya think?"

"It lies in the category of foolishness, Sam. Nothing we can use." Siber's ballpoint pen appeared instantly. He jotted a quick note.

"Write it down anyway," Sam said, detailing a M16 rifle being discharged by the cartoon mouse character. "It's...what do they call 'em? A warm fuzzy expression."

"You'll have to take it up with the Public Defender." Siber fought his annoyance. "That's not our battle. How's the arm?"

"I can't move it," Sam said, as he went on doodling with his healthy right limb. His left arm was bandaged in a sling.

"That doesn't astonish me. Do you have pain?"

"It depends. Is pain worth more?"

"To a compassionate jury, but be honest. There's no need to distort the truth. You've been diagnosed at the hospital as suffering from a chronic or, worse yet, a degenerative condition because of that sniper's misplaced shot. You'd of probably been better off had he just finished you there and then. Now look at the condition your in. I'm bringing a specialist here to examine you shortly. He'll be on our side, so make sure you're helpful!"

"Can the doctors call me a fraud?"

"You've been called a lot worse. I can manage the doctors."

"What do you know about medicine?" Sam challenged.

"I know that medical science in certain areas hasn't surpassed the Dark Ages, and proving or disproving your case will be nearly impossible."

"I am smarting."

"It's called hurting. You'll have to convince twelve smart people, though."

Sam released the pencil, making no effort to prevent it from bouncing off the table onto the tiled surface of the floor below. If you win, how long 'til we get paid?"

"I'll win."

"Why?"

"We have nothing to lose. The city can't counter sue, because you have nothing to take. It's hardly a gamble, Sam. I think an out of court settlement would be in line."

"When?"

"I don't predict dates."

"Give me a rough idea."

"Between two and five years."

Henry flopped his note pad on the table and stuck his pen on top of his ear. "The money's not the issue with you, Sam. It never was. You'd be content to let this whole thing run on for the next forty years."

"That's a matter of opinion."

"That's a matter of fact. You like to badger. There's no reason for us to harbor any falsehoods."

"Yeah, we're like family," Sam mocked.

Henry spoke apathetically, "That's your delusion, not mine."

"Delusion," Sam repeated. "Would you mind writing that on a piece of paper for me? I want to pass that along to my defense with the college stuff you mentioned before. He's educated too, but sort of weak from the neck north."

"And you're a liability to a man's career, Sam."

"Why are you bothering with me, if I'm such a liability?" Sam spouted off.

"I told you, I have no skin in the game either."

"They call fellas like you parapsychs, don't they?"

"The word's parasite."

Sam bumped the table as he stood and went to an adjacent corner of the room. He revolved his head only to encounter Henry's cool, demeaning glare. A glare he interpreted to be one of inquisition. "You're thriving in this, aren't you," he said, accusingly.

"You hired me, Sam. I didn't hire you. Which brings me to why I'm here. We'll be setting you up for a deposition. I want you to give all of your statements forethought. No tripping over yourself!"

"When?"

"I'll be in contact," Henry said, darting to his feet and making for the door. He was toting his note pad and briefcase.

"Will that dumb cop be there?"

"What cop?"

"The cop who lunged at my arm."

"Not true, Sam. Emphasize "shook". He shook your arm, setting into play a chain of events that resulted in your being partially crippled. If we go to trial, I can't vindicate perjury."

"Will he be there?"

"Read the papers. Lieutenant Barns scattered his brains six ways from shinola two days ago. He did it right there in the police station. Sick, if you ask me." Henry almost slithered away without saying goodbye.

CHAPTER 27

"He's been freed!"

"Who's been freed, Emmitt?"

"Norman, Bert! He called. "They've paroled him!"

"You scared me, Emmitt. Thank God, it's not Sam Rhiggs."

"For me, it's worse."

"Don't panic!" Bert said, knowing full well the terror in Emmitt's plea was legitimate. Had it been Sam, the fright would have belonged to Bert. He was relieved beyond words that it wasn't Sam Riggs running lose to bloody the streets. "We'll handle it," he said. "Where is he?"

"He's in the hills, Bert. There's a cabin. I can find it in the daylight." It was not yet 5:30 in the morning, and Norman had only three minutes earlier informed Emmitt of his release.

"What did he say, Emmitt?"

"He said that I was a rotten brother. On top of that I didn't deserve his loyalty. He's bitter. Then he said that he held no grudge and insisted that he wanted to prove it by campaigning for me!"

"OOPS! How long has he been on the street?"

"I didn't ask. Can you believe the gall of that man? I'm a wreck, Bert!"

"Listen to me, Emmitt! Today's Tuesday. In all likelihood, they released him yesterday morning. He's just warming up by sticking a burr under your saddle. It's his way."

"I've dreaded this day!"

"Bring him home, Emmitt. He'll ruin you if he's not contained."

"Will you go with me? I'd rather not confront him alone."

"I'll be there in fifteen minutes."

Bert arrived in ten minutes. He found Emmitt at the wheel of his Lincoln, ready to take to the road. "Get in," Emmitt prompted, shifting the transmission into drive, as Bert slid onto the passenger seat.

"Have you eaten yet?"

"I'm frantic! My stomach's in no condition for food. You?"

"I crammed a Danish."

"Norman won't be happy 'til he destroys me." Emmitt was on the main highway, cruising at seventy.

"They write tickets for this," Bert cautioned, as he zeroed in on the speedometer. "You'd better slow down."

"Thanks."

"Where we off to?"

"Past the county line, to Fairview Mountain. It's an abandoned cabin. We'll have to park the car at the bottom of a trail and rough it from there."

"How far?"

"You'll be home for lunch."

"You're sure?"

"It's a cinch. My parents owned the property. They used to haul Norman and me to the woods on weekends. I knew where he was a soon as I heard the familiar sound of the dinner bell on the front porch clanging."

"They have a telephone. It can't be too remote."

"The phone's gotta be cellular."

"Oh."

"Bert, it's a great spot for country mischief. Emmitt's apprehension temporarily receded. You can roll your shirt sleeves as high as you like. Once, Norman bought some moonshine, and we stored it in a hollowed tree stump. Whenever the old man took a snooze, we'd head for that stump. There's a fishing hole, too. The bass weigh in at eight pounds!"

"You ever catch one that big?"

"Twice, but Norman reeled them in. He said my arms weren't strong enough. I could've done it!"

"It's odd, you're chirping like a nature boy."

"Don't be misled. I'm a city boy at heart. Norman can have the hills. If he'd only stay there."

Emmitt's foot was lighter on the peddle. He swung into the slow lane, and touched the power control to the radio. A symphony blared. It was Tchaikovsky's Fourth. Marian was constantly playing with the stations. She listened to everything from classical to forties' hits. Her restless fingers searched for new music relentlessly. When one song ended, she jumped to a different station to catch another. It was perturbing, but for the sake of their relationship, Emmitt endured her flighty preferences.

A man with a tractor was cutting the growth on the median strip of the highway. The sight of it averted Emmitt's thoughts to the Jameses farm. The geological testing was in progress, and with each passing day, Emmitt's anxiety was climbing to a new peak.

"Bert, the land analysis is due on the Jameses place."

"Overdue."

"What if it fails?"

"Then your campaigns in default. We'll sneak you out of town after dark on a convenient night."

"Be serious, Bert. What's plan B?"

"Plan B doesn't exist."

"You're pretty cocky about all this."

"You betcha," Bert professed with confidence.

"Well?"

"I've been keeping tabs on the mineral samples since the drilling began."

"And?"

"The first few feet were top soil and clay, Emmitt. Farther below was a wide layer of sandstone. It stretched infinitely."

"Is that substantial?"

"No, but granite is. They've chewed their bits smack dab into that sweet stuff everywhere they bored."

"Sounds encouraging."

"Manhattan was built over granite, Emmitt! You won't be leaving Malfaxe in your pajamas!"

A crossroads appeared in the distance, and Emmitt eased to a full stop at the intersection. He went left and drove over a stone bridge spanning a shallow brook blemished with jagged rocks. The hard single.lane road split into a fork, where Emmitt took the lesser route onto a dirt tract. An abandoned springhouse could be seen hovering atop a trickling stream. Emmitt let the momentum of the car come to rest where a knoll was sprouting a white oak tree. The tree's branches were huge and low. They spread over the dilapidated springhouse, creating for it an enormous autumn leaf umbrella.

"It's a gentleman's hike, Bert. The cabin is in that pine grove." He pointed toward a hill that was heavily populated by evergreens.

"Is he alone?"

"Don't expect it. He attracts grimy company."

"Emmitt, is this safe? Norman's been with a tough lot."

"No meaner than himself. That's why I brought a gun." Emmitt lifted a twenty-two caliber automatic that was concealed inside of one of his rubber boots. "If it gets unpleasant, we've got insurance."

"Emmitt, Emmitt!" Bert pleaded emphatically. "He's your brother, man! Don't be idiotic. Give me the gun, or I'm outtta here! Now, Emmitt!"

"Don't forget you have it, Bert." Emmitt instructed, as he reluctantly handed the weapon to his friend. "We'll approach from the rear of the cabin."

Emmitt assumed a slow lead. Together, they trudged northward, each man engrossed in his own fears of what awaited them. Inwardly, they shared a common hope, that there would be no rendezvous. Oblivious to the dense foliage and poison ivy that spiraled the trees with its magnificent fall scarlet, they pushed onward, at last coming to the aft of the cottage.

"That's queer," Emmitt said. "We used to have a wooden porch." His eyes were fixed on the back door which opened above a steep drop.

"We had a real cold spell last night, Emmitt," Norman remarked, edging his way from the side of the cottage. "I sent one of the troops for firewood. That's as far as he looked."

Emmitt froze in his steps, causing Bert to stop quickly in his own.

"It's disgraceful," Norman continued "one of the girls was knocked unconscious this morning trying to take that route for a potty call. They say most accidents happen around the home, but I'll bet that'll be a new one for the books! Emmitt, I want to introduce you to the committee."

Norman wrapped his arm snugly about Emmitt's ribcage, and with the strength of a boa constrictor, gleefully commenced to diminish his brother's circulation. A rag doll couldn't have been more agile as Norman then hastily swept Emmitt off to meet his friends. "I want you to see the committee too, Bert!" He prompted. "A finer bunch of comrades you'll never acquire, Emmitt. Folks, I give you my brother, Emmitt, your future mayor, and the distinguished Reverend Dixtzon!"

"Pleasure meeting you," Emmitt gasped for air as Bert made a head count to himself and calculated the number of bullets in the gun. It was a well diversified number of lost souls, Bert concluded. Three women, two of which were Caucasian, and expecting. The other was Hispanic and toted a machete that was attached between her full skirt and a wide cinch belt. Her frazzled hair had dried blood in it, and Bert had her figured to be the one who'd crashed off the missing porch. One of the men was also Hispanic. He had fresh deep scars embedded in his cheeks. They were long, sometimes extending under his sideburns. Reflecting on the machete, Bert rapidly assumed the pair were a not so happy couple.

Five men were huddled around a blanket. Two were Negroes and the other three were white. They had been shooting dice and seemed put out by the interruption. Norman picked the blanket off the ground and thrust it at the torso of the heaviest man, who was endowed with monstrous biceps and had tense, hateful slits for eyes.

"I'm sorry you saw that, Reverend," Norman said, registering high on the sincerity scale as the men scattered.

A man who was garbed in a denim vest and no shirt underneath labored eagerly in the nearby brush. His cut offs were tattered at the thighs, and he was wearing two sneakers, neither of which matched. The man was digging a pit with a broken handled shovel. The sight of which caused Emmitt's bladder to weaken.

"Stop working, Josh," Norman said, none too loudly, although confident of his control. "You're hollowing us a garbage dump, not a landfill!"

Josh scurried to Norman, panting with each pace, prompting Bert to view the freaky little man as he would have a misguided black sheep, all the while evaluating his intelligence to be considerably less than that of a retarded June bug.

"My brother's anxious to make your acquaintance, Josh," Norman said.

Josh presented Emmitt with an energetic handshake, and Emmitt reciprocated with two fingers extended and two folded in. It wasn't until contact that Emmitt realized Josh had severed the two fingers Emmitt had mistakenly held back himself for what he thought had been a Scouts greeting. Before it passed, Emmitt felt like a penny waiting for change. "I'm Josh," the mousy, little man with the straggly beard emphasized, "but nobody ever calls me Arnold"

"I'm sure they don't," Emmitt agreed, somewhat perplexed.

"Emmitt," Norman said joyfully, "these people are at your disposal. We want to help you get elected."

"I'm happy for any aid you can muster, Norman."

Emmitt began scrutinizing appliance boxes that were cut into rectangular posters and nailed to chopped tree branches. They were newly fabricated election signs. The posters were hand drawn with red chalk, portraying Emmitt as a stick figure and very small. The artist had given Emmitt an egg-shaped head, four hairs, enormous ears, and a cucumber nose. "Vote for Emmitt" jinxed the signs in capital and small letters mixed, making the aspiring politician's knees quiver at the prospect of a public viewing.

"Neat, huh?" Norman said, with an abundance of enthusiasm.

"Excellent," Emmitt said, folding his arms. "I'd love to take them with me."

"That's not possible. We're marching in front of city hall today."

"Norman," Emmitt felt the enamel on his canines grinding over his bottom dental caps, "I want these signs."

"That's what I figured you'd say. We lay all the ground work, Emmitt, and you wanna come in for the gravy. You're gonna owe us big time for this!"

"I already do, Norman, Can't you see I'm practically on bended knee?"

"I'll have to run it by the committee."

"What committee? Is this your committee, Norman?" contemplating the bizarre band of misfits, Emmitt was in a state of wild disbelief.

"We're the Committee Representing Unanimous Democracy. You can use our abbreviation if you so desire."

"Thank you, Norman. I'd like that. Does CRUD have a charter?"

"We're not literary people, Emmitt.

"That simplifies everything. You, as the chairman, are entitled to expedite critical decisions in the interest of progress and/or individual welfare."

"I'm not the chairman. Josh is."

Flashing a gold earring from under a sweaty, black bandanna, Josh expanded his chest to a hefty thirty inches at the mention of his name.

To Emmitt, he resembled a bowlegged pirate. A pirate, who had just dug a garbage dump, and would, no doubt, burry his finest treasures there. If anyone was more deserving than Norman to be the spokesman for CRUD, it had to be Josh. Emmitt surmised that one day the world would be immune to epidemics like CRUD and disparaging illnesses like Josh, but, in the meantime, mankind must work day and night to formulate an antidote. It would be a tiresome job, probably costing billions of dollars.

"How 'bout it, Josh?" Emmitt almost whined. "It'll be a shot in the arm for my campaign."

"They're yours, if you never call me Arnold," Josh responded.

"I won't, Josh. Honest, I won't. What kind of person do you think I am?" Emmitt asked in devious humility.

Emmitt wasn't warmed by the gesture as much as by the anticipation of a sign burning ceremony in his brick barbecue. His car would be crammed full, but all of the signs were going home with him, even if he had to haul two separate loads. For the present, CRUD would have to be discouraged from producing more.

"I'm glad I arrived when I did," Emmitt cheerfully commenced to carry the signs to the car's trunk.

"You'll really make a name for yourself with that kind of publicity."

Norman scratched his groin.

"We've dozens of boxes," the woman with the machete reminded Emmitt.

"Don't move too fast," Emmitt uttered. "These signs will all have to go up first."

Emmitt's knees buckled simultaneously with a sly nudge afforded by Bert. The charade would have to advance. Emmmitt swallowed hard at the notion of what he was obliged to do. "Norman, you're my brother," he said.

"I wish you'd come home."

"Refresh my memory, Emmitt. Who asked who to leave?"

"Norman, I wasn't myself. My demands on you were inexcusable. A man does foolish acts sometimes, Norman, and he has to be forgiven."

Tucking in his shirttail, Norman stretched at the girth of his pants. "I can relate to that. Golly, I'm in need of forgiveness myself, Emmitt. I've done some capers I'm not so nuts about."

"You're human, Norman."

"I've been a rude and belligerent drunk. I've pissed the best part of my life away. The last few years there was only one thing between me and the toilet."

"The Lord!" Bert professed, with pastoral jubilation.

"Nope. It was Emmitt's phoney mustache," Norman candidly revealed.

"You're courageous for repenting, Norman," Bert said. "I'm sure Emmitt respects you for it."

The older brother's focus narrowed on Norman's jugular vein. "I do, and I forgive you," Emmitt blatantly lied from behind the diminishing, yellowing strip of hair.

"Give him another chance," Bert suggested to Norman.

"Trials and tribulations. Yes, I'll go home. God only knows, it's not gonna be very easy. Norman approached his brother, hardly allowing a paper-thin gap to separate their noses. "But that's just the kind of guy I am," he was glad to assert. I suppose I'm a chump, but I'll do it for Emmitt's sake. "He ain,t no weasel, he's my brother."

CHAPTER 28

"I'd be rich, if I was to pocket a bill each time you chucked a hand full of that dirt. How's it look?"

Hal Bagley casually allowed the clumps of soil to thump onto the bare field from where he'd gathered them. "This hardly counts for scientific analysis, Reverend. Feeling it won't tell me what's below. It's what that auger connects with that matters." He said tilting his head in the direction of the idled drilling machine resting several yards away by a pile of pulverized earth.

"You've been popping holes all over my property, mister. When's it end?" Lester grew agitated.

"How's a week strike ya?"

"Too long."

"We're ordering in a different piece of equipment. May take four or five days for it to arrive."

"What's it do?"

"It takes pictures."

"My camera can take pictures."

"It's a submersible camera."

"How's that gonna tell anybody about this ground we're standing on?" The minister grumbled.

"Probably nothing, but we don't want any oversights. Today I'd have to approve your property for Alcatraz, that is, if they were able to move it. We'll have the information we need soon." The penologist spoke with apparent sincerity, leaving Lester Jameses temporarily wordless. Alcatraz was built on a rock, everybody knew that. The trouble was, shy of being a tourist attraction, it was a diversion, and at the present the topic had no purpose.

Lester allowed his attention to wander to the lower slopes, where a plowed ridge of farmland embraced the soft muddy banks of the lake. Stu Emery, a geological engineer, was setting a bucket of mud into the rear portion of an open Jeep. "What's that for?" Lester inquired, thinking that the whole land analysis procedure was ridiculous. The land was solid, and it was ready for construction. What else was needed?

"A histosios test!" Hal almost snapped. "We've got to examine the consistency." Hal Bagley, himself, was becoming ticked. It had been a rough day, and the minister was trying his patience. It had all started when their last drill bit had broken twenty feet beneath the surface from where he and Lester were now standing. While waiting for a delivery of replacement bits, Hal received a call that his wife was involved in a minor traffic accident. Worried that it may have been worse, he left the job site in a panic. His fears were laid to rest while he was on his way to the accident. His wife called him on his cell phone to tell him the damage was minimal, a dented bumper and a crunched tail pipe. Hal returned to the farm immediately, and decided to try a shortcut through the woods to the section of land being drilled. Winding cow trails proved to be his demise. A flat tire, with no spare, cost him two frustrating hours. Shortly before five, the shift ended on another bad note when a brand new bit chipped. With his gut churning from the preceding events, Hal was in no mood to defend his position as a conscientious state engineer.

"Mr. Jameses, histosios is marsh goo."

"Why bother with mud? Up there, that's where the prison's gonna be." The preacher pointed beyond an acre of dried entangled corn to an expansive stretch of unharvested spinach. "That's the spot."

"We're taking samples from an adjoining ten acres. There's more to this than I care to explain, Reverend."

"How large of a prison are ya contemplating?"

"They're housing two thousand inmates. It'll be big. What'd they tell you?"

"They told me half that many." The minister's heart grew lame. It showed itself, when he paused and swallowed.

"Does it upset you?"

"No, well...Yes."

"If you're smart, you'd make 'em buy the whole farm and move as far away as you can."

"My grandparents are buried on this land. My parents, too."

"Oh, I see," Hal mocked, "and you want to get yourself buried out here with them."

It was a point well made, hitting Lester Jameses squarely between his two blue eyes and sinking deeply into his conscious fears. Hal resisted gawking as the minister opened his heavy flannel shirt and raised his undershirt to uncover a swollen, ugly scar on his bare chest.

"Chest surgery?" Hal felt compelled to pry.

"No. It was Hector, the bull, and I've been on loan in this world ever since. You might say every day's an extra prize for me."

Lester's message was clear. The engineer scooped a small amount of topsoil into his palm and began spilling it again slowly in front of himself. "I don't want you worrying unnecessarily Reverend," he hesitated.

"But."

"It's like this. There are three horizons of ground to be investigated, organic matter," Hal retrieved more dirt, only to fling it aside repetitiously. "The middle layer, that's all the mineral deposits that have filtered through your topsoil from run off. From the conditions of this ground and that lake down there, I'd say the runoff is extensive."

"Always was."

"Normally in the third layer we encounter bedrock, which we did. What's surprising is the amount of granite we've struck. Reverend, It's endless!"

"That's good, right?" Lester smiled.

"In this case, it's great! We've been drilling deeper the last couple of days though and tapped into water."

"And?"

"And I think it's nothing more than a cavern with a small underground spring. It's to be expected."

"When will the city get the go ahead to set up their jail? Lester asked, hunching low to tie his shoe.

"I hav'ta be non-committal. We'll be boring holes for a while yet, but we'll be finished our testing within the month."

The minister didn't bother to lift himself. He crouched in the field, with his knees vertically tucked near his bosom. The earth was cold, and the furrowed gully Lester Jameses had staked out was rigid, forcing him to twitch his buttocks. His memory strayed to when he was a boy. His father without fail had always sent him into the pasture after the cows before night set in. Winters were bitter in those years. To capture the warmth, he would often place his frozen hands on the ground where a cow had been laying. The Almighty always provided an answer, he thought. Usually it was simple.

As dried leaves blew by him and crackled in the breeze, Lester wasn't remorseful for the spent summer. He had learned long ago how to endure the oncoming weather. The snow would be deep, and the ice treacherous. When it thawed, the same land that had drained his body's strength for sixty years, now promised to be his salvation. He was finding peace in the certainty that his life was on the rebound. His church would be restored. Lester's faith told him righteousness would prevail. Regardless though, that firm, undying, faith neglected to tell him that insurmountable obstacles were rapidly accumulating.

Glimmering sporadically across the distinct sky, stars, countless numbers of them, dotted Emmitt's span of view. He'd originally sprawled himself on a padded lounge in the back yard to engage in a self-consultation. It was to be a private meeting with his own mind, where Emmitt would evaluate his campaign progress and devise a strategy to win the election by a landslide. He'd never done this before so late in the autumn, laid outside, that is. It was very brisk, and Emmitt brought a quilt to unfold over himself. He pulled the quilt up to and around his arms as he gazed at the lucid specks that were spooking his imagination with all kinds of questions. Creation was a marvelous phenomenon, he thought, scratching his brow. Emmitt started to wonder where it all had begun.

Specks, incredibly tiny specks, were dispersed randomly throughout the alluring midnight sky. They were everywhere as far as Emmitt was able to see. Emmitt embraced the notion of their being hundreds of thousands of them, and he was aware that that had to be a conservative estimation. The greatest scientist in the world weren't able to tell if the universe ended or where, so it wasn't feasible, Emmitt pondered, to venture a wild guess as to the number of stars there potentially could be in existence. To try and visualize the universe with its myriad clusters of celestial possessions was just simply more than Emmitt was capable of. It was possible, he tried to imagine, that it went on forever, but where did it begin? It had to begin somewhere, sometime. Was the big boom theory, which was advocated by a significant fraction of modern astronomers the start of it. Emmitt found it preposterous to comprehend the magnitude of such a colossal event. Astronomers with degrees up the ying-yang were totally inept on the subject. They were baffled without a clue. It vexed Emmitt's mind to lay still with his eyes fixed straight upward, trying to comprehend the extent to which it all reached.

Life, Emmitt concluded, was absolutely the greatest, most absorbing mystery feasible, and why Emmitt mused was the government opposed to the admission of extraterrestrial life. Didn't the government know that people weren't buying the propaganda it fed to the masses. Cover-ups depicting weather balloons, or mistaken manmade aircraft, for alien vehicles were less than inadequate to Emmitt's way of thinking. Deception by the authorities wasn't working. It should end. People were too informed about sightings these days. They'd been well publicized from every part of the globe. "Unidentified flying objects" were presently being accepted as vast life support systems that transported advanced beings from one remote world to another. It seemed foolish to

Emmitt that international leaders could expect to conceal the existence of visitors from worlds not yet conceived by only a few pea brained scientist. Misleading babble is what Emmitt construed it as, just plain dishonest.

Bugging Emmitt even more was the idea that if God made earthlings, how were the space natives created. Did the same God who created man design the aliens with their peculiar eyes and egg shaped heads? Their skin was weird too and judging from the majority of similar accounts they were extracted from a single mold. Discounting some distinction, they looked close. Emmitt thought they were creepy. Reproduction between these species was no doubt a chore instead of pleasurable bodily contact. Emmitt surmised that maybe they grew their offspring in glassware, or a unique derivative of a closely related substance. If so, it would certainly relieve God, if there was a God, of unwarranted flak. And presuming there was a God, a single true God, he'd dwarf all other creation. There was no alternative answer. So why would God permit strange freaks of this sort to share in man's universe? Weren't men numero uno? If so, why did aliens retain superior technology above man? Apparently they zoomed around in their space ships gathering data, but for what purpose? Animal mutilation had occurred in the sixties. Cows, along with various other creatures, were left dissected in open fields indicating empirical information had been sought. Later came the rash of crop circles. Incidents of this type were inevitably linked to aliens scrutinizing planet Earth. It was unproven speculation, yes, but what about the scores of reputable witnesses who'd seen and testified as to the validity of flying space craft. The law of averages dictated to Emmitt's common sense that a healthy percentage of sightings had to be legit. Therefore, additional life did exist elsewhere. Were some of these aliens a breed that had landed on Earth thousands of years ago, as thought by some, and because of their advanced knowledge looked upon as gods by primitive man? Well, Emmitt picked his brain, why weren't they continuing to reveal themselves to people? Were Earthlings too uncivilized for interplanetary travelers these days?

When Emmitt was a kid, television was in its infancy. Aliens invading Earth were often portrayed as sinister intruders. They'd swoop down in their rocket ships, which resembled giant aluminum foil footballs, and blast the pleasant unsuspecting humans with terrible ray guns. Emmitt had marveled at the prospect of taking them on when he grew up, only now he was certain that space beings were fine inhabitants of the universe. If they were to select his yard for a landing pad at this precise moment, Emmitt knew he'd jump at the chance to explore the universe with them. It could be within the realm of possibilities that two or three universes were on their itinerary. After all, who could tell where one massive entity began, and another one ended. The skies were bigger than people could ever imagine. It was mind boggling, but he did feel like at the focal point of all creation their had to be one and only one central force of intelligent design. Emmitt was becoming intrigued with where they'd fly to. More than that, he wondered again where it had all begun. Instantaneously, Emmitt's mental faculties lost gravity, and he found himself the inventor of a new galaxy. It was the galaxy of Zeb Lamon, where Emmitt's ship the "Happy Odyssey" navigated among pristine quasars to claim undiscovered territory. Emmitt reigned as the undisputed ruler, Emmittrio. He explored clandestine planets, where he frequently encountered pigmy communities who were constantly intimidated by his astonishing height of barely five and a half feet. A few planets had giants. Those planets were uncommon, besides, no matter how large the foe, Emmittrio remained unshaken. He'd tame the fiercest opposition with his paralyzing intelligence and infinite wisdom. He'd be the boss guru. His gift to the galaxy, no the grand universe, would be himself. Cosmic order would be his self-ordained goal. It would be a magnanimous job requiring the enlistment of dedicated loyalists, better yet, disciples. Emmitt conceived that the conclusive results were destined to be remarkable. His universe would be in a constant state of regeneration, forever expanding. Constraints nonexistent, a ship traveling at billions of times the speed of light for trillions of light years would still make killions and zillions of his galaxies unobtainable. It was perplexing for Emmitt to contemplate an actuality as incomprehensible as all of this, but it must be real. What caused it to happen? Emmitt was filled with wonder. He just couldn't fathom what caused it to happen or where it all started. Where did it all begin, he kept asking himself over and over again. Where did it all begin?

CHAPTER 29

What irked Peter was the manner in which Emmitt had chosen to dismiss him. He would've quit by November anyway, but Emmitt had mailed him two weeks advance pay and wrote Peter a brief note explaining that his services were no longer necessary. He'd gone on to say that because of the bank's austerity program, "part-time help was being eliminated". Emmitt elaborated on the subject reminding Peter that the bank was in a continuous state of cost-cutting, but if and when money became more available, Peter'd be the first person to regain his job. Emmitt closed by saying what an outstanding employee Peter had proven to be. With a personal touch, he wished Peter the "best of luck" in the forthcoming election. The envelope containing the letter had been dropped through Peter's door slot without a postage stamp, on Friday, late. That was yesterday, Peter's usual day off. Peter laid the check by a bowl of artificial fruit on his sink counter to linger in the company of two previous uncashed checks. Then he finished off a cup of instant cappuccino. True to form, Peter recognized rubbish when he saw it. He discarded the note in a litter bin on his way out to nab a quick breakfast. Daylight was an event in the making. It was to be a busy Saturday. Peter was in a rush.

When he scurried in, Peter was given a warm greeting by the hostess at the diner. Since living in Malfaxe, he'd been eating toast and hash browns there each morning without fails. It was three years minus fourteen days. He kept track of such details, just as he did the number of times a waitress would frequent his table to heat his coffee or bring packs of jelly for his toast. He was hard to please, and he allotted his gratuities accordingly. He had no favorite waitress. He had no special people. Rewarding reliability was strictly business. Special tasks needed to be accomplished in set time frames. It was not unusual for a waitress, who struck Peter as being a little on the bitchy side, to earn a handsome tip just by hustling her services to the old man's fancy.

With his appetite satisfied, Peter departed the restaurant. He went to a transit stop where he hailed a taxicab instead, instructing the driver to deliver him to the Nineteenth Regiment Armory. Today was the eighty fifth anniversary of the Army Reservist Installation. There'd be a verbal presentation preceding an arms display. He could count on a crowd being there. In all likelihood, the Armory was going to be packed. The weather channel was predicting a fifty percent chance of rain in the afternoon, inducing Peter to tote an umbrella. Between the ribs of the closed umbrella, he tucked a brown leather case holding his campaign cards.

Arriving none too soon, Peter found the Armory already filled. Onlookers meandered about the huge chamber curiously, taking in the military hardware that was positioned from the extreme entrance to the far exit. Peter couldn't have asked for an environment more conducive for dumping his cards, cards which had graduated to a glossy white, and cast his name proudly with gold fancy lettering.

He began on arrival, and in less than two hours, he had given out hundreds of his cards. By noon, he was frazzled from pushing himself in the front of what seemed like battalions of non-interested, but prospective voters, who were totally preoccupied with the military agents of rapid destruction. "I'm Peter Ghudd," he'd render his hand in hopes of a receptive counter. "I'd appreciate your vote on election day." Peter would follow through by submitting his card for what he wished might be more than a courteous examination by the recipient. It was discouraging that an inner voice was telling him that he was simply blowing time. This wasn't the way politicians swayed elections. Elections were won by impressing the masses through modern technology. Soon enough, he consoled himself, soon enough. For the present, one on one contact was the extent of his capacity. It would have to suffice.

Once he broke away from the arduous task of trying to gain individual votes, Peter became involved himself in the weapons display. The tanks were the peak attraction. There were three of them. One was a World War Two Sherman. Two tanks of greater interest were the later models. They were the Army's M60A1 tanks, and to Peter's sense of logic, impressive war machines. A recorded narrative described their ability's. They attacked armored vehicles, as well as infantry and ground targets. Aircraft, also, was in their realm of duty. Each tank carried a 105 millimeter cannon forward of two machine guns. In times of combat, they were sturdy muscle, to say the least, capable of delivering devastating punishment. Altogether the tanks were superbly offensive and well-suited for heavy operation, for Peter's purposes though, they were too cumbersome, and not at all practical.

Peter was weighing the future of conventional weaponry when a sleek guided missile caught his peripheral vision distracting his thoughts. For a change, he began dodging people as he steered himself straight for the missile exhibit. The four Redeye Stingers were small. A single infantryman could haul and launch one. These were ground to air missiles. Two surface to surface missiles were positioned nearby. To Peter's marvel, they were just as small and equally as interesting as the Redeyes. Their air speed of four hundred miles per hour totally intrigued Peter, and he envisioned dire consequences if revolutionaries ever acquired access to such formidable tools with the incentive to turn them on anybody they pleased. Certainly there were safety precautions to prevent such atrocities, but Peter knew atrocities didn't need to happen haphazardly. With a helping hand they were often produced. History was a valid teacher.

The bazookas, mortars, and machine guns randomly cluttered the remaining display setups which had been located in scattered sequence. Peter brushed by them hurriedly, as he went for the exit. He was behind schedule. Before long, he'd be attending an affair, a reception in his own behalf. It'd be a crab feast, perhaps the last crab feast of the season. The weather was getting cool, undeniably cool, even to Peter. Environmental conditions were changing. Soon the blue, green crabs would be heeding their instincts and take refuge in the protection of the Chesapeake Bay's silt laden mud.

"Home for Easter, soldier? Sound appealing?" The doctor studied the corporal's medical record before he ordered for additional medication at the bottom of the last entry sheet. "You can be grateful for the reprieve. One out of every seven of you Purple Hearts dies." The disability checks had been paid regularly since then, hundreds of them.

Serial number B280398 was alive. The well part didn't apply. If the mortar had landed a foot closer, the soldier's dead body would have been sewn together, stuffed inside of an aluminum coffin, and sent to the States for burial. Given a choice, the soldier would have preferred that to his ensuing fate. It would have been more dignified, he confided to himself as he sat by the steps at Dumph's Beer Garden. He was in his VA-provided wheelchair. Two stubs, where legs had once been, were making people turn their heads to avoid staring. Sometimes the opposite happened, but not too often. Occasionally, someone might embarrass themselves by gawking. He detested that as much as he did the government. Nam had certainly ruined his life. Now it was up to death to save him from his misery by claiming what was left of his wretched self.

Years ago his goal had been to counter the enemy, not end up like this! Originally, he was comfortable with the idea of basic survival. Why become overly callous towards anyone who'd never done a thing to him, he had frequently asked himself. Loading body bags onto planes changed his perspective though, and with each bag containing a dead GI, his wartime conditioning had improved. Increasingly, he learned to hate. Hate was his motivator. It had let him kill with no qualms or guilt. It supplied him with enough stamina to endure the war and go on existing in civilian life. If hate nourished a faint determination to stay alive, shame became his tormentor. Having lived to remember his dead comrades would shadow his conscience into eternity.

The advisory stage was history when he'd found himself in southeast Asia. At seventeen, he glorified the Marines. He read books and dedicated hours searching for articles pertaining to the Corps. A Marine was what he wanted to be, and he would settle for nothing less.

His mother despised the idea. His father saw him attending college. Upon graduation maybe he'd be accepted into dental school.

The Marines offered him a future, too. Didn't the Marines build men? The recruiters were striking men who stirred his ambitions. Their dynamic presence alone pushed all of his right buttons and gave him the self-assurance he'd need to become "One Of The Proud Few." He was sworn into the military in April of '63. Twenty-seven days later, he was flown to Camp Lajeune for basic training. He was granted leave, marking three months in the Corps, and returned home to visit his parents briefly. A week went by, and his father hugged him at the airport. His mother kissed him goodbye. He flew to Los Angeles, commercial. From there, he boarded a military transport. Two days later, he was in Saigon. At that point, his life began to run parallel with the grotesque.

In 1964, there were fifteen thousand American troops bolstering the South Vietnamese regulars. When Ngo Dinh Diem was assassinated, his government was replaced, and when that one fell, it also was proven expendable for a replacement regime. However, the government of Ho Chi Minh in the north, not only showed itself to be firmly established, but unwieldy with its aggression toward the south.

In August of 1964, it was suspiciously announced that two US destroyers were fired upon in the Gulf of Tonkin. The White House addressed the incident by flexing the biceps of its military muscle. By 1968, the number of US soldiers in South Vietnam exceeded five hundred thousand. The Gulf of Tonkin incident had set the gears in motion for a futile confrontation. Approximately one million South Vietnamese, a minimum of half a million North Vietnamese, and fifty-eight thousand Americans died. An estimated three hundred sixty-five thousand GI's were wounded.

Randomly the vet became obsessive with recollections of less fortunate men. During those intervals, he would nourish his anger, while recalling the captive flyers who were rumored to be laboring, still, in North Viet Nam. The pertinent facts weren't available, but he had seen for himself how the Cong had beheaded and disemboweled villagers. Comrades had been tortured before they were shot. A buddy was cannibalized. Guerrilla warfare was treacherous, and anybody who lasted through those atrocities lost a sizable portion of their humanity. He sacrificed his nine days after the Tet Offensive. That was the morning his legs were left to rot in a rice paddy, somewhere along the Me Kong Delta.

Now he was feeling the pain where his legs had once been, even though it was vacant space. A man passed by him briskly and disappeared into an alley that led to the employee's locker room inside the beer hall. A faint hint of steamed crabs filtered out, stirring the Vet's anguish for want of a taste.

He rolled his wheelchair to a chain fence that was securing a stairwell to the lower floor of the building. The veteran sold his pencils and pins there. That usually kept his mind occupied, and it was certainly better than staying in his three room apartment, cursing the idiot tube.

Among others, a man with a brown hat greeted him politely and leveled a five dollar bill to the veteran's chin. The man ignored the pencils, but took a tie pin with a miniature replica of Old Glory mounted to it. The pins had been selling well this afternoon, and the old fellow seemed delighted with his. When the soldier held out the change to the man, he was already gone. The patron was ascending the steps where he was being motioned inside by a heavy woman, who was wearing a black rubber apron. She was obviously an employee. The vet watched with curiosity, as droves of people filled the vestibule. From there they vanished altogether. Soon, the hall was packed and hummed with the garble of fragmented conversations.

It wasn't long before a mug tossed from the hall shattered onto the sidewalk, alerting the vet to a brawl. Two men rolled to the steps in a flurry of punches. Clearing the bottom step, they tumbled to the walk. Neither man releasing the other from his grip of fury. Miraculously, they fought themselves to a vertical position, only to fall over a wooden bench. Hastily, the vet wheeled back to the steps to avoid the skirmish. He'd quickly found himself behind a third man, who blocked his view. The third man was joined by two more heavies. One of the two was wearing a shoulder harness with a gun. Only briefly did the vet suspect the joiner may have been an off duty policeman. The man made a futile attempt to hide the gun by swinging his forearm inward to conceal his thirty-eight automatic beneath his unbuttoned blazer. Like the man involved in the fight, all three wore navy blue blazers with white shirts, and red ties.

Within the blink of an eye, the odds increased four to one in favor of the blazers. Kicking and slapping him fiercely, the four men drove the loner from the walk, where he quickly found himself dodging hectic traffic. Bleeding and disoriented, the victim limped to the safety of a mini-mart. The victor nursed his cut mouth with a handkerchief, while his comrades darted challenging glares at various bystanders.

To the veteran, it was a light discord. He'd seen cat spats in whorehouses that looked more intimidating, but when the four men approached him, his pulse raced. It wasn't Nam, but then again, he began to wish it was. He had two legs then. Now the option of running had been taken away. After lasting five decades of being handicapped, the truth had never struck him as severely as it did at this time. He was genuinely helpless.

The men surrounded his wheelchair, and two of the strangers gathered his pencils and plastic box of American flag pins from his lap. His heart pounded, as the two largest men lifted his wheelchair waist high. There was a ramp near the steps. The men hoisted the vet above the steps and onto the ramp, from there, to the main hall. The disabled soldier defied his fear by remaining mute. He was afraid, but refused to yell. His dignity was injured enough. When they sat him down, his pencils and tie pins were returned to him.

There were pitchers of beer everywhere, and orange, steamed crabs resembling giant spiders were layered four tiers high over the brims of flat trays. They were brought from behind two swinging double doors that led from a busy scullery. The crabs were delivered to wooden picnic tables covered with folded pages of dated news sections. There, hungry people were cracking the fresh hot shells to gnaw at the juicy white meat that goaded their appetites. Crab mallets continued pounding loudly as a crew of waitresses scurried to fold piles of broken crab shells in wads of brown paper so they could replenish the tables with a fresh supply. The beer garden was jammed full. As he scanned the hall, the vet viewed the chaotic scene with guarded interest.

In contrast to the vigorous atmosphere, there were some customers who appeared sedate. Six of them were sitting at a front table. All but one appeared to be in their forties. The other was on the shorter end of life's stick. He looked a solid sixty-five. This senior puffed leisurely on a pipe and sipped brew from a multicolored stein. He deserved no further attention. The vet then cast a thankful eye to a free beer that was handed him by one of the strangers who had brought him in to the festivities.

The beer was colder than what he had stashed in his refrigerator. When he polished it off, the same man gave him another. Neither of the men attempted to make conversation. It was too noisy, even for introductions. The ex-soldier guzzled a third beer, and was wheeled to the side of a table, where his benefactor had a dozen crabs dumped. A bony lady seated across from him with blonde hair and heavy rouge smiled and poured herself beer from a green tinted picture decorated with ornate designs. Meantime, the vet's newly acquired friends hung close by and watched as the disabled warrior came to life.

At nine-forty, a man sporting a golfer's shirt and wire rim glasses worked his way through the muddle. It was clear that he had something important to say. When he made it to the center aisle, he breezed to the front of the hall, and banged a crab mallet loudly on a tabletop. The speaker became audible as the garble tapered to a menacing drone. He was presenting a crusader. A man, he said, that was renowned by his own possession of common sense. "Malfaxe was in a state of political shambles," he said. "This crusader would unravel ghost leadership, thread by useless thread. He would revitalize a malnourished economy and resurrect criminal discipline." An elderly man then took the floor. The vet could see him better now. He was the senior citizen, the older man at the front table. He was the generous donor who had left his change after buying the tie pin. It grew quiet, extremely quiet. Then the vet watched as an overwhelming current of interest in the old man became apparent. Peter Ghudd removed his beret. When Peter flopped his hat on an empty cart, it was as if a high voltage circuit breaker had been activated. A charge was in order. A charge would be made.

CHAPTER 30

R. Mackey Hall constitutes the bulk of Maritime City College. The college, despite its name, has nothing to do with seafaring, vessels, or marine biology, as one might expect. At one time, it did. In those days, it was simply Maritime College. It was a private school. That was prior to the early nineteen hundreds. Young men who couldn't gain a seat in the Naval Academy often settled for this lesser of the two schools before being granted a commission in the fleet. Maritime college was a highly honorable institution, but it lacked the prestige of Annapolis. Eventually, with the passing of events that dictated a need for more capital, the college became liberal arts oriented. For Maritime College, it was strictly a ploy of survival. The board of regents came to terms with reality and utilized alternative sources of finance to keep the school operating in the black.

With the help of sound business practices, government grants, and minimal private donations, Maritime City College had no trouble remaining lucrative. It consumed five spacious classroom buildings, two dormitories, a gym, cafeteria, and R. Mackey Hall, the five story administration building. A library and bookstore are located there, also. The Hall protrudes skyward with the elegance of the Washington Monument. A notable difference being in the modern silver-tinted glass that encases the Hall's mass. The height of the building, along with the fact that the terrain under the edifice is disproportionately elevated, it was often joked that on a clear day, with a decent set of binoculars, a person could see Nevada from the top floor. It was the top floor where Art Towson was being interviewed by a local news station.

"Mr. Towson," Brenda Stevens, a petite woman reporter asked, "why are you seeking the office of Mayor, since you have tenure at Maritime City College? Bluntly speaking, some people interpret teaching to be a cushy way of life."

"Cushy, no. Rewarding, absolutely! Brenda, I totally cherish my position at the school. I'd hate to leave it. I'll answer your question by posing one of my own, if that's all right."

"Certainly."

"Brenda, do you regard Malfaxe as a progressive, dormant, or regressive town? If your response is not progressive, then you've got to recognize the need for aggressive leadership."

Brenda brushed her sandy bangs aside, as she forged ahead with the interview. "In regard to what specifically?"

"You name it! Public transportation, slum elimination, hospitals, law enforcement. These are but a few of the services either provided or supplemented by the municipal government. If I dared to be kind, I'd say a sick dinosaur has a better prognosis than this town."

"You have a doctorate in political science. Is that correct?"

"For twenty-two years."

"How can that be advantageous in solving urban problems?"

"Brenda, formal training is an asset that I'm proud of. However, it's a tool, not a solution. What's happening here is the result of depressed interest by our city officials. If I myself had earned ten college degrees, I'd still be no match for the job without the proper incentives. I'm prepared to tackle the job as soon as I'm sworn in. Assuming that were the case, my goals are obtainable! In three years you're going to see undeniable changes!"

"Goals?"

"Goals!" Art was quick to emphasize "Our city needs a direction to pursue. I'm committed to urban revitalization. With me it's a passion."

"Starting where?"

"You know where." Art coughed to clear his throat. "Do I have to say it again?" "Emmitt Braedeikk and yourself are strongly opinionated on moving the prison to the city line. Is that at the front of your immediate priorities, as it is his?"

"Yes, it'll be the first obstacle dealt with. I'm sorry for sounding curt a second ago Brenda," Art went on to say, " but we do need to keep in mind that unification coupled with expediency are mandatory factors! It'll be a huge undertaking requiring a magnitude of cooperation by all involved!"

"Does anything separate you from Mr. Braedeikk on this seemingly uncontroversial issue?"

"Emmitt Braedeikk deserves two thumbs up. I'll go one step further, Brenda, and you can plaster this on every billboard in town. I'm totally committed to situating the new penitentiary at the Jameses farm."

"No reservations?"

"None!" Art stiffened his six foot three frame, as he verbalized the cry for a new prison site. While he removed and folded his glasses the camera remained on his gaunt serious expression. It was a nice effect, since Art wasn't the kind to shield himself behind a pair of flimsy spectacles. It wasn't his style.

Brenda avoided asking Art the question she herself wanted to cover. That being Art Towson's opinion about Peter Ghudd's third-party candidacy. She had been given orders to leave it alone. As news appeal, Peter was overhead. Brenda Flashed a smile and probed on in the prearranged direction.

"You anticipate no stumbling blocks for the prison relocation then?"

"As soon as the geological analyses are made known, whoever is elected can advance forward with the appropriate measures."

"Which are?"

"Petition for Federal aid, and start to work. We'll get busy, pronto!"

"Is there any possibility of the Federal government hedging?"

"Do giraffes lay eggs?" Art tittered. "Not likely, the President's crime bill has allotted financing for penal institutions. We've got influential congressmen from three districts, who lobbied hard to get that bill passed. Now, if I'm not mistaken, it's pay back time!"

When Brenda tilted her mindful gaze to an angle, it was accentuated by fluffy, wavy hair and a milky complexion. Her next question appeared spontaneous. "The election is in eight days, and yet most voters are confused. They're commenting that they cannot distinguish between your campaign and Emmitt Braedeikk's."

"There's one major variance, Brenda. Urban renewal is what we're buying into. Emmitt Braedeikk tallies beans. I don't!"

"Will you elaborate?"

"At the debate Wednesday night."

Art Towson's interview had been broadcast on the six o'clock news. As soon as it had ended, Emmitt hit the button on the remote to blacken the screen. He was in the den. Koepy was there, too. He had stopped by to have Emmitt write a check for material. Insulation, and drywall were priced higher than what Emmitt was expecting, but after Art's appraisal of his bean tactics, the banker was too embarrassed to object. Casting the remote onto a pile of magazines, he went to the bar where Koepy was and poured himself an apricot brandy. "Want one?" He asked the contractor, who was waiting patiently.

"Not before eating. It's a rule of mine."

"I'll fix us something to chew on." Emmitt headed for the kitchen.

"More coffee, huh?"

"No. You like roast beef sandwiches?"

"With mayo, salt, and pepper."

"You got it," Emmitt said, opening the refrigerator. "I'll tell you what. You're a builder, assemble your own," he said, withdrawing a platter of assorted sliced meats. He laid it beside a jar of mayonnaise and rye bread that were already on the table.

"Do you feed all of your hired help, or am I building another room?" Koepy bantered, as he smeared his bread with mayonnaise and dabbed on a hearty portion of beef.

"You're easy to get on with," Emmitt said, unscrewing a jar of dill pickles he'd taken from his pantry. "Besides, this house has bunches of rooms. I'll give you a tour in a second. Milk, water, soda?" He asked.

"Same as you."

Emmitt twisted the cap from a bottle of grape soda. Tipping the bottle, he watched cautiously, as the purple bubbles fizzled over two ice-filled glasses. "Why didn't I get a brother like you?" He mumbled.

"Norman doesn't impress me as a bad draw." Koepy tried to lighten the mood.

"He's a snake, Koepy!"

"There are different species of snakes. Some warn you, others blend in with their surroundings, they harm without warning."

"He's conceited, self-serving, and belligerent!"

"Could be he's just rattling you for the sheer pleasure."

"Worthless, that's Norman!" Emmitt crunched a pickle with the dedication of a hungry crocodile.

"No man's worthless," Koepy rendered. "You can only find out who you are by having to deal with other people, good or otherwise. I'd say that gives everybody some degree of value."

"Dealing with 'em and living with 'em aren't the same to me!"

"This house is large." Koepy proceeded to distract Emmitt.

"My father did it. He drew the plans and raised it from the ground."

"The masonry, too?" Koepy asked, taking account of a stone fireplace. The pair of them were walking their sandwiches into the living quarters.

"Yep, he was gifted." Emmitt beamed with pride. "This way," he moseyed into the den, with Koepy close behind. From there, they climbed an oak stairway to a finished attic.

Koepy tapped his heel twice on the tongue and groove flooring. "Nothing like a sound spot to stand on," he said admiringly. "He gave this house some real class!"

"He put three rooms on this floor, Koepy. Two bedrooms and a study." Emmitt led Koepy into the study, where a cherry desk instantly caught the carpenter's eye. The desk was covered with dust. Koepy burnished a tiny portion of the top using the cuff of his shirt sleeve, and saw that it was polished to a brilliant luster.

"It's a shame to hide perfection," he said. "Did your father make this, too?"

"This house and practically every piece of furniture in it, including that desk. Not slouchy for a banker, huh?"

"Praise deserving for a craftsman," Koepy returned, as he sighted the crown molding attached to the ceiling. It, too, was oak.

"We never use this part of the house," Emmitt needlessly revealed.

"It's wasteful. Why did your father do all of this?"

"He'd wished for a larger family. My father had a tremendous heart. I'm sorry he's gone."

"He's around," Koepy insisted. "Your father's here, in every board he cut and every block he layed."

"In that particular sense, I'd have to agree. You care for a nip yet?" Emmitt conveyed boredom, as he patted Koepy's elbow in a gesture for them to leave the upper floor.

They descended the stairs, and Emmitt opened a narrow closet and spun a lazy Susan shelf one quarter of a revolution. Two bottles of whiskey and three of brandy crammed the highest shelf. Emmitt had barely touched a full bottle of apricot brandy when Koepy caused him to stop.

"Save it," Koepy insisted. "I've been meaning to give you a sample of mine. It's my specialty." After disappearing to his truck, he returned with an unlabelled brand.

"Moonshine?"

"'Fraid not. You won't be disappointed though." Koepy poured Emmitt a thrifty ounce of the bright colored liquid into an awaiting snifter, and paused for Emmitt's reaction.

Emmitt sipped the drink, then he swallowed twice the amount. "Boy, it warms your insides!"

"You've struck on its virtue."

Emmitt was happy to offer Koepy an empty snifter, but the contractor waved a refusal. "No thanks," he said.

"What's it called?"

"Wine, dandelion wine."

"Emmitt recalled the conversation he and Koepy were engaged in at the lamp post weeks before. It was then that Koepy compared Norman to a dandelion. "Good can be produced from every existence," Koepy had mentioned.

Possibly, Emmitt conceded to himself, but he would rather Norman dry up and blow away with the rest of the weeds. "You know how to stress a point, don't you?" Emmitt yielded, taking a larger sip.

"It's a genetic talent," Koepy said, breaking for the door. "I'd better cash this check, or I'll miss my chance." He left without further conversation. Emmitt tipped the bottle for a second shot. He pondered on Koepy's variety of talents, do gooder came to mind, before he gladly added wine maker to the list. If he could, Emmitt would have liked to borrow Koepy's magical powers temporarily. They were his favorites. Wednesday night was the scheduled debate, the election was creeping closer, and he was dreading it. He'd love to have the power to make Art Towson vanish.

After Koepy departed, Emmitt doubled over the younger man's trail to the curb. He'd enjoyed Koepy's company nearly to the extent of forgetting he'd arranged to connect with Marian at an out of the way club. It was on the east side of town, a geographical section Emmitt was never thrilled about visiting. Seeing no sign of Marian when he arrived at the reclusive nightclub was hardly a novelty. Being late was a prerogative she adamantly exercised. It seemed that no matter how late Emmitt was, Marian was perpetually later. He walked into the club suspecting to be greeted by a blend of clientele ranging from mangy drug pushers to available guns for hire, but his assumptions had misled him. The people inside were all black, and they were all men, none of which seemed to need to rely on pistols or revolvers. Naturally, Marian was nowhere to be seen, and Emmitt had never felt so alone in all of his born days. He was scared to death. He astounded himself by not backing out of the door though. In retrospect, Emmitt would attribute his impudence to temporary insanity. He sat down at the bar, and in his lowest voice asked for a draft. If Marian had selected this place as a cute stunt, it didn't qualify. He'd surely be smarter the next time.

Emmitt barely drank a third of his drink before a man came over to where he was sitting. The man was powerful and scary looking. His right earlobe was surgically pierced to accommodate a lady's, silver, ring sporting a big hoop. A rolled chain was wrapped across his knuckles. His facial features were blunt, maybe even nefarious from what Emmitt was able to distinguish of them. A sparse beard, along with Emmitt's lack of concentration, was blurring the man's chin. He looked Emmitt up, then down, grinning as he rolled a toothpick from one side of his mouth to the top of his tongue, then to the original location again. He steadied a harsh, sinister fix on Emmitt's rump. It didn't deceive Emmitt for a second. This hairy creature, originally to Emmitt's displeasure, seemed to be seeking a meaningful relationship.

"Colleen says she wanza dance," he spoke, as if daring Emmitt to refuse.

"Colleen?" Emmitt spilled a portion of his beer as he twisted on the barstool trying to get a glimpse of the two hundred and seventy five pound enormous, lady who was snuggled close to a stripper's pole. She was above where the billiards were, on a tiny platform, and wearing a pink tutu with gray tights, and, yes, she was gawking towards Emmitt. Somehow he'd missed her.

"Ah, you're kidding me?"

"No, it's your dance partner," the man answered, inserting a quarter into a sixties replica jukebox. "Are you declinin'?"

"I'm not the best on my feet."

"Ya don't have ta be no Gene Kelly. She'll teach ya. Make certain ya don't step on her toes with your shoes 'cause the last partner got outta step, and she snapped his neck."

"Listen here!"

In less than a second it takes to squeek a sour note on a toy violin, the man was joined by three bar patrons, obviously friends. When the guy pressed two buttons on the jukebox, a fast tune accompanied Emmitt's search for an even faster exit. There was none. The door, he saw, was blocked by a heavy bouncer, and Emmitt had no inclination to question where his loyalties rested either. Emmitt would have settled for the window, and not bothered to open it first, but it was partially obstructed by a potato chip display.

The prospective city executive began to envision himself being tossed savagely about, as scores of sadistic barflies hastened in line to feed the jukebox from a robust supply of coins. He began to untie his shoes with one single thought on his mind. He'd never written a will. Now Norman would inherit the house and the addition he'd been paying Koepy, quite handsomely, to build!"

"He ain't dancin' with Colleen!" Marian rescued Emmitt. She was coming from the lady's restroom, engaging the men with a solemn expression.

"You know this twerp?" The leader with the earring didn't wait for a response. "Where you been Sweetie?"

Marian flouted the man with no reluctance. "Working," which is likely more than I can say for you!"

"Hey, I got a job."

"Doin' what? Harrassin' my chums?"

"We'd a yanked the plug in a song or two."

"I'm obliged to your sensitivity." Marian turned from the obnoxious intruder and addressed Emmitt, "Baby, this is Tyrone. Tyrone, this is my Emmy." Tyrone kept his hand to himself. Emmitt did likewise. The three men with Tyrone dispersed into the shadows of the drab interior, leaving Tyrone to fend for himself.

"How 'bout the skins you owe me, Tye?"

"The check's in the express. I told ya last week, I'm workin', Sweetie. What're ya drinkin'?"

"Pop, the thing is we're leavin', Tye." Marian embraced Emmitt's arm in the crook of her own and whisked him away with no effort whatsoever. They reached Marian's car in a flat minute. Without the smallest desire to avoid a citation, Marian had parked in a "No Parking" zone.

"You take too many liberties," Emmitt cautioned her. "Fines are expensive."

"A tad of risk gives your life extra spice."

"Incidentally, your friends are a scary bunch. I left my fingerprints embedded in the beer glass back there. Thanks for being punctual!"

"Colleen is a prop, a robot, silly. Tye's buddies swiped her from a carnival."

"Yeah, well, Tyrone's a creep who weakened my bladder. Why do you mingle with those type of people?"

Marian, somewhat hurt, remained quiet for a while. She drove eighteen miles to the Severn River, a tributary of the Chesapeake Bay, then returned to the east section of town.

The brief ride had allowed Emmitt to lapse into a rumination of the past. It had been brought on by Tyrone. His demeaning examination of Emmitt had made Emmitt remember the service and 'Nam all over again. It was a place where if he knew what was good for himself, a soldier maintained a low profile. Emmitt, to the end, had tried his best. His tour of duty was within days of expiration. He'd complete his final field maneuver at dawn, so Emmitt, being nervous, had taken two sleeping pills. He succumbed to their power, with the intentions of waking, eating chow, and fading into the protection of the surrounding infantrymen, who were regularly at his front, back, and flank on these dangerous expeditions. It was not to be. During his sleeping hours, somebody with a creative sense of humor had painted Emmitt's fingernails with an elegant red polish. By morning, it was completely dry. Emmitt was sizzling! He stood in ranks, with no option but to await last detail orders and reviewing by his company commander. Then it came. Each and every enlisted man not counting Emmitt, ninety-six to be exact, bit his tongue to avoid laughing out loud. The brass had zeroed right in on Emmitt's splendid nails.

"My, my, Private," the commanding officer declared, "you look unusually ravishing today." His eyes darted to Emmitt's, whose purple blush was trimmed abundantly with liner pencil. In the heat of his frustration, it was a personal upgrade that Emmitt had failed to detect for himself. "Boy, Private, if the Cong getta hold a you in the jungle, this war might very well end on a pleasurable note." Emmitt wanted to bayonet the smart young officer, but he didn't flinch. "You'll be our point man on this detail, Braedeikk! You know what that means. You'll lead the men into the bush. Be alert! If anything arouses your instincts, don't be shy," he gleefully told Emmitt. "Ninety-six crack shooters are there for the sole purpose of bringing up your rear. I'm confident you won't deprive them of any action," the CO chuckled at the mental picture forming in own his mind. "Good luck and happy hunting. Emmitt didn't hear the "good luck" segment, nor did he recall whatever else may have occurred in the field. It was a blank. He did, however, remember the flowers and box of chocolate candy he'd found laying on his bunk when the deployment was finished and the platoon returned to the barracks. Thousands of miles and five decades later had done little to erase the injured pride he'd suffered at the hands of his peers that day. Life went on though, maybe not for the company commander or a significant portion of his platoon he'd left in Viet Nam, but it went on for Emmitt. So tonight he was with Marian and when she swung her Ford into a secluded alley, he knew he'd better damn sure well get his thoughts back to where they belonged.

CHAPTER 31

In the midst of the twilight, Emmitt parked his car at a secluded grove and proceeded to lumber undetected around the Jameses barnyard. A light was flickering in the reverend's house. Marian had lit a candle in the kitchen. It was her signal to Emmitt that her father was either asleep or gone on an errand. On previous occasions Emmitt welcomed the invitation, but tonight he didn't know if he'd take advantage of Lester's absence.

He was heading for the lake. The air was heavy with the smell of dead vegetation giving fair notice of autumn's departure and winter's forthcoming assault. The Farmer's Almanac was predicting a dreadful four months, accompanied by stabbing winds and mounds of snow.

Emmitt's progress was sluggish. He wove awkwardly through the underbrush, as he did, he imagined himself to be a giant Kodiak without a care or worry. At this point, he would have traded his retirement to be able to crawl inside of a cave and hibernate. When the spring reawakened him, he'd eat berries and catch salmon. If he became angry, like he was now, he'd roar. Tonight he was angry, and he wanted to roar loud enough to vibrate the bark free from the sycamores that were flourishing by the lake. Emmitt was all but there. He pushed on, until he was at the lake's edge. Then he arched his spine against one of the sycamore's broad trunks and waited. Paper, twigs, and an osprey feather floated beneath his gaze. He wasn't aware of them. His mind was troubled. Emmitt only saw the water. Clearwater Lake had become part of Emmitt's political sea. A sea in which Emmitt was unable to even tread the water.

The debate with Art Towson had been scheduled two months in advance. There was no chance of a cancellation. Emmitt's challenge was well defined. Art was confidant, aggressive, and suave. In short, he was nobody's chump. Emmitt dared not underestimate Art's charisma in the least. The outcome would be mortifying. It would be difficult, but somehow Emmitt would have to conceal his fear and attack Art on any front available. Art was an intelligent man. It was going to be a tough sixty minutes.

According to the polls, Art was in the dominant position, with approximately fifty two percent of the electorate in his corner. Emmitt had forty four percent. The remaining four percent were undecided, or Ghudd people, as the press had labeled them. To Emmitt, the Ghudd people were the blind fools. They'd rather waste a ballot on a protest vote for Peter, knowing full well they'd be better rewarded by staying home and taking in a bad soap opera.

Ten minutes passed. Five more ticked away. Emmitt's soles gradually seeped into the mire beneath his meek weight. His gut told him to leave. Peter Ghudd was riff raff, a buffoon. Any collaboration with him would only serve to reduce Emmitt's own personal self-esteem. He was about to leave, but he'd convinced himself a tad late.

Emmitt's pulse quickened with the movement in a thicket. From the secluded trail, dieing foliage was spreading as a man's form emerged from a clump of young white birch. Peter Ghudd ducked an obstructing willow branch that towered above them. He sprang upright to confront his former employer.

"You're tardy," Emmitt informed him.

"My bowels don't move with your imaginary whistle," Peter quipped.

"As Mayor, Peter, you'll have to be more punctual."

"Kind of premature for a concession speech, ain't it?"

"Peter, I thought we were taking pains to keep out of one another's hair.

Wasn't that our arrangement?"

"It was," Peter emphasized the past tense. "We had a truce, as I remember."

"Peter, I've kept my end of the bargain."

"Three stars for you, Emmitt, but the truce is off."

"Why?"

"Number one, we have a debate to attend."

"Number two?"

"Number two is that I have more on you than you have on me." Peter balked temporarily to engage the stirring mist sweeping in from the lake. He didn't mind the raw, penetrating air. It aided in chilling his lack of sensitivity.

"Mister you're bluffing. You need a reality check." Emmitt joined Peter in the view of the restless body of water. His poise was shaken. "Your ship sailed years ago, Peter. You scuttled it!"

Peter withdrew his pipe and packed it was tobacco from a worn leather pouch. Each man is his own captain.," he said. "and every new tide carries another ship."

"You'll sink us both!"

"I'm on a salvage journey," Peter said, as if any kind of remorse were unthinkable. If this ship lost I'll commandeer another one."

"I won't, metaphorically, or otherwise!" Emmitt exerted." I can't!"

"You sound uninformed." Peter lit his pipe. "If you're leveling with me, you're gonna get hurt."

Emmitt's emotions overcame him. The veins in his neck enlarged and a flash of rage betrayed his poor facade of self-assurance. "Peter," he yelled, "your intervention is costing me the election! Why don't you drop out?"

"I want my turn," Peter hurled back. "It's my destiny. It's unavoidable, now that I'm this far."

"Why, Peter? How have I brought this on myself?" Emmitt regained his composure. "Was I that much of a louse?"

"Not totally."

Emmitt was caught off balance, not to mention shocked. "When wasn't I?"

"Well, let me think," Peter said, allowing himself the luxury of a brief lapse. "The morning after that lame party that you indulged in. You dirtied your hands, by helping me with the trash. That was the day I almost connected with you. You didn't whimper once."

"You mean, because I dragged a few pieces of trash to the street, that made you like me?"

"Did I say like? How's your hearing? You took care of more than your share of the trash that day. Your brother, for instance. Most men would've left him in jail and been happy if he died there."

"He's my brother, Peter!"

"He's unflushed sewage!" Peter bit a tiny dent into the tube of his pipe. His ill mood receded only when Emmitt made no objection to his slanderous remarks about Norman. "Excuse me," he said, not very convincingly. "I'm rambling. You'd wanted to bury the ax, not grind it."

"Peter, if you pull out, I'll be able to nab crucial votes that I won't receive otherwise. If I'm elected, I'll appoint you to a full time janitorial job with the city. Forty hours a week, with unlimited overtime. A bird in the hand is better than none in the bush, Peter."

"It's a tempting bribe," Peter said sarcastically, "but, for all I care, you can keep your bird in your slick hand where it belongs!"

"You're a beaten drifter!" Emmitt strained his vocal chords, as Peter began fading into the woods. There was no response. At last their relationship, whatever it was, had ended. Emmitt was alone. He trembled with exasperation. To him, Peter was an enervated spoiler, who dared to force himself into his, Emmitt's, election campaign. Peter had the knack of inciting mass attention, whether it be good or bad, enough of the former would result in lost votes for Emmitt. The numbers were small, but to Emmitt, they were critical. In order to upset the polls, it would require Emmitt to lock onto every vote that Peter was courting and then some. Emmitt's peace conference with Peter had gotten off to a horrible start, and due to Emmitt's inferior tact, it had come to an abrupt finish. He likened Peter to an inept yodeler in a New York opera. Emmitt was upset with himself for bringing the encounter on. Peter had made just one stipulation, that being they meet at the lake. The Jameses farm was on equal turf, and Emmitt's delayed insight told him that Peter, from the onset, had no inclination to make any concessions. The original strategy had to prevail. Emmitt needed to dismiss Peter's existence one hundred percent. His logic would be centered on taking the offensive and refuting Art Towson's liberal reasoning at the debate. In the heat of it all, Peter could stand by and rot!

As he fringed the lake, Emmitt's anger tore at his insides. He didn't notice the beads of vapor on his unprotected skin. His gloves were pushed into his coat pockets. He left them there. Emmitt was detached and unmindful of the cold when he found himself at a familiar clearing in the woods. It was the exact location where he and Marian had cycled to in mid-summer. He was reminded of how he'd presented her with a flimsy job offer also, and she'd thumbed her nose at his reckless effort of chivalry by abandoning him and leaving him to the mercy of his scrawny legs. Emmitt was bewildered by the plain truth. He'd learned little since that incident. He trudged toward the Jameses farmhouse, gauging his own absence of empathy. He concluded to himself that it was significant.

To the north, a hound bayed. It was quiet. It barked. Lester's dog was alerted. Emmitt visualized Marian feeding it scraps from the table. With Marian, it was a ritual that she carried out each night. Emmitt knew this because he had been there to see her on three instances, when the reverend wasn't home. He pictured the dog snuggling close to her as she entered the pen. Emmitt quickened his gait. He forged a hill littered with dry corn stalks. His view was hindered by the density of the stalks. He shortened the range, and she was there. A harvest moon gave sight to her curvaceous silhouette. Her motions were playful. The dog lapped at his food, hooked around, and pounced up to paw at her. Marian surrendered a hug. She patted the dog's fur, and the dog, content that she was nearby, sprang for the pan of food again. Then Emmitt descended the hill as an oncoming threat, who prompted the hound to set his fangs in a vicious growl.

"Where've you been?" Marian asked, once she recovered from the initial jolt of seeing Emmitt. She exited the cage and pecked Emmitt on the side of his ruddy cheek.

"Nowhere, actually." He answered. "Is your father home?"

"No, he'll be busy 'til eleven," Marian seductively enlightened him. She embraced him and pulled him into her warmth. "You're frigid," she said.

Emmitt coaxed her affection on with a gentle kiss. "It'll pass," he said, and it did.

CHAPTER 32

Malfaxe Senior High School was erected in nineteen thirty-nine. It was occupied fifteen months before the Japanese bombed Pearl Harbor. Originally, the school was meant to educate eight hundred students, sophomores, juniors, and seniors combined. World War Two ended in forty-five. By fifty-nine, Malfaxe Senior High began acquiring the ripple effects of an American victory. When the GIs had been returned stateside, their offspring became the baby boomers. The school was forced into an expansion program that lasted three years. By nineteen sixty-two, it had increased in size by one third. The five floors included thirty-six classrooms, a cafeteria, an auditorium, and an office. Each level had one girl's and one boy's lavatory. There was a lower basement with a boy's restroom. Except for an occasional drug deal, it usually remained forgotten.

Peter Ghudd was primping in front of a row of filthy porcelain sinks. He wasn't offended by their grimy condition. Peter was too busy evaluating his own appearance. A long rectangular mirror was on the wall over the sinks, and Peter used a paper to remove the smudge marks that were blurring his reflection. He opened his shaving kit and retrieved talc, deodorant, mascara, and a plastic bag of facial makeup, all of which he'd bought on sale. He was bare from his belt line to his hairline. He'd laid his suit coat, shirt, and tie neatly on top of a radiator. At eight o-clock, he would have to be dressed and looking sharp. The debate was to be televised locally. The old man wanted to project the best image possible. He was filling the make up into the crevices ingrained in the corners of his mouth and eyes, when the lavatory door squeaked open. It was Emmitt. The two men traded glares.

"What do ya want?" Peter went back to the mirror.

"I want to know something."

"Whiz it by me fast. I go on in ten minutes." Peter smoothed the powder on his cheek. Then he swiped more on the opposite side and began patting it vigorously.

"Tuesday at the lake. You said something about having more on me than I had on you."

"It's haunting you?"

"I've heard the wind before, Peter."

"You're in for a twister!

"You do hate me, don't you?

"No. This is strictly politics, fella, but when the dust clears, you're gonna know you've been through a storm.

The sound of accumulating people began to penetrate the basement. It was a droning noise that Emmitt could hear getting louder by the second. He was scared to death, and he was aware the fact wasn't lost on Peter. Emmitt left abruptly. He dashed for the corridor beyond the door. From there, he made the steps to the wing of the auditorium stage. Art Towson was already there. The television camera crew was in place. A female moderator sat on a chair off the stage in front of the three podiums to be occupied by the candidates.

The auditorium was packed, and Emmitt saw people barging through the side entrance to cram the aisles. The moderator cued for Emmitt and Art to position themselves at their podiums. Emmitt went blank from fear. Eventually, he found himself next to Art on the stage, where he was assigned the podium to the right side of Art. Peter would be to the left.

As usual, Art was composed, and, if anything, he was basking in the attention that engulfed his presence. Emmitt was frantic. He hoped the valium would kick in to get him through the hour. Then it happened in a flash. It was simultaneous with Peter's arrival. Peter was the key to his confidence. He was a nobody strolling into view with the casual grace of a stray mongrel. Emmitt felt ready. If Peter could stand in front of hundreds of thousands of people making a spectacle of himself, Emmitt saw himself as doing extremely well. Using Peter's incompetence as a crutch was going to be Emmitt's miracle remedy.

They were on the air. The moderator, Cindy Trupp, introduced Emmitt as Mister Emmitt A. Braedeikk, the successful businessman and bank manager. She introduced Arthur C. Towson, as a professor of Political Science at Maritime City College. It was stated that, although his credentials were basically academic, his knowledge of local and city government was renowned. At last, the camera zoomed in on Peter. His credentials were ignored, because he had none. It wasn't publicized that his education went no further than the sixth grade. Peter's life was an enigma, tainted with unplugged gaps and missing pieces. In the private sector, it was clear that Peter had come up short, and because of this, Cindy Trupp secretly viewed him as a rogue. She paused and then presented Mister Peter B. Ghudd.

Live coverage of the debate began. Cindy ran through the format. There would be a question, the same question posed to each candidate. He was to take no more than three minutes to answer the question. After every candidate gave his answer, there would be a two minute rebuttal by the candidates. The initial question landed on Emmitt first.

"In your opinion, Mister Braedeikk, what is the most serious crisis facing our city today, and how would you correct it?"

Emmitt steadied himself. "That's easy, Cindy. Our city is crumbling. Buildings are falling apart. Roads need to be repaired. Businesses are leaving, and our tax base is declining. We've got to manage our money in such a way as to benefit from it as lucratively as we can. Urban renewal has been my theme for a long time. We're going to petition the federal government for aid, but that won't pay the whole tab. We've got to lower taxes on businesses, making it attractive for them to operate here. Cindy, we've been starving the goose that lays the golden eggs!"

"Mister Towson?"

"What Emmitt Braedeikk said is true. What he proposes, though, requires detailed negotiations. It's difficult to reduce taxes in a city that's in dire need of revitalization, without cutting municipal jobs and services. Lowering taxes on businesses and corporations is justifiable, if it's done within a favorable time scale. I'm formulating a plan to reduce taxes over a thirty-five-year period and will simultaneously target and invite certain types of businesses, along with manufacturing, into the city. All companies accepting the terms of agreement will be guaranteed a tax break through the year two thousand fifty.

"Mr. Ghudd?"

When his name was mentioned, Peter was leaning over to scratch the itch on his ankle. When asked what he considered the most urgent problem plaguing Malfaxe was, Peter astounded everybody. He attacked the cold weather. When sardonically asked what he would do for relief, he replied that he honestly didn't know. He'd love to move south, and, if he lost the election, it might happen.

On rebuttal, Emmitt stated he could reduce taxes effectively in a fifteen-year period. Art accused Emmitt of fantasizing. Peter yawned.

The moderator asked, if a sports arena were built, how would it be paid for?

Art said he would buy a major league baseball team. Emmitt asserted that a football team would be necessary, too. Peter said he liked baseball and football. He'd have to think seriously about voting for Emmitt.

The subject of a streetcar museum was dealt with. The cars had been stashed in an abandoned bus garage. Art wanted to renovate a vacant can factory and exhibit all of the city's valued antiques there with the streetcars. He said it would take him two years. Emmitt said he'd hire a work crew and get the job done faster. Peter returned to scratching his ankle.

The next issue was over the inferior conditions of the roads. Emmitt blasted the previous mayors, saying they were horse and buggy minded. He wanted the roads repaved, new signs erected, and the number of traffic lights increased. Art insisted on the same and called for updated crosswalks. Peter appeared as though he might be withering under the warm overhead lights. When his input was requested, he waved the question off, and so it went on, and on, and on.

The final question was posed, none to soon for the audience. It had been a boring display of sorry wit, and, due to his silly answers, Peter had seemed set on transforming the debate into a fun poking event. There would be extra time left in the allotted hour. Therefore, a lengthy commentary would have to be inserted to cover the space. Cindy leered at Peter with profound contempt. She'd learned that dealing with the prankster in an earnest manner had been at the expense of her own dignity. He'd altered what should have been a sophisticated encounter between three serious candidates into a total disaster. The old man was a flake, and she wanted to scream obscenities in his face. She would have too, but her common sense intervened. She grudgingly continued.

"I believe we are at what is the greatest concern to the city's residents. We have a prison that is not capable of restraining convicts. Its walls are three feet thick and ten yards tall. Guard strength is formidable. They monitor cells, work areas, and the prison in its entirety. One would be inclined to assume that our residents are being protected from the inmates, but that's not the case. Instead, prisoners are freeing themselves at an alarming rate, and they're right at our doorsteps. The truth, gentlemen, is that something has to be done! It can't wait! A museum can wait. A sports arena isn't an urgent priority. Citizen welfare and peace of mind are essential, and our city leadership has to address the problem now! When can you move the prison, and what will it be like? Mr. Braedeikk?"

Art was unconsciously thumbing a button on his vest. Emmitt wondered how smooth Art's response was going to be. No matter what he said, Emmitt was sure that Art's delivery would be clever. Then his eyes met Peter's blank gaze. He agonized over Peter's entrance into race, wondering whether it had been a sheer hoax or a remarkable ploy of genius by phantom interest. "Give me twenty-two months. The prison will be transferred to the city limits," Emmitt insisted. "Construction at the Jameses's site will begin no later than May. That'll give city officials adequate time to secure and register the documents pertaining to the purchase and division of the property. As everybody knows, the new location is far removed from the major population." Emmitt's confidence increased, and his voice was gaining range to enhance his dialogue. The audience was attentive. A cough couldn't be heard. They were buying into his promise. Emmitt was slinging pure, undiluted horse dung. Nevertheless, he believed his dung to have class, and, because the audience was unified in a defensive mode, he could hardly wait to sling a bigger load. "What will the prison be like, you ask? A fortress! It will have three foot-thick walls, forty-two feet high. Clearwater Lake will border on one side of the penitentiary. There will be four guard towers, one at each corner of the prison. The likeliest way an inmate will ever leave that place, without authorization, is going to be on a slab!"

"The interior of the prison will be a credit to penal installations of the past. Each inmate will occupy a single cell. To be honest, I don't know the size of the compartments. Keeping in mind that a highly secure prison is our objective, we have to assume that the smaller the cell the closer the inmates can be scrutinized. The cells will be either six by eight or possibly eight by ten feet. If elected, I'll encourage the smaller confines. That makes a difference of thirty-two square feet per inmate. If you multiply it by one thousand, we're at an extra thirty-two thousand square feet. What does this mean? It means," Emmitt cleared the dryness from his throat with water given to him by an aide. He had no trouble taking up where he'd left off. "It means more footage for essentials. A commissary, cafeteria, a prison yard, and a medical facility have to be considered. Prisoners need a place to work. The drawings I prefer show a miniature industrial complex. Jobs can be learned and practiced there. It'll be a threshold for integration into the community. Suttler Penetentiary is little more than a dungeon. It oughta be condemned!" Emmitt searched the audience for expressions of approval, a subtle gesture of any kind. There was none.

"Mister Towson?"

Art's body language contrasted with what Emmitt had stated. He went to the side of the podium with his hands on his hips, and daunting an air of authority. Emmitt feared the worst. He knew Art would make a strong case for whatever it was that he was about to lay on the public.

"Apparently," Art began, "Mister Braedeikk and myself have been reviewing different drawings. Six by eight cells won't be sufficient. He knows that!" Art accused. "What he doesn't know is the reason why. If he did, I still don't believe he'd understand. You see, studies have shown there's definite proximity's between human beings living close together and violent behavior. Are we to extinguish violence in people by forcing them into an environment that promotes the very same? I think not! Yes," Art admonished, as though he himself weren't being taken in by his own philosophy, "these people are dangerous, at least a fraction of them are. Separating them from society is mandatory." Art was completely solemn now, and he besieged Emmitt with a glance of recrimination.

"Many of these people have succumbed to criminal behavior through no conscious, personal desire. To use an old analogy from the Bible, if a seed is sewn in non-fertile soil, how can it develop properly? No! What has to transpire is for that seed to be replanted and cultivated in order for it to mature. It's never too late to modify criminal behavior. We've a responsibility to the inmates, which will ultimately enrich social welfare! The drawings I'll recommend show a seven story prison with eight by ten cells. A library will occupy the sixth floor, along with a computer classroom. The seventh floor is optional, however, for the sake of venting suppressed hostility, the inmates should have a gym there. College and vocational training will be taught, also. The latter will be done at a miniature industrial complex. Yes, my ears are buzzing already. Too many of you will protest that these resources I've mentioned are luxuries! Think about this. Our prisons are not rehabilitating. When we lock someone away in the age old clink, we're just prolonging the dire effects of a faulty system! Rehabilitation isn't a snap by any means, but, if we can plant the right seeds in the correct environment, our city will profit! Thank you.

"Mr. Ghudd?"

Peter rendered no opposition. He appeared weary. His lax posture was a sign of severe fatigue. It was an embarrassing scene for everyone to witness, for Peter mimicked the epitome of a ravaged man. Never before had any local politician given such a poor account of himself.

On rebuttal, Emmitt attacked the computer room, calling it frivolous overhead. He said a library was a lavish expense. He labeled education as a privilege and pointed out that convicts would fare better if they were indoctrinated with a healthy work ethic. Productive tasks, that was Emmitt's resolve, and, to Art's dismay, Emmitt accused him of "wanting to cuddle convicts, as if they were lost sheep instead of the town's unfair burden".

Art came back in a flash. He blasted Emmitt for lacking imagination and foresight. "Emmitt Braedeikk," Art said, was "penny smart and dollar dumb." The advantages to educating prisoners far outweighed the repercussions of isolating them in a condensed element of criminal consciousness. Art was glib, and his rhetoric seemed to possess a depth that deemed Emmitt as shallow. As their closing statements became a heated squabble, Emmitt was beginning to squirm.

"Mr. Ghudd?" The moderator moved to Peter in an apparent exercise of uselessness. Peter's face was half visible. He'd been propping it on his open hand, which was spanning his forehead. To everyone's amazement, Peter came to life. He straightened, then walked to the most outer edge of the stage. Another step and he might have fallen into the lap of Cindy Trupp. It was quiet, quiet enough that a cricket could be heard chirping beyond the auditorium's exit corridor. It was as if the ignorant little creature were ushering in Peter's revival, for the pathetic little misfit wasn't dying after all!

When the television camera encompassed Peter's entire length, the trim, blue suit he wore screened as being tasteful. It had been tailor made only three days earlier, and he'd matched it to an off, white shirt and a crimson tie. Peter's shoes shined like black lacquer, and they caused the floor to creak as he ambled in Art Towson's direction. Since he was about to resurrect the rationale of every prospective voter within earshot, Peter seemed to be spilling over with confidence. "I'm jealous," Peter said unemotionally, as he lashed a piercing stare first at Art, and then at Emmitt. Peter then engaged the camera. "Forgive me," he went on. "I'm not as well spoken as my opponents. I don't have their talent for political gab. If I'd known that all I had to do to get a formal education was commit a crime, I'd have done it years ago! I like the idea of individual quarters, too. When most men are in the Navy serving their country, they sleep in a cramped bunk. Think about it, twenty sailors in a sleeping compartment which, by the way, isn't much larger than many people's bedrooms."

Peter shook his head sideways with disgust, as his words brought no pleasure to Emmitt's ears and less to Art's. "It's awfully nice, the way politicians take care of convicts these days. What's the word you used," Peter asked Art, "proximities? Military men must not be aware of proximity's. If they were. it wouldn't matter none. They're much too exhausted from a hard day's work to bicker, let alone fight out of sheer boredom or because they hav'ta share their lodging. No, I don't have your finesse with the English language, Art. Just common sense."

"Thank you, Mr. Ghudd."

"Thank you for not interrupting," Peter snubbed the moderator. "When's society gonna avenge this foolishness? That's what I wanna know!" Peter retrieved articles that he'd brought along and left at his podium. He read the initial caption. "'Man Shoots Neighbor Over Parking Space', 'Grandmother Mugged and Raped', here's one, 'Teen Gang Wars Erupt in City'. I guess everyone's read one of these by now," he said, "'Dead Fetus Found in Restaurant Wash Room Some Body Parts Missing.' How 'bout this," Peter said, his voice gaining magnitude, "'Robbers Kill Store Clerk, Take Six Dollars.' It's more than a minor nuisance, and this is not the national news, folks! It's in our city, and it's lurking right outside those doors there, waiting for us, and the law of averages says that some of you stand to be victimized before you even get home tonight. Oh, I forgot this beauty," Peter held the last article high in the air for the audience and viewers to see. He read the caption slowly to emphasize each word. "Convict Sues City and Officer's Estate for Reckless Capture.' Technically speaking, Sam Rhiggs's last victim was a sixteen year old boy. Before that," Peter cried out, "he'd been incarcerated for other killings. The truth is, Lieutenant Barnes died as much from scholarly taught lunacy as he did from a self-inflicted bullet through the brain. So what do we do with scum like Sam Rhiggs? We award him with a fancy psychological profile, and send him to the city prison again, which happens to be not such a bad place!"

"Mr. Ghudd, your time's up and..."

"You owe me time," Peter cut in. "I'm gonna finish!" His face tightened, and his flesh became vivid. Peter wouldn't relinquish the floor.

"Too many of our legislators and educated people think prison should be lenient. They'd like us to feel as though we're the criminals for making prison tough." Peter was ripping into Art's territory, and he drew a sharp response.

"Are you a mind reader, Mr. Ghudd?" Art asked.

"Could be," Peter returned, from the side of his mouth, showing no inclination to stall.

"All right, Mr. Ghudd, what am I thinking?" Art pressured him.

"You're thinking you'd make a better Mayor than me. Isn't that right?" Peter smiled.

Art had been snared in the same kind of trap he'd set for Peter. However, he realized too late that his jaws, unlike the jaws of Peter's trap, were a notch loose. He tightened them. "Maybe," was all he said.

"No maybe to it!" Peter corrected him. "You're wrong though. Your whole concept of reformation is stupid!" Peter screamed. There was a positive reaction from the audience. It was brief and Peter blazed on.

"Sam Rhiggs is a monster, but what do we do with him? We furnish him with decent food and shelter. He's got a clean, dry cell with a fluffy pillow to lay his nasty head on at lights out time! When his cell becomes a hair cramped, we worry about abusing this poor, misunderstood victim of society. "He needs more room we say." It doesn't matter how many people the guy's killed, we have to make sure Sam stays comfortable! In prison, he gets taken care of!" Peter's anger was overflowing, and his words went through the auditorium like steam from a boiling cauldron. "I sure hope Sam's getting along well!" He roared.

"How 'bout the gym Isn't that a winner of an idea? We want these cons to be nice and strong. That way, they won't have any trouble molesting us when they're released. Right, Art?"

"How much does an education cost?" Peter began pacing the stage. "How many of you people have paid for your kids' college education lately? What did you sacrifice for it?" The silence was intense, as Art feared the inevitable. Emmitt himself was filled with bewilderment. Peter, the restroom commandant and the impossible candidate, was captivating the audience with the exact skills that he had just moments earlier denied possessing.

"Does it flatter you to have your tax dollars spent to give a trade or college education to a criminal? Educate them for what?" Peter squared off with Art. "So they can be released early by a wimpy parole board and take a job away from some poor person who's been struggling all his life. Where's the logic? Where's the justice, folks?"

A large man with a prosthesis was in the middle of the audience. He rose awkwardly and clapped. He was joined by an enthusiastic applause. Peter surged on.

"We've been duped, friends, by the so called humanitarians, the professionals, the sellout politicians. They've got fancy names and labels for people who hurt other people out of meanness. They've made it difficult for us to sort through the falsehoods of a collapsing society and trample down the bad guys. Well, I may not be book wise or have their way with words. My instincts are guided by the basics of survival though. Even the animal kingdom has codes to exist by. Many of the lowest forms of life have laws that dictate their behavior. If the laws aren't obeyed, the offender is dealt with quickly, and harshly. There are few reoccurrences! What do we do?" Peter's tempo was escalating, as Emmitt remained petrified. He and Art were witnessing a new, strange Peter. A Peter with charisma, who was operating on a different level. A level of logic that both Art and Emmitt had neglected to entertain.

"What is it we do?" Peter asked for a second time. "We send cruel, heartless devils to campus type prisons! We pamper them. We give 'em food, clothes, medicine, and legal representation. They get days off! They get their time reduced. Why they'd want their sentences cut is a mystery to me! Is jail really a deterrent, folks? If it is, why do we have so many criminals in this country? Why do we have repeat offenders? Are the animals smarter than us, or is it just the human breed of animal who has us baffled?"

"Mister Ghudd."

Peter was oblivious to the moderator. He brought his fist equal to his face and clenched his teeth. When his fingers straightened, his anger was skyrocketing.

"Prison, my friends, what is it? It's nothing more than a kindergarten for mean spirited, destructive bums, who won't get with the program, and don't intend to! Art Towson and Emmitt Braedeikk are right! We do need a new prison. Our visions are different though. The prison of the future ought to be a hell hole that gets the point across." Peter paused to dab a handkerchief on his brow. When he stuffed the cloth into a deep pocket of his dress trousers, front row listeners heard his bus tokens meshing. To Emmitt, the following quiet was as nerve retching as an interval between thunder booms.

"No more 'Babes in Joyland! That's my platform!" Peter rebounded. "When the judge tells somebody they're going to jail, they should have tears in their eyes. They'll want to get down on their sorry knees and beg for leniency. They'll be willing to do anything if the judge won't... send... them...to...JAIL! That's the kind of prison we have to build! Let's make the big house a rotten scene." Peter erupted again over an enthusiastic applause, "Convicts should be computing their minutes in the penitentiary, not their benefits!"

People, men and women, were leaving their seats to shake his hand. Peter requested that they be calm and allow him to finish. "Don't be taken in by Emmitt Braedeikk or Art Towson," he continued. "They'd like to build a new prison with all those fancy extras. The truth is, they can't! The land for the prison is similar to them. It has no integrity! It's on a king sized shoal, a ledge, folks. It rest on top of a gigantic, water filled, cavern, and it can't take on the weight of the job!"

"The tests aren't conclusive!" Emmitt interjected.

"They are conclusive. The data is in. You're prolonging the truth!" Peter yelled. "Art is too!"

Art folded his arms. "You're crazy!" He grumped.

"No, you're crazy!" Peter went into a rage. "What makes you think convicts are so special?" And, if you want to quote the Bible, here's one for ya. You can wash a swine, but it'll always go back and wallow in the mud."

The entire auditorium became an explosion of chants for Peter. Emmitt was disoriented. He wanted to shrink into total obscurity. The election was lost, and he'd be glad if nobody ever remembered who he was, or what he'd apparently tried to sneak past the voters.

As for the old meddler, politically speaking, he'd proven to be quite a handful for Emmitt and a crowd pleaser to boot. At last the community viewed him as a standup member who'd come just in the nick of time to establish himself as a serious frontrunner. So if it was accurate to report that by nine PM on Wednesday, Emmitt had gone down from the strain of the massive outbursts. It was equally true that it was Art Towson who had been mercilessly creamed.

CHAPTER 33

Whipped! You're image is somewhat tarnished, Emmitt! Whipped is nonsense!"

"Cut the fanfare, Bert. Will ya? You're insulting what's left of my dignity, pal. I oughta deserve a little more respect, but I guess I don't." Emmitt's plea trickled into the festering of a vulnerable friendship, one that had consumed half of his lifetime. It was eleven o'clock on Thursday morning. The polls would open at noon. The two of them were in Bert's parsonage, the study to be exact. Bert was leaning against a bookshelf. He raised a delicate china cup to his mouth, sipped the tea, and gave Emmitt a toast.

"To the future Mayor!"

"I'm not listening to any more of this gibberish, Bert! Save your hurrahs for Peter Ghudd." Emmitt was set to walk. He was still licking the agonizing wounds inflicted from Wednesday's disastrous exchange. Knowing that he, himself, was nothing less than a liar, Bert was now telling him he'd be the big cheese in City Hall. Emmitt knew that the entire concept wasn't a novelty. In today's world, politicians were often elected on their ability to lie ,and sometimes miraculously recover. Nonetheless, reassurances from Bert about his being elected were degrading to his common sense.

"Wait, Emmitt," Bert said, inducing him to prolong his departure. Bert chipped his cup when he brought it higher to meet the book shelf. "Peter Ghudd's pulling out!"

"I've also been told that bulls sprout utters!"

"No, it's true. Tune into the news. You'll see! He's agreed to quit!"

"Agreed to who, Bert?"

"Who, Emmitt? Who requires no explaining." Emmitt was stunned by Bert's brashness. When Bert saw Emmitt was speechless, he resumed. "As soon as you leave here, go straight home. You'll be interviewed, Emmitt. Don't blow it!"

"What do you mean, Bert? Have you been in orbit for the last two days? I have blown it!"

"I mean it. You're to endorse every syllable that Peter Ghudd's ever pronounced, especially everything he's said in reference to the penal system. Be sure you sanctify it with endless blessings. You'll be elected, Emmitt!"

"What about Art?"

"What about him? He's too ultra-liberal for the voters. We can't waste precious energy trying to save his bacon."

Emmitt wondered if his ears were betraying him. "That's not why I asked, Bert. Why'd you think I'd expect you to throw Art a lifeline?"

"Art was high in the polls. I'd of said he was the man until the debate."

Emmitt was graduating to cranky. "Why'd you run me, Bert? I'm not a politician."

"Why not?" Bert returned apathetically. "You...Art, either one's as helpful as the other." Bert retrieved a book that was laying on top of the television and placed it on the shelf next to the chipped cup.

"Helpful," Emmitt's guts were churning. If what Bert had insinuated was true, then he, Emmitt, would have to know where he'd stood all along. A flash of insight entered his mind. "Art and I were sponsored by mutual people, weren't we?" Emmitt's lips quivered. "The tacky strings always lead back to the same puppeteers, don't they?"

"This isn't national politics, Emmitt! Whoever's elected is irrelevant. Basically the programs are chiseled in stone. They don't change, not for you or Art, and certainly not for a coincidental joke like Peter Ghudd!"

"He's no joke anymore!" Emmitt was quick to respond.

"He's done. If it hadn't been for Sam Rhiggs escaping, Peter Ghudd wouldn't of had half the steam coming out of that old engine of his." Bert was getting steamed himself. "You might as well know something, Emmitt. Sam's escape was a blunder. The two men he rode out with that day were allowed to get loose. It was supposed to add to the prison's already fallible reputation. Sam just happened by when he shouldn't have. Now it doesn't matter. The puppeteers, as you call them, have decided on a new place for their high rise. Suttler Penitentiary can stay until it crumbles or the next three millenniums pass, whichever comes first."

"It doesn't matter, Bert," Emmitt angrily repeated Bert's sentiments. "It doesn't matter that two people, a sixteen year old kid and a policeman, died for a stupid building that became obsolete on a whim?"

"The people mattered, Emmitt. God knows that some of us will take them to our graves and further."

"God, if there is a God, Bert, and I rather doubt it, certainly has strange advocates!"

"Watch your slurs, Emmitt. The Lord's always been my inspiration."

"Malfaxe has an inspiration too, Bert. His name is Peter Ghudd. People can see and touch him. He talks out loud, Bert. He tells them logical things they understand. If you want a practical, modern day God, Bert, catch Peter's sermons! He's on the proverbial mount, and he's preaching from his own, hard to dispute, bible."

"Peter's not altogether a saint. He's left some sinister skeletons in his closet. We've agreed not to dust them off by staying mum. Do what I tell you, Emmitt!"

"Tell me this, Bert," Emmitt was getting even more roused by Bert's arrogant attitude. "What am I supposed to tell Reverend Jameses about his land? He was counting on selling that ground. It was essential to saving his church."

"A congregation can convene anywhere."

"Then great. His parish can come to ours?"

"Ours, Emmitt? Ours? I built that church, not you!" An abrupt exasperation terminated Bert's willingness to play along. "Don't push!?"

"I won't, but if I ever go inside of a church again, it won't be one a black man can't worship in."

"Be real. Religious segregation went under in the seventies. A black woman is what you have in mind! Am I rankling you?" Bert didn't really care. He opened his collar, as if to release the heat. "Your evening deposits have drawn interest. Half this city knows you've been tapping into Lester's daughter. It's wholesale knowledge. You're not fooling anybody."

"Let me ask you a question, Bert. How long were you in love with Lester's wife before he took her away from you? Marian believes her mother may have had your engagement ring for almost a year when you were young, only suddenly she married Lester! This wasn't a hundred percent about politics. You knew that as long as I needed Lester Jameses's property, I wouldn't be able to foreclose on his church. What were you afraid of, unwanted guests? Lester's wife wasn't only white, but she was your fiance He got her pregnant right under that self-righteous nose of yours, Didn't he?"

"There's a great number of churches in Malfaxe."

"Yes, but you and Lester were tight. You've said that to me on a hundred different occasions."

Bert flicked on the television and channeled in the news. "Go home, Emmitt! Do what I said."

"I'm a little slow, Bert, but I'm not your lackey anymore!" Emmitt flared back. "Screw City Hall," was the last thing Bert heard as Emmitt barged outdoors and into the grief of their broken friendship.

Emmitt arrived home half sick. The election was in progress, and winning was a slim possibility that wasn't remote enough for Emmitt. Given the opportunity, he would have conceded to Peter and saved himself the embarrassment of one last humiliating defeat from the conniving eccentric. He wanted to stick Bert, also. Concession would've been a double edged blade. A blade Emmitt conceived as rather late to pull. The polls were open. Continuing on seemed to be his only option in order for the final chapter of his loss to be written. Either way, he was destined to be the object of harsh criticism. He'd be branded a loser and a liar, not a very attractive combination for a bank manager. He was considering early retirement, when he met the press at his door step with a bashful 'hello'.

"Is there any truth to the rumor that Peter Ghudd is no longer a candidate?"

"You'll have to ask him."

"If he confirms it, how do you see this election?"

"With or without Peter, it's a circus!"

"Did you try to conceal the results of the Jameses's' land analysis? Are you presently in favor of a different city prison?"

Emmitt had had it to the hilt with the nagging. He was in the process of entering his house, when he did an about face and unloaded the baggage, he'd been burdened with for what seemed an eternity.

"Yes, I held onto information!" He dubiously admitted, unleashing his anger. "And I'll tell you something else," he continued. "Peter Ghudd's right! Prison life needs to be less attractive. If it were, we'd all breathe easier. With that, Emmitt slammed the door behind himself, leaving five reporters temporarily stunned, however, at no loss for something to print.

Emmitt paced to the den. He went through the kitchen. When he reached the bathroom, it occurred to him that he wasn't alone. Norman was in the kitchen serving breakfast to a stranger. Emmitt's curiosity guided him to the archway dividing the den from the kitchen. A lanky black man in a terry cloth robe was sitting at the table. His ear was bandaged and his movements were sluggish. Emmitt wanted no part of him and went straight to his bedroom. He consumed six shots of whiskey and fell unconscious for five hours. As the noon faded into the evening, he awoke. It was dusk. Emmitt sat motionless on the edge of his bed, waiting for the inevitable darkness to encase him. He wanted to hide from everything, including himself. He rousted when six chimes from the clock in the den banged hard on his brain.

Returning to the kitchen. He'd bumped into Norman's visitor in the hall without exchanging a word. Norman was adamantly glued to the stove. He was pouring soup from a can into a pot. Emmitt collapsed onto a wooden kitchen chair and began scrutinizing his brother's clumsy technique for lighting a stubborn burner.

"Who's the riffraff, Norman?" He began demolishing table crumbs with his tender knuckles.

"Name's Boomer. He's a fighter."

"And I'm the mayor to be. Weird friend."

"You have your friends, I've got mine. It's normal."

"Tell me, normally, normal, Norman," Emmitt slobbered, "When's he un cooling his heels?" He meant to prop his elbow on his leg. He missed. Emmitt's head jerked almost plunging into his lap.

"Can't say. Norman was being inattentive to Emmitt while he was tampering with the knob to the burner.

"He's a winner, Norman?"

"Quite the contrary."

"What's the story?"

"You want the story, Emmitt? I'll see if you can comprehend it. While you were being made a fool of last night, me and Hank went to the Iron Worker's Hall. We saw some good fights, much better than the one I heard you put on. Are you still with me?"

Emmitt blinked twice for yes.

"This was the last fight, see. Some oaf of a squirrel trips into the ring lookin' lost. He's very plain and ordinary...nothing special. A few minutes later guess who struts out? It's Boomer. He's flashy. He's workin' his way to the ring lookin' sharp. Boomer's wearin' a red robe and white shoes. The shoes have these red tassels on 'em. He's shadow boxin. He's bobbin' and weaving, and flicking jabs Joe Louis would've been proud of. Boomer must've had twenty or thirty people escorting him to the ring, his entourage, or best friends is what poor Boomer probably thought. They were all right there at his side. When he finessed his fighting machine of a body into the ring, they eagerly rooted him on at the bell." Norman stopped to try lighting the stove again.

"Get along with it. I've things to do," Emmitt weakly groaned.

"Okay, pal. The bell rings and Boomer's already in the oaf's corner for action. Thirty seconds later Boomer's in la la land, flat out, Emmitt, but that's not the best part. The best part is this. Those friends of his, who went ringside with him when he was on his feet? They all snuck into the crowd. Not a single buddy wanted to help him. Can you draw any comparisons, Emmitt? It's an old story"

"Huh?"

"Forget it!" Norman focused on the stove again. "Give me a match."

"A what?" Emmitt's stupor progressed.

"A match, Emmitt. I'd like a match, if you got one."

"I got one." Emmitt was at the peak of his being plastered. "A match, Norman, is my face and your ass, your saggy, hideous, brainless ass. Now do ya have your match?" Emmitt paused and reconsidered his statement. "I didn't say that right," he huffed, removing saliva from his chin with a swipe of his forearm.

"Oh, you said it right, Emmitt," Norman was boiling mad, as he stomped out of the kitchen. "I'm sick and tired of the insults I've had to take around here, Emmitt! Sick and tired! Next time I need a match, I'll ask somebody better lookin'.

As for Emmitt, he'd waver from conscious to unconscious during the remainder of the evening. Then he slept peacefully for five hours straight, providing himself with the break he desperately needed before he could bolster up for the challenge of a brand new day. Presented with a choice, he'd preferred lapsing into a coma, though it wasn't to be. When he managed to drag himself to the shower to rinse the sweat from his body, the clock was stalking midnight, and Emmitt was groggy. He didn't learn about the election results until later. He'd won by a landslide. It was his fourteen hundred, and sixty-two votes to Art's three hundred, and ten. It was the worst voter turnout in the city's history.

CHAPTER 34

It was late Saturday and Emmitt had found the Jameses house darkened. Isolated by his shame and ridden with tortuous feelings of overwhelming guilt, he'd posted himself outside of Marian's bedroom window. He tapped on the pane, a shallow tap. He paced, reversed his strides, and paced more. Marian was in there. The bedroom curtains may have been opaque, but Emmitt was aware of her presence by the vibrations that prickled his tender skin like a million thorns. At last, she cracked the window four or five inches and greeted Emmitt with a nasty reception.

"Leave!"

"In due time."

"My daddy catches you here, you're vulture scrap!"

"Marian, I'm sorry. It wasn't my fault! I didn't want him to find out the way he did."

"I'm sure, go scatter your razzle, dazzle elsewhere. " Marian grumbled, slamming the window.

Emmitt pecked on the window loudly, then much louder. When Marian ignored his pleas, he cursed to himself. As he continued to knock with reckless determination, he didn't have the faintest idea that Lester was about to nab him.

"You're being a pest!" Marian returned through the bitter cold sheets of glass. In an instant, her anger turned to fear. She closed the curtains nervously when she saw her father pressing the muzzle of his twelve gauge shotgun into Emmitt's ribs.

"The shop's closed," Lester said, volunteering a sly innuendo in reference to his daughter's line of work. "You'll be doin' business with me tonight!"

Emmitt smelled the liquor on Lester's breath. It was potent, even in the outdoor air. When Lester pointed the gun at Emmitt's head, Emmitt saw the brown paper bag that assumed the shape of a pint of whiskey. It was stuffed under the minister's belt.

"Come with me." Lester prodded him toward the kitchen with the discomforting blue steel of the firearm. When they went inside, there was a second whiskey bottle on the table. It was empty. Lester staggered to a chair, not neglecting to aim the gun straight at Emmitt's groin. "I oughta neuter you with this, only if I wait 'til mornin', it'll be more fun!" Lester's grin was sinister. It beamed with pure contempt.

"I came to square things away, Reverend. I want to level with you."

"You want to level my church! That's the kind of leveling you've got in mind!" Lester tilted the empty bottle above his mouth to reassure himself that it was positively drained. It was.

In the many years, Emmitt had been acquainted with Lester Jameses, he'd never seen him this affected. The minister was gloating with the prospect of sheer revenge. He was on the brink of a major crisis. His church would be confiscated and the proceeds divided and auctioned off, Emmitt, in all probability, if he survived, would be blamed for the misfortune. What worried Emmitt more was Lester's comment about the shop being closed. Apparently, Lester wasn't as naïve as he'd pretended to be about his daughter's lifestyle. Emmitt realized he might have to answer for the mood it had put Lester in. Worse yet, there was the fact that Emmitt, himself, had been indulging in the fruits of Marian's labor. Emmitt concluded that he'd definitely pay for that. As he had done so often in the past, he contemplated a quick break for the door and assessed that he'd never reach the knob. Instead, he cracked. Tears invaded his eyes, and his chin trembled. He couldn't restrain himself, as the drops of his tears fell one by one at his very own feet. Emmitt hadn't cried this profusely since he was a boy.

"I just thought I'd come by and try to be friends," he babbled incoherently.

"Friends? Is that what you call it? You lied to me about my farm. You're taking my church. Oh bye the way, mister, I'm also aware that you've been humpin' my daughter! I am not a happy friend!"

"You're drunk, Reverend," Emmitt kept sobbing.

"You're goin' with me," Lester dictated while Marian concealed herself in an adjoining storage pantry.

"To where?"

"To the barn for starters…enders, too! Take those fancy clothes off!"

"Why?"

"I don't wanna ruin 'em when I plug ya."

"You're crazy, Reverend!" Emmitt whined.

"You'd do well to hold that thought. I'm in a killin' mood, mister. Now get them duds off, jump!"

"Underwear, too?"

Lester viewed Emmitt's scrawny physique and fought hard to avoid laughing. "Nah, you'd rather be dead than to be seen like that! Wear your shorts if you want. You won't be going anywhere."

As Emmitt undressed, Lester threw Emmitt's clothes across a kitchen chair. When they left for the barn, Emmitt was clad in briefs and a sleeveless undershirt. It was thirty eight degrees, and Emmitt had abandoned all hopes for reconciliation. Even Marian had forsaken him. She'd not shown herself since he and Lester had left her at her bedroom window.

"There's your accommodations." With the two loaded barrels of the shotgun, Lester pushed Emmitt past the barn's planked door. Another poke with the gun made Emmitt trip and find himself on a pile of empty feedbags. "Enjoy your visit," Lester taunted him. "Watch out for

Mister Gobbles, though. He's my black snake next to your elbow there, and he thrives off rats!"

Scared half to death, Emmitt jumped to his feet as Lester stumbled away. Emmitt heard the clanging of the outside bolt being locked into position. One by one, he went to every window in the barn. There were six, and all six were boarded to prevent him from climbing through. An hour crept by. Emmitt folded his body into a fetal position. He'd taken refuge in an unoccupied cow stall on the opposite side of the barn from where Mister Gobbles would reign perfectly unchallenged. His efforts to maintain warmth were futile, but it did thwart his concerns in regard to being shot. By morning, he'd be frozen solid, and Lester Jameses would have to forfeit his plans and accept Emmitt's death by freezing as a fair trade.

The following hour was miserable, and the hour after that was unbearable. Emmitt, by then, was lying between two bundles of hay, hoping his life would end fast. As the door to the barn creaked ajar, Emmitt began to welcome a swift blast of lead. When he saw Marian, he was too numb to be tense, she'd brought him clothes. They weren't his.

"Wear these," she fussed.

"Where's mine?" Emmitt asked, frowning at the wide dungarees and immense, patched blazer that Lester had worn only two days earlier while clearing timber.

"Daddy's sleepin' on top of yours. You'd better be lost when he wakes!" "How 'bout some shoes?" Emmitt was panicky only Marian didn't answer him.

Emmitt reluctantly pulled the hat over his ears. It was extremely large for his head, but it was no more out of proportion than the rest of the preacher's wardrobe.

"My keys, Marian?"

"Haven't seen 'em."

"You drivin' me home?"

"Can't. I gotta rise early. You either walk or take the cycle."

"You get me on the main drag."

"Nope. I need my rest. I've got choir in the morning with Reverend Mickey. We need the money, remember? The state penn pays a lot better than you ever did!"

Emmitt trailed Marian for approximately two hundred yards to where last summer's produce stand had been. There, under a tarpaulin, was Emmitt's transportation. It was the same motorcycle he'd seen leaning against the house the first day he'd ever spoken to Marian. The rubber handle grips were rotting to pieces, and the wheels had several missing spokes. One of the tires had an expanded wall, and the cycle was rusty from the front to the rear.

"Is this the best you can do?" He complained.

"No, it's the best you can do," Marian replied, nonchalantly.

"Call me a cab."

"Call your own cab."

"How do I operate it?" Emmitt retreated, shying away from the prospect of encountering Lester Jameses again.

"Here's the key." Marian touched the ignition. "Keep it in neutral to start. Give it the choke there, twist the throttle on your handle grips." Marian rotated the throttle to show Emmitt how. "Hop on," she said.

Emmitt straddled the cycle with hesitation. Use your heel and kick your start," she coaxed.

Emmitt kicked with his bare foot. Nothing happened. He kicked four consecutive times before smoke puffed into the air. It was quickly consumed by the pitch dark. The fifth try brought ignition to the motor.

"When I tell you," Marian proceeded loud enough to overcome the noisy engine, "jump into gear."

Emmitt was vibrating with the machine. He'd never been in control of this sort of raw jarring power before.

"Move on," Marian insisted over the roar of the engine. "You can return it however you want as long as I don't see you anymore!" She disappeared abruptly, leaving Emmitt just the way she'd found him, forlorn. Her rejection had cut through Emmitt's flesh and penetrated his chest like a jagged saber. He was devastated.

With no alternative, Emmitt shifted the cycle into gear and spun onto the awaiting asphalt. Three blocks later he fell incurring a bruised hip. He remounted and pulled the hat down low once again over his ears. It would be daylight prior to his reaching home, and Emmitt held the belief that the hat would aid in concealing his identity. It wasn't that he expected to be recognized, he simply didn't want to risk the slightest chance.

Thirty-five, forty-five, accelerating to fifty two miles per hour was Emmitt's top speed as he saw illumination in the foreground. The sun was climbing. Emmitt was becoming distracted by its splendor. The sun's magnificent rays tinged the highway with a pleasant amber cast that seemed to be drawing him into its increasing rapture. It was intoxicating. The new dawn pulled at him harder and harder. He didn't want to go home. He didn't want to be the Mayor. Emmitt would have given anything just to be able to ride straight into the horizon and keep going.

With his exit drawing near, He skidded to an abrupt halt. As he evaluated his circumstances, he pulled his hat down tight one last time. He thought about how complicated his life had become in six months. The two best relationships he'd ever known were now severed, first Bert and now Marian. He had a job that he didn't deserve. His brother was constantly antagonizing him, and nobody would ever believe a word that he babbled again. The long highway that was stretching ahead once again was gaining appeal. However, Emmitt chose his regular exit. Life was brief, he told himself. His hurt couldn't last indefinitely. For the present, he'd go home, try to handle his botched affairs, and bear the consequences for all of the gross dishonesty.

Emmitt sputtered onto a single lane road and turned right at a mini-mart. From there, it was two lefts and a right onto his street. When he made it to his front yard, he dismounted the cycle and pushed it to the back of the house where he propped it against one of eight large, heavy posts that were bolstering his deck. The addition to his bedroom and sun deck had been finished Friday afternoon. Koepy had collected all of his gear immediately afterward and hurried off without being paid. He'd also mentioned to Emmitt that he would return on the weekend to collect his final installment for the job. Emmitt had given Koepy a key, telling him the check would be on the kitchen table, and he could leave the key there in its place. Upon entering his home, somehow with all that was happening Emmitt had remembered this. He temporarily regained a small fraction of his composure. As he was endorsing the check, he realized how trusting he was of Koepy, a man who was little more than a stranger to him. One thing he didn't like though was the cement pad that Koepy had never removed as Emmitt had wanted done. Emmitt would scrutinize the bill later to make sure it didn't appear on the itemized list. If it did, he knew he'd take pleasure in making Koepy rectify his mistake. Even now, nobody was going to screw Emmitt.

Hours were lost when he found himself sprawled on the sofa, still in the same outfit that he'd worn home from the Jameses farm. Somehow, it didn't bother him. What did bother Emmitt was Norman. Norman was in his own bedroom with the television's volume so loud that the house was almost vibrating. He dragged himself from the living room to Norman's bedroom door and began kicking the bottom panel of the door. "Are you deaf?" He shouted.

Norman's approach bordered amicable. With a shifty grin tainting his diplomacy, he showed Emmitt into his untidy domain.

"You oughta hear this." Norman's grin was accompanied by an arched left eyebrow, which Emmitt had learned to interpret as problematic. Resisting the urge to ignore the comment, Emmitt submitted to his own curiosity.

"Can you increase the sound, Norman? I don't want to miss anything," Emmitt yelled from the bottom of his lungs.

"Sure."

Plaster could have crumbled from the ceiling. A newscaster's voice flooded the house to the highest rafters. There was a riot in the city prison. Six guards were taken hostage. Emmitt was stunned. The newsman's words droned in his ears with minute to minute updated information about the seizure and demands of the convicts. Emmitt advanced to the television and decreased the overpowering noise. Seconds later the newsman was given another printed brief which he promptly read. Emmitt listened intently as the news of the Reverend Mickey, and his choir came through the set. They'd been doing their program from the city prison when the violence erupted. In the middle of the minister's sermon, a prison revolt had been unleashed. The condition of the guards was unknown. Reverend Mickey, himself, was unharmed, freed, and apparently involved in the negations. It was thought that a singer in the choir was severely injured. Reverend Mickey had pleaded for the man to be released. He needed medical attention badly. The convicts were taking an unmerciful stand. Nobody else would be freed unless a bargain were ratified.

Emmitt's terror was building with every additional statement on the crisis. Marian was in that prison with Reverend Mickey's choir; and, for all he knew, she was either dead or dying. The convicts wanted the right to unionize. They were demanding a fair day's wages for a fair days labor. They wanted no longer to be called convicts. Their title would be changed to associate denizens, and they weren't refuting on the new prison. Along with it being Art Towson's version, a modern coffee lounge had to be an unconditional part of the deal. Their last demand struck Emmitt profoundly sour. He, the Mayor to be, would have to renege on his latest, relatively hard-line opposition statements about prison reform. He would do this unconditionally or the body count was set to begin at midnight.

Emmitt's vocal cords were strained. "They're nuts!" He squeaked.

"Can't ya do what you usually do, Emmitt?" Norman asked, with apparent earnest. "Lie to 'em. Then, after they do what you want, stick 'em with the truth."

"Funny, Norman. They know I can't tell them I've changed my mind. They want blood."

"So what? It's not yours. People are expendable creatures, Emmitt."

"I envy you, Norman. You're the pinnacle authority on life."

Norman cocked his head far enough back so he'd have no trouble gazing down his domineering nose at Emmitt. "I am life," he haughtily declared with the utmost of candor.

Emmitt didn't respond. Instead, his mind slipped into a faraway state where Norman wasn't allowed. His brother was an insensitive ogre all right, but he had one attribute that continually prevailed. Norman had the uncanny knack for telling things exactly the way they were. He was truthful to the extent of being repulsive. Emmitt's hatred for his brother was an undeniable product of that trait. Nonetheless, Norman's remark had well defined Emmitt's potential role in the prison riot. Emmitt commenced to reason that people seldom died on their own terms. Whether cremated or buried, human corpses became no more than dust for the worms to wiggle through. He wasn't going to alter the process, nor was he capable of prolonging it. The hostages, including Marian, had no business in the prison to begin with. Why should he feel responsible for the lives of dummies, who chose a viper's nest to sing the praises of a God who didn't exist? They'd have to work their problem out as best they could. In the meantime, Emmitt planned on writing a speech. It would be sympathetic. He'd haggle for the release of the hostages, knowing beyond the smallest doubt, the prisoners wouldn't concede. If a massacre ensued, it would be the convicts fault. Ultimately, they would be the culprits. Emmitt felt that he would have no trouble living with the consequences. Norman's voice shook him back.

"On the other hand, Emmitt, by showing up at the riot, you'd reap sensational press."

"What kind of jerk do you think I am, Norman? There are lives at stake here! I won't play games!" He'd have to write his speech expeditiously, in order to deliver it prior to the midnight deadline. The speech could be televised, and there'd be no face to face settlement between himself and the prisoners. A parlay, such as that could be exceedingly dangerous.

"Emmitt," Norman's posture slumped with the gross disappointment, "Emmitt, think! This is the opportunity governors are weaned from, man! If you'd get in the thick of it all, it'll be font page!" You'd look like a regular David and Clyde all over again."

"Whose Clyde?"

"You know, the giant, who got himself killed by that little squirt. He was about your size Emmitt."

"You mean David, and Goliath."

"Whoever."

"You're saying I should meet with the convicts?"

"It's the chance of a lifetime."

"They'll tear me apart, Norman, besides I don't want to be the freekin' governor."

"You're wasting precious time, Emmitt!"

"Absolutely not!"

"It's your career."

"I told you I don't want to be the governor. What do I look like, a raving maniac?"

"Yes," Norman yelled back, as he scanned Emmitt's attire. Each piece of clothing, from his floppy hat to the outdated and tattered pants he wore screamed to be sanitized. Every stitch of clothing was many times Emmitt's regular measurements. His feet were bare. His eyes were glazed, and he was developing a case of hives. Emmitt's mouth also began twitching in silence. Norman, who was as far from being a therapist as one could get, gave into the notion to dabble in the profession of psychiatry. He quickly appraised his brother as a man who'd lost it. He'd have to get Emmitt out of the house or else start sleeping with a high powered revolver. For now, Norman would work on convincing Emmitt to leave by adopting a different strategy. "Marian's name was on the list of hostages." Norman revealed in an off the cuff manner.

"It would be," Emmitt returned, much in the same tone.

"Yeah, if my girlfriend were a five buck an hour act, I'd let the jailbirds have her too. You can always try and collect your money later out of their wages."

"Norman, your account is overdrawn. I think we'll settle it!? Emmitt was getting sucked in.

"What you need to worry about is her, Emmitt, 'cause I'll bet you're an awfully easy number to fill in for, so to speak! Buddy once those studs get a hold of her, she'll never wanna go back to you!"

"You're begging for a lesson, Norman!"

"How's the garage sound?" Norman persisted. He sought to entice Emmitt to the garage where he'd tie him up just as he did when they were kids. Well, not exactly. There was no rope, and obviously no tree in the garage. Duck tape would do fine though. Norman's scheme was to bind his brother's arms and legs from the roll, and then with hardly no effort, tape Emmitt to a spare tire. Thereafter, Norman would secure affidavits from two doctors on emergency duty at a hospital recommending Emmitt be committed to an asylum. Norman preferred it be a done deal by suppertime.

"I've dreamed of this day," Emmitt confessed, without any distinct insight.

"Me, too." Norman swiveled himself a half a revolution to engage the adjoining hall. From there, with Emmitt in hot pursuit, he'd file through the house, past the rear porch, and into the garage. Emmitt's fate would be sealed when Norman locked the garage door.

The scuffle, Norman calculated, might last five quick minutes. He was used to bullying Emmitt. To Norman, it was a finely tuned science of repetitive action followed by repetitive reaction. He'd enjoy getting Emmitt's goat for a random slaughter. As a past time, it broke the monotony. Today there were greater rewards in the making. He looked forward to ousting Emmitt for at least a year. With minimal effort, he'd have him classified mentally incompetent and sell the house in no time at all.

It was all very clear to Norman, but what he didn't see was the ingrained madness that had accumulated over their lifetime. It was festering into a major eruption. Norman didn't see the bickering and foul arguments as unnecessarily divisive. He didn't see the agonizing torment he'd forced Emmitt to endure on a daily basis as an unconscious wish for his own personal demise. Regrettably, Norman didn't see any of these things as he strutted for the hall. Least of all, Norman never saw the heavy porcelain lamp that crashed into his skull, sending him tumbling to the floor.

Emmitt let the remainder of the lamp topple to Norman's motionless feet. A lifetime of insults and one up man ship had irrevocably been answered. Emmitt vowed to himself never to forget the satisfaction that was rushing through his veins. He concluded that revenge was more gratifying than sex. Emmitt nudged Norman's belly with a stiffened foot. He welcomed the lack of response. An unanswered challenge came from the same dirty foot to Norman's ribcage, no movement. His brother was a helpless mass of fat, and Emmitt noticed that Norman was as sloppy in mindlessness as he was when conscious. The drool was running from Norman's mouth. It began to puddle on the floor. Emmitt leaned over to shake him. It was useless. He placed an inquiring thumb to Norman's neck for a sign of life. That, too, was futile. Norman was gone, this time really gone!

CHAPTER 35

He claims he's the mayor. The pudgy sergeant announced, "Says he can defuse this bomb."

"Not a chance. The mayor's having another well timed heart attack." The irritable police chief never lowered his binoculars. Instead, he kept them sealed to his eye sockets while he searched the prison yard for the slightest movement. It was still.

"Says he's the new mayor," the sergeant laughed.

Chief Drake was a tall imposing hulk. At six feet four inches, and two hundred and forty pounds, his size alone intimidated people regardless of which side of the law they were on. He was a thirty six year veteran. In his prime, he'd been trimmer around the middle. When he was twenty years old, his hair was auburn. Over the years, it had retained only a few traces of its youthfulness. Mostly gray, but quite full, the chief kept it cut close to his scalp. Because he always wore his cap on duty, for the average cop it was difficult to imagine the chief with hair. Other than a severe widow's peak extending from beneath the cap's bill, the chief's hair, ordinarily, remained a well-covered secret. If anything, it was his heavy facial bone structure that caught one's attention. He had broad, hollow cheeks and a strong hawkish nose. It was rumored that on his mother's side he was part Cheyenne Indian.

His paternal grandparents had immigrated from England at the end of World War I.

His grandfather had told him about the Great War, and how No Man's Land had transpired from routinely quiet to a butchering field. The soldiers had rallied out of their trenches with guns and mounted bayonets to fight hand to hand in the open terrain. There they'd slaughter one another, retreat, then collect themselves for another attack. Sometimes they might wait for days. Then they'd go at it again. His grandfather had described how gas warfare had made its debut on a dismayed and fragmented planet during the First World War. Due to that the chief had acquired a scaled down mental forecast of what was about to transpire in the confines of the prison. It wouldn't be a pretty picture before the last inmate, or cop, or unfortunate hostage fell. The guns would blaze flashes of blue streaks into the barrages of cons, but the gas grenades were to be launched first. The charging police, with their protective masks and air pack canisters would command a huge advantage, and although some of them were bound to die, the prisoners were going to be slain in their tracks, bunches of them. The chief was suffering from emotional fatigue. He let his binoculars dangle from a strap around his aching neck as he met Sergeant Ferguson's frown. "Where's this nut at?"

"The grocery store." The sergeant answered. It was the one on Brentwood Street, which was temporarily being used as command central because of its close location to the prison. The sergeant waited for the chief to order him to send Emmitt away. This was not the night to be bothered by weirdoes or groupies.

"Bring him here!"

Ferguson grinned an affirmative acknowledgment and left the observation tower that was attached to a guard shack below, and inside the prison confines. He left in a black and white rookie driven patrol car and went to the unoccupied food store. Unoccupied except for droves of policemen, who were huddled around the building in clusters. The lights had been dimmed, and the employees sent home. Command central now had shopping carts filled with guns, ammunition, and all of the proper essentials for a lofty killing spree. Every blue uniform available was there. At eight thirty five pm., and less than four hours remaining before the rioters promised to make good on their threats, options were becoming extinct. Inevitable death was rapping at the gates of Sutler Penitentiary.

The chief was talking on the phone in the guard shack when the cruiser returned, its lights dormant and motor barely audible. It parked beyond the huge iron grill that prohibited traffic from entering or leaving the prison. The sergeant stepped from the car first and extended a steady arm inside for Emmitt to grasp. Visibility was low, but not so bad that the chief overlooked the horribly disgusting figure that began trekking ahead of Ferguson. It was certainly gross and unkempt.

Emmitt stubbed his toe on the threshold entering the guard shack. His feet were bare under the bedroom slippers which were open at the tips. His clothes were the same ones he'd worn home from the Jameses farm. Emmitt was a physical mess and a mental wreck. He'd just bludgeoned his younger brother to death. Norman was never going to hassle him again. A thousand righteous acts weren't capable of erasing his greatest single atrocity. Emmitt wanted to be punished, and he could think of no better way than that of sacrificing himself to the inmates.

Not being overly concerned with trivial pain, Emmitt did lift his leg and began massaging his toe spontaneously. "I'm the new mayor," he said, poking his grimy foot across his thigh.

"What do ya do for an encore?" The chief asked, "gargle onions?"

"Seen enough?" The sergeant proceeded to shuffle Emmitt toward the door.

"Not yet," the chief stopped him. "I want the name of his tailor before he leaves." He paused. "Where's your identification?" He asked Emmitt.

"Home."

"And where's that?"

"I'm granting you a favor, Chief." Emmitt scoffed, taking a pen that was tied to twine on the wall. "This is my social security number." He wrote the nine digits on a miniature cereal box that was on top of a mound of trash in an overflowing basket. "Check it out. Your job depends on it. Also, run down my Lincoln's tags. It's adjacent to the supermarket."

Although Emmitt's appearance seemed to speak for itself, suggesting he were a person of no consequence, the chief examined him for a few awkward seconds. Emmitt was unshaven and his blotchy skin was indicative of a two day binge. He was also smothering the guard shack with the essence of animal scented straw. The chief pondered Emmitt's fate. He was seriously considering why anybody would want to be the mayor and dare involve himself in such an unforgiving predicament. Emmitt's face held a resemblance to the new mayor's all right. The chief had seen him on the televised debate, and there were always pictures of Emmitt in the papers. If this man were driving a Lincoln, the possibility of him being the mayor wasn't totally nonexistent. Perhaps it was Emmitt's arrogance that swayed the chief.

"Do it, Sergeant!" Chief Drake said, remembering how bizarre others had become in their final years. "When you return, have either a confirmation or else a permanent, reliable chaperone for this man."

"Got cha!" Ferguson scrambled for the door.

One minute led to another, five minutes passed, then ten. Emmitt looked past his own reflection in one of the guard shack's bullet proof windows and settled his gaze on the cramped city structures hovering atop the rows of gooseneck lamp posts. Under the lamps were news vans and police cars. They were everywhere, but the buildings themselves, as if in a removed world, seemed detached. Lights in the apartments switched on and off intermittently and high resolution television sets flickered brilliant colors from almost every visible unit. Emmitt's attention soon dwindled, and his interest returned to the streets where the formation of scattered crowds was gaining momentum. The crowds were larger than when he had pushed his way between them and forced himself on an unsuspecting policeman with the seemingly hideous tale of being the future mayor. Had it not been for the precinct's slammer housing a full load, Emmitt would have been booked for his bad breath. The fuzz laughed instead, and eventually Emmitt was relayed from one cop to the next. It had been cheap entertainment for them. The police gawked at him and made jokes that temporarily diverted their own accumulating stress. Emmitt was unaffected, as one smart cop sat him in the rear of the sergeant's police transport. Emmitt endured the humiliation. He'd take it all in stride if it meant getting an audience with the cop at the lead. It did, and he did. Sergeant Ferguson, for some strange reason, had consulted the chief and then returned to fetch Emmitt.

The crowds weren't permitted to within three city blocks of the prison. As Emmitt kept vigil from inside the guard shack, he considered them as nothing more than show seekers.

They multiplied rapidly. Several hundred people, that's how many he guessed were there, maybe more. They gradually divided as the sergeant's car slowly went in between them. Then two mobs became one again, obstructing Emmitt's full view of the car.

The chief's attention was elsewhere. Keeping one hand in the vicinity of the telephone, he ignored Emmitt while the two of them were alone. If ever the phone rang, the chief's primary objective would be to pounce on it, then he'd have to stall Jimmy Sloane, the riot leader. He'd try. If it didn't work, Jimmy would start mass producing angels. Up until now, the chief had demonstrated good faith by converging his men at the market. Jimmy had demanded it. For insurance, Jimmy had blackmailed a local television station into covering the chaos at the prison live. Whenever Jimmy wanted, the station would be expected to air the outskirts of the prison from any angle. A refusal would bring instant death to a hostage. Jimmy was in the boss's seat! He'd taken control of the warden's office, and the reception on the forty-six-inch flat screen proved to be exceedingly sharp.

Meanwhile, the chain of events were unceasingly grinding away at the chief's confidence. He'd never been bullied by criminals. Now he was dancing to the tune of incarcerated thugs of every kind. Departmental jealousy had been running rampant. The individual and personal resentment of a lot of cops would surely dictate that he'd occupy a permanent position on the department's mockery totem pole. It was no wonder Emmitt had been brought to him. It wasn't useful policy, or even precaution, to present straggly slime to the chief of police in any criminal environment. Tonight his men had sent him a gift. Emmitt was a symbol of the expanding sentiment in the department.

The grimy, counterfeit buck stopped with the lowly chief. The chief, it would seem, had little else to do other than interview a deranged loafer.

Meanwhile Emmitt didn't pursue a dialogue with his disinclined host. He assumed their bond, provided that they had one, was going to be temporary. With the best outcome possible, the chief was destined to become Emmitt's jailer. Emmitt had committed murder and was no better than the ruthless people he himself had condemned earlier. If he lived through the riot, he'd forfeit a trial and plead guilty, saving the city's time and expense. After all, cost reduction had been a major segment of his platform during the campaign. Nobody then would be able to call Emmitt Braedeikk, a hypocrite.

The idea began to strike Emmitt as meaningless. The cons were going to kill him, hopefully fast. That would be his fate. He'd already formulated his plan, and he'd stick too it. Emmitt would trade his miserable self for a hostage. An insignificant life for a valuable life. He'd be laughing at the cons from his cheating grave. It'd be a fitting slap in their mean, ugly faces.

The mobs at the outskirts of the boundary had forced their selves to the vicinity of the police occupied super market There they reluctantly separated for a second time to allow the sergeant's car access to the guard shack. Its lights remaining out, the cruiser advanced slowly, slowly enough that Emmitt felt Ferguson should have walked, and conserved the city's gas. The driver stayed seated as the stout, pear shaped sergeant with the aviator's square framed bifocals and beet tinted complexion wobbled himself to the small structure. When he trudged, and with a noticeable hesitation. Emmitt knew he'd gotten the truth. Yes, Emmitt, the butt of dozens of policemen's wisecracks was in actuality the newly elected mayor. In all probability, the sergeant was afraid there would be a departmental down sizing. The sergeant strained at his vocal cords camouflaging his dread with artificial glee. "He's the mayor! Lucky for us, Chief!"

Lucky was hardly the chief's opinion. He was facing a crisis that, if not subdued peacefully, had the potential of becoming a media horror movie with around the clock reruns. Hashing out an agreement with the cons required expertise. It would take intelligent dialogue spoken by a man endowed with charm, a man who'd regain trust for the establishment's side. A man of stature and composure, wielding the image of infinite authority might persuade the inmates to humble themselves. The chief looked at his main negotiator, who by now had returned to massaging his toe. He'd rather have taken his badge and pinned it through the sergeant's fat tit than do what he was about to do. Then the ringing telephone intensified his misery.

"Chief Drake," he answered quickly. "What'd you say? We're ready to negotiate. The mayor's here, too."

"Why don't you send him in?" A voice asked.

"It's been a rough day for him. He's set on sprucing up."

"Excuse me, I have to shoot somebody."

"You've not seen him. Hold tight. I'll see what I can arrange." For the chief, it was time to continue with his ongoing nightmare. "The inmates are tired of waiting," he said to Emmitt, not bothering to cover the phone's mouthpiece. "Will ya bargain with 'em?"

"I'll go in," Emmitt astounded the chief, "but they're to release the people who are hurt."

"You hear that?" The chief relayed to Jimmy.

"Nobody's hurt real seriously."

"Nobody's hurt," the chief told Emmitt with justified skepticism. "Seriously" was a relative term he'd avoid bickering over.

Emmitt blew his decaying cork. "Tell them if I'm going in, I want two female hostages released! I'm a good trade. I'm worth that, maybe more!" He added.

"The hostages will walk by you in the middle of the prison yard in two minutes," was part of Jimmy Sloan's message to Emmitt. The remainder of Jimmy's statement was best not repeated by the chief.

CHAPTER 36

Jimmy Sloane, in his forty-six warped years on earth, was accused of a seemingly infinite number of crimes. Robbery, assault, drug trafficking, and grand larceny were part of the list. He was a classic case of trial and error. Error meaning he should've never been released from prison following his third conviction. It was the one for stealing a forty two foot yacht out of a Maryland marina and using it to transfer cocaine to Fort Myers. There, the drugs were stored and eventually divided into small lots before they'd be sold.

A self exalted man with an endless supply of cash, Jimmy always possessed a high opinion of himself. He was always quick with a smile. His biggest problems resulted from being equally fast with a knife. When he was apprehended in the outskirts of Baltimore, he was mellow and amicable enough to encourage one of two vice officers to relax. Jimmy sent four inches of steel through the officer's chest, barely missing a descending aorta by a slim three quarters of an inch. The policemen weren't going to arrest Jimmy. They'd merely wanted to drill him about a past acquaintance.

In the con game, Jimmy was an experienced abuser. His personal esteem derived from his acute ability to use people. If it meant gaining a pittance of self enhancement, he'd lie better than the average person could spit out the truth. Now he was leering at Emmitt with a combination of rage and embarrassment. He'd relinquished two healthy hostages only to be given skid row material in exchange. He'd asked for the mayor. Emmitt was a total waste. Nobody would give a buffalo chip whether the tramp in front of him lived or not, otherwise they'd never allowed him in. Had he known what Jimmy was thinking, Emmitt's sentiments would've coincided. The two men were locked in a contest of eye contact when Jimmy began spouting off with morbid disapproval.

"You're repulsive," Jimmy said upon completion of an objective appraisal. "I've seen healthier miscarriages!" Jimmy closed in on Emmitt's face, scrutinizing the aftermath of an adolescence that had left Emmitt's face mildly scarred from acne. "You look like you were ambushed in the womb, and left to rot. The doctor who botched your mother's abortion must have been workin' with a jackhammer. By tomorrow you'll be late for an overdue funeral."

"Suit yourself," Emmitt returned, calculating the status of the hostages. He counted fourteen remaining, seven men and seven women. They were seated on the floor of the warden's office and next to the two walls that were adjacent to the television set. Emmitt assumed it was so the news surveillance and the hostages could be watched by the convict together. Just one of the captives was hurt. A middle aged black man suffered a terrible head wound. He was propped in a corner, and Marian was dressing his forehead with a piece of her shredded choir gown. The man's name was Teddy. His bleeding contained temporarily, he rested his head peacefully on Marian's arm. As he fazed in and out of consciousness, Marian soothed him with tender words, making Emmitt wish it had been himself who the convicts had slugged. When Marian refused to even glance in Emmitt's direction, he began to flirt with his pending execution.

"The only wrong thing these people have done was try to bring some happiness into your lives." Emmitt grumbled. "Show a little decency, please. Let them leave. I'm the mayor. Spare them, whack me! I'm extremely unpopular. You'll be celebrities in this stinkin' town!"

Jimmy had been consumed in his anger. Insulted by the police, he was preoccupied with an insatiable thirst for blood. He wasn't impressed with Emmitt's babble. The hostages were going to be killed. He phoned the chief in a flashing heat. "They're dead!" He forewarned.

"Don't injure anybody, Jimmy, please! What did the mayor say?"

"Listen, if he's the mayor, this town's got more to grieve about than a dumpy prison."

"He's not always as shabby as he is tonight, Jimmy."

"Sure, and I'm not doin' fifteen to twenty for cuttin an ignorant cop!"

"I'll send you an old newspaper with his picture."

"Swing the camera to the west yard. Give me cinema," Jimmy insisted. He dissected the television screen with microscopic vision. He'd not have to worry about the hostages. They were being watched by two cronies. Mickey Eli was a petty thief, who'd never amount to a fraction more or a decimal less. Jerome Tille was an altogether different kink in a string of seemingly mediocre inmates. He equaled Sam Riggs in a variety of criminal aspects. Labeled the "Photographer", he killed people, as many as Sam, but they were usually of a racketeering breed which was why his hits weren't as provocative to the social order as in the ordinary sense. Also, once the victims were terminated, the bodies were seldom discovered. His tactics were concise and effective. He'd stalk his prey, sometimes for weeks, corner them in a secluded area, and plant a twenty-two shot in the left section of the recipient's brain. He'd dispose of the corpse, but provide his employer with adequate proof of a task well done. It was the four by six photos Jerome developed himself and thoughtlessly stored in a metal box in his apartment that convicted him. The gun was there, too. Each photo showed the deceased with a flow of a bloody ink like goo streaming down the head, onto the neck and throat, and usually coagulating at the deceased person's shirt collar. Jerome never had time to conceal the body of his last contract. The hit was found slumped over a dryer in a Laundromat. Hence, an investigation was begun, which spawned the "Photographer's" downfall. Jerome's reputation preceded his incarceration at Sutler, and his nickname caught on. Thus, the "Photographer" became a proud and feared resident upon his arrival at the city lockup. Primed on cocaine, he was intrigued by the opportunity to demonstrate his skill with no fee required. He was eyeing the choir with a hungry lust. Jerome was in transit to an out of state penitentiary, where he'd be administered a lethal injection. As far as he was concerned, they could stick him with a hundred needles, he'd never feel a thing.

The west yard of the prison revealed an abandoned macadam. It was identical to the north, south, and east yards. Content that he was in control, Jimmy demanded the exterior of the prison's walls be reviewed. He was appalled at the magnitude of the crowd outside of the walls. The police, themselves, were in danger of being squashed under the heels of thousands of irate men and women wielding everything from kitchen knives and garden tools to automatic weapons. The crowd was immense. It girded the prison like an army of savage Huns. The camera advanced in an attempt to reach the edge of the crowd, only to zoom back to the prison walls where Peter Ghudd monopolized a spotlight. Peter was on top of a news van he'd commandeered, talking through a bull horn. Jimmy realized every head was directed in the old man's direction. The police weren't allowed close to him. The men in the blue blazers, who protected Peter's space, were too many in number. Peter's arms flailed in exasperation. Peter raised his hands to his torrid face to claw at thin air. It seemed clear that he wasn't promoting tolerance. The phone in the warden's office rang twice before Jimmy heard it.

"Jimmy?" The chief lacked self-confidence, and it was obvious. "We've met problems on this side of the wall, Jimmy. This city's rabid. I don't think we can hold them. Jimmy, we've brought a bishop here. He'll be on the wall in a minute. I need you to switch the loud speaker system on. Let this irate mob of fanatics know you're a compassionate guy, Jimmy! There's the bishop now. He's by the amplifiers. Go ahead! Just speak slowly to the bishop, so everybody can understand you're not such a bad guy."

"How's this?" Jimmy spoke into the telephone. He complied by flipping the amplifier switch to the on position. A long blur was heard. "Testing, one, two, three, get yourself laid, padre!" He emphatically relayed the words. It made the crowd angrier. They began pushing harder toward the prison walls.

"Not smart, Jimmy!" The chief rehemently traded back. By the time he'd regained his temper, Peter Ghudd was on the ridge of the prison wall himself. The amplifier was blaring like a jet engine, prompting Peter to remove his knee length cashmere coat and stuff it into the gray cone shaped hole. Peter had brought the bull horn. Looking stern, he put it to his mouth.

"This is Peter Ghudd," he notified Jimmy Sloane, "and I'm not fuckin' around! We've got a mess of angry people here tonight. Every breath you take, Jimmy, adds a hundred more angry people. I'm havin' the camera give ya the picture. It's kinda bleak."

True to his word, Peter commanded the camera to be swung to encompass as much of the mob as possible. The station crew complied. Jimmy Sloane's underarm deodorant began to fail.

"The police ain't gonna interfere, Jimmy. We're seizing the prison!"

"Are you done, grandpa?"

"Nope!" There was a brief hush. Peter gloated, "We aren't takin' any prisoners, bub." His soldiers were clamoring in the shadowy backdrop of a city reborn. The hour had emerged to dismantle the vermin infested nest, and Peter was not bluffing. If anything, he was wallowing in the prospect of a gallant fight.

Jimmy was convinced that he was no longer in a bargaining position. Peter led a legion large enough to stampede the prison and every inmate right into oblivion. Jimmy needed no great imagination to etch a mental picture. They'd likely sweep up what was left of Sutler Penitentiary and pour it into a waste basket. It would be worse than the Alamo.

"Peter's a tad hyped," Emmitt said, reading Jimmy's mind. It wasn't difficult.

"You know him, huh?"

"He cleaned my toilets at the bank I managed. Hates filth with a vengeance."

"Peter's his name?"

"It is," Emmitt acknowledged.

"He's the half wit who wanted Sam Riggs's hide."

"Now he wants yours."

"Sam's to thank for this!"

"No, you are. Sam's just the fuse. You happen to be the dynamite. Your timing's lousy!"

"In the few long minutes I've known you, you've confessed to being a banker, the mayor, and you talk like a fruity poet. Let's just say you're the messenger. What's the offer?" Jimmy temporarily relented.

"It would be a waste. Peter's the government in power, and dishing out pardons isn't part of his program. You'd be wise to free the choir though. Sparing them might persuade him to reciprocate."

"Is that the best you can do?"

"Keep me. If Peter makes a blitz on the prison, kill me!"

"I am snuffing you! I've listened to enough of your dopey dribble." Jimmy turned to engage the "Photographer." Sam's fixed us nice! Fetch him. We owe him a huge favor."

Like vapor in a cyclone, the two cronies vanished, leaving Jimmy totally alone with Emmitt and the choir. The con squeezed the pearl handle of the forty-five automatic with a bonding grip. Ignoring Emmitt, he stepped closer to the hostages. Jimmy was seeing red. It was the sort of red that accompanies heathen savagery, but the red transformed to a brilliant white as the white took on the glow of a distant star exploding in Jimmy's skull. Darkness followed, and Jimmy became a black hole, crumbling within himself. Emmitt had literally struck again. He'd floored Jimmy with a bookend that had been setting on the warden's desk. It was a geode, sawed in half and mounted on a brass angle plate that had brought the aspiring killer to his demise. Jimmy lay on the carpet, his body was limp. By now Emmitt's technique was perfected. Again he'd proven himself as nobody to be trusted with a heavy object in his hand. Jimmy groaned once in sheer agony, prompting Emmitt to slug him again with the bookend. Instinctively, Emmitt then dove to the door. He locked the bolt while the stunned choir sprang to their feet. Their fear had jumped to hope. They embraced one another. They'd been rescued, it appeared, by a magnificent undercover agent impersonating not the mayor elect, but a penniless drifter. Everyone there assumed that it was obviously the plot of a genius.

An inmate, trying to enter the office, was hampered by the locked door. He pounded on the door with his knuckles, and when nobody let him in, he yelled for help.

A swarm of frantic inmates dashed to the door, which was no more than a thin layer of corrugated plywood. It began splintering fast under the assault. Emmitt picked up Jimmy's gun and fired two rounds through the door. A body thumped, and blood seeped beneath the door's kick plate. The choir's reprieve then hung on one gun with a dubious amount of bullets.

Seconds were crucial. It was Marian who rushed to the door behind the warden's encased golf trophies. She eagerly tipped the transparent case and, with an urgent heave, she thrust the warden's finest memories down into the shattered glass. Marian clicked the latch on another door that was made accessible from behind the trophy case. It led to the prison roof by way of a tight passageway that was laced with cobwebs, and dust caked together much like furnace soot. The choir scurried along with Emmitt in the rear.

When he heard the inmates bash the first door to pieces, and heave themselves into the empty office, Emmitt's throat felt as though he'd swallowed for the last time. He heard Jimmy yelling orders again from down below. Emmitt wished he'd finished the riot leader off when he'd had a chance. They'd be on him in thirty steps. Emmitt fired two more shots into the unlit stairway. The "Photographer" fired three shells from a thirty-eight Smith and Wesson in return, inducing Emmitt to draw the third and upper door shut. It was two solid layers of steel barrier. Emmitt's sweaty hand searched for the bolt. There was none, at least not on the outside. The door locked from the stairway.

There was a wall less than two feet opposite the door. Emmitt wedged his delicate body in the middle of the door and wall, bracing himself for an impact sure to pulverize his bones. It happened quick, knocking Emmitt to his tumbling side. Emmitt wasn't aware of the helicopter bellowing in the raven sky. He crawled on his knees, then he pressed the bottoms of his feet to a six by six piece of hickory that was laying between his feet and the wall behind himself. The hickory was cut square at the ends. It served as a solid brace for his legs, providing minimal space for the inmates to jostle open the void they needed.

Using the door, they hammered at Emmitt's knees persistently until the pain thrashed at all of his caving joints. Within a few heartbeats, the helicopter landed on the roof. Immediately a crewman dipped his arms to help the women climb in. Marian remained. She'd sent Teddy instead. He was delirious. His head wound dripping profusely, she wouldn't leave him behind. It had been a miracle that he'd made it thus far.

The chopper soared airborne, assaulting the remaining hostages with a heavy blast of wind while Emmitt absorbed two more crunching onslaughts from the inmates. His feet were diligently stuck to the wood, reinforcing his knees, which were being battered by the door. His knees were swollen and knotty. The pain was unimaginable, but like iron anchored to the roof, his knees never faltered. Stronger men would have collapsed. After delivering the first hostages, the helicopter left the parking lot, zooming toward the prison roof again. By the time Emmitt had the door hammered on his knees nine more times, the chopper had landed. With a reckless haste, the men in the choir boarded the helicopter ahead of Marian. She climbed in last, then, giving no warning, she sprang back out onto the roof. The chopper was poised for lift off, but she ran to Emmitt, stopping just once to unsnag her ragged choir gown that was caught on an upright vent.

From the helicopter, Marian had seen the wood bolstering Emmitt's feet was the proper length needed to jam the door. As his strength was weakening, she pried the block loose and twisted it to lodge it between the door and the wall. A microsecond later, there was a violent thrust of pressure colliding with the door. It was wasted energy. The door couldn't be budged. The inmates doubled their manpower at the door, as Emmitt came to rest letting his arm and right side bear the burden of his body's weight. His reprieve was short. The cons were pounding an ax at the inner hinges of the door, and the door was beginning to unfasten at the frame. With all the strength she was able to collect, Marian wrestled Emmitt to his feet. His legs were numb, but she persisted relentlessly. A hinge on the door snapped. The door was starting to lean outward. Emmitt was dragging himself in Marian's wake now, magnetized by her apparent concern for his life. He'd forgotten his true reason for coming to the prison. He'd have to work on dying later.

When they reached the chopper, Emmitt boosted Marian into the puny fuselage. It was packed. Emmitt's body, as small as it was, just couldn't fit, and a third trip by the bird was out of the question. The inmates were almost on the roof.

One of the crewman secured the end of a harness to a bulkhead in the chopper. He looped the harness itself over Emmitt's back. It laid under his armpits and swung up to meet just above Emmitt's face. Emmitt's arms were dangling at his sides, keeping resistance on the yoke, which would allow him to be hauled through the air without falling.

The crewman automatically juggled his thumb, signaling the pilot. It was a smooth lift off for everyone except Emmitt who was jolted by the acceleration of the helicopter as it jerked his cable. The chopper's motor screamed like a thousand banshees, and its blades bludgeoned Emmitt with tornado propulsion.

The chopper sought altitude momentarily while Lester Jameses's dungarees did the opposite. They hung low on Emmitt's waist. Emmitt tried in vain to clinch them with probing fingers. It was no use. They had slipped below his reach. As the chopper made a beeline for the supermarket parking lot, Lester's pants were hugging Emmitt's shins. Above the crowd, they flew. Ninety feet dropped to seventy and stabilized at sixty, with the new mayor's boxer shorts intact, a television news team was knocking itself out to render on the spot coverage of the event. It was being broadcast that Emmitt Braedeikk, the mayor elect, was responsible for the dramatic liberation of the hostages. It was, also, made known that he was the skinny little fellow dangling from beneath the helicopter.

The Reverend Jameses's dungarees flapped wildly while flash and video cameras labored to preserve Emmitt's heroic flight. Soon Emmitt would give a whole new meaning to the phrase "gone with the wind". Emmitt's slippers had been retaining the jeans with miserly effort, but at last the slippers and jeans tore free, allowing Lester's pants to sail wildly into the clutches of admirers who skirmished to inspect the pockets thoroughly for any spare change that belonged to the dumbfounded mayor.

Perhaps the kindest act the press was capable of exercising, might have been to disregard Emmitt's remarkable descent from above. Instead, his insufficiently clad anatomy was allotted priority. The Malfaxe Tribune provided him with front page status. Below his half nude picture, the article went on to paint Emmitt as an unusual political figure basking in the glory of unrestrained heights. He was, also, awarded the title of the town's most eligible bachelor. The story wasn't seen by Emmitt until two days later. In the meantime, things progressed from pandemonium to the unthinkable.

Chapter 37

As the driver chugged to nearly twenty feet away from the prison's entrance, Peter was riding on the running board of the tractor trailer. The driver was preparing to ram the gate. Diesel exhaust mushroomed over the vertical pipes of the eighteen wheeler's cab section, fogging the yellow lights on the guard shack with a heavy gray smog. The air was clouded with a gagging smell as a legion of thousands awaited Peter's command to level the gate. It wasn't midnight, however, the deadline for the inmates had arrived. It was Peter's deadline, not theirs.

Chief Drake posted himself outside of the guard shack. He'd never felt this belittled. The chief was dazed and frazzled. His militia was outnumbered, hundreds to one. From all appearances, the police were nonexistent. Their uniforms couldn't be seen anywhere among the rapidly growing hoard of angry people surrounding the prison. The Governor had been notified about the crisis at the prison, but, as of yet, there'd been no reply from the state capital. The chief's nausea swelled to his chest. His sight was being blurred by smoke. His legs were unsteady, as he gazed into the torrid face of Peter Ghudd.

"You'll be prosecuted for this!" The chief ranted.

"Go back to your telephone and call somebody who cares!" Peter mocked.

"People will die! The police can't protect your pack of animals!" The chief warned.

Peter's eyes became infected with contempt. He looked Chief Drake up and down as though he were a hill of decaying sheep dung. "Get lost! The police can't even protect themselves," he ridiculed, returning his attention to the gate.

Peter's hold on the mob was staggering. As long as it was Peter cracking the whip, anyone of the thousands of people would follow him into a den of underfed lions. The chief, himself, felt the allure of Peter's charisma. Thirty years earlier, he would have probably dogged Peter's tracks himself. Peter was an alpha wolf, and behind those fierce eyes of his laid a mind as sharp as butchering fangs. Tonight Peter exceeded being lethal. He was programmed to annihilate. The chief dashed for the phone. He'd try and reach the governor again. The National Guard had to be activated. In just fifteen minutes, the throng had doubled in size, and the deluge of Sutler was ready to begin. Peter shouted to the truck's driver. "Take 'er down!"

The truck banged the two sides of the gate hard onto the inner walls of the prison. Peter had anchored himself to the running board, and was thrown free as the truck had surged to the gate, ripping it apart at the middle. The crashing blow battered the gate into shambles, and the truck sped into the prison yard and came to a rest inside the entrance to the prison's main lobby. Gunshots had penetrated the truck's windshield and the driver slumped dead over the wheel. Peter wasted no time in getting to the lobby, He quickly climbed into the truck's cab and propped the slain driver over the dash. A stray bullet pierced the radiator. Peter reversed the gears to clear the lobby of the truck. His mob began gushing in. An inmate fired two shots, causing two men to fall and be stomped under the weight of the crowd. When the vigilantes caught him, they beat the inmate first with their fists. One vigilante began choking him, as another hammered him with the same gun he'd tried to use on them. The convict died on his feet. Three more inmates were dragged off of the elevator and bludgeoned.

Motioning the attackers ahead, Peter climbed onto the hood of the cab, an ornament of savagery, as the prison became a stage for homicidal mania. Guns crackled through the perpetual rage. Most of the inmates were taken by surprise, completely overwhelmed by more of a fight than they had bargained for. The prisoners were hopelessly doomed. The convicts on the ground level were being stabbed, beaten, or shot to death. Eight of them survived by pretending to be dead. Seventeen of the town's people died in the first five minutes. In the building chaos death was proving to be a two way street. The convicts on the third floor opened up on the raiders below with assault rifles they'd taken from the guards. They were shooting from behind barred windows with the glass broken out. Six more men fell along with two women, who were trampled beneath the wave of marauding angry people. The siege of Sutler Penitentiary was gaining tremendous force.

A good many of the inmates had stayed in their cells. Some were shot right there. Others were being busted out and rounded up.

The convicts on the third floor scurried to the fourth level, where they joined a few remaining diehards. Ammunition was running low for the inmates, but not the vigilantes, whose guns were spewing non stop cascades of hot lead. It would be one more floor for the cons, then they'd have to stand or die on the roof. Likely the later.

It was Jimmy Sloane, who tugged the first mattress from a vacant cell and hauled it to the roof. Three mattresses followed that. Taking the shape of a barricade, four additional mattresses were laid on top of those. The idea caught on fast. Some of the inmates began firing into the tide of vigilantes, while the others relayed the mattresses to the roof. A five foot mattress wall was built in three minutes. It spanned the entire width of the prison roof.

By the time Peter's brigade was able to storm the roof, the inmates were firing back at them from behind the mattresses. The townspeople suffered more casualties. They were stalled temporarily. The inmates would fight come hellfire, and that's exactly what happened. Like meteor showers, Molotov cocktails were hurled onto the wall of mattresses by the mob. Flames stirred up into the night's breeze. The convicts were being trapped between the heat and the steep fall to the prison yard. They were battling insurmountable odds. It was useless! Their ammunition was depleting, as the fire eagerly ate at their barricade.

The 'Photographer's' clothes were the first to catch on fire. An inmate futilely slapped at his torched comrade, but then went back to the problem of his own survival. Molotov cocktails were landing everywhere around him, he'd do well just to save himself. The "Photographer" who by now was engulfed in flames, darted to the edge of the roof and fell six stories to the prison yard. He flared like a Roman candle all the way down.

Jimmy Sloan's leg was shot out from underneath himself. He tried crawling across the roof to breathe cleaner air, but was stopped by a burst of fire that exploded in his face. The heat was unbearable, as the smaller fires joined to become a huge fire that sparked the heavens with its amber ash.

At 2:17 AM, a one-alarm fire brought two fire engines skirmishing for a furniture store. The store was downwind of Sutler. It was a frame construction. The fire had migrated from the burning mattresses and ignited paper in a dumpster. It burned the wooden exterior of the building, working its way to the second floor, where expensive bedroom furniture had been displayed. When the firemen arrived, they found the building demolished.

By 2:25 AM, the inmates were using their last cartridges. One prisoner sucked the barrel of his thirty eight just prior to blowing out the top of his skull. The others were shooting at Peter's army in delayed sequence. With their mattresses burning, the convicts only protection was literally going up in smoke!

At 2:45 AM, an alarm box was activated one street north of the burning furniture store. A row house had been ignited. The homes were over eighty years old. Fire walls had not been installed. The fire had kindled five additional homes. A third ladder truck squealed to the scene. The second fire station was now emptied.

A burned and frantic inmate leaped over the incinerating mattresses, his lungs gasping, his hands charred, he surrendered. It was the same with the nine who followed him. Then a convict was doused by an exploding cocktail. He aimed his gun at his heart and pulled the trigger. By the time he realized the gun was empty, the plastic handle had already melted to his hand. He, too, jumped sixty feet to his death. In all, twenty-six inmates spared themselves by dropping their weapons. When the prison's rooftop eventually dwindled into a smoldering heap of fabric, the rest of the convicts who'd retreated to the roof died. The twenty-six survivors had their arms and wrists bound with wire, cut from the top of the prison wall. They were taken to the prison yard, where Peter Ghudd was waiting.

Sirens were heard screeching in the distance. A paint store was ignited for the third alarm. More Ladder engines amassed at the two story building from six miles away. The fire was a disaster! It was feeding on cans of paint that were popping open like chestnuts in a microwave oven. There was an adjoining Goodwill store. It also caught fire. Beside the Goodwill store was a warehouse.

To the rear of the prison was the basketball court. The convicts were gathered there. They were badly beaten. Broken noses and fractured skulls were common injuries. Those convicts were fortunate compared to the inmate who'd been kicked repeatedly until his spleen was ruptured. Another had his back broken by a steel pipe that was torn from the prison's plumbing. Peter's enforcers had done their job well. The criminal community suffered a traumatic shock, but it was early yet. Malfaxe was a town set on quenching its fury in a vengeful pool of rectitude. The pace was set.

There was a casualness accompanying Peter as he strolled through the ranks of the prisoners. They were made to stand erect. Their head count was increasing to nearly a hundred eighty, and growing rapidly. Inmates who resisted, but managed to live, also had their wrists bound with wire stripped from the top of the prison's wall. Peter had ordered that all the prisoners in their cells be sawed out if necessary and brought to the yard immediately. They'd be appearing before the new judge in town, Peter, and their sentences promised to be a grim, if not a foregone conclusion. Every eye, mind, and particle of energy in the yard zeroed in on the old man as he roved by the inmates one by one inspecting their ragged condition.

Peter would do with them what he pleased. Nobody would challenge Peter's authority. His henchmen, in their patriotic red, blue, and white attire, were behind him. Behind his henchmen was a town of crusaders long overdue for the past forbidden fruits of justice. They were jammed inside the prison walls, and thousands more stayed outside of the open gate. High over the crowd, the nocturnal sky was turning aglow above the burning city. Worse yet, all fire stations in the town had been depleted of their equipment as certain doom was eyeing the unscathed portions of Malfaxe.

There were search lights mounted on each of the four prison walls. The light on the east wall was shining directly on Peter. He planned on making good use of the effect. He didn't feel December's crisp chill penetrating his skin and working its way to his bones. The meteorologists were hinting of a white Christmas to be. If it snowed tonight, the overlay would last for another five or six days. Enough time for Christmas to come and go. It was cold, but Peter was warmed by his mounting power. He moved into the shimmer of the light, not once noticing the man fidgeting with the light's wires. Koepy was as inconspicuous as a patch of mortar. Peter had no concerns. He sauntered to the nearest inmate, a frail man, probably in his fifties. The man was Caucasian. Except for a small frame, he had no distinguishing characteristics. Peter was relaxed and confident. His mission had been well defined by a slew of speeches he'd given in taverns, halls, and outdoor assemblies. Television was the tool that had established him though. It had made him famous, surpassing even his wildest expectations. Now, by his own mandate, it was time to deliver on his intentions.

Peter removed a 357 magnum that was wedged between the small of his back and his belt. He flattened the bore of the muzzle to the convict's head, then, without firing, brought the gun to rest parallel with his own leg. "Bring me all of the murderers, he dictated to the convicts.

Four inmates were gathered by some of the cons who were gambling for a reprieve. Peter sustained his place in the light. He had the men line up according to their height. The shortest inmate was on the extreme right end. The tallest was on the left. Peter went to the right of the line. He raised the gun, and at a slight angle, shot the first inmate through the side of the head, killing him and the other three inmates instantly. They became contorted globs of death. Scarlet flesh had splattered in a million fragments, as the single bullet made its trajectory through the heads of all four inmates. It pinged off the prison wall and lodged itself in another inmate's arm. He fell, screaming in agony.

"Attempted murderers," Peter called out to the inmates. There was no response. "Shall I begin guessing?"

The prisoners didn't budge. Except for Emmitt, it became eerily quiet. Emmitt was probing a path toward Peter. He'd barely gotten to the outskirts of the crowd, when he was stopped by two of Peter's men in their matching, blue blazers. Emmitt's frail body was no equal for Peter's guards. He made a feeble effort to bully his way past them, but it was useless. Once again, Emmitt was being mauled to his sore and bumpy knees, when he was rescued by Peter's intervention. "Let 'em up," Peter ordered his men. Peter closed in on Emmitt, suave and confident. They were inches apart, and Emmitt could see that Peter's brashness was a coat of armor that he'd never be able to penetrate. The one time janitor turned politician was now a demagogue out of control. Emmitt saw the reflections of a city on fire burning in Peter's sweaty, glossed face. The core of the city was to Emmitt's back, but he sensed that Malfaxe would more than likely run through with a dozen mayors before the residual effects of Peter's rampage might be repaired. Emmitt was thankful it wasn't going to be his duty. For the present, he had enough to worry about with the old man staring a tremendous crater in Emmitt's half, brave facade.

Peter broke the silence. He was obviously in no state of mind to mince words. "Well, if it ain't Mr. Bullshit!" He greeted his former boss.

Emmitt's ribcage stirred as though it had a threshing machine inside. He'd seen executed men, only that was in 'Nam. 'Nam was a sick episode in his life. This was home, where trials, plea bargains, and stays were granted. Life had meaning here. As Emmitt's attention was fixed on the four convicts who had been decapitated, he briefly tried to reason away any significance their lives may have served. In spite of his feeble efforts to save their lives , it wasn't difficult for Emmitt. They were all murderers, why brood over them? Then he looked at Peter for a hint of remorse. There was none to be found. Peter's lips separated, his words confirming Emmitt's horror. "You can destroy a man," Peter said, "you'll never abolish an inspiration.!"

Then Peter immediately approached another convict. It was the same convict, the small one, he'd neglected to shoot earlier. He shoved the gun under the man's chin. Emmitt's hands tightened with nothing to cling to, least of all a heavy object. The gun discharged, transforming the convict into a faceless corpse.

Peter was ignoring the few citizens who'd deserted his legion. They were spreading out into a city being ravaged by fire, a fire fanned by the winds of Peter's own doings. Sheer rage rose to the old renegade's neck, settling in his eyes. They were the most evil pair of eyes Emmitt had ever engaged. "You're deranged!" Emmitt shouted, lunging at Peter's eyes. He wanted to rip them out of their sockets, but his assault was deflected by Peter's swift, nasty elbow to Emmitt's jaw, knocking him into the guards, who then propped Emmitt up to his feet.

Peter reloaded the spent cartridges in his gun's chamber. Six more convicts died in the wake of Peter's pistol. His guards remained stoic in the presence of the mob. In the background, sirens could be heard screaming from emergency vehicles. They were echoed by another string of ambulances tearing through the city. With the potential of becoming a vast furnace, Malfaxe was in a state of mounting destruction.

Peter still failed to see Koepy, who'd deserted the spotlight on top of the prison wall. Koepy wove through the crowd, making his way to the extreme edge, just shy of where Peter was beginning to reload the magnum. The light went out momentarily. Peter hesitated. A fight had erupted between two of his guards and a man three feet from where Peter stood. They'd rumbled their entangled bodies right into Peter so hard that the pistol was knocked from Peter's hand. It was kicked, stepped on, and disappeared for an instant. The brawlers were separated by five more of Peter's guards. It was Koepy who'd been fighting. The guards knocked Koepy into the mob, where he vanished as discreetly as he'd appeared.

When Peter had his gun given back, the light was sputtering inconsistently. He browsed through the ranks of the terrified convicts. It was a fact that every possible class of criminal had fair representation at Sutler. The murderers were dead, at least most of them. It was the thieves, rapists, and ordinary thugs who swelled the prison's population to a disproportionate extent. Peter wasn't differentiating. He was about to become an equal opportunity executioner. Actually, he'd searched well for Sam Rhiggs. Sam wasn't there. Somehow, if only temporarily, Sam had avoided Peter's wrath. Prisoners were still being hauled from their cells though. Peter would be watching for Sam. In the meantime, he'd randomly pick his victims.

Peter made a choice. He escorted a prisoner to the spotlight. The light was oscillating faster. It went out, but flashed back on. Off, on, off, on quicker and quicker. It was like a concert strobe light shining on the old man as he pistol whipped the convict whose wrists had been bound behind his back with the razor embedded wire. The man was young, maybe just in his twenties. He was already losing a dangerous amount of blood from his wrist. Passing bad checks was his crime. He was petrified, as Peter spun the gun's cylinder. The rapid clicks whizzed by the chamber, stopping abruptly along with the light which had settled on Peter.

A shocked crowd of onlookers questioned their sanity, while Peter's appearance had somehow altered beneath the unstable light. As the tempo of the irregular light slowed only somewhat, Peter's looks began to mimic that of a sinister masquerade. Infamous leaders, diabolical in every sense of the word became captured in the light. At last Peter was now dressed in dark bottoms with a light brown shirt. He wore an arm band. It had a morbid insignia. Peter wasn't aware of his change, as he aimed the gun at the convict's head. He pulled the trigger once, twice, then tree times. The gun didn't discharge. "You're a two faced, double talking weakling!" Peter began slurring Emmitt, who was trying to break free of the two henchmen. "Social outcast think they don't need to conform. They'll need permanent persuasion!"

"So now we're killing people for what they think, Peter?" Emmitt was hysterical. "What's next, a little genocide?"

Totally in the light, Peter's cheeks hollowed in the shadow of his protruding brow. His eyes were dilated with fury, dancing wildly, they rolled upward to expose their marble whites. He'd acquired what looked like a mustache, actually two mustaches, and in reality, two that Emmitt couldn't envy. The one atop Peter's upper lip finalized the image. However a rowdy Iraqi veteran had taken the liberty to bounce a piece of charred debris off of Peter's forehead, leaving a second smudge the size of a large postage stamp. Although it had made him look silly, the light had captured Peter's grotesqueness. His uniform, the symbol of pure undiluted hatred, was mimicking Peter's atrocities. In the light, the newly acquired uniform revealed its blood soaked sleeves, and the blood seemed to be flowing excessively onto Peter's guilt laden hands.

As word of Peter's atrocities flooded outside of the prison walls from those within, the crowd began to thin. In the beginning, it was slow, but the momentum gained quickly until there were only a few of Peter's guards left. Except for the light that had flickered out of control, all of the lights on the prison's walls stayed on. The faulty light had faded out, as if to signal that somehow Peter's spellbinding hold had been broken.

At last, the police were penetrating the crowd. They began restraining the prisoners, only inexplicably Peter, himself, had disappeared. Strangely enough, he'd evaded, not only the police, but also Emmitt who'd been keeping tabs on Peters movements. It was uncanny. Peter was nowhere to be found. Emmitt had last seen him stepping out of the light's focus. It was as if he had evaporated, not leaving the smallest trace of his macabre existence.

It was pushing 4:00 AM by the time Emmitt reentered the guard shack. A hint of snow trickled in the cool, moist atmosphere. Emmitt tucked his chin lower to occupy the gap left by a missing top button on Lester's borrowed shirt. Lester Jameses was certainly a big man, Emmitt told himself. Had the button been there, Emmitt would have still needed three more inches on his neck size to allow for the difference. Emmitt pulled the collar of Lester's jacket over his neck and folded down the wool knit hat he was wearing to meet the collar. In the chaos, he'd lost Lester's fedora. The wool hat Emmitt was wearing, he'd gotten off the basketball court. It was laying there unclaimed. Emmitt's head was cold, prompting him to put it on. Pleased that it had fit so well, he decided he'd keep it. He was craving warmth. The temperature had dropped to a frigid twenty two degrees.

The door to the guard shack had been ripped away and the windows were broken. Heat was an unobtainable luxury inside the flimsy outpost, although the telephone was still working. The chief slapped the telephone in Emmitt's palm before he made his way to the prison yard to supervise his men. With the fire on the prison's roof thoroughly extinguished, the inmates were being jailed again, only this time it was to their relief. There were no complaints or comments about retaliation coming from any of the inmates. Tonight the convicts were happy to be returning to their cells. Emmitt spoke into the phone with an inquiring "Hello?" A pause occurred, and Emmitt was about to put the phone down, when he heard a gruff voice. It sounded like Norman's.

"Emmitt?"

"Norman! I thought you were dead!"

It was quiet for a brief period, making Emmitt feel foolish to himself for succumbing to false hope. "Emmitt..." It was Norman's voice.

"Norman, you're alive!"

"Emmitt, is this you?"

"Yes, how'd you know I was here?"

"I called the police station. They gave me the number."

"If you're calling to tell me you're swearing out a warrant for my arrest, Norman!" He was interrupted by Norman.

"Arrest you. Emmitt, for what?"

"Decking you, and if your head wasn't scrap iron, I'd a killed you!"

"You ain't man enough, Emmitt! I gotta say, though, you hit me kinda hard. That was a lousy trick you played on me."

"How is your head, Norman?"

"Terrible! I'll live."

Emmitt breathed easy. He'd been dealt a reprieve on life. Best of all, so had Norman. He tried to hide his elation, but it was difficult. "Why'd you take forever to call, Norman? I could have used some of your daring, bravado here!"

"I've...never mind."

"Come on!"

"Okay, Emmitt, tell me the truth, just this once."

"Just this once, Norman. You've got my word."

"Have I ever lied to you, Emmitt?"

There was a pause. "Norman, you've done more to me than I'd want to remember. I have to admit, though, you've never lied, not ever. I wish you would've sometimes."

"I was there, Emmitt!"

"Where, Norman?"

"I've, I've been beyond Emmitt. Beyond everything that's ever seemed important to me. It's too awesome to describe! That's why I needed to talk to you. All of that talk about ongoing life, it's true, Emmitt! God is Real! I never believed in God, and in all honesty, I don't think you did either. I've been embraced by his eternal compassion! It's big enough to shame Everest! It's better than anything that you can imagine! An angel told me!" Norman halted in mid sentence.

"What? Go on, Norman. What did the angel say?" Emmitt's concern with his brother's mental condition increased.

"The angel said...the angel said, Emmitt, that God wanted me to walk with His hand on my shoulder. The angel promised it would happen if I walked closer to God!"

"Norman, listen. Is your medical insurance paid up? If it isn't, I'll accept full responsibility for your convalescence."

"Cut it out!"

"I'm not trying to be smart, Norman. I guess it's this new job. It's shaping into a huge bummer. Do you suppose God can reach over to my shoulder once in a while? I could use some help!" Emmitt aimed at the subtle approach. Norman's persistence was genuine. Another argument wasn't necessary.

"Weren't you taking any of this in, Emmitt? How damn wide do you think your shoulders are? If I have to walk closer to God, you will too! Your no more privileged than I am! It'll be a challenge, Emmitt. I don't know if we're up to it."

"I'm bushed, Norman. We'll talk at home."

"Fine." A click led to a dial tone. Norman's head was throbbing.

CHAPTER 38

"Sit here, boy!" Emmitt had ordered. He was there to clean out his desk when he'd led Vernon through the bank's main lobby and into his partially abandoned office. There were six desk drawers in all to be emptied. They were crammed full. Emmitt was able to open the most stubborn of them by shimmying the drawer side to side and persistently pressing the jammed papers down hard. The five remaining drawers were less trouble because they didn't contain magazines he'd been stashing away for the last three years. Wondering why he'd kept so many trivial items, he emptied the contents onto the floor into one large mess.

Emmitt rummaged through the mess, sorting similar things and laying them together on the floor. Pens and pencils numbered in the dozens. He kept those by themselves. There were hundreds of paper clips, index cards, and even six spare neckties. He'd hastily separated the mixture and placed those on different blocks of linoleum. Realizing he'd amassed a defunct collection of junk, he quickly began scooping everything into a plastic leaf bag that he'd brought along for the dumpster. The new mayor planned on arriving fresh at a City Hall that was lean and clean. He'd be bringing with himself no excess paraphernalia.

Emmitt double checked the bank's security system, then he and Vernon left by way of the rear office exit, dumping the leaf bag into the green metal dumpster directly outside of the building. It was Sunday afternoon. A week had passed since the riot at the prison. His installment into office would be tomorrow. He'd arranged to return his private set of the bank's keys by registered mail to the headquarters in Chicago first thing on Monday morning. Margaret Simpson was the bank's new manager now. Emmitt consoled himself that she would do a fine job. She had worked diligently to keep the bank a competitive enterprise while lately he had been little more than a complacent overseer preoccupying himself with political aspirations. He'd wished her all the best two days earlier.

Breathing deeply, Emmitt rounded the corner of the alley with Vernon in close pursuit. Eleven inches of snow made walking difficult, especially for Vernon. The dog's belly had bottomed out in the last six inches of snow. It had caused him to hop with his hind legs in a frenzied effort to stay with Emmitt, who at the moment was paying Vernon little mind. Finally, Emmitt turned and lifted Vernon into both arms and began lugging the dog to the bus stop.

The buses were understandably late. It was no wonder. The streets were only randomly plowed, forewarning Emmitt of some of the undeserving employees who were drawing nice city salaries. If the roads weren't cleared, the entire city might as well fold until they were. Emmitt, himself, had had to ditch his own car three quarters of a mile from the bank and trudge the remaining distance. While he was in the bank, he had thawed somewhat, but now, with the wind slashing across his face, the sixteen degrees stung him to his tonsils. Keeping Vernon as close to himself as he possibly could in the numbing temperature, he buried an agonized expression in the dog's matted fur. By twelve thirty-five, he was still waiting for a bus, and had lost all faith in the mass transit system. He'd been waiting for what had seemed an hour, actually, it had only been fifteen minutes. He was taxing his mind for an option, when a horn honked. He raised his head from the dog's fur. It was Lester Jameses.

Lester's stoic body language deceived Emmitt. The minister sat erect, intently looking straight ahead. Emmitt wasn't even sure who it was at first. Lester's truck, with it's multiple dents and vanishing paint, was covered by a hefty coat of snow. It didn't help that Emmitt's vision had become blurred by the wind. In apparent frustration, at last Lester leaned to the passenger's side of the truck and spoke through a missing window. Emmitt could see him quite well now.

"If you're waitin' for a bus, you'd better go with me."

Emmitt approached the truck cautiously, his eyes searching for a gun that the preacher might be concealing. "I'm out of your way, aren't I?"

"I'll drop you anywhere that's convenient," Lester promised, making Emmitt squirm. "What I mean is," Lester corrected his terminology, "I'll take you home. Come on, get in!"

Emmitt didn't argue. He was afraid of coming across as ungrateful. It was obvious that he was stranded, so he got into the truck with Vernon on his lap, expecting either a choice sermon or an overdue payment of lead. If Lester was armed and bent on revenge, it would still be warmer inside of the truck. Emmitt preferred being shot today, just as he had on that frigid night in Lester's barn. Given a choice, it would certainly be better than succumbing on a street corner with his face frozen tight onto Vernon's middle section. The mental picture was more than Emmitt wanted to bear, forcing himself to consider the brighter side. His spirits were harkened by knowing that the press was likely to be cheated from another one of their revealing photographs of himself.

Lester brought the truck to a steady ten miles per hour, keeping his grip tight on the wheel and his attention straight ahead. An awkward few minutes milled passed as Lester drove his truck between abandoned cars left on the slippery roads. The city had been thoroughly immobilized by the snow, which was approaching blizzard status in rapid time. The eleven inches of white powdery snow that Emmitt had walked through to get to the bus stop was quickly nearing thirteen. Except for the National Guard sent in to maintain order, nothing else of any significance was moving.

Sometimes as many as six soldiers were patrolling every square block, as their army green Jeeps powered through the snow and ice to carry on with a show of strict regimental control. They were everywhere. As he scrutinized the many singed buildings, the new mayor to be was glad the Guard was there. These were the lucky buildings he was looking at. They had warded off the fires set by Peter's followers. Other structures weren't that fortunate. Emmitt was fully aware that Lester's church had been reduced to charred lumber. While touring the city to assess the damage, he'd seen its remains two days earlier. Emmitt desperately wanted to apologize, but he found himself to be rather speechless, and Lester didn't seem too prone to making conversation either. In the meantime Emmitt would just stay quiet. He could see that it was all the minister could do to keep the truck on the disabled roads without having an accident.

Emmitt's thoughts turned to Marian, and he questioned himself as to whether Marian ever wanted to speak to him again. After all that had occurred between the two of them, it was heartening that she'd helped him escape to the helicopter. Back then it seemed a true act of caring, only Marian was the kind of person, Emmitt reasoned, who'd have done that for probably anybody, except maybe someone like Sam Rhiggs. It was a shame, Emmitt told himself, in the most sardonic sense, that Sam didn't have a protector like her. They'd found Sam on the previous Tuesday dangling beneath the prison's gallows. As of yet, the coroner hadn't decided if it was homicide or if Sam was his own executioner. He did exhibit a strong death wish though. Emmitt figured that the truth would never be known, especially since Sam's hands were never tied, but he also knew the cons were too afraid of one another to talk. Sam's death crept from Emmitt's mind, reviving his tender feeling for Marian. In the future, he'd work hard at being a good mayor and even harder at becoming a better human being. Over time, maybe Marian's faith in him might be restored. The whole situation with the Jameses, as bleak as it looked, only served to make Emmitt more determined to accomplish what he knew he'd have to do. From now on, he'd be as honest as the falling snow was thick.

Emmitt was peering now at the rows of scorched houses. Their dirty exteriors were blasted with cinders and flames that had been hurled upon them violently by the wind. The flying ashes and heat had been thrashed on them relentlessly, only somehow these homes remained upright. This was no thanks to Peter, who'd come close to bringing the entire city to its demise. Peter had proven to be a smooth talker with seemingly honorable motivations. The history books were loaded with characters who possessed Peter's verbal talents, Emmitt surmised, not to mention deceptive motivations. Many of them had famous names that school children could blurt out. He decided that Peter was a social mutineer ingratiating himself by exploiting basic horse sense only to exploit it to achieve his evil intentions. Peter had used the convicts, very well in fact, to propel himself into the limelight. Who, in their right mind, would have disputed Peter's logic? He was a smart cookie, to say the least, but extremely dangerous. Had Peter been elected, his sinister way of influencing people may have been catastrophic, and who knows where it might have ended. It was imperative that Peter be hunted down. If he couldn't be caught, Emmitt concluded, Peter would have to be chased into the darkest of caves where the vampire bats could feast on his decaying flesh. Otherwise, Peter would be the one feasting, and likely it would be to the expense of any good that a benevolent, and respectable social order might offer.

In the prison yard, it had never occurred to Emmitt that he'd witnessed a class act steeling Peter's cagey hold on the town. It just didn't seem possible, but Koepy had given an outstanding performance. Koepy may have been an amateur magician, but he was the best Emmitt had ever witnessed. And then there was the night Emmitt had bludgeoned Norman's skull. He'd have bet his life on Norman being dead. In fact, when Emmitt had showed up at the prison to intervene for the hostages, he'd done just that. Norman told Emmitt when he came to that he'd seen Koepy leaving. It was in the wee hours of Monday morning. A strange time to be picking up a paycheck and returning house keys. That was the only explanation for Koepy being at Emmitt's place. Emmitt regretted missing him. He wanted to pay him more. Koepy had actually assembled steps on the cement pad that Emmitt had instructed him to break apart. The steps to Emmitt's sun deck were broad with fancy wooden railings. They were connected to posts topped with decorative knobs. It was obvious to Emmitt that the carpenter had left his signature, for even a layman could see that the entire structure was built to withstand the assaulting climate of the forthcoming years. A note was tacked to the bottom post. It said, "Your Father's house has many rooms. May your journey begin here." Koepy, Emmitt noted, was much more than a handyman. The carpenter was a specialist, who'd given Emmitt's concept of "home improvement" a brand new meaning. A meaning that, in reality, for years had been lost in Emmitt's materialistic view of everything he'd ever considered worthy. The idea occurred to him spontaneously, in Lester Jameses's truck. It had happened right when the tires clawed their treads into a rare patch of solid road that Emmitt grasped what Koepy might have meant. It may not have been Emmitt's biological father that Koepy was referring to when he wrote "Your Father's house has many rooms." It may have been an invitation for both himself and Norman to enjoy superior dimensions, anyway that's what Emmitt was starting to take from it. The words were similar to a Biblical verse, John 14, although Christ had used the word "rooms." The word began to stir Emmitt's mind to the limit. If the word" rooms," were symbolic, were there an assortment of plateaus that earthly man wasn't aware of? Emnmitt soon realized, and quite intently that the God he would always try to please was as intangible as the air he was breathing only much more life giving. Was there anything as mysterious as the universe, or its wondrous creation? "No way", he'd told himself. It didn't just happen. Nothing occurs anywhere without a catalyst. Emmitt felt dazed by his own stupidity, and Koepy's youthful insight. He even wrestled with the bizarre notion, but only briefly, that Koepy was the product of another, but elevated rebirth. He was so different from anybody that Emmitt had ever encountered. Peter was too, for that matter. Maybe Koepy was a protector of some kind and had been sent to stalk Peter's harmful trail, and influence the outcome of his pending deeds. Emmitt instantly dismissed the idea as crazy and allowed his thoughts to move on. For the rest of his life, however, he'd never forget Koepy for saving an angry city from its near uncontrollable anger and helping to turn Emmitt's own ruffled life one hundred eighty degrees from a domestic war zone.

Norman had mellowed, also. Emmitt didn't know how long his brother's mood might last, but Emmitt was doing all he knew how to do to stretch the diplomacy. They'd gone to Baltimore the day before to see a hockey game together, and Emmitt had enjoyed the excitement with a youth like enthusiasm. He continuously yelled griping complaints at the visiting team, ate endlessly, and bought lunch for Norman and snacks for some of the other fans. Norman later bought ringside tickets for a boxing match at the Steelworker's Hall. That would be next week. Emmitt was thrilled with the prospect. He'd never seen a live bout before. Emmitt promised himself to keep his official business in order in the meantime. His duties as the new mayor promised to be demanding, so he'd have to skillfully balance his official responsibilities with brotherly tact. Besides, his ironclad rule dictated that the job come first. The roads were at the top of the list. They'd have to be brought up to par in record time. They'd need all kinds of repairs and improvements, but for the present, Emmitt would settle for a good plowing.

Just as the truck climbed a small hill, Lester's tires spun in the slush and then grabbed fast again. Emmitt's head jerked and his knees buckled a little. His knees were improving since he'd used them to bar shut the metal door on the prison roof. By all rights, they should have been splintered to shreds. While he was on them that night, he'd been praying hard, something he'd hadn't done in years. And like Norman, he'd embarked on a religious excursion following that terrible night of the riot. Since then, Emmitt had found the devout posture not discomforting at all. It seemed to be a sacred honor. The humility of it all bolstered his soul and upgraded his self-confidence to the point of being obvious.

From the top of the hill, Emmitt scanned a portion of the city. Although he was thankful there were no fatalities among the general population, it was, nonetheless, a disappointing sight. He confided to himself that the firemen and the police were truly earthly guardians who deserved a whole lot more than a simple "thanks, or a perfunctory paycheck." As it had been said so many times before by so many. "They were the true heroes, the unsung heroes, who risked their lives day after day," only recently they'd given so much, and gotten so little back in return. They deserved the utmost of respect. Emmitt wanted desperately to do something significant to express his personal gratitude along with that of the city's. It would be a monumental task, and he'd probably come up short, but he was determined to try anyway. He'd, also, need more than one term in office to transform Malfaxe into an appealing town for businesses, let alone a thriving metropolis. If he got re-elected, it was going to be interesting to see just how much he could accomplish with an extra term. As the truck rendered its momentum at an intersection, the future mayor was thinking quietly about how the prison issue needed to be resolved in his first term. After all, his word was his promise. He knew society had to banish its recurrent evil doers, but maybe that wasn't enough. Exile, why not exile? There were remote places all over the world that the meanest and most incorrigible criminals could populate. He thought about prison ships, and distant mountain locations as alternatives. For now, he'd have to either build a new prison or renovate the old one. In the mean times, it wouldn't hurt to lobby Congress for a change in penal policy. For many cities, what happened in Malfaxe was likely a prelude of things to come. He really believed Peter was right about reform. His prison needed to be a deterrent not a reward system. Emmitt wasn't lying when he'd sided with the shrewd troublemaker on the prison issue, but some things he knew could be carried way too far, as Peter had already shown. He'd even re- think the exile solution along with the other two possibilities he'd pondered. There was no immediate remedy for the problem, none at all. Only he knew that in ample time an honest analysis would provide a proper answer, and it would take some trial, and error.

Lester Jameses braked the truck. It nearly slid out of control, descending the hill and leveling off on a straight road that traveled by eight additional blocks of row houses which were divided by an abandoned brewery. The houses were quite old, most of them built in the nineteen twenties. They were of box design. Emmitt noticed that they didn't even have rain gutters. Their brick was scorched from the fire and their wooden trim was engraved with old paint that had bubbled from the intense heat of the flames. A little Asian girl, maybe six or seven, was jamming a straw thin stick with an American flag under a second story window. The flag was no bigger than a regular mailing envelope. When a terrific gust of wind tore shingles from an adjoining house and blew a flower pot off of a step to its broken demise, Emmitt was flabbergasted! The flag remained waving in the distance, never leaving its fragile post which was still positioned where the girl had stuck it. Emmitt watched the flag rippling in the freezing cold wind. Soon he became overtaken with immense pride in the fact that America, with all of its problems, was still a great country with extraordinary people, and these people were the steel in an unfolding web that spread across the United States like a chain link fence coiled infinitely around itself. Yeah, it was true, he reminded himself, that Malfaxe was hurting, but just as a child with an injured leg stands up to run with a devilish resolve, Malfaxe would not be hindered by a few bad setbacks!

Two blocks later, the Reverend slowed his truck. They passed an adult bookstore, after that was a beauty salon, and each still intact. Then they came to a halt at Lester's destroyed church. It was burned to its foundation. None of it made any sense to Emmitt. Why'd a pornography shop avoid being set ablaze, but yet a church was totally ruined? The church had stood next door to the porn shop. Emmitt continued to be speechless.

In the past he'd read about a church in the Mediterranean Sea area. It was on the island of Malta. For the allies Malta had been a strategic stronghold during World War Two. It was centrally located, and used for regulating shipping lanes. It had air strips, and anchorage for Allied ships and submarines. The church, Emmitt remembered, had been bombed on a Sunday morning during a service. Fortunately, a miracle had taken place. The huge German bomb that had crashed through the ceiling and came to rest near the pulpit never detonated. The church was spared, and nobody inside was killed. The bomb to this day, still occupies that very spot where it had landed. It's been disarmed and serves as a monument to a merciful God. Emmitt was still baffled as to why a righteous God would let such a dispiriting consequence befall on Lester's church. If anybody didn't need the heartache, it was Lester Jameses.

For several uncomfortable seconds, Emmitt wrestled with his inability to talk. It was Lester who broke the silence with a single sentence as if Emmitt wasn't even there. "I'm gonna rebuild my church," he said, with a strong, solemn conviction.

It was then, and exactly then that Emmitt understood the reason why Lester Jameses's church had been reduced to gray ashes. He knew he'd finally come upon the truth as to why God would permit such a terrible mishap to occur. Lester Jameses had to be corrected. There was no possible way that Emmitt was going to let Lester do what he'd said. It was time to take the offensive.

"No, you're mistaken!" Emmitt said. "I can't allow it!"

"I'm what?" Lester came back, quietly daunting the heat of ten thousand Hells in his narrow black eyes.

"You're not rebuilding your church," Emmitt reiterated, choosing to meet Lester's stare. "We're doing it together!"

"What?"

"I said, we're rebuilding the church together, Reverend. I won't be robbed of the opportunity, not by anyone!"

A few more moments passed by, and a peaceful quiet lingered between the two men as Lester drove the truck to a main road. Three quarters of a mile further, a posted sign marked the border of Malfaxe. The streets were improved here. They'd been plowed and salted. Traffic was flowing at a reasonable pace. Emmitt reached for the knob on the radio. The music being played was becoming extremely loud. He'd wanted to turn the volume lower. Emmitt began to guess that they'd traveled very close to the station's transmitter. No matter which way he rotated the knob, the music's high volume persisted. Emmitt, after fruitless attempts finally realized that Lester's radio, true to form, was actually broken. He couldn't imagine where the music was coming from. He didn't mind though. The melodies were sounding better by the note. He began to want more until every cell in his body was exploding with them. Emmitt couldn't get enough.

It was the side view mirror that caught Vernon's attention. The dog braced his paws against the upper part of Lester's truck door, putting his head past the vacant window. He pressed his nose to the mirror and began barking loudly. Vernon's ears flopped in the whispering breeze. When Emmitt tried to make him stop barking, Vernon only became more encouraged. "He's trying to find himself out there," Lester said.

"Aren't we all, Reverend," Emmitt responded, as the truck went further and further into the undying harmony, "aren't we all?"